THE SAVOY TRUFFLE

Patrick Harpur

SKYLIGHT
PRESS

First published in Great Britain in 2013 by Skylight Press,
210 Brooklyn Road, Cheltenham, Glos GL51 8EA

Cover image: detail from linocut *Violet Cream*, by Merrily Harpur.
www.merrilyharpur.co.uk

Designed and typeset by Rebsie Fairholm
Publisher: Daniel Staniforth

www.skylightpress.co.uk

Printed and bound in Great Britain by Lightning Source, Milton Keynes.

British Library Cataloguing in Publication Data.
A catalogue record for this book is available from the British Library.

ISBN 978-1-908011-65-7

To my sister and brothers, Merrily, John and James

part One

1

'DABS am werry brilliant when Dabs's brains am up,' claimed Dabs in her high soppy voice. Her tongue half-protruded feebly. Her eyes, half-closed with dimness, were full of self-satisfaction.

'All right then, Dabs – what's your I.Q.?' enquired the Moo. Dabs's veiled eyes swivelled with sudden uncertainty, perhaps even panic.

''Bout a millionteen,' she decided, fluttering her eyelashes complacently.

'No, Dabs. Your I.Q. is about four. You are a big flabby fool.'

'Amn't.'

'Yes, you are. Are your brains up now?'

'Yis. They am up.'

'In that case I'm going to ask you an easy-peasy question. So easy that even a slow worm could answer it. If you get it wrong, Spiv will be forced to punish you.'

Dabs and the Moo were sitting up in their parents' bed, legs under the eiderdown, facing Dada and Maman who were drinking tea and reading the Sunday newspapers. Neither was disturbed by the ritual exchange between Dabs and the Moo, who now sternly put his question:

'Who's the captain of the England cricket team, Dabs?'

Dabs's eyes moved from side to side in their crinkled sockets, evincing an effort of thought. Suddenly light broke over her face:

'Muffin the Mule!'

'No, Dabs. You are an imbecile. Get 'er, Spiv!'

'Ow! Ow!' squealed Dabs theatrically, as Spiv savaged her upper arm.

Unable to pronounce his own real name, the Moo's nickname for himself had stuck. He was tall and heavy for his five or six years, with a large domed head and dark, deep-set eyes. Spiv was a stuffed toy, probably a fox if his faded red hunting coat, to say nothing of his smell, were any indication. He was the Moo's inseparable companion; and, ever since he had gone AWOL in Dorothy Perkins – the Moo distraught, search parties dispatched – he had been attached to his master by a blue ribbon worn ambassadorially across the body so that Spiv dangled handily at the Moo's waist like a six-gun, able to be drawn on Dabs at a moment's notice.

'You are an *imbecile*, Dabs,' the Moo insisted – Spiv supporting his view – 'you don't know *anything*.'

'Dabs knows what she knows,' piped Dabs, her eyes shifting from side to side to suggest mystery.

'It's not easy to gauge the exact extent of Dabs's ignorance,' said Dada. 'Certainly her knowledge of cricket is little better than sketchy.' He put down his paper, took up from the bedside table a pair of hairbrushes – one of five sets he kept about the house – and began to groom his thick, high-standing head of glossy hair. Dermot Blyte was a stocky man of forty-five with strong eyebrows and a weak mouth. His face, attractive enough when animated, was nondescript in repose; and the more so for being overpowered by his rampart of hair. 'But what, one wonders, of her grasp of the political scene?'

The retarded face of Dabs, her flat tongue protruding farther between her teeth, turned expectantly towards the Moo. His brow furrowed as he strove to frame a testing political question. Just as he was beginning to look perplexed, Dabs intervened with a timely idiocy:

'Ban the Bomb,' she murmured, blinking rapidly in the expectation of praise. 'It am werry Dodgy.' Spiv struck at once. 'Ow! Ow!'

'No, Dabs. You are a spastic imbecile. The Bomb is *not* Dodgy. It is Swinging' – the Moo raised a thumb – 'don't you know *any*thing?'

In common with the rest of the country, Dabs and the Moo were quoting Norman Vaughan, compere of *Sunday Night at the London Palladium*, whose strictly dualistic – almost Manichaean – system of philosophy divided all human experience into that which was

Swinging and that which was Dodgy, the terms to be accompanied by a Nero-like thumb raised and lowered respectively.

'Ow! Ow! Dabs am only joking. The Bomb am Swinging,' amended Dabs so emphatically that her thumb went up a nostril.

'Dabs is an awful eejit,' said Dada fondly.

'Should the Moo be using a word like "spastic", Dermot?' Maman belatedly asked her husband, laying her portion of the paper across her knees. 'It's not a word the Moo should use, I think. Nor any of us, if it comes to that.' Lorna Blyte, once famously petite, was now a short woman of forty whose celebrated waist had been destroyed by child bearing. Her chief sense of loss, however, centred around the catastrophic thickening of her ankles. Notwithstanding, her face, still unlined, was pretty; her eyes, grey; her nose, retroussé like the Moo's. Her light brown hair was, to Dermot's dismay, invariably in disarray.

'What do you say, mavourneen?' asked Dada, using one of his two Irish endearments. 'Who's spastic?'

'Dabs is,' said the Moo.

'Dabs is almost certainly not spastic,' contradicted Dada. 'An imbecile, yes. Perhaps even a cretin. But not spastic, which refers to the physical rather than the mental side of things. We are privileged, the Moo, to speak the language of Shakespeare, and it behoves us not to abuse that privilege. I dare say I have, if nothing else, set an example to all my children in that respect. No one has a higher regard for the language of Shakespeare than I. Of my command over that language, modesty forbids that I utter a word. I say only that Dabs may well escape the charge of... spasticitude because she is physically sound. Unless one counts the lolling tongue, the shifty eyes.'

'Beautiful eyes,' murmured Dabs, twinkling them beguilingly.

'*Hideous* eyes, Dabs,' the Moo reminded her.

'Oh! Oh!' squeaked Dabs indignantly. 'The Moo's words am pincering Dabs!'

'Spiv'll give you pincering, Dabs,' promised the Moo. 'Give 'er one, Spiv.'

'Ow! Ow! Spiv am making Dabs's brains go down.'

'They're *always* down,' said the Moo roughly. 'You've got no brains at all, Dabs.'

'Dabs am werry dangerous when Dabs's dander am up,' threatened Dabs with a sudden show of spirit.

'You couldn't knock the skin off a rice pudding,' replied the Moo scornfully. 'You're a big flabby fool.'

'Dabs am werry important. She am a member of the Sloppy Club,' said Dabs smugly.

'What's this?' cried Dada. '*Dabs* a member? Is everyone in this household a member of the Sloppy Club, the Moo, apart from your poor dear loving Dada? Surely this is criminally unjust?'

'You're not sloppy enough, Dada,' explained the Moo, who was both Sultan of, and final arbiter of admission to, the august institution.

'On the contrary, the Moo. There can be no rational explanation for my exclusion from the Sloppy Club. One can only suppose that – whether through some congenital defect from your mother's side of the family, or through some petty childish grievance – your judgement has been impaired or obscured. I am not one to draw attention to myself nor in any way to blow my own trumpet, but I dare say common decency cries out against the shabby way I've been treated after years of labour and self-sacrifice to procure the comfort of my family – and not least of you, the Moo. Besides which, I'm a bloody sight sloppier than Dabs!'

'*Enfin*, Dermot. Language.'

'Dabs isn't a member either, Dada,' the Moo assured him. He was quite used to his father's flights of incomprehensible rhetoric. 'She's lying. As usual. She's a steaming great nit.'

'Oh! Oh!'

Hugh Blyte, the eldest of the four children, was lying in bed, thinking about his novel. Hearing the faint sounds of Dabs's protestations from the other end of the long upstairs corridor, he smiled and heaved himself out of bed to join, as was the custom on a Sunday, the gathering of the Blyte clan in and around the parental bed.

As he pulled on his short paisley-patterned dressing-gown, he stared idly out of the window at the back garden of the Blyte residence, Cliff Acre. He could see the big tree-encircled lawn flanked by flower-beds, borders and paths, one of which led into the rhododendron bushes and thence to the gate that gave on to the cliff path. Half way up, there was a summerhouse. In front of the house there were two garages on either side of a short curved sweep of gravel drive; at the sides, an orchard, sheds and a greenhouse. The house itself was a large rambling pile of mellow red brick which included two huge bay-windowed rooms on the ground floor; six bedrooms above; and, on the top floor, the flat rented by Theo Hamilton, who taught music at the local girls' school, and lived there with his father, Charles, and the Colonel. Dada had bought the place for a song in the early fifties when everyone wanted smart and convenient maisonettes. Now, large houses within striking distance of London were highly prized, especially such houses as Cliff Acre which was part of an exclusive Edwardian estate complete with golf and tennis clubs. Built on a series of hills – but called, simply, St Michael's Hill – it had originally been the home of ex-colonial types, but had now begun to attract a racier kind of resident: Americans, self-made men, showbiz people, even pop stars.

Hugh turned to the mirror and applied Clearasil to an incipient spot. Then, as an afterthought to needle Dada, he pinned to his dressing-gown a badge, home-made out of a safety pin Sellotaped to a circular piece of cardboard cut out of a cereal packet, on which the words 'SLOPY CLUB' had been printed with a leaky Bic. On his way out, he paused at his desk to scan once more the letter from Bloggs, all the way from exotic Notting Hill. Then, half-wishing that he were Bloggs – engaged in Life instead of stuck here in Wyebridge – he went along to his parents' room.

'Ah, here is the Young Master,' cried Dada, suspending the action of the hair brushes at Hugh's entrance, 'doubtless ready to dazzle us with his wit and learning!'

'Good morning, Luh'le Shuggy,' said Maman, smiling. Hugh's glottally-stopped nickname derived from a remote Glaswegian charlady's stab at pronouncing 'Little Hughie'.

'Morning, Aged P.s,' said Hugh world-wearily. He poured himself half a cup of tea from the large pot on Maman's bedside table, picked up a section of newspaper and crossed the spacious and sunny bedroom to slump on the small sofa covered in lemon silk, one of the few remnants of Maman's French upbringing. On the front page of the paper was an exhilarating photograph of a common-looking blonde who had swum naked, or something, with a Cabinet Minister. Not much older than himself – he was sixteen and a half – the blonde could've been someone out of *Tit-Bits*, not a sober Sunday broadsheet. What was happening to the world?

There was silence, broken only by the rhythmic smack of hair brushes as Dada renewed his preening.

'Dada am having lovely red hair,' remarked Dabs in tones of wonder as she gazed enraptured at Dada's glossy coiffure. Dada smiled indulgently. He was proud of his hair. However, it was not red. At best, and in certain lights, its chestnut colour acquired an auburn sheen. But Dada saw in the mirror a smouldering red mane, embers of those ancient flames that crowned the Celtic warlords he claimed as forebears, despite his actual rank as the son of well-to-do Anglo-Irish shopkeepers from Kilkenny.

'Dabs seems able to perceive easily what others labour to see,' muttered Hugh.

'What's that you say, Luh'le Shuggy?' asked Dada sharply.

'Nothing, Dada.'

'You will do well not to provoke me, Luh'le Shuggy, or I may not be answerable for my actions. Do I have to remind you what the burning redness of my hair betokens?'

'No, Dada.' Indeed, everyone knew what the red hair betokened: a berserker-like rage, fatal legacy of the warlords, that Dada only managed to suppress from moment to moment by the greatest will-power.

'In fact,' pursued Dada, 'I feel my temper rising now. Of its own accord. I won't be responsible for the outcome, I tell you.' Blood was indeed flowing into Dada's face.

'Calm yourself, Dermot,' urged Maman anxiously. 'Luh'le Shuggy is baiting you. Don't rise to it. And you, Luh'le Shuggy, will not upset your poor father.'

'Dada am getting batey,' wailed Dabs. 'Dabs am werry frighty.'

'You needn't be frighty, Dabs,' the Moo, apprehensive himself, tried to reassure her. 'Dada won't lose his temper. Will he, Maman?'

'Please, Dermot…' said Maman, alarmed at the continuing rise in his colour and the beginning of heavy breathing. Like the H-bomb, the temper was a fantastic deterrent but nerve-wracking to have in the house lest it accidentally trigger a holocaust. Dada had warned

Maman about it: his temper – or, rather, its loss – prevented him from forming human relationships, let alone marrying. Maman had promised him that there would never be any cause in their marriage for irritation, let alone anger. If this was an assurance she had not been able to fulfil, she had devised early on methods of soothing and appeasing which had so far kept the rage at bay. 'Please. Luh'le Shuggy will apologise to you at once.' She gave her eldest son a severe look.

'I regard it as a failing in myself, Dada, that I can't appreciate as Dabs can the praeternatural redness of your almost unnaturally abundant hair.'

'Hugh!' scolded Maman.

'Sorry, Maman. I mean, Dada, that I apologise. You have the most beautiful hair, beside which my own greasy lank deplorable locks –'

'That will do, Luh'le Shuggy,' warned Maman.

'Well, well,' said Dada, still nettled but – his colour returning to normal – no longer on the verge of detonation, 'it is perhaps understandable, if mean-spirited of you, Luh'le Shuggy, to envy my hair. It has been a sadness to me that my son and heir should, as he says, possess such thin, bloodless, measly hair, with all its suggestion of moral degeneration or even premature baldness. But we must look on the bright side. Perhaps your hair signifies that you have escaped the curse of the Blyte temper, just as you have unfortunately escaped the Blyte gumption and vim – but what is that infernal cacophony?'

Everyone listened. From the floor above there could just be discerned the dissonant sound of someone plonking through an elementary piano piece.

'It's not actually a cacophony,' said Maman. 'But I think even Sabrina might be a little disappointed in her own efforts.'

'Sabrina? Who is this "Sabrina"?' Dada was aggrieved.

'Sabrina Cholmondeley – the daughter of our neighbours,' added Maman in anticipation of his next question.

'We tell you this every week, Dada,' the Moo pointed out. 'Theo is giving her a lesson.'

'Sabrina am like Spiv,' opined Dabs. 'Her Bach am worse than her bite.' Unsure as to whether this was an insult, and deciding to play safe, Spiv came down on Dabs like a wolf on the fold. 'Ow! Ow!'

'Stop that, the Moo. And be quiet, Dabs,' reproved Maman. 'You are beginning to get on my nerves. I slept badly and they are frayed. I have the wretched Sunday lunch to prepare and already I'm quite worn out.'

'Lunch at two o'clock sharp,' stated Dada with tight lips.

'Yes, well, we'll see,' replied Maman, her defiant tone undermined by a tremble in the voice. 'It may not be possible. I am *fatiguée*.'

'May I remind you, macushla, that while my preference has always been for luncheon at one, I have conceded to you an extra hour.'

'Yes, yes, but you have all been extremely trying today. I'm a bag of nerves.'

'You have Carla, remember. I do not mention the expense of bringing a Mother's Help over from Italy.'

'Is three pounds a week an expense?' wondered Hugh.

'If you were educating four children at private schools, Luh'le Shuggy, you would know that an extra three pounds a week was very much an expense.'

'Three children, Dada. You forget that I'm no longer at school. I'm saving you a fortune.'

'I sometimes think,' said Maman, pursuing her own line, 'that I'd be better off without Carla's help and with an extra three pounds towards the housekeeping.'

'You see, Dada, you could give the school fees I save you to Maman for housekeeping. I don't think you realise how she struggles.'

'She has ample housekeeping. It is all a question of management. For my part, I am known for my liberality with money.'

'On the other hand, "liberal with money" is not an exact description of a man who keeps his Remembrance Day poppy from one year to the next in order to avoid unnecessary expense on charity.'

'Well, well. Let us see how profligate you are, Luh'le Shuggy, in the matter of poppy-buying when you have four children and an au pair to support.'

'Stop it, both of you. As if my life were not exasperating enough, having to produce huge meals at a moment's notice and with absolute punctuality...'

'You think I ask too much of you? Hm?' Dada was affronted.

'You think it too much to ask that I be fed in reasonable time when I labour the entire week to –'

'No, no, no,' cried Maman, tears filling her eyes. 'But I can't cope, I can't cope –'

'You see what a state Little Lorna gets into when she doesn't take her tablets?' said Dada gently.

'I don't like them.'

'You didn't like your Librium either. Do I need to remind you, mavourneen, that when your fool of a doctor refused to prescribe anything for your nerves, I went to some trouble to procure this new Valium for you, almost a wonder drug with its strength minus the old side-effects.'

'Not that much trouble,' said Maman. 'You got them off David Siskin, your old army buddy.'

'Well, if that is the line you are going to take after all the trouble I've gone to…' said Dermot huffily.

'No, no, Dermot. I'm grateful, really I am. It's just that…' Maman hesitated. 'It is as if one's emotions are removed.'

'Well, we cannot ask much more of a simple tablet. Now swallow one down with your tea and we'll say no more about it.'

'I thought perhaps… that I might, well, see how I got on without a tablet today.'

'Well, if that is your final decision, so be it. Only, we have already witnessed a distressing display of nerves, and one dreads to think what further spectacles the day will bring. You do not consider, of course, how much your family suffers from the consequences of your nerves, nor how much it takes out of your husband who has, I dare say, more than his share of anxieties – but let that pass.'

'All right. I will take the Valium.'

'No, no. You are at perfect liberty not to take it. I will not have it said that I in any way forced medicines, however beneficial, on my wife.'

'I'm taking it now. Look, it is gone.'

'Well, well, that's better, macushla.' Dermot leaned sideways and nuzzled his wife's neck with his sweep of hair. 'Little Lorna doesn't mind taking the helping medicine for her Prince Flasheen Eyes, does she?' he murmured beguilingly, working his eyes in a manner to suggest the origin of the nickname. 'She knows that she is powerless

15

to disobey the commands of Prince Flasheen Eyes, who only has her welfare at heart.'

In spite of herself, Maman smiled. Then, as Prince Flasheen Eyes continued to croon endearments, and to add fierce pecking kisses up and down her arm, she began to giggle.

2

HUGH contemplated the photograph of the little blonde. The newspaper said that she could bring the Government down. Nothing like it had ever happened before. Hugh pictured her, swimming naked; and, himself wearing only the short dressing-gown, hurriedly crossed his legs. The blonde was a reminder that, while the nineteen sixties were technically well under way, they had only actually reached such places as San Francisco and, well, Notting Hill where Bloggs bathed in asses' milk. The Home Counties in general, and Wyebridge in particular, were still stuck in the fifties. While Hugh was condemned to eat antiquated Spam and semolina and salad cream, Bloggs dined on food smeared and spiced with garlic and black pepper, soy sauce and mayonnaise. While Bloggs wrote of atheism and anarchy, in Wyebridge everyone still went to church at Christmas and Easter, and even the Secondary Modern kids wore uniforms. Bloggs casually mentioned things such as deodorants and divorcées; but Hugh was a little shocked to hear that divorce (to say nothing of sexual intercourse) had spread beyond the legendary fleshpots of Mayfair and Brighton. The most exciting thing he had seen, apart from Elvis and his pelvis on the TV, was the versatile Charlton Heston winning the chariot race in *Ben Hur*; and, later, parting the Red Sea in Cinerama. Bloggs meanwhile had seen a fight with knuckle-dusters outside a The Who gig; and had travelled to the far North to hear the Liverpool sound. Just as David Whitfield singing 'O Sole Mio' on a frangible 78 rpm had been swept away by Elvis singing 'It's Now or Never' on a 45, so now The Pelvis himself was being ousted by the Animals, the Kinks, the Rolling Stones and, above all, the Beatles. While an LP was out of reach for Hugh – even a 45 cost six and eight – Bloggs had both Beatles' LPs; both 'albums'.

Still, the sixties were coming. Only Dada now dared to wear baggy grey flannels and to play Liberace records. And, while parents still did the Twist – fathers briskly like Chubby Checker, and mothers more sexily like the French – their children learnt the myriad Mod dances they saw on *Ready, Steady, Go* ('The Weekend Starts Here!') every Friday. Polio and whooping-cough and pea-soupers were dissolving; health and air were blowing in. Cabinet ministers were being cheeked by little blondes. As if on the cusp between civilisations, everything was changing. The very air was altering from oxygen to something headier – either maddening or illuminating depending on the predisposition of the individual lungs. The post-war world, grey as an archive film, was – like television itself – trembling on the verge of colour.

The bedroom door swung slowly open and a German helmet of Second World War vintage appeared.

'No, mein Fuehrer!' shouted Maman at once. 'Take that thing away!'

Just visible underneath the helmet was the intense white face of a boy about nine or ten years old, small for his age – scarcely taller than the Moo – and as thin and wiry as the Moo was well padded.

'But Maman,' protested the boy. *'Ich bin ein Berliner.'*

'I don't care. You know that thing gives me the willies. Take it away!'

The boy's head withdrew, tortoise-like.

The helmet-less boy re-appeared, marching briskly into the room and trailing behind him a collection of wires.

'Well, mein Fuehrer, come and give your Dada a kiss. You are not too big for that? I hope you will never be too big to give your father a kiss.'

'Die, Englander pig-dog,' replied the boy, drawing freely on the language of his beloved war comics. He removed the pin from an imaginary grenade with his teeth, tossed it as if into Dada's lap and supplied the sound of the explosion. Then, holding up his wires, he said calmly: 'Will you help me with my death-trap please, Janey?'

'Janey isn't 'ere,' said the Moo. 'Dabs is.'

'Dabs will help the Fuehrer,' promised Dabs rashly. 'Her brains am up.'

'No, they're not,' said the Moo, readying Spiv.

'Janey, *please* help. This is serious.'

As if by magic, the retarded expression of Dabs gave way to that of a normal girl of about thirteen or fourteen. Her face, quite pretty, was as full of candour and character as Dabs's had been shifty and vacuous. Its owner, however, was inclined to conceal it behind twin curtains of shoulder-length brown hair.

'I might do,' said Janey. 'What's in it for me?' It was not always easy to understand Janey because, as well as partly hiding her mouth, she often spoke with it barely open, being self-conscious about displaying the wiring of her dental plate.

'The satisfaction of seeing my Enemy maimed or perhaps killed.'

'Really, dear...' demurred Maman vaguely.

'I am tempted, mein Fuehrer,' said Janey.

'It's the problem of wire, you see, Janey. Piano wire would be best. That's what you read about. It's so thin, you see, that the motorcyclist can't see it and it snips his head off.'

'Yes, I see,' said Janey to her brother. His name was George. He had acquired his nickname at the age of three when he had been exposed to an old newsreel of Adolf Hitler, orating. George had been nearly sick with laughter; and, at tea, had surprised everyone by suddenly reproducing the speech with uncanny accuracy – the same mechanical arm movements, the toss of the head, the ranting scream. Even the cod German had sounded authentic. Everyone had laughed. Only Maman had noticed with uneasiness the authentically insane fire burning in her third child's blue eye.

'But we haven't got a piano, have we,' George went on. 'So, anyway, I found these' – he held up his wires – 'and I thought that we could join them up and string them across the cliff path. I mean, they're too thick really, but if the Enemy were going fast enough on his bike, he might not see them in time and crash over the edge, aaaargh.' He simulated the cry, dying away, of a boy falling from a great height.

'Best little brain in the family,' said Dada admiringly. 'Are you listening to your brother, Luh'le Shuggy? He will not go to Oxford University like you, but see how he thinks things through in a fashion so different from your own intellectual, airy-fairy approach to the world. Oh yes, the Fuehrer's university will be the same as his father's.'

19

he university of the Bogs,' said Hugh, not looking up from a raging review of a new novel by one of the Angry Young Men, ess young and more petulant than he had been five years before.

'I was referring, as well you know, to the University of Life. It ill becomes you to mock at this institution. And yet I am not ashamed to say that hot tears prick the backs of my eyes when I think that you, Luh'le Shuggy, will be the first Blyte to go to Oxford University – go *up* to Oxford, as Oxford men say.' Dada gazed unseeing out of the window, picturing his eldest son's ascent. Hugh looked uncomfortable.

'What you and Maman don't understand, Dada,' he said, 'is the English educational system. I need at least three 'A' levels, all with high grades, if I'm to stand a chance of –'

'I can see myself now,' went on Dada, regardless, 'proudly visiting you in your college "rooms" and partaking of cinnamon toast and exotic teas while bantering philosophically with your fellow students...'

'You will not be visiting me in my rooms, Dada – supposing I should ever acquire such things – because you wear a grey cardigan and then you tuck that grey cardigan not only into your trousers, but also into your underpants, whose flaccid elastic therefore shows above your waistband.'

'Ah, the dress of Shakespeare,' surmised George.

'Even you must see,' continued Hugh, 'that I cannot have someone of such perverted appearance visiting my rooms. Someone might see you, and I would be forced to turn my face to the wall and die lingeringly of shame.'

'Don't be brutal to your poor Dada, Luh'le Shuggy,' said Dada. 'He cannot shake off overnight the attributes of his race – all Irishmen are raised to tuck their ganseys well in. However, as so often, you underestimate me. I would not dream of wearing such an article *up* at Oxford. I shall purchase Oxford items: bags and brogues and stiff underpants with properly turgid elastic. I shall be in fine fig, and a credit to you, Luh'le Shuggy.'

'Oh, Dada,' said Hugh sadly.

'The problem is,' George was explaining earnestly to Janey, 'that I can't join up these wires I found into one long wire. They spring apart, you see, as soon as I knot them together. Can you help?'

'Jesus wept!' exclaimed Hugh.

'*Enfin*, Luh'le Shuggy. *C'est malheureux*,' scolded Maman.

'You will *not* blaspheme,' added Dada sternly.

'All right, all right – but can't you do something about that squalid Fuehrer? He's *taken my guitar strings*. Every single thing I've ever cherished, that little Nazi has smashed up, and you never do *anything*. It's a monumental injustice. It's blatant favouritism.'

'You must *not* take Luh'le Shuggy's things without asking, mein Fuehrer,' said Maman in a tired voice. 'Put them back at once.'

'He can't put them back,' expostulated Hugh. 'He can only take things apart. Does *no one* remember my cricket bat? Which he used to bang in the metal parts of his guillotine? Ruined. And what does he get? A feeble slap on the legs. Here, give me those strings, you little Hun.' Hugh leapt up and, clipping George round the head, seized the guitar strings.

'Ow! *Achtung!*' protested George. 'Did you *see* that?'

'No,' said Maman shortly.

'It's so *unfair*.' He rubbed his head dramatically. 'Nobody cares if Luh'le Shuggy gives me brain damage. I don't know why he needs the strings anyway – he just goes plink plink all day, the same note, the same soppy wet song' – he broke into a deep quavering imitation of the song, at whose accuracy Maman, in spite of her irritation, could not suppress a smile – '*Out in the West Texas town of El Paso, I fell in love with a Mexican girl…*'

'Luh'le Shuggy wuvs a Mexican girl,' sniggered Dabs, making a surprise reappearance.

'Don't you bloody start, Dabs,' said Hugh furiously.

'No, don't you bloody Dabs,' echoed the Moo approximately.

'Do *not* swear in front of the Moo,' reproved Maman. 'You know how he imitates. In fact, do not swear at all, Luh'le Shuggy, or I won't have you in the house. I mean it.'

From the floor above there now came the sound of a Bach concerto being expertly played on the piano.

'For Pete's sake,' shouted Dada, 'is there to be no peace on a Sunday morning? I can hardly hear myself think.'

'I wish that were what we all could hardly hear,' muttered Hugh.

'It is beautiful, Dada. Theo got a scholarship to the Conservatoire in Paris,' said Janey. 'Don't be a Philistine.'

'Oh, oh, so I'm a Philistine, am I? Well, well, I know it is stylish to look down on a man such as myself – for, yes, I shall say it: your father is a business man – but he is not ashamed to be such, no matter how fashionable it becomes to mock and sneer at him because he has not been to Oxford and the Conservatoire. And yet, while you all mumble and sieve your impoverished syllables through your teeth, who has done more than I to promote the language of Shakespeare in this household? I spare no expense to encourage you in your Art, Janey, and Luh'le Shuggy in his literary endeavours, neither of which activities will ever afford you a decent living, yet you have the neck to call me a Philistine. Oh foul! Am I not entitled to lament in the words of King Lear: "How sharper than a serpent's thanks it is to have a toothless child"?'

'Don't be silly, Dermot.'

'Oh, so you defend your pelican daughter, Little Lorna? But was it she who spurred you on to write your little stories? Was it she who took them off to be appraised by powerful men of letters? No, it was not. It was your own Prince Flasheen Eyes, whom you now turn on with cries of "Philistine!". And when your writings were spurned by the journals to which he submitted them, did he not dry your tears and urge you never to lose heart?'

'But I did,' said Maman.

'Spiv likes Theo's music,' said the Moo, looking into Spiv's eyes. 'It's sloppy.'

'It soothes Spiv's savage breast,' said Hugh.

'Luh'le Shuggy said "breast", Maman,' said George righteously.

'Be quiet, the pair of you. And we all like Theo's music, the Moo. Even Dada does really.'

'Does he? I see. And you secretly wish, O wife of mine, to number among his pupils? Is that it?'

'No, Dermot.'

'You suppose I would object?'

'No, dear.'

'You objected to Maman's French conversation with Theo,' Janey reminded him.

'That is ancient history,' said Dada .

'Before the Moo was born,' said the Moo cosily.

'Not at all, the Moo. Not even your birth could stop your mother nattering away nineteen to the dozen in the language of… of Marcel Marceau –'

'*Parlez-vous Français, Monsieur?*' interjected George. '*Non, non, je suis un crétin.*'

'Best little brain in the family,' said Dada, his admiration giving him pause. 'Speaks good working French, mein Fuehrer, on top of his fluent German… And then, of course, Muggins comes home after an abominable day at the office, hacking away at the rock face in order to put food on the table – only to find that there *is* no food on the table: Muggins's wife has been too busy ooh-la-la-ing all day with the French scholarship boy. Any sane man would have put a stop to it.'

'As you did, sane or otherwise,' said Maman. 'And Theo is *not* French. His father is of Scottish extraction, as you well know; and his poor mother was a German Jew. He only *speaks* French. Do try and hold these distinctions in your mind, dear.'

'And you wish to resume French conversation with this effete piano-player of mixed race?'

'Did I say any such thing? You deliberately misunderstand me, Dermot. You are impossible. And Theo is *not* effete.'

'Just because he doesn't have dandruff and B.O. like the other teachers at school,' added Janey indignantly, 'doesn't mean he's effete.'

'Very well. I only venture to suggest that a single glance at his appearance – the foppish scarves, the suspicious corduroy – I do not mention the girlish skin – is enough to ascertain that Theo is very far from being, ahem, a ladies' man. I do not use the expression "bum boy" –'

'Ah, the language of Shakespeare,' said Hugh.

'Dermot! *Pas devant les enfants!*'

'Theo is perfectly manly, Dada,' said Jane.

'And he dresses very nattily,' agreed Maman.

'Ah, I see. You approve of the absence of neckties at Sunday luncheon? Well, well, I suppose we should all be grateful that Herr Hamilton of that Ilk does not sport a natty skull cap or a natty little kilt.'

'Don't be absurd, Dermot.'

'Speak French, Dabs,' ordered the Moo.

23

'*Zut! Zut!*,' cried Dabs at once. 'Dada 'as made in 'is pantalons ze poo *formidable!*'

'That is simply a preposterous suggestion,' exploded Dada. 'And even if it were not, it would not be as funny as you, the Moo, seem to think. I see your hysteria has rendered Spiv unable to strike at a moment when for once he would be more than justified in doing so. However, I am ready to pass over the whole subject of the dubious pianist who in any case cannot bear comparison to your own darling Prince Flasheen Eyes, can he Little Lorna?' The eyes flashed; the lips pursed prissily; the head of hair was poised for nuzzling. Maman smiled in spite of her nerves.

'Am Prince Flasheen Eyes a bum boy?' enquired Dabs.

'Right, that's it!' bellowed Dada. 'Out! All of you. Go and make your beds.'

'Luh'le Shuggy is in love with a Mexican girl,' taunted George, evading his brother's swipe with agility and scampering out of the bedroom.

'Where are you going, Dabs?' asked the Moo, trailing after his sister.

'Dabs am going outside to think about Art,' said Dabs with dignity. 'And to burn with a hard gem-like flame.'

'Oh,' said the Moo, impressed.

3

HUGH shivered in the thin sunlight. Autumn was around the corner. He went into the tool shed, sat down on the lawn mower, lit a stub of cigarette and took out Bloggs's letter again. He had fagged for Bloggs at school – Bloggs was not, of course, his real name – and Bloggs, after a half-arsed attempt at hanky-panky with Hugh, had become something of a mentor. When Bloggs left, Hugh's scholarly decline had accelerated.

Bloggs was sharing a flat in Notting Hill. He had a girlfriend; or, as he put it, a bird. He was birded up. He was in love. Hugh could not suppress a severe pang: he had never been in love, not even – and contrary to popular opinion – with a Mexican girl. He had, of course – like all right-thinking, red-blooded boys – been half in love with Binnings minor, whose Desdemona in the school's staging of *Othello* had maddened most of the sixth form. But Binnings minor was not, contrary to popular opinion, a girl, let alone a bird; so Hugh was left to pine for Audrey Hepburn in *The Nun's Story* and to seethe over the drawing of Ursula Andress on the *Dr No* poster. The untameable beast in his underpants, scarcely dormant for more than twenty minutes at a time, stirred restlessly.

Hugh groaned and, folding up Bloggs's letter, put it carefully away in his jacket pocket. He rose from the lawn mower and checked his reflection in a piece of broken mirror. The spot on his chin was breaking through its coating of Clearasil. His hair was annoying: he had no sooner exchanged his Billy Fury quiff for a snazzy Tony Curtis Boston, than the Beatle cut became the only thing birds gave the time of day to. He took a comb out of his back pocket and scraped his hair forward. It came nowhere near his eyebrows, as it should. It'd take ages to grow. And then Dada would probably force a short-back-and-sides on him. He pushed down his nose to lengthen it and screwed up his eyes to simulate myopia: yeah, surely he looked just like John Lennon. With a bit more fringe he'd be the spitting image. Absent-mindedly he began to sing in the cowboy bass of Marty Robbins:

'*Out in the west Texas town of El Paso…*' Then, remembering the Fuehrer's penchant for listening at doors, he lowered his voice almost to a whisper:

'*I fell in love with a Mexican girl.*' But the song sounded old-fashioned to him. Besides, like the Beatles, he was writing his own songs. Well, song. It was about alcoholism and despair and the meaninglessness of life; because, if the Beatles had a fault, it was their lack of a social message.

The sound of heavy footsteps outside made Hugh hurriedly stub out his cigarette and wave the smoke frantically in all directions. Dada appeared in the doorway.

'Ah, so this is where the young master has his place of business. Still, it is refreshing to see that he has roused himself from his bed of indolence, doubtless to mend the fence on the cliff path as his poor father has begged him to these last weeks.' He sniffed the air distractedly.

'I'm afraid I'm rather busy, Dada.'

'You have been busy all month, doing nothing except stay in bed until all hours, rising only to eat and drink at my expense.'

'I don't do nothing,' protested Hugh. 'I devote myself to Art. It is very wearing. You would not have me give up the quest for Beauty and Truth, I hope.'

'You know I would not, my boy. Have I asked you to contribute to the expense of maintaining the family, as any normal father would? No, I have not. I understand that you must be free when you are young, as I was not free at your age, but breaking my back in the potato fields, with nothing on that back bar a little grey gansey that offered scant protection from rain and wind. However, I do not mention that now, just as I do not reproach you for failing to put food on the table. I ask only that you do one or two little chores about the place, which I would not need to ask of you if you had any consideration or respect for your poor fond old Dada –'

'Dada, I will mend the wretched fence. But can't it wait?'

'Yes, yes, it can wait. It can wait until some passer-by, perhaps some superfluous member of this very family, leans on that post and plunges to their death. By all means let it wait.'

'I'll do it now, Dada,' sighed Hugh.

'Well, well, thank you, Luh'le Shuggy. You are not a bad son.'

While Dada withdrew the lawn mower and wheeled it away, Hugh began to rummage vaguely about for the sledge-hammer he'd need to mend the fence. Typically, it wasn't there. Sighing, he fished out the claw hammer and some nails instead. Then he left the shed and began to make his way up the garden.

Janey was sitting on the grassy bank which gave on to the verge which separated Cliff Acre from Chestnut Avenue. Sometimes it helped her to think, to be outside the oppressive purlieus of house and garden. Plus, she hoped someone famous would pass by. For ever since a feature in the *Sunday Times* had dubbed St Michael's Hill the 'Beverley Hills of London', rumours had flown about that stars were moving in. The Who had been mentioned, and Tom Jones. Cliff Richard was already there, at the western end. But although he'd been momentarily groovy (when the papers blew their tops over two kids who'd eloped on his advice in *The Young Ones* not to 'wait until tomorrow'), his crooning in the film *Summer Holiday* had done for him, and, in six months, he'd be forgotten. At any rate, Dada had rubbed his hands with glee at the prospective rise in property values. At the same time, though only on the verge of senior management, he could believe himself on a par with the rich men surrounding him. There were gates at each entrance to the estate, half-closed to discourage, without actually preventing, the ingress of plebeians. Outside the gates, down the hill that Maman toiled up on her bicycle, the houses became progressively smaller until they spilled up against the village – rapidly growing into a town – of Wyebridge.

As the silence deepened, Janey gave up the hope of a passing pop star. Perhaps, instead, a battalion of Mods in fur-trimmed anoraks would zoom through, scootering down to Brighton for a rumble with the Rockers. But St Michael's Hill was not on the Brighton route. It was not on the route to anywhere. And, in Chestnut Avenue, cars were practically non-existent. If only something would *happen*.

27

She had seen a tramp once. She'd longed to speak to him because 'tramp' was a profession she was very much drawn to. But she'd been too shy. Not that she'd confessed her aspirations to Miss Whitley, the careers mistress. On the contrary, when asked what she had in mind for her future – technical drawing? Secretarial work? Nursing? ('I'm afraid "air hostess" might be a little beyond you, dear.') – Janey had known instinctively that she could not say 'tramp'. She knew she was required above all to be sensible. She wondered if she could hazard 'show jumper'; but, knowing in her heart of hearts that this was as far removed from her capacities as 'air hostess', she said firmly, and as sensibly as possible, 'I'd very much like to work with guinea pigs.' Miss Whitley's face indicated that she might have misjudged the situation. 'Or, in fact, any small, er, rodents,' she expanded sensibly. Miss Whitley's pursed lips silenced her. Both of them sat speechless for a while, looking out of the window, until Janey felt that she could decently slip away.

Her dental plate made her front teeth ache. It was supposed to. It was correcting the tendency towards goofiness. She took it out. Pieces of bent wire forced her side teeth backwards and a single band of wire forced her front teeth inwards. Resting on the palm of her hand, the pink plastic plate, moulded to fit the roof of her mouth, had two startled 'eyes' where the wire was fixed in circles to the surface of the plate and its own set of steely 'teeth', bared in a ghoulish smile. It was quite sweet in repose, like a flat fish or squid; but if she whipped it out after meals, it was a monster from the deep, encrusted with barnacles of meat and trailing long seaweed-like strands of vegetable. In this state it became Foody Fenella – who spoke, oddly enough, in a French accent – and an ultimate weapon against any small child who annoyed her. Meanwhile, it was also a deterrent to anyone wishing to kiss her. Not that she wanted boys to kiss her, yuk; but, just lately, she had begun to think that it might not, given the right person, be so bad.

Janey turned over on to her stomach and began to make chains out of the last of the daisies. She was wearing what she always wore. At the dawn of tights and mini-skirts – that confusing combination of the chaste and the wanton – she stuck with her Dark-Age drainpipe jeans and ankle socks. On her feet she wore plimsolls. With an autumnal nip in the air she wore a duffel coat over her loose charcoal-grey jumper, a sloppy joe similar to the ones Maman favoured to hide her decaying figure. Her shirt was white Aertex. This ensemble did not imply a lack of fashion consciousness so much as a loyalty to one of her life's defining moments.

Some years ago she had been taken after school by her friend Bernice, who was two years older than she, to The Big Toe. This was the first (and last) coffee bar in Wyebridge. Bernice had hitched up her grey school skirt, put on some lipstick and marched boldly in. The place was empty except for the proprietor and his girlfriend, a deathly pale woman with dark lipstick and a cigarette holder, who was dressed in a tight black polo-necked sweater and tight black three-quarter-length trousers. While Janey huddled at a corner table, Bernice ordered two frothy coffees. The proprietor nodded. He had a narrow intellectual beard running around the outside of his face. He wore a sloppy joe, black drainpipe jeans and, of all things, a beret. Like a French painter. Janey asked herself, with beating heart, whether he could be, of all things, a real *beatnik*. Her question was answered when he came out from behind the counter – Janey saw, with a sharp intake of breath, that he wore no shoes. He shuffled over to the juke box in nothing but a pair of nylon socks, nodded civilly to Janey as if it were quite natural for her to be drinking frothy coffee in this shoeless Bohemian underworld, and pushed a coin into the machine. He pressed some buttons and – ecstasy! – *Tell Laura I Love Her* began to play. Janey and Bernice looked at each other, their mouths open in silent screams. Then Janey pulled a Bic out of her blazer and began to scribble down on her bared arm the words to this most banned of all pop records.

In the following days, whispering in the cloakroom, she would initiate classmates by ones and twos into the forbidden lyric of *Tell Laura I Love Her*. For a brief delirious period she was even known as Laura. It took her two weeks to muster the two shillings needed for another coffee and another play of the juke box. Then, plucking up all her courage, she returned to the Big Toe. It had vanished. Outside the sign-less, boarded-up building only a squashed empty packet of Gaulois remained as evidence that the experience had not been only a dream.

Holding four or five daisy chains, Janey turned lazily over on to her back. Her curtains of hair fell away to let the weak sun on to her face. She closed her eyes. Apart from a blackbird singing away in the tall bushes, there was silence. Then she heard a distant, and distinctly thrilling, roar.

As usual, tension was building between Charles Hamilton and the Colonel as they walked simultaneously through the portals of the St Michael's Hill Tennis Club. The entrance drive passed straight in front of the club house, which overlooked the best grass courts outside Wimbledon. Behind, there was a wide terrace where members carried their drinks from the bar to sit beside the extensive lake, towards which the two pedestrians now headed, converging on the footpath that led off the drive to the right. Neither was willing to give way and so some unseemly jostling was inevitable. But the real battle of wills took place where the path forked. Both branches led to the terrace; but while to the left it was short stroll, to the right a circle of the entire lake had to be made. Beyond the narrow water-side path lay acres of uncultivated trees and brush, with only a few rough trails on which Charles had never, bar the club's Secretary, met another soul.

At these encounters, the Secretary, whose name was Lamb – also by coincidence a colonel – would barely acknowledge Charles while greeting the Colonel heartily; and the latter would often linger to hob-nob with his peer, leaving the excluded Charles to continue on his way alone. It was a little, well, crushing. As if he were not good enough for his companion. And he had to struggle against the irrational feeling that the Colonel – his Colonel – was being disloyal. God knew, you gave a fellow house room, you fed a fellow, you were entitled to something. Not thanks – nor did Charles require thanks – but to the odd acknowledgement. Surely. Would it kill the Colonel to give him a nod or tip him the odd wink? Apparently. He didn't even like being seen with Charles. Yet, perversely, he always accompanied him on his pre-prandial Sunday constitutional. 'Accompanied' was not perhaps the word – the Colonel waited until Charles left the house and then he would yawn and saunter out also, as if by chance. Outside, he walked at the same pace as Charles but on the opposite side of the avenue, as if anything more intimate would somehow compromise his independence or dignity. The Colonel was almost Japanese in his refusal to lose even the tiniest fraction of face.

Thus, at the fork in the path, the Colonel, who had taken the lead, paused and pretended to examine a discarded sweet wrapper on the ground. He was reluctant to take either path lest Charles did not follow him and so cause him to lose face. But Charles always did follow him, somewhat irritably, having been forced to lose face himself rather than forgo the Colonel's company. The reverse scenario, however, did not obtain: if Charles took one path the Colonel was just as likely, with a show of indifference, to take the other. He could never allow himself to be perceived as *following*. Sometimes the Colonel would even feint left, making Charles go that way – and then jink right, leaving Charles looking a fool. For all his stoutness the Colonel could be quick enough on his feet when it suited him.

Today, Charles edged slowly and with great tact towards the right-hand path, giving the Colonel plenty of time and space to nip past him, as if the choice of route had been his all along. It usually worked; but, today, it didn't. The Colonel suddenly took it into his head to set off on the opposite, shorter path to the terrace. Charles instinctively made as if to follow him and then changed his mind. He was damned if he was going to alter his course to suit the Colonel's whims. He had humiliated himself often enough as it was. The balance of power was already too heavily weighted in the Colonel's favour. Damn it, a chap had to retain some self-respect, didn't he? Bitterly disappointed, Charles held his course and began the long circumambulation of the lake alone.

Hugh traipsed lethargically up the long garden path towards his rendezvous with the broken fence. He passed through the Bad Lands, the scrubby zone on the west side of the house where the old sandpit was and the bonfire place and the monkey puzzle. This was the Fuehrer's area, where he built his go-carts out of old planks, crates and pram wheels; where he fired his crude clay pots and worked on his inventions. This morning he was spluttering over an old saucepan in which lead was being melted. He wiped his streaming eyes, tipped back his German helmet and looked up long enough to flick Hugh a V-sign, which Hugh absent-mindedly returned.

George thought of his activity as smelting. The lead was coming to the boil over the open fire. Using an old metal spoon he began to skim off the creamy scum, like marshmallow melted in Horlicks, which rose to the surface of the pure silver liquid beneath. He saw himself as purifying the lead. He had a whole batch he had melted and re-melted many times, but no matter how often he removed the scum there always remained some impurity to cloud the clear mirror of the silvery surface. It was almost as if absolute purity were impossible. Also, of course, the amount of lead shrank after every operation so that he had to augment it occasionally from lead twisted off the windows of the Ruined House; and this, in turn, set the purification process back.

Crouched over the saucepan he began to feel a bit dizzy, even a little sick. He stood up and reeled away, gulping fresh air until he felt better. Once the scum was removed, the pure – or pure-ish – molten lead would be poured into a bucket of cold water where, hissing, it solidified immediately into a silver sculpture. George was in the middle of a long sequence of these experimental works of art – pouring, dripping or dashing down the lead from different heights to create different shapes and effects. Then he would melt down his creation and start again. Obscurely he felt that, at the moment when he reached the final purification, at the same moment he would hit upon the shape of perfection.

Hugh plodded alongside the wide lawn where Dada was attempting, with a martyr's expression, to start the lawn mower. He straightened up and beckoned Hugh over; but Hugh held to his course, merely pointing to the claw hammer and then in the direction of the cliff path. Dada raised a thumb and mouthed 'Swinging'. Then he pulled the cord on the mower once again – and it sprang into life. The tinny whirr of the engine always startled him. It was reminiscent of enemy aircraft. And, as always, he had a brief moment of panic, a powerful impulse to dig a slit trench and throw himself into it.

Dermot was shaken by a spasm of rage at his own weakness. The same rage he had experienced when his platoon captured its first German bunker high in the Apennines. Allied Command had assured its troops that the Krauts were demoralised and on the verge of flight. But the bunker he peered into had been beautifully wall-papered. How close to flight is a soldier who bothers to wall-paper his bunker? By the holy fly, best fighting troops in the world, those

Germans! Thus his heart had not pounded with rage at the enemy, but at the ignorance or duplicity of his superiors – pounded and then sunk.

'Tell me the story of Little Lorna and Prince Flasheen Eyes,' said the Moo, who had crept back into the parental bed as soon as Dada had risen to mow the lawn.

'You must be tired of that story by now, the Moo,' replied Maman, pleased.

'No. Tell it.'

'I haven't time now, darling. You know that I have to spring up and make lunch or else Dada will be cross.'

'Not yet though,' said the Moo, who knew his mother.

'Well perhaps not *quite* yet,' agreed Maman, who had the greatest difficulty getting up. Especially on Sundays when the big lunch had to be cooked. It wasn't that she couldn't cook; it was because Dermot was such a stickler for punctuality. It made her so fraught that, ironically, she became unable to put the meal on the table. If there were any danger of its being ready on time, she would drift off to arrange flowers or iron napkins. Dr Siskin's Valium helped in some respects by reducing anxiety; but in others, it did not help because it was only anxiety that drove her even to approximate the punctual completion of a meal.

Dermot was very good. He hardly stickled about anything, not even the nerves which had been the bane of her life; and which he had been alone in diagnosing when they first met. But lately he had begun to look thunderous when he returned exhausted from the office to find his dinner not waiting for him. He had every right to sit there in silence, his drawn hungry face speaking volumes, because after all it was little enough to ask that a hot meal should be ready for him when he slaved away all day and was so patient with the children and so good about her nerves. Plus, he shelled out money he could ill afford on Mother's Helps. But, somehow, all this only made matters worse – the meal more impossible to serve up, and Dermot's face, blacker. If things didn't improve, thought Maman, he might even *lose his temper*. Her neck grew stiff and painful at the very idea, and she felt slightly sick.

Still, there was time for a little story with the Moo. A story always

33

helped to assuage the slight bitterness she still felt at having failed to publish a single one of her literary efforts. Of course, her inferiority complex had always whispered to her that her efforts were vain, her stories valueless; but some other part of her had rebelled and remained hopeful. Alas, the complex had been proved right. When she told stories to her children, therefore – as she had to each in turn when they were young – she could live again briefly in that Golden Age before her ankles had thickened and her literary hopes been dashed.

She drew the sheet over both of them to make a tented world in which the enchantment of the tale could be held. It had a square patch of thinner cotton, like a magical window through which the Moo could watch the action of the story unfold. The Moo was suspicious of fantastical stories; he preferred the romance of the True Life tale.

'Little Lorna stood outside the large hall and listened to the sound of music and dancing which drifted into the night,' began Maman, thinking to herself that her last-born child would soon be too old for these intimate sessions and that, thereafter, there would be no more. She and Dermot had decided on two children. It may have been literary failure which led her to beg for a third. To have then given birth to a fourth had been a wholly unexpected blessing. 'She had been invited to a ball at the Regimental Headquarters near where she lived, and it was there that she met a dashing young Irish Captain.'

'Prince Flasheen Eyes,' sighed the Moo.

Half-way around the lake Charles Hamilton stopped at the gap in the undergrowth which fringed the lake's perimeter. Because of some quirk of topography, some tilt of the earth, the water was at its deepest here, practically – it was rumoured – unfathomable. And beneath the black surface, it was said, there lurked an ancient pike. A member who had once angled for this legendary denizen, and caught it, had been dragged into the water. He would have perished had not his screams alerted a men's four, who landed him with a fallen branch and half a rotting tennis net. Even today, just as people were beginning to say that the enormous fish was dead or, perhaps, imaginary, an occasional and massive perturbation of the lake's waters at twilight seemed to confirm the continued existence of the Leviathan and its unabated health.

Charles crept to the edge – he could not swim – and peered into the depths, as if he might glimpse the submarine monster ghosting through the weedy murk. He experienced a frisson of fear, like vertigo. Quickly he stepped back and raised his eyes to the far shore where men were sitting out on the terrace in the weak September sunlight, drinking their halves of beer or gins and it, before sloping home to the roasts their wives were cooking. Moving among them was the distinctive figure of the Colonel, cadging drinks. No one seemed to resent it. Charles saw him pause at the Secretary's table and accept an offer of pork scratchings. How the Colonel could pass the time of day with that man, let alone seek out his company, was beyond him – a man whose chief pleasure lay in blackballing any candidate for club membership who was not a replica of himself, namely: a purple-nosed ex-military bigot, who strove to scotch the membership hopes of anyone he suspected of being Jewish, Roman Catholic, American or connected to show business. Anyone, in fact, whom he accounted 'second eleven'. Fortunately, his bigotry was matched only by his lack of perspicacity. Dan Rose had been welcomed owing to Colonel Lamb's belief that the Roses were an old Yorkshire family; Dan's friend Eugene McCarthy from Cork had slipped through the vetting procedure simply by laughing incredulously when asked if he were a bloody Catholic. Both names therefore had been passed up for approval to a Committee increasingly puzzled by the apparent lack of applications. Charles had managed to secure Theo's membership only by concealing his son's maternal roots.

Charles thought of his beloved wife. It distressed him that he couldn't remember her face. But then, occasionally, he caught a sudden expression of hers as if out of the corner of his eye. She was smiling sceptically at him with a little twist of her mouth, and flicking back her dark luscious hair. How ironical it was that she had left Germany long before the other Jews, only to… well, it didn't bear thinking about.

Across the still surface of the lake wafted the sound of laughter. Doubtless the Colonel was working his damnable charm. Charles couldn't suppress the suspicion that the laughter was aimed at him.

Stung all over again by the Colonel's desertion, he turned his back on the lake and pushed his way into the undergrowth. He had never before ventured so far off the beaten track and so he was surprised to come across a clearing in which there were signs of habitation. A crudely-built lean-to had been constructed on one side of an ancient oak. Another, like a mirror image, had been assembled on the opposite side of the clearing. Could some primitive people actually be living here? The sun was really quite hot now, almost uncomfortably so, and the air was very still. Charles even found it a little difficult to breathe. He pulled out a handkerchief and mopped his brow.

The silence was rent by the harsh cry of a macaw. It startled him. His heart skipped a beat. Silence descended again. Charles became irrationally reluctant to move. Defiantly he forced himself on, acutely aware of the clumsy noise he was making as he pushed deeper into the wilderness, trampling down bracken and briar. Suddenly, he was frozen in his tracks by one of the most ominous sounds in Creation.

4

THE path sloped upward ever more steeply towards the garden gate. At the top it was overshadowed by massive rhododendron bushes whose blooms in early summer, blood-red and white, were as big as a boy's head. Under their canopy the sound of birdsong and lawn mower alike were muted. Hugh paused in the chapel-like hush to wonder what exactly he was up to. Not at this moment, walking up to inspect a broken fence, but in general. In Life.

He had always been clever. That is, he had always passed exams two years early, always been the precocious youngest in the class. He had won a scholarship to the brutal Public School chosen by Dada on the strength of its rugger reputation. He had passed his 'O' levels when he was barely fifteen. Dada used to read out his reports as proudly as if they were his own:

Hugh is as bright and questioning in class as he is thoughtful and meticulous in his written work. The examinations held no terrors for him.

And,

Another outstanding term's work. The examinations hardly tested him. We should be thinking about Oxbridge colleges! Well done indeed.

But something went wrong in the sixth form. Hugh began not to mind if his Latin unseens were less than perfect. He began not to care about Henry VII's foreign policy or whether Satan was the real hero of *Paradise Lost*. He had sat exams every term since he was seven, and he was tired of them. He wanted to read and write without always having to look over his shoulder at the predictable, old-fashioned curriculum. He wanted to be left alone to scowl over Sartre and the Beat Poets, Aldous Huxley and the Angry Young Men – none of whom, naturally, were considered suitable for school. His reports

37

recorded the sorry tale:

Hugh seems lackadaisical... does not contribute to the class... written work careless and late... early promise sadly unfulfilled... lost his spark... unlikely to achieve the 'A' level grades necessary for...

When the deputy head, Foggo Parkinson, gave him detention for reading *Saturday Night and Sunday Morning* as if it were pornography, it was the last straw. Hugh grew sullen, scuffing his feet in a slovenly way as he paced the endless corridors. If he couldn't get blind drunk in the North of England and get into punch-ups and have sex behind dustbins in alleys, he could at least leave his boring priggish school. But the school got there first:

Hugh's attitude leaves a great deal to be desired... I have had to speak to him on several occasions... letting himself down... smell of tobacco... deplorable 'protest' in the School Necessities... unhealthy influence on younger boys... school morale... obviously feels we have nothing further to teach him... best if we part company...

Nothing so dramatic as expulsion, then – just a sort of fading away of his stellar future, not with a bang but a whimper.

To their credit, Maman and Dada (both of whom lacked, and were slightly suspicious of, an English education) had not made as much fuss as Hugh expected. A bout of nerves, a threatened loss of temper, certainly; but also a kind of relief that their son had ceased to drive himself so hard and competitively towards academic perfection. It was vaguely agreed that his education would continue, but that for the moment he'd 'take a break', 'sort himself out', and so on, prior to fulfilling Dada's dream of fathering an Oxford man.

While Hugh suspected that he was destined to disappoint Dada, another part of him was so relieved, so light of heart, to be out of prison that he could believe anything possible, even admittance to Oxford. His alternative plan, however, was to get a best-selling novel (or, at least, a hit record) under his belt before Oxford time arrived, thus cushioning the blow to Dada's hopes. Unluckily, he found it tricky to get started in the mornings, preferring to lie in bed and think about birds; and then, when he did get started in the early afternoon, he had to work first on his Nobel Prize for Literature acceptance speech – which, with some severe editing, he had got down to under an hour. Foggo did not come well out of it. Typically, he began work on the novel when everyone else was asleep.

Hugh went through the rickety gate, out on to the cliff path. He turned left and began to walk towards the back of the Cholmondeleys property, checking as he went the fence to his right. It was roughly built: wooden posts hammered into the ground were connected by cross bars nailed closely together so that a child could not slip through – and over the cliff. For, while the hills of St Michael's Hill were mostly clay, there were seams of sand that were vulnerable to erosion. The clay path marked just such an abrupt transition; but the sand beyond it had subsided and been washed away long ago, leaving a sheer drop on to the famous, but now defunct, Brickland Race Track. No one used the path much except for the Fuehrer and his Enemy, who waged war along its length on their bikes. It was a short-cut to the Tennis Club, but not much of one; and in any case people mostly went by road. Nevertheless, all the Blyte children had been banned from the hazardous path until they were at least eight. It was out of bounds, of course, to the Moo.

The novel. That was another bloody thing. No one mentioned how hard it was to write a novel. It looked easy when you read them. And it *was* quite easy – to start with. Hugh had started several. His latest was set way back in the past, more than ten years ago, where his hero Rex Darkling was attending his parents' funeral. They'd been horribly mangled in a train crash. Rex's funeral gear was tight black jeans and a black leather jacket, like M. Brando's in that motorbike film. His hair was black and greased back. His expression was brooding. He had felt nothing when he identified the mutilated heads of his parents. He felt nothing now as he dispassionately catalogued the blind futile movements of a worm wriggling at the bottom of the grave. His heart was a stone. He was incapable of feeling. A monster. He scowled around at the other mourners. Lady Isabella was watching him from under her veil. Her black eyes were burning suggestively. At once Rex knew, with an almost visionary clarity, that he would possess her…

Hell's teeth, it was spastic. Barbara Cartland in bed with Albert Camus ('Don't start,' Hugh warned, as his underpants were stirred). Basically, it was impossible to write a novel, realised Hugh with an almost visionary clarity, until he'd had sexual intercourse. It was all so *typical.*

～

39

'The brave soldiers were getting ready to snatch Europe back from the Hun,' continued Maman, feeling obliged to add some educational detail to the story. 'For the war was in its third year and it was dark days for the British who had fought alone against the mighty German war machine. We had been living under air raids and threats of invasion, severe rationing and much hardship. But now the tide was turning. The Americans had come with chocolate and nylons to help us; the Germans were beaten in the Sahara by the Desert Rats; and we were ready to free Little Lorna's beloved but cowardly France from the tyranny of the Fuehrer.'

'Not *our* Fuehrer,' interjected the Moo comfortably.

'No, not our good little Fuehrer, but the cruel Fuehrer Hitler. Now. There were a lot of parties and balls to cheer us up at this time, and Little Lorna had many admirers because she was pretty and vivacious, with lovely slender ankles.'

'She was a sheik.'

'Nearly, darling – she was *chic*. Especially in the velvet skirt and little bolero she'd made out of curtains, like Scarlett O'Hara.'

'And she put tea on her legs.'

'That's right! To make them look as if she had stockings on. Which they did once she'd drawn a line down the backs with an eyebrow pencil. Oh yes, men fell at her feet, which was, frankly, a bore. She had turned down three proposals of marriage. But she was nearly twenty-three, and ready to settle down.'

'Before she became an old maid.'

'Well, she would never be *that*. Anyway, she was greeted at the door by the adjutant of the Regiment, who had organised the ball.'

'Prince Flasheen Eyes.'

'Exactly. But of course Little Lorna didn't know his name yet or who he was. She only saw a rather young-looking man with thick hair –'

'Bright red hair!'

'Well, redd*ish* hair, who said in an Irish accent, which he had in those days: "My name is Captain Dermot Blyte, but you can call me Prince Flasheen Eyes." And he did this thing with his eyes, and didn't say "flashing" but put on a soppy voice and said "flasheen". It was so unexpected and silly that I laughed even though I didn't mean to. Then he said: "I've been waiting for you all my life, and you shall dance with no one but me!"

'He was cocky,' said the Moo. 'Like Cassius Clay. "Ah em the gradest!"' he elaborated.

'He was *very* cocky. So Little Lorna bantered right back at him: "What a pity I shan't be dancing at all then!" But he only smiled, and looked deeply into Little Lorna's eyes so that she felt a bit queer. Well, of course, after that, she was determined not to dance with Prince Flasheen Eyes; and she planned the biting things she'd say to him when he asked her.'

'But he didn't ask 'er.'

'No, he didn't.'

'She was cross.'

'Yes. She was rather. Especially as he was dancing all the time with other girls. Little Lorna watched him out of the corner of her eye. Then she realised: although he was handsome and dashing, he was not dancing with the pretty girls but with the girls nobody was asking to dance.'

'The walleyes,' said the Moo.

'The wall*flowers*,' corrected Maman.

'He was *kind*,' exclaimed the Moo.

'Yes. He felt responsible for the success of the ball and he wanted everyone to have a good time. Little Lorna's heart melted.'

'Then at midnight came the spot dance,' said the Moo impatiently.

'Yes. Do you remember what that is?'

'The lights go down, a spotlight comes on and whizzes about the dancers, and when the band stops playing the spotlight stops too. Then a man calls out orders to the dancers: "Everybody move four steps to the left, everybody move three steps back, everybody move six steps to the right, everybody –'

'That's it,' said Maman hastily. 'And when he has finished sending everyone all over the place, whichever couple is standing in the spotlight wins the prize!'

'An onion.'

'*Three* onions. Because onions were rationed and so they were a great treat.' Unable to believe that onions were a treat, the Moo pictured a fabulous cluster of Fabergé onions.

'And Prince Flasheen Eyes asked Little Lorna to dance,' he said. 'And she said: "I don't mind".'

'She did. And the Prince took her in his arms and they wafted around; and Little Lorna was excited because she longed to win the spot dance. But she was also sad because she knew she wouldn't win, because she had always longed to win something but had never won anything in her life. And she mentioned this to Prince Flasheen Eyes, who said very calmly: "We shall win tonight."'

'Then the band stopped playing and the moves were called out,' said the Moo. 'Everybody move forward five steps, everybody –'

'Yes, yes. And Prince Flasheen Eyes was whispering in Little Lorna's ear all the moves a second before the man called them out, as if he knew what they would be or as if he was pulling the man's strings. Step by step, left and right, backwards and forwards, they edged towards the magical pool of light. Then, just as they moved into it, the man announced that they were the prize winners. And everyone crowded around and admired the onions and said how lucky Little Lorna was, meaning lucky to dance with Prince Flasheen Eyes as well. And Little Lorna felt that if she stayed with him, she would be from then on a lucky person, who won things, instead of standing against the wall watching the winners dance past.'

'And she married him,' sighed the Moo. 'And he went off to fight the Germans, and came back again. And they had four children – the first three hideous and, frankly, a bore, but the fourth one lovely and Little Lorna's favourite.' Maman laughed and kissed the Moo on his firm, chubby, wonderfully edible cheeks.

The distant roar ceased, leaving a strange echo in the charged air. Janey sat up, her hands still festooned with daisy chains. She listened intently. There was nothing but the distant lawn mower, the nagging of a wood pigeon and the cry of a jay. She might be in Wiltshire, she reflected, or Dorset – those mythic places where all girls had ponies – instead of only a couple of miles from the ever-expanding girth of Greater London. If only something would happen. If only a passing band of gypsies would bundle her into a highly-painted caravan and bear her away to a life of flounced skirts and horse fairs. Then she heard the sound again. It was clearly an approaching car. But not a normal car. Its high-pitched rev and deep bass roar were like a racing car's; like Mr Cholmondeley's red sports car, but more so. As it drew nearer, Janey's heart raced.

Around the corner of Chestnut Avenue swerved the most glamorous machine she had ever laid eyes on, and all the more snazzy for its simplicity: a black Mini Minor.

Of course, a Mini was in itself – being all the rage – Swinging. But black was not among its standard colour schemes, and so this one had been specially made – a deduction borne out by its souped-up engine, its thick tyres, its twin exhausts, its wealth of chrome and – *the coup de grâce* – its blacked-out, smoked-glass windows.

It stopped abruptly beside Janey. The invisibility of the driver made it seem autonomous and alive, like an intelligence from the future. It stood there, throbbing, veiled in its own mystery like an omen. Then, as if satisfied by her gape of admiration, it shot off – zipping up the avenue, veering right at the end and thrumming away into the far reaches of the estate.

Janey was left feeling excited and a little uneasy. What did the Black Mini portend? What did it mean to be singled out by such a creature? It was marvellous but also uncanny – laden with a meaning she couldn't fathom, like a foreboding.

The path was slippery after yesterday's drizzle. Side-stepping an outcrop of rhododendron branches, Hugh found himself skidding down a concealed dip in the path where the sand had subsided more dramatically, taking part of the path with it. Instinctively he reached out for the fence post, but it wasn't there. Or, rather, it was there – but it had come loose from its crumbling footings and was leaning outwards so that its whole section of fence hung at an acute angle over the precipice. The post had to be pulled in, and righted, and fixed with a good sledge-hammering. Since this was impossible at present, he'd just have to do what he could.

The more pressing question was: how did you get to have sexual intercourse? Plan A – to get drunk in the North of England etc. like in *Sat. Night and Sun. Morn.* – was not practical: he'd simply be beaten up in a pub for being a sissy Southerner. It had better be Plan B: the hit record. Result: knee-deep in tasty birds. He'd got a lot of the words and some of the tune. It was to be sung in the classical manner – fast and raw like *Hound Dog*:

I've given up thinking and I've taken to the drinking sang Hugh in a low voice, glancing around to make sure the Fuehrer wasn't

43

within range,

> *But I'm sh-sh-shaken by the D-DTs*   (Roger Daltrey stutter).
> *I've given up the girlies, got me by the short and curlies*
> *So I've taken to the mar-tee-nees...*   (swivel legs)

The trouble was, 'short and curlies' would be banned from the radio like that bloke telling Laura he loved her while dying in a stock car race. Sex and death were the two things you couldn't get on the radio; but what else was there? Hugh sighed deeply. In any case, he couldn't sing 'short and curlies' in public. Not till Maman was dead anyway. Typical.

He knelt down and, leaning tentatively forward, grasped the skewed fence post. Then, together with its section of fence, he pulled it towards him. For one moment he thought he was going to topple forward and pitch over the cliff to his doom. However, breathing heavily, heart beating, he hauled the post upright. He stood up and bore down on it. He didn't like to use his full weight because the post was beginning to rot, and he was afraid it would snap; but at least it was more or less vertical. What was really needed was a whole new fence, preferably chain link. That would settle it. Meanwhile, there ought to be some sort of notice. A warning sign.

> *One for the road, bubble, toil and trouble*
> *One for the road , now I'm seeing double*
> *Swallow the TOAD*   (Del Shannon falsetto)
> *Barman says "Nope, you know now it's closing time*
> *CLO-OSING TIME".*   (Frank Ifield yodel?)

Yes, the chorus of the hit record was coming along. Except, it needed a key change. But, hell's teeth, how did you change key? *Play Guitar the Bert Weedon Way* didn't say; and, besides, Hugh did not want in any way to play the guitar like B. Weedon. One of the merits of falling in love with a Mexican girl was that you didn't have to change keys. But now he needed to, and couldn't – and couldn't anyway until he re-stringed the guitar after the Fuehrer's ravages, and tuned it. Which he probably wouldn't be able to. Oh God, what did it matter? He shouldn't be writing pop songs anyway. He was only doing it for profoundly ignoble reasons, viz.: to pull birds. He should be devoting himself, Keats-like, to Beauty, Truth etc. But, oh God, he was so sick of battling with the beast in his underpants, so mortally tired of it all. *Weltschmerz* came down on him like a drowsy numbness; and he began to walk dully back towards the garden.

Passing the summerhouse, as Maman called it, Hugh could hear the Moo banging about inside. It was a hexagonal wooden structure, slightly raised, where garden furniture was stacked. Unfortunately it was also full of the furniture, old trunks and boxes which had overflowed from the house, rendering it unusable for the gracious shady teas Maman had envisaged. Suddenly, the Moo burst out of the doorway and down the three steps. He was brandishing two Dinky toy cars and uttering muted plosive sounds, his eyes unseeing as they focused inwardly on the imminence of a violent car crash. His brow furrowed as he strove to reconcile his intense desire that the tiny E-type Jaguar would triumph, with the worrying suspicion that, in fact, its long bonnet would crumple horribly in collision with the solid Wolseley of the police. Its driver, Jack Pluff, reached a hand out to his trusty companion, Fray Bentos the tame wolf, who bore the same relation to Spiv as Pluff bore to the Moo. 'It's all right, boy,' murmured Pluff grimly, 'the cops are going to get more than they bargained for because... because I've reinforced the bonnet so as it's *a battering ram*.' The Moo's face brightened as he trotted blindly past his eldest brother, reproducing the sounds of a high-performance car accelerating, and the cacophony of metal striking metal at great speed. Having disposed of the police car, Jack Pluff – soldier, cowboy, Surrey cricketer, Number One recording star and, now, jewel thief – raced on towards the Tower of London where the Jag battered through the gates. Fray Bentos seized the Crown Jewels in his powerful jaws as Jack fought off the army of fat Beefeaters with their puffed-up pants. As the twosome made their getaway, the Beefeaters stared wonderingly at the receding E-type, their punctured pants slowly subsiding.

'*What the hell are you playing at?*' The E-type was stopped in its tracks by Dada's furious shout. Both the Moo and Hugh watched, surprised, as Dada abandoned the mower and raced towards them. 'What are you doing in there, the Moo?' said Dada sharply and a little too breathlessly. 'You know the summerhouse is out of bounds,' he added before the Moo could protest.

'I don't think he did, Dada,' said Hugh. 'I certainly didn't.'

'Well... well you know now.' Hugh was taken aback by Dada's vehemence.

'The Moo was doing no harm, Dada.'

'Well, that's as may be…' Dada's anger had given way to a softer, almost appeasing tone which made Hugh suspicious. 'But I won't have him, or any of you, mucking about in there.'

'Why not?'

'It's… dangerous.'

'I don't think a summerhouse is all that dangerous, Dada.'

'Oh, I see. So you wish to see a large stack of furniture fall on the Moo's head before you have second thoughts?'

'I don't think that looks likely.'

'Likely? Likely? You will perhaps forgive your father if he takes a less cavalier attitude towards his children's lives. Even if the chance of death or maiming were the remotest possible I would still forbid entry to this building. Besides,' he added irritably, 'I'm not going to stand here arguing with you. You will simply do as I say for once in your life.'

'But Dada,' piped up the Moo, 'we've *always* played in the summerhouse. You never said anything before.'

'I most certainly did. And even if I did not, I am saying now. It is out of bounds.' Hugh was struck by his father's shifty look. He wondered why Dada was being so defensive. He didn't for a moment believe the dangerous furniture story. Dada was hiding something. Almost certainly something squalid. But what?

'I thought I'd locked the bloody place,' Dada was muttering to himself. 'Where are my keys…?' He rummaged in his pockets for his key ring, pulled it out and, selecting one, locked the summerhouse door with a flourish. 'There! Now we'll hear no more about this.'

The Moo was not perturbed. He was already revving the E-type prior to an explosive departure. Hugh observed his father almost pityingly. The man clearly had no idea that the window on the left of the door, although warped, was unlocked and easily prised open. A thing Hugh made a mental note to do, when he had a moment. But then it crossed his mind, out of the blue, that Dada was keeping something illicit in there. Magazines, perhaps, like *Health and Efficiency*; but worse. The shame attached to this idea made him turn away from himself – made him, in fact, put the whole incident away. On reflection, the last thing he wanted to find out was what Dada had locked in the summerhouse.

He left his father to resume mowing and wandered off into George's zone.

'Mein Fuehrer! The sledge hammer. Where is it?'

'Dunno,' said George, looking up blearily from his pan of molten lead.

'Yes, you do. Think. Where did you leave it?'

George frowned with the effort of recollection.

'It's up at the Tennis Club. At my camp. I needed it to hammer in the shoring.'

'Dada'll kill you if he finds out. You know what he's like about tools left out. He still hasn't forgotten what you did to all the house keys,' warned Hugh, glad that for once it was not one of his possessions which lay rotting or rusting in George's workings.

'Don't tell him. I'll get it. Straight after lunch.'

'Squalid Hun.'

The low rumbling sound was more like distant thunder than any noise an animal could make. Yet Charles knew that it was an animal because he had heard it before in the rain forest. It was the throaty roar of a tiger – that indescribable ripping sound, like the tearing of a membrane between this world and some other world of terror.

Charles peered through the thicket. He saw that he had come to the boundary of the Tennis Club grounds, where they abutted on to the property next door. He had heard that the new owner, a man who had made a fortune out of managing pop music turns, had built a private menagerie. This accounted for the cries of macaws, the distant rumpus of monkeys and, above all, the roar of tigers. They were supposed to be sad, clapped-out old cats whom the impresario had saved from the knackers' yard.

He edged forward, holding his breath. There, beyond the rotted remains of the Club's fence, now lying flat on the ground, were six tigers burning brightly in their chain-link run. The animal who had spoken detached itself from the group and slunk towards him. It did not look at all clapped out. In fact, with its enormous head and paws, its heavy muscles and brilliantly painted coat, rather the reverse. It rested its amber eyes calmly on Charles Hamilton and, barely six feet away, began to walk to and fro, riffling its fur against the wire of the cage. But even during its smart about-turns it never once took its eyes off him. Mesmerised, Charles was rooted to the spot. The rippling of the black-striped orange coat turned the fur to flames that burnt into Charles, bringing to mind his mortality.

He cast an uneasy eye over the cage. Before the war he had engineered bridges in India and Malaya, a job which not only enabled him to assess the security or otherwise of the structure; but had also familiarised him with the capabilities of tigers. Thus, although the fence was high – more than twice as high as he – with an inward-slanting overhang, he knew that a tiger (even a clapped-out tiger) could escape quite easily if it had a mind to. Fortunately the tiger in front of him now, he told himself, would be too well fed and lazy to wish to exert itself. All the same, Charles was scared.

He made to move away. At once the tiger flung itself with a terrible snarl against the mesh of the cage and hung there by the claws as if crucified. It stared hard at Charles before dropping back to the ground and resuming its patrol. Charles didn't dare move again. Didn't dare incite the beast. Having seen its claws he didn't doubt that it could not only bound over the top, but also tear down the cage any time it wanted. So Charles just stood there, every inch of his skin prickling, unable to take his eyes off the eyes of the tiger, fixed on him as dispassionately as a god.

And he felt overwhelmingly that it was the tiger who was free and he who was caged, just as he had been caged for so long in that unspeakable jungle camp after the fall of Singapore. No wonder the Colonel regarded him with, at best, indifference and, at worst, contempt. Seeing himself clearly in the mirror of the tiger's jewel-like eye, he understood that he was as miserable a specimen as his captors had always maintained. A worthless sort of a chap. No wonder he had no friends, and a son who put up with him out of pity.

Charles felt momentarily close to tears – more evidence of his weakness and lack of worth. The tiger stopped dead. As if its work was done, it turned on its heel like a sergeant major and ambled away. As it did so, it lifted its tail and, in an act of scorn, fired out of its nether regions a jet of vile fluid that would have hit Charles right between the eyes had he not flinched in time.

In the bar, Charles swallowed a large whisky. Several people edged away from him. He realised that he stank of tiger. Through the window he could see the Colonel, still working the terrace. The boom of the Secretary's laugh filled him with violent emotion. Normally he would wait until the Colonel was ready to return with him for Sunday lunch at the Blytes'. But today he slipped away, leaving his companion – if that was the word – to make his own way home. On the whole, he thought, he wouldn't mention the business with the tiger. There was too much attached to it, too much of something very like shame.

5

MAMAN was rooting around in the larder, selecting vegetables and naming them under her breath in French. *Pommes de terre, carottes, oignons, petits pois...* But what was the French for cabbage? She experienced a moment of pure panic as the word – which she knew as well as her own name – failed to arrive on her tongue. It was like the first symptom of some ghastly disease. She pressed her forehead against the cool mesh of the meat safe and willed the French for cabbage to come. It wouldn't. And there was no one to help her with the cooking. It was typical that just when Carla, the so-called Mother's Help, was needed most, she disappeared to Mass – a luxury Lorna couldn't afford because, even if her Catholicism hadn't lapsed, mortal sin was less costly than the wrath of Dermot at an unpunctual lunch.

'Are you all right, Mrs Blyte?' asked a voice. Maman jumped.

'What do you want, Sabrina?' She didn't snap exactly, but the shock made her short.

'I've come to help you with dinner. I said I would, after my piano lesson.'

Maman blinked. She was at a loss as to what to say to this child, more than a year younger than Janey yet so composed as to seem an adult. And so immaculately turned out in her fresh print dress that Maman felt momentarily – absurdly – dishevelled beside her. Once the picture of French fashion, putting the frumpish English to shame, she dressed carelessly now, in voluminous skirts, sloppy joes, cardigans and sensible shoes that emphasised as if out of self-spite the tragedy of her ankles.

'Did you, dear? I don't remember.' She raised an unconscious hand to the wisps of hair which had escaped their grips and which contrasted sharply with Sabrina's hair, severely pulled back and hanging in a glossy pony tail. Her eyes were a spectral blue, almost violet, like Elizabeth Taylor's. It was disconcerting to find that the child, perhaps because of the slight heel on her white shoes – too old for her, Maman disapproved silently – was an inch taller than her own five feet two. Petite, Dermot called her; but 'dwarfish' was how she thought of herself when the black dog of self-dislike bit. 'And you really mustn't creep up on people like that. I might have had a heart attack. Didn't you think to knock at the back door?'

'It was open,' said Sabrina. 'I like the way you leave your doors open. So inviting. I like informality myself. At home Cheryl and Roger are always locking doors.' She tilted her finished little head to one side and smiled patiently, like the hairdresser Maman dreaded going to.

'I don't think I need any help today, dear – thank you all the same.' What was the matter with the child, always coming round, always at her elbow, offering help? It was as unnatural as the beautiful, spooky colour of her eyes.

'Sunday lunch can be such a struggle,' said Sabrina, still smiling.

'Oh it's pretty straightforward,' said Maman, irked that Sabrina seemed to have divined the truth. Out of the window she could see the Fuehrer reeling back from the fumes of his molten lead and clutching the German helmet to his head. She clucked her tongue in exasperation.

'You must be the last people on Earth not to have a fridge,' smiled Sabrina, going into the larder and opening the meat safe which stood on a low table with its legs set in bowls of water to repel ants. 'My, that was a big fly.'

'No, dear. It wasn't,' said Maman quickly, although she had perhaps seen something fly out.

'I think it was a bluebottle.'

Maman's heart convulsed. This was the word she least wished to hear.

'I don't think so, dear.'

'I wonder if there's another.' Sabrina peered in at the joint of beef. 'Cheryl says they're not hygienic.'

Maman felt inclined to scream. She said:

'Can you carry the joint over to the table, Sabrina? Without dropping it?'

'Of course I can.'

'Thank you. Now, if you really want to help, you could make a start at peeling those potatoes. And don't forget to gouge out the eyes.'

While Sabrina was tipping spuds into an enamelled bowl in the sink, Maman surreptitiously scrutinised the joint. The kitchen was narrow and dark, so it was difficult to see what damage the bluebottle – if it had been a bluebottle, which was by no means certain – it might not have been a fly at all – what damage the hypothetical insect had wrought. She couldn't see any eggs. But that didn't mean much in the circumstances. She had a brief vision of her poisoned children turning blue at the lunch table, slumping face down into the lovely brick of Wall's (the new Raspberry Ripple!) she'd bought half an hour ago from the van; a brick, *zut,* that was already spreading in the warm larder.

She ought to chuck the beef out. She would chuck it out. Or, she could wash it. This was no guarantee of safety, of course, but better than nothing. Oh, but all this hoo-hah – *nom d'un chien,* she felt exhausted already – was quite unnecessary if the unidentified flying object had *not* been a bluebottle. And besides, a good roasting would surely burn any noxious germs to a crisp. She'd leave the *sacre* beef. The crucial thing was simply to get it in the heated oven *now* if it was to be ready by Dermot's two-o'clock-at-the-latest.

'Have you any rubber gloves, Mrs Blyte?' Sabrina was asking.

'No.'

'Cheryl always wears them. So do I, actually. Otherwise one's nails suffer rather.'

'Mon Dieu.'

'I wish I could be more like you, and not care about nails and things. Perhaps it'd be better if I made the Yorkshire pudding.'

'Shouldn't you be helping your mother with the lunch?'

'Cheryl doesn't really like help. She's more of a one-man band. Besides, we only have spaghetti Bolognese or something else simple on Sundays. But I think it's nice to have an old-fashioned meal. Your kitchen is old-fashioned, too. Nice. Not like ours, all clean and shiny and convenient.'

'Spaghetti Bolognese,' thought Maman, who had only ever heard of such a thing and certainly never eaten it. Even Carla, who was Italian, had not suggested it. It was like *La Dolce Vita* over at the Cholmondeleys, with their refrigerators and rubber gloves and spaghetti. And children in high heels with, now she came to look more closely, a touch of make-up. At Sabrina's age. Really, it was most… *unsuitable*. Still, it was not the child's fault. And she meant well.

'Do you know how to make a batter, dear?'

'Oh yes. Well, sort of…'

'We'll make it together, shall we?'

'Oh *yes*.'

'*Chou!*' exclaimed Maman, suddenly remembering.

'Bless you.'

'No,' said Maman, laughing with relief. '*Chou*. Cabbage.'

At five minutes to two the children convened to be inspected before lunch. Dada stood in front of the mirror over the fireplace buffing his hair to a high sheen with the set of brushes he kept in the hall. Swoosh, swoosh, went the brushes alternately.

'It's little short of tragic that none of you kids has inherited my hair.' He sighed and, with a sorrowing expression, turned to face them. 'Ah, the Young Master. Have you washed your hands and brushed what is left of your hair?'

'I have, Dada,' replied Hugh.

'That's my boy. You are excused inspection. You have grown too old for it. And besides, if I cannot accept the word of my son and heir, this family would be in a sorry state indeed. Now, Janey. You look very nice, my darling girl. Can you not brush your hair out of your face a little? Just this once? For your proud Dada? It's such a pretty face if people were allowed to see it.'

'Oh Dada, shut up, please.'

'Oh well, if you cannot do such a little thing to please your poor old father who, God knows, does not ask anything of his children except that they are honest and try to do their best in all things –'

'All right, all right – is *that* better?' Janey scraped her hand across her face and flung her hair back.

'Yes, yes, that's much better, my beloved daughter.' He kissed the top of her head as wisps of hair began, in a trickle at first and then in a cascade, to curtain her face once again. 'Now, mein Fuehrer. Let's see.' George had wet his comb and slashed once at his hair so that the front lay in a fat diagonal slick across his forehead while the back remained matted. Whether he had intended an approximation to his namesake's famous hairstyle was not certain. 'This will not do, mein Fuehrer,' said Dada. 'You must comb your entire head. Before you do so, you must stimulate the follicles, like this.' Dada placed the tips of all his fingers on George's scalp and, putting on his Stimulating-the-Follicles face – the one he used every morning on his own head – he vibrated the fingers nervily. 'Night and morning, mein Fuehrer, if you wish to hold on to your hair. It is too late for your older brother, but you may yet avert baldness for many years if you do as I say.'

'Like this, Dada?' said George, advancing on the Moo with rigid, claw-like fingers and a hideous rictus set on his face. The Moo shouted and hid behind Janey. 'Comenzi here, fat little Englander,' suggested George, 'und I vill make you squeal like zer pig you are.'

'Well, George,' said Dada. 'Frankly I am disappointed. You make a joke of this, but you will be sorry when your hair begins to fall.'

'Resistance is useless, you weakling,' pursued George. 'Your FOLLICLES ARE MINE!' He lowered his hands and reversed the claws so that they pointed upwards. Then he lunged at the Moo's genitals. The Moo let out a scream and cowered farther behind his sister.

'Stop, mein Fuehrer! If you don't stop, I'll *go sloppy* on you!' George still advanced but with less vigour. He didn't want to be seen to fear the Moo's threat; but, in truth, he was apprehensive. The Moo had developed this habit of going sloppy in self-defence. The first time he had gone sloppy on George, George had thought it easy to shrug him off and dispatch him with a bayonet thrust. But, strangely, he could not. It was not so much that the Moo was immovable, heavy though he was; it was more that there was a special quality to his bulk as it leaned on George, a kind of positive force born of its very negativity, its passivity, which sucked the strength from him. George felt weak, slightly hysterical, as if he had been laughing uncontrollably, and he found he could not even raise his hands to poke the Moo in the soft places which made him squeal and beg

54

for a mercy the adamantine Fuehrer would only reluctantly – and after a good long poke – extend to him. He pretended that he was voluntarily giving in to the Moo's leaning; but he knew it was only a matter of time before the Moo twiggez-vous-ed, and then... what? It didn't bear thinking about. His brief ascendancy would end, the Reich would topple, and he would be once again at the bottom of the pecking order, as he had been before the Moo came into this world. He made another half-hearted lunge at the Moo's underbelly, saying: 'I vill spare your miserable follicles zis time, podgy pig-dog, but please to remember zat I vill strike when you least are expecting it. Heh, heh, heh.' George retreated with diabolical laughter to the dining-room.

It had gone two. In the kitchen a fraught Maman, having at last sent Sabrina home, was locked in combat with the Mother's Help while the vegetables quietly boiled down to a pulp.

'I'm only asking you, Carla, if you happen to know where the ten-shilling note is that I left on the window-sill.' She did not look at the short, hairy, middle-aged Italian woman for fear of seeing her lip begin to tremble, as it so often did. It was all too trying. Carla had only arrived a month ago, smiling unctuously and showing a gold tooth. She had pinched the Moo's cheek so painfully that he had set Spiv on her. Hugh had wrinkled his nose fastidiously. Janey had found a greasy black hair in her scrambled eggs, and gone green. The Fuehrer lobbed hand grenades at her under his breath. On top of it all, she was not a Help to Mother. She was slovenly. And when she was not smiling in an ingratiating and, frankly, *épouvantable* way, she was crying. Her moustaches were quivering now.

'Scusi, Signora,' whined Carla. 'No understand, no understand.'

'I put money here,' said Maman, stabbing the window-sill. 'Now it is not here. Have you seen it?' She pointed to her eyes and then to Carla's, and then to the window-sill. It was all so exasperating. Sundays were bad enough without this. On the very day when she most needed help, Carla bunked off to church and, in the evening – when the children's supper needed doing – Carla would come down from her room in her best clothes and announce that she was off to take part in the *passegiatta*. With a peasant's inability to imagine a culture different from her own, she persisted in this folly every Sunday, pacing the deserted avenues of St Michael's Hill, peering over fences and through hedges in order to locate the grand procession she was certain must be occurring only a few feet away. Last week she had been brought back in a police car.

How Maman longed for her old Help, the pretty Swiss – and Protestant – Marietta, who spoke perfect English and French; who cleaned the whole house cheerfully before bringing her employer coffee and thin toast in bed; who understood that the English had *no idea* of what a real meringue consisted. Who had gone home to marry her childhood sweetheart.

'I no take moneys,' wailed Carla. 'I no take. Aiaieeee!'

'I'm not suggesting –'

'I no robber! You bad Signora!'

'Calm yourself, Carla. *Restez tranquille…* tranquilo. For God's sake –'

'Carla knows who take moneys,' said Carla, ceasing to cry and looking crafty. 'I see with these eyes.'

'Who?' asked Maman wearily.

'You no believe Carla…'

'Yes, yes, I believe you.'

'Fuehrer take money. I see with these eyes. He very bad man.'

It was the last straw. The only one of her children who would always be above suspicion was George. He was as incapable of stealing as he was of lying. Even Hugh's belongings, which he freely appropriated, were always left in full view, broken or dismantled, but never stolen and hidden. Carla, perhaps confused by his nickname, had picked the wrong child to accuse.

The four children gathered in the dining-room to watch Dada carving the beef. He had a special face for sharpening the knife with the steel – mouth pursed, cheeks puffed, veins outstanding – as he thrashed knife and steel together in the time-honoured berserker tradition of the Blytes. Then he tested the blade with his thumb, wincing at its acuity. Then, fork and knife poised over the joint, he cried 'Snippets!' His Sharpening Face changed abruptly to his Carving Face – eyes wrinkled, jaw jutted, lips stretched over his teeth – as he began to cut off the toothsome brown pieces of meat from the outside of the roast beef, offering them in turn to his salivating brood.

56

The question of turns was a vexed one. The usual order was: Janey because she was a girl; the Moo because he was the youngest; Hugh because he was the oldest; and then George because he was left over. Occasionally the order might change if the Moo was especially importunate or if Hugh suddenly asserted what he held to be the inalienable rights of the first-born; but George was still last. Yet he was the only one who never complained about his place in the order of snippet dispensation, either because he accepted the eternal fate of the third child among four, or perhaps because he suspected that he was Dada's favourite. This suspicion was not allayed by Dada's capricious behaviour two or three times a year when, casting aside all order and tradition, he cut an enormous snippet and, oblivious to all complaint, presented it to George as if the favouritism he suppressed for most of the year could no longer be contained. Such was the case today.

'Here is the best snippet for the best little brain in the family...'

George accepted the morsel of meat but did not eat it at once. Ignoring the howls of protest, he calmly flaunted it, taunting his siblings in the language of the Master Race:

'Dribble on, puny Englanders. Resistance is useless. You must bow before the power of the Reich...' Thus did the ceremony of the snippets make briefly visible the covert relationships which would obtain between the children for all of their lives.

'Dabs am going to have a 'nippet,' announced Dabs, making one of her unexpected appearances.

'It's *snippet*, Dabs,' corrected the Moo. 'Go on, say "snippet".'

''Nippet.'

'*Snippet.*' Spiv flew over and batted her in the chest.

'Ow! Ow! Schleppit! Suppit! Snookit!' cried Dabs in a panic.

'Calm down, Dabs,' said the Moo, surprised by the degree of hysteria.

'No, no! Dabs can't calm down. Dabs am werry frighty.'

'Whaddya frighty of, you village idiot?' said the Moo, trying to sound rough.

'Spiv bit Dabs. Dabs am bleeding to death,' said Dabs in a small voice.

'*I* don't see any blood, you steaming great nit. You're a big flabby liar, Dabs. And liars must be punished, mustn't they, Dada?'

'What's that? Punish liars? Yes indeed, the Moo. With extreme force.'

'Y'hear that, Dabs? You're going to be punished.'

'No, no! Dabs am bleeding inside. Dabs's infernal intesticles am frighty and moving about inside her and bashing into each other! And bleeding!'

'Calm down, calm down,' reiterated the Moo, a little alarmed. 'You don't have to be frightened. Look, Spiv's gone away now. I'll protect you from him.'

'The Moo loves Dabs,' sighed Dabs happily, her eyelashes fluttering, her tongue lolling affectionately. 'The Moo gives Dabs his 'nippet.'

'No, 'e does *not*,' emphasised the Moo.

'Oh!'

Maman appeared. She was red in the face.

'I've sacked Carla!' she said tearfully. 'You will have to drive her to the station, Dermot.'

'Certainly, mavourneen. And never fear – your Prince Flasheen Eyes will soon find a replacement for her.'

'You! When have *you* ever taken an interest in the running of this great big draughty house? Never! *I* will have to do it, as I have to do everything else, working my fingers to the bone!' She gesticulated violently with her plump fingers. 'Oh, my nerves are in *shreds*. I can no longer cope. I'm going to bed. Please have the goodness to remove that odious creature from my house.'

'Spiv is going to kill Carla,' announced the Moo.

'Spiv is not going to kill anyone,' said Dada firmly.

'He is.'

'That animal is a bad influence on the Moo,' opined Hugh. 'What began as a justifiable, Dabs-oriented series of retributions is becoming a senseless slaughter. Stalinesque.'

'She had the neck to accuse mein poor Fuehrer of stealing the ten shillings I left on the window-sill,' elaborated Maman. '*Nom de Dieu*, it is too much. Frankly, she is a sly creature. I might have believed it of Hugh or even the Moo, but not mein honest Fuehrer.'

'The very idea, macushla!'

'Actually,' said George nonchalantly, 'I thought the money was mine. The Enemy and I needed ten bob urgently to buy bangers.'

There was a short silence.

'Penny bangers. For pogromming ants,' George explained.

'In God's name,' cried Dada, 'how many of these fireworks did you need?'

'One hundred and twenty,' calculated the Moo. Dada paused to look with admiration at his youngest son, before exclaiming:

'And this for killing ants? Oh Lord, let me remain calm. Let me not lose my temper.'

'He puts the bangers in the ant hill and makes the Enemy light them and then he laughs when it blows up,' said the Moo, while Spiv squinted confirmation from over the edge of the table.

'How can you be so cruel, mein Fuehrer?' said Janey indignantly.

'They're *ants*,' said George pityingly.

'They are living creatures who have as much right to live as you do,' retorted Janey, looking upset.

'Ants have no rights. Even the Enemy knows that and he is a clot,' said George calmly. 'At least, the red ones have no rights. They sting. I only blow up red ants.'

'You'll have to say "sorry" to Carla, Maman,' said Janey. 'After all, the Fuehrer did take the money.'

'Yes, yes,' said Maman tetchily. 'Really, it is too trying of you, mein Fuehrer. You can't just help yourself to ten shillings like that. It is dishonest.'

'Well now, in all fairness, mavourneen, it was honest of him to own up at once,' said Dada.

'And he did assume the money was his in the first place,' Janey chipped in.

'Albeit an assumption he very often makes in relation to other people's possessions,' remarked Hugh.

'It is all very vexing,' said Maman, dabbing at her eyes with a hankie. 'I will have to apologise to Carla. Although, she should not have accused the Fuehrer of theft when, as he freely admits, he merely mistook the money for his own. There was a quickness to blame, a slyness, that is most unappetising.'

'She is not an appetising person,' suggested Hugh.

'That is a vile thing to say, Luh'le Shuggy,' said Maman. 'She is a poor creature, unblessed with attraction, but that is no reason to be unkind. You have all been unkind to her, a wretched woman far

59

away from her own country. Really, I am ashamed of you all.'

'She smells,' stated George.

'That is typical, mein Fuehrer. I won't have you speak in such terms. Frankly, I wash my hands of the lot of you.'

'It's true though,' said Janey. 'It's quite off-putting, especially first thing.'

'It may be true, Janey, but I should have thought that you, of all people, might show a little milk of human kindness.'

'I show milk,' said Janey, indignant.

'Well, yes. Very well. But you do the least possible. You show her no warmth.'

'Neither do you.'

'*Enfin*, that's enough. I will not have you speak to me like that. You can be cold, Janey. I do not like to say it, but it is true. If you are not careful, you will grow up to be a cold person and people will not like it. You will repel them.' Janey's eyes filled with tears. 'There, I have said it. I have issued a warning. Now let that be enough. Don't cry, darling. I did not mean to be severe. I was merely warning you for your own good. You are not an unfeeling person and I dare say you have done your best with the wretched woman.'

'I deplore the fact that Carla has caused nothing but resentment in our happiest of families,' said Dada. 'We have none of us taken to her.'

'She tried to steal Spiv,' hazarded the Moo.

'She did no such thing, the Moo,' said Dada. 'That is a wicked thing to say in order to cause trouble. I don't know where you get it from. Certainly not my side of the family. If you tell lies again, I will thrash you within an inch of your life. I will not have it said that any child of mine is a liar.' It was the Moo's turn to approach tears. 'There now. You see where untruths lead? They lead to loss of temper. And, I promise you, you do not wish to make me lose my temper. Already I feel my blood stirring –'

'Don't lose your temper, Dada,' begged George.

'I'm sorry, Dada. I'm sorry,' said the Moo, pressing Spiv to his brimming eyes.

'Well, well, we'll say no more about it.'

'If only that were true,' murmured Janey.

'Since no one here is capable of putting one thought after another,' sighed Hugh, 'I suppose it's my duty to summarise the situation. As I see it –'

'Do not say another word, Luh'le Shuggy,' said Maman. 'You are terribly clever, I'm sure, but you are not old enough to know when it is appropriate to speak and when it is not.'

'I was only going to remark that Carla cannot possibly be happy here and that therefore it is our duty to release her from whatever contract exists between her and Dada.'

'What on Earth do you mean?' exclaimed Dada. 'What contract? I know of no contract. She is an au pair. Au pairs do not have contracts. Has she spoken of a contract? I assure you there is none. I will not have her implying that any binding legal agreement exists between us. In fact, I shall tell her as much. And she shall leave this house. Are we all agreed that we do not like Carla?'

'We are, Dada,' confirmed Hugh. 'Although we have not heard from Dabs.'

'Whaddya think, Dabs?' asked the Moo roughly, readying Spiv. Janey's face became slack, the mouth falling open, the tongue lolling; but the slit eyes had a starriness in them.

'Dabs am adoring the Carla,' she sighed. 'Carla am werry appetising. Dabs loves to smell her.'

'Get 'er, Spiv.'

'Ow! Ow!'

'Trust Dabs to be controversial,' said Hugh.

'I will eat my snippet now,' announced George. 'I will eat it slowly in front of you Englander *dummkopfs*. And you will be powerless to do anything but drool.'

'Good day to you all!' called out Charles Hamilton from the doorway. He still had a trace of a Scottish accent.

'Hello, Mr Hamilton,' said Maman.

'Good afternoon, Hamilton,' said Dada.

'Hello, Hamilton,' said the Moo.

'*Mister* Hamilton, the Moo,' corrected Maman.

'Wotcha, Mr H.,' said George.

'It's "Good afternoon, Mister Hamilton", mein Fuehrer,' said Maman. 'Really, Mr Hamilton, I do apologise for my ill-mannered children. It is inexcusable.'

'Not at all, not at all. I enjoy George's colourful vernacular. And besides, it is I and Theo who apologise for our tardiness. I had to change my togs after… well, after my constitutional.'

Charles and his son traditionally lunched with the Blytes on Sundays. In accord with his mercurial nature, the Colonel sometimes attended, and sometimes did not. Charles was a small wiry man in his late fifties. Dressed in a tweed jacket, mustard-coloured waistcoat and bow tie, he cut a neat, almost dapper figure; and, if his face was a little too red and his moustache a little too clipped to be entirely *comme il faut*, he was nevertheless, and unlike Carla, what Maman called an appetising little man. Theo was a tall man of about thirty-two or -three. He had a pale face, deep-set eyes, a prominent nose and thin brown hair which touched – even hung over – the collar of his brown corduroy jacket.

'Say "Hello" to Theo, children,' prompted Maman.

'Hello, Theo,' they chorused.

'Ah… um… trust everyone… um… tickety-boo…? Ah… good. May one…?' He addressed Janey, indicating the chair next to her, as if he did not sit there every week. Janey coloured slightly and nodded.

'Theo,' said George.

'Um… yes, mein… Fueh…?'

'Did you know that Luh'le Shuggy is in love with a Mexican girl?'

'One had… um… inkling… Misplaced, um… affections…?'

'Shut up, mein Fuehrer. I'm not, Theo. The Fuehrer is being annoying as usual. Little meat fly.'

'You have missed snippets, gentlemen. I am about to carve in earnest,' said Dada, his Carving Face bearing him out. 'Is that a silk scarf you are wearing, Theo, under your open-necked shirt? It cannot be, ahem, a *ladies'* scarf, can it – although, to my failing eyesight, it seems to resemble one.'

'Um… unsure… May very well, um… be.'

Dada gave vent to a plosive sound.

'Theo is Bohemian,' said Maman breezily. 'He has lived on the *Rive Gauche* and cannot be expected to uphold your English *petit bourgeois* conventions.'

'I'm not English,' protested Dada. 'Nor do I have any pretensions to French culture. But I hope I can still dress decently when the occasion demands.'

'This from a man who tucks his cardie into his underpants,' mused Hugh.

'Do they wear ties in the Bogs, Dada?' asked Janey innocently.

'What, pray, are these "Bogs"? You know perfectly well that I am of an extremely ancient and noble family from county Kilkenny, Janey,' said Dada, striking a defensive attitude. 'We were poor certainly – but we were not from the Bogs.' It was a fancy of Dada's to conceal the modest rank of his family and the comparative ease of its circumstances.

'Dada is from the Bogs,' George explained to Mr Hamilton. 'He lost two toes to trench foot. They didn't have gum boots when Dada was a boy. He had nothing to wear but a little grey gansey. Show Mr Hamilton your deformed foot, Dada.' He fell to his knees and began to untie Dada's shoelaces.

'It pleases my children to torment their father, ha-ha,' laughed Dada with false heartiness, shaking his left foot to free it from George's nimble fingers. 'I assure you that I have the full complement of toes –' he adopted his cod Dublin accent – 'Oh yes. Be da Holy Floy, I'm okay so in da toe department.'

'"By the Holy Fly" is a Bogs' expression,' Janey explained to Theo. 'It is like "Begorrah" – something no Irishman has ever said.' Theo changed colour in acknowledgement. Much of the communication between him and Janey took place through different shades of blushing, like octopuses.

'Your father is *not* from the Bogs,' said Maman irritably. 'And even if he were it would not matter.' She turned to Charles. 'Really, I have no idea where my brats get this snobbery from. We give them all the advantages of an education that neither their father nor I were fortunate enough to have, and, *zut alors*, we find they have turned into little snobs. Too clever by half. *Nom d'un chien!* The vegetables!' She pattered out of the room to retrieve the rest of the meal.

'What's your job, Hamilton?' the Moo asked Charles abruptly.

'I used to be an engineer,' said Charles, smiling indulgently, 'but I retired early. Bad health, you know. Too long in the jungle, ha-ha!'

'In the hands of cruel Japanese guards,' elaborated George, adding 'Banzai! Aaaargh!' by way of colour.

'Yes,' said Charles.

'With Theo,' decided the Moo.

63

'No. Theo was in England. With my wife, you know, who had escaped from Germany. Who died of pneumonia while I was a guest of the Japanese.'

'Being forced to build railways, like a slave,' said George, not without a certain relish, and drawing on such history as his war comics provided.

'More or less.'

'Didn't you dig an escape tunnel and get rid of the earth down your trouser legs?'

'No.' Charles added: 'It was too hot.'

'That wasn't very British of you.'

'I suppose not.'

'If you'd been more British you'd have dyed your hair and made snazzy fake Jap uniforms and strolled out of the front gate, whistling a Jap tune!'

'I wish we'd had you there, George,' said Charles with a twinkle.

'Is the Colonel not joining us, Mr Hamilton?' intervened Janey tactfully.

'I'm not sure,' said Charles heartily. 'I took him up to the Club for a pre-prandial snifter –' here, with bravado, he partially pulled out of his pocket the leather lead he always carried, but which the Colonel had never agreed to wear – 'but I let him run free on the way back. I must say, he *is* taking his time.'

But at that very moment the door swung open and in marched Colonel Bogey. He gave a peremptory bark of greeting and then went over to Dada, where he studiously avoided looking at the roast.

'Welcome, Colonel,' said Dada, cutting him a handsome slice of beef. It was hard to say exactly what sort of stock the Colonel came from. The mass of short brown woolly fur on his long body and his stumpy legs suggested more of the sheep than the sheep dog. The wrinkled face and lugubrious expression implied a touch of bloodhound. The guarded eyes were human.

'What kept you, sir? Eh?' called Charles, anxiously eyeing the slice of beef lest it was larger than his own. 'Looking for me, were you? Hah! Gave you the slip. What do you say to that? Mm?' But the Colonel disdained to reply beyond shooting a sideways look at Mr Hamilton. Then he fell to making short work of his meat.

Like Yul Brynner in *The Magnificent Seven*, Colonel Bogey had come out of nowhere and might, presumably, return to that nowhere at any time. He had come in like an eel through the particularly capacious cat flap installed by the house's previous owners in the second back door, next to the old servants' staircase, which the Hamiltons used. He carried no identification, and all attempts to trace his owners, if he had ever had any, failed. Although it was the Blytes who named and kept him, it was the Hamiltons he condescended to eat and sleep with. Charles had been pleased. He longed for companionship that was not of the perfidious human variety. He had been disappointed: the nearest the Colonel came to being a companion was on a galling outing like today's. Mostly, Bogey went off on his own, stumping down the hill to Wyebridge and staying out all day.

Colonel Bogey finished his meat and stared pointedly at Dada. When nothing more was forthcoming, he turned tail and, without a backward glance, stalked out of the dining room. Charles suppressed an impulse to follow. Somehow, he couldn't give up the notion that some intimacy between them was possible. If only he could find out what the Colonel got up to in town. He had not so far lowered himself as to tail Bogey, nor had he hired sleuths to do so; but he often found an excuse to stroll into town himself for a bit of shopping. His dearest wish was to run into the Colonel, to find out what his business was, to break the barrier of secrecy and silence that surrounded his life, and, yes, to share in that life. But he never had.

'Pass the vegetables to Mr Hamilton, Luh'le Shuggy,' trilled Maman, returning with a tray full of boiled-down offerings. 'He looks close to tears of hunger! Do not tap your watch, Dermot. I know that lunch is a little late. Truly I do. But this business with Carla has thrown me. Frankly, it is too much. I feel that I can't cope.' She closed her eyes tightly to master tears.

'Does this meat taste all right to you?' asked Dada, wrinkling his nose.

'Don't be ridiculous, Dermot,' said Maman. 'It's perfectly all right.'

'You shut the meat safe securely?'

'Of course,' Maman said quickly, raising her napkin to her face to conceal its stricken expression.

'One bluebottle could be the death of us all,' warned Dada. 'I saw a lot of them in the war. Terrible things, flies.'

'Unless... um...holy, er...flies?'

'It is not a joking matter, Theo,' said Dada, annoyed at the sniggers of those who thought it might be.

'They have dirty legs,' said the Moo with a scientific air.

'Precisely, the Moo. Also, they lay eggs on food and turn it putrid. Poison enters the system unawares and –'

George began to choke and splutter, his face turning a convincing purple.

'Stop it, mein Fuehrer,' said Maman mildly, attempting a vague smack which the gurgling George easily evaded.

'You will not look so funny,' reproved Dada, 'when we are all discovered dead at the table in an advanced state of putrefaction.'

'Don't, Dada. I can't bear it,' pleaded Janey.

'Well, well, I have said enough. Be vigilant. That is all. The bluebottle is a slippery creature.'

'*Alors,*' said Maman, clapping her hands as a distracting tactic, '*aujourd'hui il faut qu' on parle français!*'

'Parley-voo, twiggez-vous!' exclaimed Dabs excitedly, before disappearing behind Janey's hair again.

'Do not make a mockery of your mother, Janey,' said her mother. 'You will be glad of your French when you come to do your exams.'

'Oh do we *have* to speak French,' groaned George. 'It ruins lunch.'

'Nonsense, mein Fuehrer. *Alors, tu commenceras. Dis moi quelque chose.*'

'Le Français est murd.'

'Don't be disgusting, dear. Disgusting and silly. And it is *merde*. Rrrrr. *Tu comprends?*'

'Oui, oui, Maman.'

'George said wee-wee, Maman,' protested the Moo.

'Oh, for God's sake. Luh'le Shuggy, set an example.'

'I'll speak French, Maman, if Dada does too.'

'Dada is entitled to a day of rest.'

'Janey will speak French,' said George innocently. 'She longs to speak French... to Theo!'

'*Shut up,*' hissed Janey.

"*Sank 'eaven for leetle girls,*" sang Dada, twirling his fork and tipping an imaginary Maurice Chevalier boater.

'You are no better than the children, Dermot. Be quiet the lot of you. You try my nerves. Very well, you need not speak French. But you will all live to regret it.'

'When I've eaten my peas,' said the Moo in an announcing voice, 'I will make a new member of the Sloppy Club.'

'Wait until after lunch, dear,' said Maman.

'He need not, I think, mavourneen. We'd all like to hear who the new member is. It seems likely that the Moo is going to rectify a certain glaring omission – I won't use the word "injustice" – in the roll call of sloppiness. Isn't that so, the Moo?'

'Who is it, the Moo?' asked George.

'You'll see.' The Moo breathed heavily through his nose as he balanced peas on his fork.

'Is it Dabs?'

'No!'

'It *am* me!' exulted Dabs. 'Dabs am werry sloppy.'

Theo's shoulders shook.

'Morons are banned from the Club,' the Moo reminded everyone.

'The Sloppy Club is very exclusive. Only Janey, the Fuehrer and myself are members, I think,' said Hugh.

'Wrong,' said the Moo.

'Well, who else?'

'Colonel Bogey.'

'Good grief,' said Mr Hamilton.

'And Robbo.'

'Who is Robbo?' asked Dada suspiciously.

'The dustbin man.'

'I see. So you grant membership, the Moo, to a comparative stranger, a dustbin man, over a man who loves and nurtures you.'

'Eh?'

'I'm referring to your beloved father, the Moo. I am referring to myself.'

'Robbo gives me Wrigleys to chew.'

'I see. So membership can be purchased for a price? And yet your pocket money, a considerable sum which, incidentally, comes from my pocket and not the pocket of this Robbo, counts for nothing in the sloppy scheme of things.'

'No.'

'I'm a member,' said Maman, almost shyly.

'You *were* a member,' corrected the Moo.

'Oh. Yes. I remember.' Maman tried to sound bright. 'I was unfrocked. Or whatever the word is. For getting cross.'

'I *'splained* about the crayonning. You need a big surface for it. You shouted.'

'Yes,' said Maman. She looked out of the window. 'My beautiful flock wallpaper...'

'You were not sloppy,' reproached the Moo.

'No.'

'Well, the Moo,' said Dada keenly, 'you have finished your peas. I don't think many of us will be surprised by this election, which, I venture to suggest, is long overdue – but let that pass. As long as justice is finally seen to be done, well –'

'It costs the Earth,' interrupted the Moo, rehearsing a common assertion of his father's.

'Well, well,' said Dada, disconcerted, 'I dare say funds may perhaps be found, although we have to consider that substantial pocket money is already forthcoming...' His voice trailed away as the Moo, unmoved, slipped down from his chair and walked around the table.

'Theo,' he intoned, pulling from his pockets a piece of cardboard with a safety pin attached; an aspirin bottle filled with a sickly-coloured liquid; and a much-folded sheet of paper. 'Here is your Sloppy Club badge. Here is your Sloppy Orange Juice. Here are the Sloppy Club rules. Read them out.' Theo received the items with bowed head and, clearing his throat, read aloud from the sheet of paper. The rules of the Sloppy Club, as written out by the Moo, were few but strict:

1. *You must be slopy, do things slopy, give slopy hand shakes, eat slopy ect.*
2. *You must buy slopy orange juice from the Sultan of Slopy, e.g. the Moo Blyte and drink it on birthdays and funerals and when West Ham United win matches. 2d a bottle.*
3. *You must pay 6d for a Slopy Club badje.*
4. *When you go out you must wear your Slopy Club badje.*

5. *You must help other Slopy Club members in dificluty, homework, money ect.*

Signed The Moo Blyte
Sultan of Slopy.

'Obey them,' said the Moo.

'Um… tremendous, er, honour, the Moo… quite speechless… try to deserve –'

'Eight pence in total,' said the Moo, holding out his hand.

'Ah…um… let me see,' said Theo, fumbling in his pocket. 'Er… change… um, a little short… sixpence?'

'That'll do.' The Moo took the coin and turned on his heel.

'Dermot, do you think the Moo should be…?' questioned Maman. 'It seems rather…'

'I dare say Theo can afford it,' said Dada shortly. 'One must pay for one's privileges. My own club,' he added with studied nonchalance, 'is the Combined Services which, I think it's fair to say, has a pretty exclusive membership. They know how to dress there. Oh yes, a very good class of member.'

6

AFTER lunch, Dada drove Carla to the station. Maman and Hamilton *père et fils* drank coffee in the drawing room. Hugh went to his bedroom to try and re-string his guitar, rehearse his hit record and, in between, *sotto voce*, his love for the Mexican girl.

Janey went to her bedroom to do her Latin homework and to moon about. Mooning about was a favourite activity, often taking concrete form in her many sketches and doodles. Sketches of, for example, Theo Hamilton smoking Gaulois in a beret and a string of onions.

The Moo was already in the playroom where Jack Pluff had just gone cold all over, realising that his disguise as an ice-cream man was about to be exposed at Checkpoint Charlie. His mission was to rescue the beautiful television lady, Muriel Young, who had been snatched by Communists and imprisoned in East Berlin. But now he was being asked for his papers. He'd have to shoot his way through. Grimly he removed the pins from a brace of hand grenades masquerading as ice-cream cones. 'C'mon, boy,' he murmured to the trusty Fray Bentos. Then, agile as a big cat, he leapt from the van and ran towards the border, lobbing grenades to left and right, and opening up on the enemy soldiers with his sub-machine gun while Fray Bentos tore the throat out of any Red rash enough to get in the way.

George, meanwhile, adjourned to his sloping den beneath the back stairs in order to gloat over the collection of war comics he'd won off the Enemy at marbles. Although he shared a bedroom with the Moo, he had created this alternative accommodation for himself, sometimes sleeping there in a sleeping-bag on an old mattress.

After a while he grew restless. He let himself out of the back door and scooted up the garden to the summerhouse where he had cleared part of the high shelf of its junk, including a trunk of old papers, and placed there twenty-nine apples scrumped from next door's orchard. They were rotting nicely, but not fast enough. He'd water them later. They were to be the ammo in a planned attack on the Enemy in retaliation for an atrocity that still rankled: the Enemy had made a load of mud pies, oven-baked them to a vicious hardness and transported them in a wheelbarrow to his camp in the Tennis Club jungle. Then he had lured George across the clearing from his camp with promises of a new war comic – only to let him have it. Trapped inside the Enemy's lean-to, George could do nothing but cower as pie after pie slammed into his body. He still felt the defeat, the humiliation, more strongly than the physical pain. Fury rose in him afresh and, his heart black with vengeful longing, he set off for the cliff path.

Carefully navigating the Dodgy part by the wonky section of fence, he trotted along as far as Enemy territory: the back garden of 'Ponderosa', the low ranch-style house the Cholmondeleys had built for themselves. He crept through the screen of rhododendrons and, keeping low behind shrubs and trees to avoid being spotted from one of several picture windows, he made his way to the enormous double garage, eccentrically attached to the house itself. He went in by the side door and stood, slightly awed, in the presence of two shining cars: a red Italian sports job and a spanking new snub-nosed Mini Minor. He stroked its bonnet. Why didn't Dada get Maman one? She could barely cycle up the hill from the shops with her bags heavy on the handlebars, her face getting redder by the second.

In the corner stood the Enemy's glossy red Raleigh. George inserted a drawing-pin into the front tyre and sat back on his haunches to enjoy the faint satisfying hiss of escaping air. Then he eased out of the garage and skirted along the wall of the house. He ducked beneath the kitchen window and, unable to resist, inched himself upwards to peek inside.

The Cholmondeley's kitchen was as full of shiny chrome and gleaming Formica and blond wood as the Blyte's was dingy, poky and dark. With its breakfast bar, its padded benches and table built into the wall, its coffee machine, its refrigerator big enough to be out of *The Beverley Hillbillies*, it could have been a coffee bar or diner in an American film. George had been invited to tea there once, during a truce with the Enemy. 'Hay tea,' as Mrs Cholmondeley had pronounced it. She spoke in a strange, clipped, precise way with odd vowels that suggested to George that English was not her first language. She always said 'is not' and 'had not' instead of 'isn't' and 'hadn't'. This, together with her extraordinary hair, of a blondeness never seen before in the Home Counties, made George vaguely suppose that she was Swedish. The tea had been more like supper, with cold meats and salad. Swedish food, George guessed. The Cholmondeleys ate in silence, holding their knives in their strange Swedish way, like pens, and freely putting their elbows on the table. George quite liked it, except for the moment of panic when it occurred to him that these people might be aliens who had taken over human bodies, just as Luh'le Shuggy had described after seeing *The Invasion of the Body Snatchers*. It would be like aliens to get everything perfect – and then fall down over something as silly as holding a knife.

'Ramparts having been thrown up,' translated Janey, 'Caesar attacked the Belgians with javelins.' She knew what Caesar'd be doing next – he'd be throwing bridges across rivers and carrying on war against the poor British tribes. Unless Agricola beat him to it. She was pleased that she had recognised one of those ablative absolutes Luh'le Shuggy had explained to her, but she wished she'd done her Latin homework on Friday night, as he used to. Then it wouldn't have hung over her all weekend. Then she wouldn't have had to do it, as she always did do it, on Sunday afternoon when things were depressing enough as it was. Sundays were always grey and usually drizzly. The sun always burst out on Monday mornings when you had to sit in a smelly classroom. If she could just do more homework on Friday, she'd pass her 'O' Levels more quickly and – whooosh – she'd be out of school at fifteen and off up to the Yorkshire Moors, riding stallions. Even Caesar, throwing up ramparts as he may, couldn't stop her.

She slumped back on her pillows. She was doing her homework on her knee, on her bed, because her desk was covered in old birds' nests, shells, stones, feathers and other natural debris. The floor, where she preferred to draw and paint, was covered in pieces of paper, books, and dirty clothes. The mess was not doing Maman's nerves any good. There had been scenes. She knew she should tidy up more if Maman's nerves were not to be irrevocably shredded; but she had no energy for tidying up and so she wouldn't, and so Maman's nerves would get worse and it'd be her fault. Hell's teeth, it was all so inevitable and *tedious*. Even the sky with its little puffs of grey Surrey clouds, like office workers, was boring. Why couldn't the Aged P.s just send her to Yorkshire now, to work as a groom and win gymkhanas, like Jill in *A Pony for Jill*.

She pictured the wild-eyed skewbald the gypsies had given her in return for saving the little gypsy boy from drowning. No one could ride the pony. It was a killer fit only for the knackers' yard. But Janey could see that it was only fear that made Lightning so mean. His trust could be won through kindness and trust and a sensible diet (not too many oats – bad for the withers). She rode him in the show-jumping competition and conquered evil Lucinda Low-ffolliott with her immaculately tailored habit and her cruel silver-handled crop. At the final jump – the terrifying Wall – Lucinda cut her little grey once too often and was thrown; while Janey, with the merest of touches on Lightning's responsive mouth ('Come *on*, Lightning – we can do it! Hup! *Hup!*) had soared over the Wall, the only clear round, to tumultuous applause. The grizzled Master of Fox Hounds turned to the elegant but manly music teacher beside him and said with grudging admiration: 'She's a good 'un, that.' 'Indeed… sensitive, um, hands… very good, er, seat…' murmured the music teacher in reply, entranced by the sight of the dashing young woman, her long silky hair blown back from her radiant face and perfect teeth – oh, oh, it was all so *hopeless*. She'd be stuck here for years. How could she endure the waiting?

The door opened and the Moo wandered into the room. Picking his way through the flotsam, he tapped the glass tank on the mantelpiece.

'Speedy Gonzalez doesn't move about much, considering,' he commented. ''E's dozy.'

'He's a slow worm. It's his job to be dozy.'

'Draw me a picture like the Fuehrer's,' he demanded.

'Go away, the Moo. I'm busy.'

'It's not fair. The Fuehrer's got a big picture of Nazis doing the goose step. I want one. A bigger one.'

Janey rolled off her bed on to the floor and opened her largest sketch pad with resignation. She deftly outlined in charcoal a rank of soldiers with their distinctive helmets, kicking their legs high in the air like the Tiller girls.

'Look at the one at the end,' she said. 'His leg has gone all wonky, see? He's the sloppy Nazi. He's going to go sloppy on the one next to him and they're all going to fall down like dominoes.'

'Draw it, Janey! Make them all fall down!'

'No. It'll take too long. You'll just have to imagine it.'

'I *can't*.'

'Take the drawing and go.'

'No.'

'All right, you can stay. But you'll have to kiss… *Foody Fenella!*' With a flash of the wrist, Janey whipped out her dental plate, festooned with strands of saliva and the remains of lunch, and made it advance upon the Moo. 'Ma nem eez Foody Fenella,' she intoned in a deep, French-accented contralto, 'and I weesh to keess thees oh-so-sweet leetle boy. Slurp, slurp.'

'*No*,' screamed the Moo, squirming away and blundering out of the room.

Her homework fatally disrupted by the Moo's visit, Janey trailed listlessly downstairs to the playroom in order to moon about tragically while playing Luh'le Shuggy's Everly Brothers' records, the nostalgic songs of her childhood.

Mrs Cholmondeley was standing at the sink, wearing pink rubber gloves. She was talking, her brow puckered in a frown, but George could not hear her. He could only see the red mouth moving and the blue eyelids fluttering with irritation. She was dressed in a very soft white sweater, green stretchy ski pants and high-heeled mules. She was evidently addressing her husband because Roger Cholmondeley was standing behind her, his arms at his side beginning to spread in a gesture of helpless innocence. He wore a smart new blazer – quite unlike Dada's, which was frayed with a faded gold regimental badge on the pocket. His blue shirt was open at the neck with a yellow cravat tucked in. His face was tanned, his teeth very regular, his eyes keen-looking. What Dada would have had to admit was a fine head of black hair, was swept back in a dashing way as if he had

74

just stepped out of his open-topped sports car. He pulled a cigarette out of a packet lying on a spotless Formica surface, fiddled with it nervously as his wife talked on, and then replaced it.

Meanwhile, Sabrina was dancing. At least, she was doing a few steps, her glossy pony tail bouncing up and down, and then darting forward to touch, by turns, her mother's and father's arms, trying to capture their attention. They took no notice. Her face wrinkled briefly and then, like sand smoothed by a receding tide, it regained its clean, golden, impassive surface.

Once, in the distant past, when he and the Enemy had been allies, Sabrina had insisted on playing a game with them. She had turned her brother's camp at the Tennis Club into a cottage hospital where George had been ordered to lie very still while she bandaged his head and fussed with his clothing and, suddenly – disturbingly, stirringly – 'kissed him better'. His first thought afterwards was how piercingly blue Sabrina's eyes were. Almost too blue, really, like a doll. His second was, *Gott in Himmel*, had the Enemy *seen*? He was stamping around outside the primitive dwelling and, it seemed, had not.

Bradley Cholmondeley – the Enemy – was sitting at the table, one foot idly kicking its leg. His head was in his hands. In front of him stood a tall glass, untouched, of pink fluid. George realised that it must be, of all things, a strawberry milk shake. Bradley wore round National Health specs with the left lens obscured by brown material in order, it was said, to make him use and thus strengthen his weaker right eye. At first George had thought it made him look spastic; but now he thought that it gave the Enemy a villainous, master-spyish appearance. Almost snazzy. On the other hand, Bradley's mouth was a little loose on its hinges, which made him prone to slobber slightly when he became excited.

Roger Cholmondeley had placed two cigarettes in his mouth and lit them. Then he extracted one and attempted to insert it in his wife's mouth while she was still talking. She batted it aside with an irritable flick of her pink rubber glove. The twin points of her chest in the fluffy sweater – so unlike the friendly roundnesses under Maman's sloppy joe – were rising and falling exotically. But then that was the Swedish for you, George supposed, recalling the sniggers with which the older boys at school greeted the word 'Swedish'.

But then again, when he had casually asked the Enemy what it was like being half Swedish, he had been taken aback by the Enemy's vicious attack on him for taking the Mickey. 'We're not bloody Swedes, mush. That's balls' ache. You're gonna get a poking if you call me a Swede. We're from Hounslow, mush.' Stung by the accompanying kick aimed at his genitals, George retaliated:

'*Eeyouns*low? You talk like a council kid from St James-down-the-road.' This was the Secondary Modern down the road from the boys' Prep. School whose pupils lay in wait for any posh kid who strayed from the herd. 'Eeyounslow! You want to bog off where you belong – to St James-down-the-road!' An incensed Enemy punched George in the face and thereby unwittingly confirmed that, if he were not a council kid, he had council kid blood in him. This increased George's respect for him in the East End gangland sense of the word. From that moment on, George felt that Bradley Cholmondeley's veneer of civilisation was as thin as a Prep. School uniform over council kiddery. Indeed, there was something Dodgy about all the Cholmondeleys, just as Sabrina's perfectly blue eyes were, as the Enemy had once told him, colour blind.

Exhilarated by his act of sabotage on the Raleigh, George decided to cycle over to the Ruined House, smash a few windows and nick some lead to replenish his dwindling stock. He ran home and yanked his bike – Luh'le Shuggy's old one re-painted a lumpy red – out of the tool shed and pushed it at high speed beside him before vaulting on to the moving saddle, just like the Cisco Kid used to mount his galloping pinto. As soon as he hit the saddle, he let out a shout of pain. Something had pierced his bottom. At the same time, the front wheel squelched horribly. He reined in the bike and dismounted. There was a drawing pin stuck point upwards in his saddle. And his front tyre had been punctured. '*Donner und Blitzen*,' muttered George. He smiled grimly. You had to hand it to the Enemy.

'Why am I here?' wondered Rex Darkling as he stared moodily out of the window of Lady Isabella's flat in Notting Hill. The sounds of a Caribbean steel band floated up from the grey alienated streets like laughter in the face of a firing squad. 'What's the point of it all?' A thin rain began to fall, revealing the true bleakness of the streets and silencing the forlorn bravado of the band. A mangy dog hobbled over

to a doorway and lay down to die. From the floor above could be faintly heard the muffled screams of a young girl, as a drunken quack botched her illegal abortion.

'Come back to bed, darling,' trilled Lady Isabella, her dark eyes flashing in the murk as she undid her ample brassiere. Rex turned towards her, reflecting bitterly that he might snatch a few moments of oblivion in her voluptuous arms. He liked to make her breasts swing like bells –

'Whoa,' said Hugh. It was squalid stuff. It was worse – the last line was, wasn't it?, a line from squalid old D.H. Lawrence. He'd nicked Maman's copy of *Lady Chatterley's Lover* from under her mattress and scanned it for tips. It was heavy going. That game-keeper and his John Thomas: hell's teeth. 'I'd give him bloody John Thomas,' muttered Hugh. Not literally, of course.

It was no good. He'd never be able to write a proper sex scene till he'd had sex himself. But then, of course, he wouldn't be able to publish the bloody thing while Maman was still alive. It was all so hopeless. He turned up his transistor to hear the Searchers sing *Needles and Pins*. You had to keep the radio on practically all day if you wanted to hear the record that you were obsessed by. But, oh, what a lot of dross there was to plough through while you waited. Just like Life. He really ought to work on his own hit record a bit more.

The only consolation was the thought of his first novel being published to fantastic acclaim the day after Maman's funeral. At Oxford, dons treated the precocious best-selling author with deference. In his Notting Hill penthouse, dolly birds cooked his breakfast for him. They were dressed only in – no, no, that way madness in the underpants lay. During his lecture tour of America starry-eyed blondes deserted their surfing boyfriends to besiege his hotel room. One lucky one, called… called Krystal, with the most enormous yet shapely – hell's teeth, don't start, don't *start*. Hugh sprang up in frustration and headed for the playroom.

The last straw, supposed Janey, had been seeing Carla surreptitiously putting a lit match to a daddy-long-legs; and smiling as it went up. She had written Carla's name in green ink on a piece of parchment (well, a piece of thick drawing paper), placed it in the crucible (well, a bronze ash tray), lit the candles and joss sticks, and performed the spell:

'*By the Powers of the North, I banish thee. By the Powers of the West, I banish thee…*' Quite a long incantation, actually. For a first attempt at serious witchcraft, it had been an unexpected triumph. It was sobering. She was glad she had resisted the temptation to begin with the wax doll containing hair or fingernails – she loved to mould or sculpt – because it might have been too powerful, perhaps lethal. She didn't want Carla to frizzle up like the daddy-long-legs; she just wanted her gone. And now she had gone. Within forty-eight hours. This was a power that should be used sparingly.

Janey got up from the sofa she'd been lying on, legs hooked over the arm-rest, to change the record on the old red Dansette. The playroom was perhaps the grandest of the three principal reception rooms, the others being the dining room and the drawing room – which was only for best. The family actually lived in the dark so-called breakfast room because it was warmer and conveniently situated next to the kitchen. The playroom was huge, with a great sweep of curtainless bay window. It had been kitted out with stuff that Maman had bought cheaply at auction – a heavy cupboard for toys and rubbish; two old sofas; three mattresses and a bean bag – all of which could be jumped about on. The faded brown wallpaper was tastefully decorated at George's height by a frieze of blitzkrieging panzers; and, at the Moo's, by a rough stick-like representation of Jack Pluff mowing down some stick policemen, together with various wonkily-drawn vehicles, mostly crashing. Balloons were attached to some of the figures, containing succinct ejaculations, such as 'Take that!', 'You slopy devil, Pluff!', 'Aaaargh!', and so forth.

'*My Ebony Eyes is coming to me from out of the skies on Flight Twelve-Oh-Three*,' sang Janey, along with the record. '*In an hour or two I will whisper "I do" to my bewdifool Ebony Eyes.*'

'*The plane was way overdo,*' said Hugh, appearing in the doorway. '*So I wend to the airlines desk and I said: "Sir, I wunner why Flight Twelve-Oh-Three is so late" and he said: "Oh they probly took off late or they may have rern inna some turbulent weather and had to alder their course." I wend out to the gate and watched the light from the control tower whip through the darkness as if it were searching for her.*'

78

Janey interrupted him. *'Then came the announcement over the* loud*speaker: "Would all those having friends and relations on Flight Twelve-Oh-Three please report to the chapel across the street."'*

Then, in unison, they sang:

'Then I felt a tearing breaking inside ("That's not right." "Yes it is.") *and I knew those heavenly ebony skies had taken my life's most wunnerful prize – my bewdifool Ebony Eyes.'*

'We take the Mickey,' said Janey, 'but really the Everlys are very moving. Like oboes.'

'Ebony Eyes isn't just a love song, you know. It's about the death of an era.'

'The era of talking bits in the middle of records.'

'The era we grew up in. There's a new era beginning. An era when parents will have to listen to their children for a change if they want to survive because they won't know how anything works. Let's not wallow in the Everlys. Put on *Not Fade Away.'* Obediently, Janey removed the record from the Dansette and slotted the Rolling Stones over the central column.

'Dada thinks the Rolling Stones are the end of an era. He thinks their hair is the end of civilisation.'

'Amazing, isn't it? You'd think their hair'd be one thing he approved of. There's no making him out.'

'Mick Jagger doesn't sing in the language of Shakespeare.'

'But he can make any word rhyme with any other word.'

'At school, all the girls are divided into Beatles girls and Rolling Stones girls. I want to be a Rolling Stones girl, really. But there's no getting away from it – I'm a Beatles girl.'

'Me too,' said Hugh.

'It must be our upbringing, It's harder to shake off than I thought.'

Janey was secretly mad about the Beatles. She wangled invitations after school to Petula's house. She did not much like Petula, but Petula had both Beatles LPs, which Janey couldn't afford. Most of the girls sub-divided into lovers of John and Paul; but Janey was a George Harrison girl. He seemed shyer than the others, and more wry. He played the guitar best. He did a fantastic scream on *Twist and Shout.*

'Could you make a sign for the Dodgy fence post, Janey?'

'Why don't *you* make a sign?' sighed Janey.

'You're the artistic one.'

'"Danger. Wonky Post". How much art does that require?'

'Oh go on. If I do it, it'll look squalid. If you do it, it'll look official. Lives will be saved.'

'All right. If I must.'

'Thanks.' Hugh plumped down on the bean bag, pulled out a Strand stub, put it in his mouth, lit it and inhaled deeply.

'If Dada smells that, he'll *definitely* lose his temper.'

'D'you know,' mused Hugh, shooting twin rods of smoke out of his nostrils, 'part of me would like Dada to lose his temper. Sort of get it over with.'

'Don't say that. Not even as a joke.'

Hugh shrugged and pulled a magazine out of his jacket pocket.

'Letter from Bloggs today,' he remarked. 'Wants to know how I'm doing in Bourgeoisville. He says he's shacked up with a dolly bird called Frankie over a boutique in Coolville. Notting Hill to the rest of us.'

Janey did her best to process the unfamiliar sentence.

'"Shacked up",' she experimented. 'It sounds terrible.'

'It sounds,' corrected Hugh, 'Swinging. The place is swarming with cool Yanks and Aussies and coloured cats. There's music in the streets day and night. The air smells of hashish smoke and spicy grub. Some beatnik types have declared Notting Hill a republic, and twinned it with Cuba. He wants me to come, Janey. Why don't *we* go? There'd be people we could really really talk to. Not like round here in… in Morguesville.'

'How would we get money?'

'You don't need money. It's crazy, man. All Communist. You just take over an empty house, 'parently, and the police can't touch you. You live in groups, making art and things. Plus, there's free love.'

'I don't suppose people keep ponies up there?'

'No,' agreed Hugh.

'Still. It'd be groovy to get away from this… this…'

'Loony bin.'

'Yes.' Janey's heart was pounding with possibility. She imagined as best she could her Bohemian life in the Republic of Notting Hill alias Coolville. 'I'm a bit young for free love.'

'I'm not,' said Hugh with more decisiveness than he felt. 'Bloggs knows these Californian blokes who're running a magazine to... Raise Consciousness.'

'?'

'I dunno exactly. But it sounds fantastic. Something to do with liberating the working classes. Anyway, the point is, if we're not On The Bus, he can't guarantee our safety when the Revolution comes. Take a look.' He slapped the magazine down in front of his sister.

'*Head Transplant*,' she read carefully.

'That's what it's called. Look here. Crazy or what?'

Janey looked at the smudgy black and white photo of the magazine's editor. Baz Tytherley III, it said. He was On The Bus if anyone was. He was wearing a brown corduroy suit and an obviously coloured shirt, though you couldn't tell what colour, and a scarf knotted around his neck. Also, he wore dark glasses. One hand held a cigarette; the other was resting on a girl with short hair like a boy and not much on, bar the odd bit of crocheting. Her eyelashes were as long as a giraffe's. Her eyelids were blacked out like Dusty Springfield's on *Ready Steady Go*. But the disturbing thing was that Baz Tytherley III, with his corduroy and scarf and long hair, reminded her of no one so much as... Theo. Could it be that Theo was not just eccentric, but *cool*?

The record came to an end. Neither of them changed it or put it on again. There was silence in the playroom. Hugh read his magazine. Janey mooned. After ten minutes, they both suddenly broke into the same snatch of Dionne Warwick song. '*Walk on by-y-y.*' They both laughed. It was funny to think that while their thoughts and lives had become so separate and different, their soundtracks – synchronised in childhood – were still running in parallel.

'It says here,' said Hugh, 'that the agents of revolution lie all about us in the hedgerows.'

'?'

'Fly agaric, f'rinstance. What *is* fly agaric, Janey?' His sister got up and drew him to the window.

'There,' she said. 'Under the silver birches Dada planted for goal posts. Those red toadstools with white spots. They're fly agaric.'

'Hell's teeth. We could eat them and, it says here, see through bourgeois values. See Reality. Like Lapland witch-doctors. They eat fly agaric and then have visions and… ecstasies, it says. It's like flying.'

'They don't poison you?'

'They would if you just ate them. What you do is feed them to your reindeer and then drink the reindeer's wee-wee.'

'Yuk.'

'No. 'Parently it tastes okay. Natural.'

'Where are we going to get a reindeer?'

'Oh *God*. Everything's so *difficult*.'

George, who was listening at the door, pricked up his ears at the mention of reindeer's wee-wee. This was his sort of thing. He hurried off to look up 'fly agaric' in his bible, Arthur Mee's *Encyclopaedia for Children*, where he had recently ascertained, to general amazement, that the blood in a tadpole's tail travelled at a speed of point nought nought nought nought nought nine metres per second.

7

'Come along, mavourneen,' said Dada through compressed lips. 'We are already late.'

'I'm not coming.' Dressed only in her slip, Maman was standing in a pool of discarded clothes in front of the bedroom mirror.

'Why ever not?' enquired Dada with a jollity belied by the ominous jingling of coins and keys in his pocket.

'I have nothing to wear.'

'Now that is simply not true, macushla. Here, what about this?' He picked up a summery dress with a floral print. 'You look pretty in this.'

'I look hideous in that,' said Maman with venom.

'Little Lorna will always look pretty to her Prince Flasheen Eyes,' strained Dada.

'I look *grotesque*,' emphasised Maman with a sob.

Attracted by the unmistakable accents of tragedy, Hugh came into the room and stood watching his parents.

'For heaven's sake, Lorna. It's only a drink at the Club with Roger and Cheryl. Throw on anything.'

'There's nothing, *nothing*. Nothing that doesn't make me look like a... like a *tub*. A tub with heavy, thick, grotesquely deformed ankles. I can't even wear a decent court shoe, let alone heels.'

'Maman,' said Hugh. 'You look lovely.'

'Thank you, Luh'le Shuggy. You are a good boy. But you only say that out of pity. The truth is, I look like a dwarf. A fat dwarf with no neck. In the shape of a *tub*.' She sobbed a little more.

'You are not a dwarf, Maman. You're petite. And you always look lovely whatever you wear.'

'It's only your nerves making you say such things,' added Dada.

'Is it any wonder my nerves are frayed and raw when I look like this?' She flapped at the mirror. 'I eat next to nothing, carrots and lettuce, hateful, *hateful*, and still I make Hattie Jacques look like the Shrimp.'

'Well,' demurred Dada, 'you do eat the occasional biscuit... the odd éclair.'

'You can't call those things "éclairs". I was raised in the cradle of patisserie. If I do not know anything else in this world, I know éclairs. The English haven't *the first idea* how to construct an éclair. *Mon Dieu*, they put cream inside instead of *crème pâtissière*, and then it is not even cream! It's... it's – what is that stuff for tiles?'

'Grout?' supplied Hugh.

'They put grouting in their plastic éclairs. *C'est diabolique.* Oh how I long for the food of my childhood! How I long to promenade the avenues of Paris in my red heels and my blue sash around my tiny waist! Look what the English have done to me. *Sacrebleu*, they have turned me from creamy custard into a tub of grout. It is too much. I shan't go out ever again. *You* go. *You* go and drink your flat English beer with your friends Roger and Cheryl.'

'I don't want to go without you, mavourneen,' said Dada dutifully. 'It wouldn't be the same. It would,' he added gallantly, 'be a penance.'

'And I am to stand beside Cheryl Cholmondeley, who looks like a glamorous Lana Turner, with her thin, thin ankles and her perfect red nails – my God, the nails! – and her Marilyn Monroe hair and her perfect make-up and –'

'Too much make-up,' interrupted Hugh. 'Do stop, Maman. She has to do herself up like that because she hasn't a fraction of your wit and personality. Not a hundredth of your prettiness.'

'You're a wicked boy to tell such fibs, Luh'le Shuggy,' said Maman, smiling through her tears. Impulsively, she kissed him. 'I can't go on like this,' she told her husband as she pulled one half of a lavender-coloured twin set over her head, stirring the pool of clothes with her foot for its cardigan. 'I want you to make an appointment for me with that doctor friend of yours. Sealskin... Silkins...?'

'David Siskin. Now, macushla, you know we can't afford Harley Street doctors.'

'You could afford him when it came to the Valium.'

'You know that he gave me a generous discount.'

'Well, isn't that what old army buddies are for? He can give you another discount. His brochure guarantees weight loss – and I've tried everything else, from hard-boiled eggs to revolting powdered stuff. I scarcely touch a carbohydrate. I can't go on looking like a tub. If you only do one thing for me, Dermot, do this.'

Bugger Lamb sat on a stool at the long dark polished bar of the St Michael's Hill Tennis Club. He sipped his gin and swerved his bulging eyes, frog-like, around the shabby but comfy room. The tables were unoccupied at this hour, except for the one in the corner where two young men sat in the same clothes they had played squash in, drinking expensive bottles of foreign beer. Bugger Lamb reflected on how unfortunate it was that, as Secretary of the Club, he had no say in the election of members. That was left to the Committee. Had he made a mistake in passing up the names of those two? It was beginning to look like it. They were part of an alarming influx of younger, unsound, distinctly second eleven types – more money than sense, a lot of 'em; women in the billiards room; brats in the bar. Jews, a lot of 'em, or worse – Catholics, Americans, all sorts. The Club was shot to buggery.

Naturally, Colonel Lamb had performed his duty as conscientiously as possible – difficult actually to keep 'em off the courts, but not many had the nerve to show their faces in the bar, what?, apart from those two unwashed pups, Rose and McCarthy.

The door opened and the Blyte family trooped in, followed by the four Cholmondeleys.

Something fishy about Blyte, thought Bugger Lamb, even though the fellow was rumoured to have 'had a good war.' The wife was a good sort, nothing flashy about her, more than could be said for – ah, talk of the devil. Bugger bulged glassily at the sight of Cheryl's fifties-style calf-length tight pink jeans. Bugger him. Far too done up, that filly. Still, you wouldn't say no to a few jumps around Sandown Park, what? *What?* As for Cholmondeley, well, he needed a bloody haircut. Definitely second eleven – just look at the bugger's blazer! – and well down the batting order.

'Evening, Colonel. Didn't see you in church this morning,' bantered Dada.

'Which church?' countered the Secretary suspiciously.

'Oh… any church!' laughed Dada gaily, sensing that things had immediately gone awry.

'Not a Catholic are you, Blyte?'

'Be da Holy Floy!' exclaimed Dada in a voice that was too high-pitched, 'he's asking if an Oirishman such as meself is after being a Catlick! Well, yez can all riddle me body with bullets here where I stand, and oi'll die wid da name of da Blessed Vorgin Mary on me lips!'

'Good grief,' said Bugger Lamb faintly. He reached for his stick and made for the door that gave on to the terrace.

'Care for another snifter, Colonel?' called Dada, waving his wallet as if to claw back a situation he felt had got away from him. 'A stiffener? A… a chota peg, what? Ha-ha-ha.' But the Colonel had buggered off.

'No, no, I'm in the chair,' intervened Roger Cholmondeley, withdrawing a wad of bank notes from his back pocket and beckoning to the barmaid. 'A pink gin for the missis, please, Lorraine.' Roger did not notice the glance that Lorraine shot at Cheryl, nor the snake-like flicker of the eyes with which Cheryl reciprocated, measuring the barmaid from head to foot. A bat's squeak of hostility passed between the women, too high-pitched for male hearing. 'Two pints of Red Barrel for me and Mr Blyte. And what's the little lady having?'

'The little lady,' repeated Maman with the merest of edges to her voice, 'will have a gin and Dubonnet, please, Roger.'

'Right you are. And what about Harry here?'

'Harry will have a pint, please,' said Hugh.

'No, no, no,' laughed Dada falsely, giving his son a mock punch. 'Hugh will have to wait until he's eighteen!'

'*Sorry*. Hugh. Of course,' apologised Roger. 'Still, he could have a half, eh Dermot, old man? Red Barrel – it's only piss and gas, eh!'

'Less of the "old man", old man, ha-ha,' laughed Dada. 'Well, all right. But sip it slowly now, Luh'le Shuggy,' he warned, meeting Hugh's eye. Hugh, who had been drinking beer secretly for two years, nodded soberly.

Roger organised drinks for the children, who were dispatched under Janey's care to a nearby table, beneath which the Moo, clutching Dinky toys and a bottle of Seven-Up, sank to join Jack Pluff. Roger watched Lorraine deftly compiling his order.

She was a well-built woman, no longer young but dressed youthfully in white boots, a short tight white skirt and tight white armless polo neck that did nothing to understate her figure. As she pulled the pints, her yellow back-combed hair quivered, her tongue passed over her coral pink lipstick, her eyelids flashed an eye-shadow as kingfisher-blue as her eyes. 'Common,' Cheryl had called her. She did look a bit tarty; but, then, you couldn't tell these days because looking tarty was the fashion.

'There we are, sir,' she said, laying the drinks before him. She invested the 'sir' with a friendliness, a lack of servility, an intonation just short of the ironical, that gave Roger to understand that there was more to Lorraine than met the eye. Although, as far as he could see, what met the eye was already more than most men could cope with.

'Have one yourself, Lorraine,' he smiled, passing her a pound note.

'I won't, thank you,' she said. 'I don't drink on duty.'

'Well, I hope to catch you off duty one day,' Roger flirted automatically, and then blushed in case what had been meant as gallant had sounded lewd.

'Perhaps you will,' she replied, but tartly rather than tartily, flicking her eyes towards Cheryl. Looking more closely now at Lorraine, what Roger particularly noticed was not the admirable figure, the bouffant hair, the made-up face, but the lovely, longish, thinnish and very uncommon nose.

'Here we are!' exclaimed Roger, handing round the drinks. 'That's a nice piece of material, old man,' he said, mischievously fingering Dada's blazer. 'I could have my tailor make it into a blazer for you, ha-ha.'

'Ha-ha,' responded Dada. 'That's an interesting regiment, Roger.' He pointed to the badge sewn on to Roger's front pocket. 'I don't think I recognise it.'

'Not surprising, old man,' said Roger, unabashed. 'It's probably the regiment of piss artists, pardon my French.'

'Ha-ha.'

'Ha-ha-ha.'

There were only a few years between the ages of the men, yet in another sense there was a generation; for Dermot was just old enough to have been in the war, and Roger, just too young.

'I like your stylish trousers, Cheryl,' said Maman. 'Very dashing.' Everyone looked at the jeans, as pink as the shocking pink knickers Maria Bueno had stunned the Centre Court of Wimbledon with. They fastened at the side, Hugh noticed, giving her front the stirring but impenetrable bareness of a censored photo in *Health and Efficiency* magazine; and, as she took her seat on the stool, the movement made a little susurration between her legs, causing Hugh mentally to admonish the interior of his underpants in no uncertain terms. For a single heart-stopping second, he thought he might have spoken aloud, because Mrs Cholmondeley caught his eye, drew deeply on her menthol cigarette – cool as a mountain stream, promised the advert – and slowly winked. Hugh felt confused, unmanned. Three years of training at Public School failed to prevent the blood rising to his cheeks. He felt, without knowing why, shame.

'I hear that you are something of a brain box, Hugh,' said Cheryl with a smile. 'I hear that you read many books. That is somethink I would love to have more time for.'

Hugh found Mrs Cholmondeley's genteel accents fascinating, like a foreign language. She never contracted her words, he realised. Never said 'didn't' for 'did not'. Yet the way the odd Hounslow vowel intruded was exciting, like a mucky barmaid posing as a débutante. (*Stop* that, he scolded his underpants.)

'Hugh not only reads,' said Maman. 'He writes.'

'No,' said Cheryl. 'And what is it that you write, Hugh?'

'Oh, Maman,' hissed Hugh despairingly.

'Don't be ridiculous, Luh'le Shuggy. It's affected of you to refuse to speak of your writing.'

'I don't write. Not really.'

'*Pas vrai!* You are writing a novel.'

'Ye gods! A novel,' cried Cheryl.

'I've hardly started it.'

'And what is the theme of your novel, pray?' asked Cheryl. Her inflammatory red lipstick and long red nails clashed with the pink jeans, at the end of which were half-lengths of golden calf culminating in slender ankles which she now crossed expectantly. Hugh's face turned a deeper colour.

'That is a thing we'd all like to hear, my son,' confirmed Dada. 'I'm sure.' He ostentatiously drew attention to his hair by sweeping it back with all his fingers.

'I dunno. I s'pose it's about, um, loneliness, alienation, madness and death.'

'I love a good laugh, me,' said Roger.

'No, seriously, Hugh. I think it's perfectly marvellous that you are trying to write,' reassured Cheryl.

'Hugh is an existentialist,' explained Maman brightly.

'Good God. *Are* you, Luh'le… are you, Hugh?'

'I might be.' Hugh reddened further.

'So my son and heir will be off at any second to set fire to the Bank of England?'

'No, Dada. That's anarchists.'

'Oh *well*. Perhaps you'll show a little forbearance towards your poor father, who can't tell an anarchist from an existentialist. Perhaps you will try and overlook the embarrassing fact that he has not had your expensive education. He merely fought in a World War to preserve his country from tyranny – so that you could burn it down at your leisure.'

'I think young people today are perfectly marvellous,' said Cheryl. 'So free. We could learn a lot from Hugh.'

'It's difficult to imagine what exactly,' laughed Dada.

'I think you would be surprised, Dermot. I think our Hugh's a dark horse. I think he knows ever so much about philosophy and that.' She dropped another eyelid at Hugh, whose thoughts turned, appropriately, to an early bath with hemlock. 'I mean, when did you last read a book, Roger?'

'This morning, my love. In the toilet.'

'Try not to be common, dear.' Cheryl turned to Maman. 'My husband thinks that Readers' Digest counts as a book, like D.H. Lawrence or Dostichevsky.'

'Lady Chatterley and her gamekeeper,' said Roger, rubbing his hands together. 'Phwor, eh?'

'That is typical, I'm afraid,' lamented Cheryl. 'What do you think of *Lady Chatterley's Lover*, Hugh?'

Hugh longed to talk to Dan Rose who was sitting in the corner with that teaser of an Irishman, Eugene McCarthy. He had once knocked up with Mr Rose who had said something no grown-up had ever said: 'Call me Dan, Hugh mate' – and had taught him how to serve a top spin American kicker. Dan was not American but it was as if he were, with his sun tan and gold chain and fantastic white teeth. He was old, of course – probably nearly thirty – but a cool cat nonetheless. He was a high flyer at IBM and had a leggy wife who looked like the Shrimp in that photo of her by the Oik Snapper, as Dada called him – David Bailey – in which the Shrimp was lying in hay, modelling tight – oh, *tight* – jeans open at the top (DON'T START, Hugh mentally bellowed at his underpants).

'Well, I… er…,' he hesitated.

'Ha-ha-ha,' laughed Dada uneasily. 'Hugh hasn't read that particular tome, I venture to suggest! We try to keep smutty books out of the house.'

'Many experts came forward, Dermot,' explained Cheryl seriously, 'to testify that it is not smut but Literature.'

'Literature. Phwor, eh?' twinkled Roger.

'Well, I'd be *your* gamekeeper any time, Cheryl, ha-ha,' averred Dada wildly. He knew next to nothing about the book. Except that it was smutty.

'You will support me, Lorna,' appealed Cheryl. '*Lady Chatterley* is a work of art, no?' In fact, she had been dismayed by the book. Hoping for insights into how one might approach, well, that side of things in a refined way, she had been initially repelled by the most unlady-like behaviour of Lady C. Subsequently, Cheryl had come to suppose that if you were a *real* lady, as Lady C undoubtedly was, you did not need to behave like one. You let yourself go when it came to that side of things. Cheryl determined that she would try and mend her ways in that regard.

'I rather think it may be,' said Maman, 'since all the most modern people say so. Personally, I have no idea. But it may also be that they think it's clever to call blue material Literature when in fact Dermot is closer to the mark. Really, I have no idea. I haven't read it.' She took a pull on her drink to conceal the lie. Or, at least, half-truth; for it was true that she had not read all of it. She hadn't been shocked by the sexual frankness so much as bored by La Chatterley and her pawky lover. She really couldn't be bothered with him and, *enfin*, his measly John Thomas.

'Same again for Mr and Mrs Cholmondeley, Lorraine.' It was Dada's round. 'Just a half for me and a Dubonnet for my wife.'

'Leaving out the missis's gin, eh, old man?' grinned Roger. 'One of your little economies?' Black clouds blew at once into Dada's face, presaging a storm of anger only the truth could provoke.

'Not at all,' intervened Maman smoothly, ever alert to forestall the legendary temper. 'It's just that we can't stay long. The casserole will be burnt to a cinder.'

'To hell with the casserole!' cried Dada with unfocussed eyes. 'Lorraine! A bottle of your finest champagne!'

'Really, Dermot,' murmured Maman. 'Do you think we ought…?'

'It's time we had a bit of a knees-up!'

'As the actress said to the Bishop,' laughed Cheryl, laying a long red finger nail on the sleeve of his blazer, and winking.

'Ha-ha,' laughed Dada glassily. 'That's it, Lorraine. The Bollinger.'

'My word, Dermot,' said Cheryl. 'Bolly! I love a drop of Bolly. You do not do things by half, do you?'

'You're crazy, old man. Ab-so-lutely crazy,' chuckled Roger. 'But we like people who live life to the full, don't we, Cheryl? Is he as mad as this at home, Lor? Plenty of old Blarney?'

'Not always,' laughed Maman, blinking rapidly at the 'Lor'. 'Sometimes you can hardly get a word out of him.'

'No, seriously. I find that very, very hard to believe,' said Cheryl archly, smiling at Dada.

'No, no, no. My wife speaks truly. When the black dog of melancholy bites, I can fall into a brown study for days.'

'Thinking your deep thoughts,' decided Cheryl.

'I'd re-decorate that study,' cracked Roger.

'Roger is never melancholy,' said Cheryl lightly. 'He has no soul.' She smiled wistfully, giving everyone to understand that she was very much in possession of such an article. 'You have no soul, do you, Roger?'

'If you say so, my poppet. I can only be grateful that you could bring yourself to marry someone with money but no soul.'

'I'm sure Roger has a soul,' said Maman.

'No, Lor. Cheryl is right. I don't. It's a luxury I can't afford.'

'Do not talk silly, Roger,' said Cheryl. She winked at Hugh. 'Hugh understands me.'

Hugh did nothing of the kind; but he found himself contorting his mouth into an obliging smile, and trying to hide his involuntary squirm of embarrassment. He turned to catch Janey's eye, but only caught her looking away. She was sitting hunched over her Coca-Cola as, opposite her, Sabrina Cholmondeley held forth. Her face was all but hidden behind its veil of hair, the ends of which she was distractedly chewing. Maman couldn't get her out of her black drainpipes, but the white blouse she'd forced her daughter into revealed a promising bust Hugh hadn't seen, or taken in, before. His heart shrivelled with pity and tenderness. How could Janey, who most deserved happiness, ever find it? Only he knew what treasure lay behind the scruffy withdrawn appearance. No one else would take the trouble to discover the reality. People never did. And so, unlike the annoying confident pretty little Sabrina, Janey would never get a boyfriend and would remain a lonely spinster all her life.

Janey didn't mind being relegated to the kids' table. It was better than having to listen to the grown-ups, like poor Luh'le Shuggy. Dada's carry-on was bordering on the certifiable. But, then, Mrs Cholmondeley always sort of *maddened* him, with her starlet's laugh and red nails, hanging on his every word and, hell's teeth, *winking*. Not a little crinkle of the eye, but an extraordinary drop of the eyelid like a ventriloquist's dummy. It made Janey cringe to see how her brother did not meet the wink with his best curl of the lip, but grinned in a ninnyish way, and shuffled about awkwardly. He was so much cleverer than the grown-ups, Luh'le Shuggy – knew all about really important things like William Blake and Zen, Socrates and ablative absolutes. Clever and, yes, good-looking, if you looked beyond the inane grin and the shifty way he stood, with his shoulder blades sticking out. The dab of Clearasil, clearly visible, made Janey's heart bleed.

While the Moo was busy composing violent car crashes at their feet, George and the Enemy sat opposite each other on either side of Janey and Sabrina. Both had folded their arms on the table and were hunched forward, keeping an eye on each other – in Bradley's case, literally; for he was wearing the owlish spectacles with their single brown opaque lens. Both were drinking glasses of cream soda through straws or, rather, blowing down the straws to see which of them could make the bubbles rise highest without actual spillage.

The bubbling became so intense that Sabrina had to raise her voice in order to make Janey hear.

'Maybelline. It's absolutely the latest thing. It makes your eyelashes longer and thicker.' She batted them in evidence. 'You should try it, Jane. Or doesn't Maman allow you to wear make-up?' Janey flinched at the 'Maman'. Throwing up mental ramparts as fast as Caesar, she politely replied that the subject of make-up had not come up. However, since she scarcely opened her mouth, moved her lips or ceased to chew the ends of her hair, her answer was lost under the roar of cream soda. The younger girl was undismayed. 'You should do something with your hair, Jane. It's quite nice. Pity about the colour. But I could help you. I do my own hair. Cheryl says I'm too young for a shop perm. But I'm lucky – I don't need rollers and that. I have a natural wave. You could have a bob. Then your face wouldn't be so hidden. I'm sure chewing doesn't improve one's hair…' Janey surveyed Sabrina's head, with its daytime pony tail loosed to an evening cascade, and moved her shoulders non-committally. She watched the little pink mouth working, watched how the confident bottom lip curled inwards, causing the appearance in her chin of a sanctimonious little dimple which asserted louder than any words that whatever Sabrina said was, of necessity, correct. 'I could come round after school, Jane, and give you a blonde rinse. Shall I, Jane? What? I can't hear you. Stop making those noises, boys. Are you looking at my dress, Jane? Cheryl took me up to Kensington and we bought it at Biba. That's a boutique. Absolutely the latest thing.' She stood up, twirled, and pointed to the inches of thigh. 'You see? It's a mini dress. It's a new line. It cost eight pound. Do you like it? Of course, I hate the little bow. So childish. Cheryl says she'll cut it off.' She sighed heavily. 'Still, I do sometimes wish I could just muck about in jeans and a sweater, like a boy; but I simply look a mess. I wish I could get away with it like you, Jane. You're so lucky – you don't care one bit about appearances. Cheryl's getting me a Biba trouser suit for Christmas.' She dimpled her chin self-approvingly and took a dainty sip of her pineapple juice. Janey took a mouthful of Coca-Cola and swilled it around Foody Fenella, whose presence she found oddly comforting, like a weapon.

'If you put a tooth in a glass of Coca-Cola,' said Bradley, 'it completely dissolves.' The last word was accompanied by spit.

'Say it, don't spray it, Cholmondeley,' advised George. 'And if you'd tried it, as I have, you'd have found that *actually* it doesn't.'

'Obviously *your* tooth didn't, Blyte, because your teeth are protected by yellow slime because you never clean them.' George was momentarily nonplussed by the truth of this assessment. He made do with:

'Well, you still have your baby teeth, Cholmondeley.'

'As a matter of *fact*, Blyte, I do not.' The working of his mouth occasioned further spray. 'And why are you wearing your school blazer? You must like school, Blyte. You must *love* school. You wish you were at school now. You're hoping that a teacher will walk past so that you can suck up.' He demonstrated sucking up through violently zigzagging lips.

George had been afraid of this. He was red in the face. He cursed his parents for being too mean to buy him a proper jacket and long trousers. Bradley ruthlessly pressed home his advantage:

'And you're wearing baby shorts. School shorts. Is ums wearing nappies under ums shorts? Is ums?' George kicked Bradley's shins – and let out a cry when the Enemy retaliated twice as hard.

'George!' called out Dada. 'Behave yourself.' By sheer force of will, George drained all the blood from his face and, summoning all his strength, constructed an expression of complete indifference, a Hadrian's Wall to keep back the Scots of shame and the Picts of rage.

'… *The Sound of Music*,' Sabrina was telling Janey. 'Cheryl is taking me again for my birthday. It's in the West End. Of London, you know. We go to all the shows. I'm going to be a singer when I grow up. Or a dancer. I'm good at both but I don't know which I'm best at. I know all the words. Listen: *Doe, a deer, a female deer, Ray, a drop of golden sun* – I do a dance I made up myself, I won't do it now, just the hands – *Me, a name I call myself, Far, a long long way…*'

As more people drifted into the bar, the Blytes and the Cholmondeleys held their positions, the women on bar stools, the men rocking to and fro on their feet and jingling the contents of their trouser pockets. Maman noticed that Dermot was doing a bit of Prince Flasheen Eyes on Cheryl. When they were first married, this would have amused her. For Dada had been only one of many suitors, and she had not accepted his proposals at once, far from it. Not till he had lain down in the middle of the road and refused to move until she accepted him had she, laughing, agreed to be his wife. She had had the upper hand. How had things managed to change so? How had she become so dependent on him and his opinion? How had she come to look at herself, judge herself, through his eyes? Eyes which were now fixed on Cheryl Cholmondeley.

Maman did not blame him. Cheryl was quite a sight. She was common, of course, but Maman didn't hold that against her. It wasn't the Thirties any more – and thank God: all that endless class distinction and knowing everyone's place. It was good that a man like Dermot could flirt with a woman like Cheryl.

'I adore your cravat, Roger,' said Maman. 'Very dashing.'

'Oh "dashing's" my middle name, Lor.'

'Dashing the hopes of maidens everywhere, I'll be bound!'

'That's me. "There goes that dashed Cholmondeley," the cry goes up at the factory!'

'How is the factory? I wish Dermot would work for himself. The firm doesn't appreciate him.'

'I, on the other hand, often long for the old nine to five, you know, Lor. Especially now that the valve business has gone up in smoke.' Roger laughed, but not whole-heartedly. In truth, he had been shaken by recent developments. The valves he made for wirelesses and computers had been suddenly superseded by transistors.

'I dare say your old valves are still sparky!'

'Ha-ha-ha. You know me, Lor – twiddle my knobs and I still light up! No, it's been a long slog, but I'm in transistors now. Of course, I missed the radio boom – we all did, thanks to the Japanese – but I've put my shirt on transistors for computers and, touch wood, it's working out.'

'Not for long,' said Hugh. 'Those new silicon chip things are taking over.'

'I very much doubt that, Harry my lad. They're all talk. You know the Americans.'

'Well, Dan – Mr Rose – 'he gestured towards the corner table where Dan Rose, razor sharp, caught his eye and waved cheerily – 'he says that the third generation of computers is up and running. They'll be here by Christmas. He says that, speed-wise, they'll make the transistor look like a donkey cart next to a Ferrari.'

'Ha-ha-ha.'

'I'll just go and have a word with him,' added Hugh, sauntering gratefully away. His face hurt from the smile he was forced to adopt in the teeth of their constant pointless bloody laughter.

George and Bradley drained their cream sodas simultaneously.

'I'm getting out of here,' said Bradley.

'Yeah, me too,' said George.

'You don't have to do everything I do, Blyte.'

'I'm not, Cholmondeley. *Actually*. I've got a lot of things to do.' He waved to Maman and pointed to the door.

'Be in before dark, mein Fu… George!' she called out.

The two boys had cycled over to the Club. They collected their bikes in silence, eyeing each other's tyres. Both had mended their punctures; neither admitted to puncturing or being punctured. They rode off in different directions. George took the road home. Bradley sped along the cliff path to his house, changed his clothes and ran back to the rear of the Blyte residence where he crept through the rhododendrons and down the garden path. He was executing the most daring of plans.

'We should start up a Woman's magazine, Dermot,' Cheryl was saying. 'We could do better than *Woman's Own*. I know what women want, and you, with your managerial experience, know how to sell it.'

'Yes, *do* start a magazine with Cheryl, darling,' said Maman. 'It would be such fun.'

'I doubt that Cheryl knows a great deal about knitting patterns,' laughed Roger. He took a long drink to neutralise the cold chill Hugh's words had produced. He glanced over at Dan Rose – tanned, confident, relaxed – and fear gripped him. What if he were right about the obsolescence of computer transistors? Roger had put everything into them, making a late grab for the market which, so far, was working. Just about. But the slightest tremor could send the whole edifice crashing down.

'That is why there would be no knitting patterns,' smiled Cheryl. 'The modern woman wants more than knitting patterns.'

'What does she want?' asked Dada.

'Fashion. Interior decoration. The Pill. Men.'

'Ah-ha,' said Dada uneasily, jingling his keys more quickly.

'How to Get Your Man and How to Keep Him,' elaborated Cheryl.

'I could be the Agony Aunt,' said Maman in lively tones.

'Someone a little younger, I think, dear,' said Cheryl.

'Surely, a wise head…?'

'We need to bring our readers into the bedroom,' said Cheryl easily.

'Steady the Buffs!' exclaimed Dada.

'I don't think the ladies are quite ready for *that*,' laughed Roger.

'We certainly are, aren't we, Lorna?'

'Most of us haven't got beyond the kitchen!'

'Well, that's certainly a suggestion, Lorna,' said Cheryl, winking.

'Oooh, you filthy beast!' cried Dada, his mock shock masking his shock. They all laughed with different degrees of candour, while Roger shook his head in mock disbelief and Dada and Maman both watched with fascination as Cheryl expertly uncrossed her slender, slender ankles.

George was happy to be away from the Tennis Club bar. What made him particularly happy was to be alone in the house for once and able to indulge in the secret vice that the Enemy must never ever find out about. But firstly, duty called. He filled a watering-can and hauled it over to the summerhouse where the apples he had scrumped were laid out on the high shelf. He turned the door handle but was surprised to find that the door had been locked. He pulled out his Swiss Army penknife and, inserting one of its blades in the crack of the warped window, levered it open. Then he lowered the can through the window and followed it headfirst. He clambered over a pile of furniture, stood on a chest of drawers and delicately moistened them. They were rotting nicely, most of them brown and some of them flecked with white fungus, but still some way off that precise consistency which would cause them to explode on impact and cling like napalm. How he longed for the apples to be ready, longed for vengeance on the Enemy after the humiliating Great Mud Pie Defeat. The mental image of the Enemy's ugly mug and puny body splattered with pungent rotten fruit and running with foul juices made him laugh out loud. But he was determined not to strike prematurely. Patience was the key: a slow build-up of *matériel* until success was as certain as it had been for Montgomery at El Alamein.

As he turned to jump down, he noticed that behind the stack of furniture, hidden from ground-floor view, was an old divan. It had a satin sheet on it, and some cushions. It looked as though it had been recently used. By a *tramp*, obviously. Snazzy or what. A real tramp would be... *fab.* He ought to stake out the summerhouse and see; but for the moment his secret vice beckoned, and he scampered back to the house.

Meanwhile, Bradley's plan was coming on apace. It had been formed as a result of dissatisfaction with his camp in the Tennis Club grounds. What he really craved was a *dug-out*. He pictured a large underground cave whose small manhole-like entrance was completely hidden by camouflage. The cave gave on to a labyrinth of tunnels with many secret exits so that he could pop up all over the Tennis Club, ambushing the Enemy, like the Japanese army on Iwo-Jima.

The reality had been different. Digging was arduous. Endless roots and rocks got in the way. What he needed was an existing roof he could burrow under. A mental scan of the neighbourhood revealed the ideal place: the Blytes' summerhouse. A quick recce after dark – ghosting along the cliff path (whoops! Nearly tripped at the dip) and through the bushes – suggested that it was even better than he'd thought. Digging from the rear of the summerhouse, he'd be completely out of view of the house. Also, the going was easy – no roots or rocks, just light sandy soil he could pile up behind the building or disperse in the bushes. What a coup – to build a base camp *behind Enemy lines!* He had already made significant progress after only two sessions of digging: he could already kneel upright under the summerhouse's floor. He slid down into the dug-out for a third session. It was still light outside but dark in the dug-out. He switched on his torch, and began to loosen soil with his trowel before scrabbling it back between his legs like a terrier and working it through the opening with his feet.

George settled himself comfortably in his sloping den under the stairs. At the door end it was high enough to stand; at the other end the ceiling was only an agreeable four inches or so from his face when he lay down on his mattress. He lit the oil lamp which Maman had said he must have there under all circumstances, or perhaps under no circumstances – probably the former because he had to have light, hadn't he? There were little piles of plaster here and there underneath the nails that Dada had said he absolutely must drive into the walls. Or, possibly, absolutely mustn't. He couldn't quite remember. But probably must, because how else was he to display his collection of memorabilia? The skull of an unknown animal with huge canines, probably the Surrey Puma; a gas mask; a ceremonial German dagger, looted by Dada, which hung above the German helmet; a flat lead sculpture twisted and menacing enough to give Francis Bacon the willies; a catapult carved from the forked stem of a rhododendron; a rusty machete slung up by Luh'le Shuggy's old, or possibly new, silk tie; a chrome hub cap; a cyclist's plastic bottle half full of stale lemon barley water. There were four prints: of a poster advertising a bullfight; of *Rain, Steam, Speed* by J.M.W. Turner; of a British tank in action because George was, despite his nickname, a patriot who rejoiced over Britain's win in the War, even as he silently marvelled that an army made of the likes of Dada could ever have defeated the Best Fighting Troops in the World (it could only be that God, as Dada maintained, was British); and a portrait of Danny Blanchflower, the Irish captain of all-conquering Spurs.

Using the spike on his Swiss Army knife for removing the stones from horses' hooves, George punched two holes in a tin of Nestlé's condensed milk and took a long ecstatic suck of the thick sweet liquid. He plumped pillows luxuriously around him and, at last, pulled his secret vice out from beneath the mattress. He leafed slowly through its pages, pausing for a long time at the picture of Stella who, with her pirouetting and her scraped back hair, reminded him disturbingly of Sabrina.

Each of the Blyte children was allowed one comic, delivered every week. The Moo, for example, had chosen *The Beezer.* George had taken *The Eagle.* Janey had taken *Bunty,* but was now too old for it, and had given it up. The trouble was, that George had become so addicted to its serials (*Bunty* had written stories as well as comic strips) that he had been forced to keep *Bunty* on – which meant giving up *The Eagle.* This was George's dark secret: he was subscribing weekly to *a girl's comic.* He was reading about hockey teams and gymkhanas and Stella's quest to become the youngest ever member of the British ice skating team. At the moment, he was engrossed in the diary of little Mozart's older sister as they toured England in the 1700s, wowing everyone with their musical genius. He was pretty rebellious, that Wolfgang Amadeus, and a great one for getting into scrapes. Of course George missed Dan Dare and his arch-foe, the Mekon ('Prattle on, you empty fools – for, to-morrow, VENGEANCE WILL BE MINE!!!); but the stories were read so quickly while a *Bunty* story lasted two or three days. Sometimes Mozart's sister would admire an English boy, such as the handsome pickpocket who had saved her from the kidnappers. And this had given George his first taste of romance, plus an inkling that girlie stuff might one day be of more practical use to him than a knowledge of the different planets the Mekon had subjugated for his own evil ends.

Just then he [Bradley] heard the summerhouse window being prised open, the clank of some container, followed by a body dropping to the floor. Bradley flicked off his torch and lay completely still. He recognised the scuffling footsteps of the Enemy. Little did the unsuspecting pea-brain know! He heard George clambering about, and clattering a bucket or something. There was the sound of water dripping. What was the nit up to? He heard George give a short laugh and, jumping down, leave the summerhouse.

Bradley smiled to himself. It was indescribably satisfactory to have a secret base deep within Enemy territory. But for how long? Bradley already longed to see the staggered expression on Blyte's face when he revealed the dug-out. But what then? He wouldn't be able to use it any more. The Enemy would take it away, unless – and this would, actually, be quite snazzy – they shared it. Blyte was, after all, a worthy foe. What acts of terrorism might they not plot together by candlelight in the dug-out? Who could stand against their combined force? And Bradley could take refuge whenever he wanted from his beastly home. But this could never happen. Not after the Great Mud Pie Victory. Bradley found himself almost regretting it, for there could be no truce, let alone an alliance, until the Enemy had retaliated. Not that Blyte showed any signs that he *was* planning to retaliate. On the contrary, things had been quiet;

and Blyte, on Saturday mornings at their camps, had been quite chatty and even pleasant. Too pleasant, perhaps. Too quiet.

It was almost dark outside and Bradley decided to call it a day. He was just about to scrabble his way out, when he heard a key jiggling in the lock of the summerhouse door. This time, it was not the Enemy. Instead, it was a man's heavy footsteps crossing the floor and wading through the piled junk to the divan hidden at the back. Bradley froze, face down in the earth, and held his breath. There was a creak of springs and a sigh as the man sat down on the divan. Then there was silence for an eternity. Bradley was beginning to think he had imagined the sounds, when the door opened again. A woman's shoes tip-tapped above his head. The man spoke in a voice too low for Bradley to make out the words. The woman uttered a muffled exclamation, too brief and indistinct to be identified by anyone apart from Bradley. As the springs of the divan creaked more profoundly, and then more quickly, he silently scooped earth over his head and into his ears.

There were no streetlights in the luscious avenues of St Michael's Hill. A myriad stars were visible. The Moo had long ago been escorted to bed – a nightly chore for which lots were drawn – because there were menacing ghosts on the dark staircase which could not be dispelled until the light switch at the top was reached. The next bed – Hugh's – was empty since Hugh had commandeered one of the two spare rooms. In the third bed lay the sleeping Fuehrer, whose unconscious longing for suffocation led him to scrimmage in his sleep head-first down the bed whence he was rescued, sweating and asphyxiated, by parents at their bed-time. Next to George's feet, resting on his pillow, lay Goose. To the casual observer this resembled nothing so much as a sock; but over the hand of Dada or Maman it was a mongoose that burrowed under the bedclothes and, with much snarling, 'swept' the area for the snakes that woke George, kicking and screaming, in the night. Goose's services had, happily, not been required for some months now; but George kept him on stand-by, in case.

Only Hugh was still awake, struggling with his prose: Rex Darkling could think of nothing to say to Lady Isabella but merely scowled and loured and longed for the sweetness of death, until Hugh too passed into the Dreamtime, where he had to sit an exam that was in German and so he couldn't answer a single question.

Indeed, under the dear little twinkling Surrey stars, all the inhabitants of the estate were dreaming. Some of them would be haunted by fleeting images all next day, but none of them would remember exactly what they had seen.

Maman dreamt that she was writing a brilliant story, page after page, at fantastic speed, in French; beside her, Dada, who had gone to sleep grinding his teeth over the Bollinger, was dreaming that without his knowing it his hair had been a wig all his life.

Janey dreamt that she was falling ecstatically, with bobbed hair, through the canopy of an emerald rain forest, only to be caught by the long trembly pianist's fingers of a lemur. George dreamt that under the skin of the lead he was smelting in the old saucepan lay a circular ingot of pure gold. The Moo dreamt that Spiv, very big and luminous, was smiling quizzically at him.

Charles Hamilton was dreaming that Colonel Bogey was standing six feet tall in his stockinged feet and was barking orders in Japanese that Charles couldn't understand, even though his life depended on it. Colonel Bogey was dreaming that he was endlessly searching a labyrinth of streets and alleys for the one smell that would give him peace. Theo dreamt that he stood up to receive the Albert Hall's applause for his concerto, and had no trousers on.

Roger Cholmondeley dreamt that he was in a sleigh being dragged by an uncontrollable team of huskies out on to a frozen lake whose ice would not support his weight; Cheryl dreamt that she was galloping north amidst a herd of reindeer away from the catastrophic ending of the world. Bradley was dreaming that he was in a dug-out in Hounslow which was collapsing on top of him; Sabrina was in Mrs Blyte's cosy kitchen biting into a rock cake that was empty in the middle.

Bugger Lamb dreamt that a huge turd, as if from the arse of God, fell out of the sky and smashed the dome of St Paul's Cathedral. Eugene McCarthy dreamt the smell of the smoke of his granny's turf fire, and woke with tears in his eyes. Dan Rose dreamt that his wife looked like Jean Shrimpton and was making love to him, only to wake and find that she did, and was.

part two

8

'T HE Zodiac,' shouted George. 'It's here!'
The family scrambled like Spitfire pilots and assembled on the steps of the front porch to watch Dada manoeuvring the spanking new motor car slowly up the drive. They had known it was coming – Dada had brought brochures to pore over weeks ago – but since it was the firm's car, it had taken an age to arrive and so everyone had forgotten about it, not least because no one really believed that something new and Swinging could enter their lives.

'What do you think of your old Dada now, eh?' asked Dada, climbing out of the Zodiac and looking into the shiny paintwork in order to smooth his luxuriant reflected hair. No one answered. The Moo was overwhelmed by the car's... *Americanness*; its sleekness and its brilliant fins. After the rounded old baggage that was the Austin, the Zodiac was sharp, almost spivvy, like something from the future. They all felt it. Hugh was even uneasy: the car looked so modern, so... unBlytish. Janey was struck by its colour: two-tone light blue, like something Mrs Cholmondeley might wear. The front seats were not separate and made of gloomy brown leather, but a continuous blue-grey bench with sparkly bits in the fabric. Only George suffered a pang of disappointment: he had lobbied vigorously for a black chassis and a yellow roof, but no one had listened to him, as usual, thus missing their one chance of real snazziness. However, he brightened at the sight of the plastic dashboard, with no sign of maiden-aunt walnut; and, above all, at the speedometer whose numbers went all the way up to a hundred.

'*Donner und Blitzen,* Dada! This is a *pokey* motor. Can we do a ton-up?'

'Of course, mein Fuehrer.'

'Of course *not*,' said Maman. 'It's far too dangerous to drive at a hundred miles an hour.'

'Cripes!' exclaimed George, lapsing into English in his excitement. 'It's got a Motorola!' He switched on the radio and *Poetry in Motion*, sung by Johnny Tillotson, came out of it.

As if summoned forth by the song, there rose from the back seat of the car, like Aphrodite rising from the wine-dark sea, a girl who had been lying there asleep. There was a collective hush as she opened the back door and, poetry in motion, climbed out on to her very long legs and stood smiling before them. She had black hair, blue eyes and white skin with two little blooms of pink on her delicate cheekbones.

'Are you a top model?' asked George.

'This is Bernadette O'Flaherty,' said Dada with pride. 'She has come from the Emerald Isle to replace the ill-favoured Carla.'

'Bernie O'Pair at your service,' said the girl.

'Welcome, Bernadette,' said Maman warmly. She shook the girl's hand and flashed a smile at Dada. Firstly Dr Siskin's expensive dietary régime, she thought, and now a new Mother's Help – and all without any nagging. She had been wrong about her husband. Just when she had begun to think that her marriage was foundering, Dermot had risen to the occasion. The sudden spate of thoughtfulness was as pleasant as it was surprising.

'Ah, call me Bernie, Mrs Blyte.'

'And how old are you, Bernie?'

'I'm eighteen.' She looked around at the children. 'Well, look at all of you.' No one spoke because their breath had been taken away, especially Hugh's. Hell's teeth, she was hardly older than he was. His legs felt weak. Bernie laughed melodiously. 'This'll be Luh'le Shuggy? Have I said it right, now? Well, don't you look like a good-looking John Lennon? And this'll be Janey. Sure, it's an honour to meet a real beatnik. Hello, mein Fuehrer. Your Dada tells me you're known as the Fuehrer. Well, aren't you a man after my own heart? And wasn't it a shame about the war? Sure, we'll have better luck next time. And here's the Moo. Wasn't I expecting a little boy – and here's a great big man! What's that quare yoke you have attached to you? Spiv? And what class of craytur would that be? A fox? God, he looks a dangerous customer altogether. Will he like me, d'you think?'

The Moo thought he would. Indeed, for Spiv, it was love at first sight. For all of them Bernadette O'Flaherty was sunlight and air breaking through fog.

While Maman settled Bernie in, Dada took the children for a spin around St Michael's Hill. At the end of Chestnut Avenue an old Triumph pulled up alongside the Zodiac. Dada glanced disdainfully towards it, running a careless hand through his hair. 'Good God!' The driver of the Triumph was Roger Cholmondeley. Dada had heard that Roger was having business problems; but to have fallen so far so fast, from an Italian sports car to an old banger of a Triumph – well, Dada could not suppress a shudder of pure *schadenfreude*.

Roger pointed at the Zodiac and made a face of theatrical shock. Dada managed to hide most of his gloating expression, but could not altogether suppress a superior smile. Roger stuck his thumb out sideways and waggled it slowly up and down, as if the world's verdict on the Zodiac were hanging in the balance. Then, abruptly, it plunged downwards. Roger shook his head sadly. But by the time an incensed Dada had rolled down his window and bellowed: 'No – *you're* Dodgy! *You're* Dodgy! Your car's Dodgy! Your blazer's Dodgy! *Everything about you is Dodgy,'* Roger had calmly accelerated away.

It was early on a weekday morning. Maman was up. Up and happy. Delirious. She was *slim*. Well, slimmer. She had a shape again. The Tub was no more! Dr Siskin's – David's – diet had been as simple and effective as his elegant brochure had promised: an injection every now and again in Harley Street, and then pills. One lot to combat the 'water retention' she never knew she had (no wonder her ankles – where water collected – had ballooned); another lot to, well, slim her. True, she had to go to the lavatory every half-an-hour, which was, frankly, a bore; but it was worth it – she was blissfully peeing away the pounds.

Meanwhile, the slimming pills were nothing short of miraculous. 'Eat what you like,' David had said. But, strangely, she didn't feel much like eating. She felt like smoking. Stranger still, she suffered no loss of energy. Rather the reverse. She found she could get by happily on three or four hours' sleep a night. Instead of lying in all morning, she was up and doing. Two days ago she had decided that the drawing room was a disgrace, especially the curtains, six of them, which she had pulled down in order to launder. But the Axminster had suddenly seemed in more urgent need of cleaning, and so yesterday she had had delivered one of those new Bex Bissells for shampooing carpets. Today it stood unused, foaming slightly at the mouth, beside two piles of grubby curtains while Maman, puffing vigorously on a cigarette, avidly scanned the prospectus for night-school courses.

There was a whole world of skills she couldn't wait to acquire. She ticked Tapestry, and then Upholstery (she could refurbish the sofa!). Then Cordon Bleu Cuisine (what a surprise for Dermot!) and, obviously, Spanish. Comparative Religion, of course; and, while she was at it, Philosophy. Why not. At that moment another idea for a story came to her. They were coming thick and fast. She had already dashed off the outlines to three or four on dismembered cigarette packets. Any minute now she'd sit down and write them. And send them to *Argosy*. She'd be successful this time. She stared at the wallpaper where, clearly projected, was the moving image of herself collecting amid applause the Short Story of the Year Award. She banished the picture with a shake of the head. What was that idea again? *Zut*, it had vanished. Never mind, there'd be another, better one along in a minute. She'd just have cup of coffee and a fag, and then she'd get down to writing.

She was arrested at the breakfast room door by the sound of Bernie's voice, telling one of her stories. Maman felt a pang of jealousy. It used to be she who told the stories. Now it was Bernie. And all the children – even Luh'le Shuggy who had no need – got up early for school so that they could listen to her as they munched their way through a huge pile of toast and drank huge mugs of tea. It should be she, thought Maman, who made the toast and told the tales; but she'd had her chance. And now, ironically, just when she was for the first time able to rise with the lark, she was no longer needed. Still, it gave her time to concentrate on her own work. And Bernie was a treasure. She smiled ruefully as she went in.

'It was the last bus. I was after helping Pat Tim bring in the haycocks by tractor and we'd had a drink in town and it was late…'

'Pat Tim drives a tractor,' said the Moo, impressed.

'He does, the Moo, filthy thing that it is, and he no better half the time, wiping his oily hands through his hair and saying: "Amn't I the lad now, Bernie? Amn't I only gorgeous, like Elvis the Pelvis? And wouldn't you want to be kissing a lad like meself all day long and not coming up for air?" The bold eejit. "I would not," says I, "and get away and wash yourself before you address another remark to me, Pat Tim," but, sure, I don't mean it for he's lovely hair, Pat Tim, and the big arms you'd want to wrap around yourself – but that's not the class of information I'll be giving out to the likes of you children. So where have I got to? Ah yes. I'm on the last bus, and I'm the last passenger on that bus, and it drops me off in the Windy Gap at midnight –'

'What's that?' asked the Moo.

'It's a gap between two hills where the wind howls. I've to walk down the track about a mile home into the valley. It's an awful lonely place, and desolate. No one lives there except Mad Kate.'

'Mad Kate,' repeated George with pleasure.

'Except she's not so mad. It's more that she was *touched*, or so the ould ones say. And now she can see more, and farther, than we.'

'Touched?' wondered George.

'Touched in the head,' explained Hugh. 'Simple-minded.'

'Well now, Luh'le Shuggy. Not so simple. For wasn't Kate touched by ...' She lowered her voice. 'The Good People.'

'?'

'?'

'Ah God, 'tis a quare country, England. Totally cut off from reality. Still, you're lucky enough, I'd say, not to be troubled by the likes of the Good People, who'll bring you good luck and treasure, surely, but more often than not will banjax you. They're the ould race of Irish who live under the hills. They don't like you to mention their real name, but in the Irish language' – she lowered her voice further – 'they're called the *Sidhe*.' She pronounced it 'shee', like an admonition to be silent.

'Do you mean... the Little People?' whispered Janey.

'I do,' said Bernie. 'And I don't. For they're not always so little. They can be as big as you and me – bigger – and clattering through the night on horseback like gentry, calling to their hounds and laughing, their silver eyes flashing. Kate says it's a glamour they put over themselves, or over our eyes, to make them seem big or small.'

'Dod-gy,' breathed George. The Moo nodded solemnly, his toast suspended half way to his mouth.

'Anyway, there was I, up in the Windy Gap at midnight, and it beginning to rain, when I heard a sound I hope to God I never hear again –'

'Good morning, darlings,' called out Maman as she bustled in. It hurt her to see the brief look of annoyance at her interruption pass across the Moo's face. 'Don't mind me,' she said quickly, heading for the kitchen, 'I'm just going to make myself a cup of Nescafé. Shall I poach some eggs for anyone? No? Well, don't be late for school now, children. Bernie, I rely on you.' She stopped in the doorway of the kitchen, a vivid figure wavering like a flame. Hugh noticed that her eyes were very bright, as if back-lit. Come to think of it, he hadn't seen her blink for days. Then she turned, smiling, her shiny eyes unfocussed. 'On second thoughts, I haven't time for coffee –' She lit a cigarette and puffed smoke violently out of the corner of her mouth, like a soldier in front of a firing squad. 'I'll just… just go and…' She hurried out of the breakfast room.

'Go on, Bernie,' said Janey and Hugh in unison.

'The sound you hope to God you never hear again,' prompted George.

'Yes,' said the Moo nervously, his fingers poised near to his ears, in case.

'At first I thought it was only the wind sobbing in the trees. But then it seemed to be carried by the wind, coming nearer, sounding all around me, a wild and bitter cry, keening, keening…' Bernie drew out the onomatopoeic syllables for dramatic effect. 'I ran then. I ran to Mad Kate's cottage and I hammered on the door. Cold sweat was pouring up and down me back. I knew she was there for, sure, where else would she be? But she wouldn't answer. 'Twas then that I saw it…'

'What?' said the Moo. 'What?'

'The candle burning in the window. And behind the candle, a crucifix. My legs nearly went from under me, for I knew well what the candle and crucifix meant.'

'What?' cried the children. 'What?'

110

'It meant,' said Bernie, looking at each of them in turn, 'that *the Banshee was abroad.*'

'The what?' said the Moo, wide-eyed.

'What did you do?' asked Janey in horror.

'What would anyone do, with the Banshee keening and howling after them? Holy Mother of God, I ran for me life and never stopped till I was safe inside me own house, with a chair up against the door handle.'

'It might have been only the wind,' suggested George. 'It might have been all in your mind.'

'It might, mein Fuehrer. Except.'

'Except what?'

'Except that old Mister Sweeney was only found dead in his bed the next morning. And 'tis well known that the Banshee cries the Sweeneys just as she cries the Lynch family and the O'Kellys. Whenever one of them is near death she is heard keening – a terrible mourning crying sobbing sound – and sometimes seen, by the water's side, as it might be a ford or lough, combing and combing her long grey hair.'

The children had gone to school. Hugh was in the kitchen, waiting for the kettle to boil. He was also watching Bernie who, with her back to him, was washing up at the sink. She didn't believe in wearing actual clothes for housework – she had too few to risk spoiling them – and so she had little on apart from a short grubby slip on which her Slopy Club badge was prominently displayed. Her legs and feet, which knocked the Shrimp's into a cocked hat, were bare. On the other hand, she always wore full war paint. The combination of fashion-plate face and street-urchin apparel created, if you didn't know better, a sluttish impression. Bernie's complete unconsciousness of that impression proved Maman's claim that Bernie was only an innocent country girl. Innocent – and devout. For she went to Mass weekly and only mixed with other young people at Church Socials. Hugh berated himself for the filthy Protestant thoughts that came unbidden into his mind as he looked at Bernie, swaying her hips inside her little crackling nylon slip in time to the song she was singing under her breath. He smiled mirthlessly in the manner of Rex Darkling at the irony: the girl who

111

seemed so attainable (plus, she slept *in the next room*) was by virtue of her free-spirited innocence wholly out of reach. It was like one of Shakespeare's Major Themes, viz. the conflict between Appearance and Reality; which not only led inevitably to a Tragic Outcome, but also to the transformation by imagination of loose-fitting Marks and Sparks Y-fronts into a stiff codpiece that sent Hugh scurrying back to his bedroom with a lukewarm cup of coffee to crush his passion like rose petals into a long and over-perfumed poem.

While Bernie was putting away the unused Bex Bissell and re-hanging the drawing room curtains, Maman was looking at herself in the mirror belonging to the bathroom cabinet. She had a spot of trouble focussing: the little yellow flashes of lightning in the corners of her eyes had become more frequent and more intense. Rather a bore, frankly. Quickly she swallowed another pill.

Also, something, perhaps someone – at any rate a sort of shadow – kept creeping up on her from behind. She could sense it – sometimes, looking in mirrors, almost see it. But no matter how quickly she jerked her head around, it always managed to dart away in time.

Her eyes, though, were pleasing. Very large and clear and grey-blue. But as she looked at them looking at her, they looked a bit funny. They seemed to have no pupils, like an old blue-eyed blind dog. A bit funny. It didn't do to look too closely at them, actually. She switched her attention to her pleasingly sunken cheeks. She had cheekbones! But below the jaw-line her plump, smooth neck was now unaccountably ravaged, a charnel-house of hanging skin. David had warned of this. Weight loss could lead to loose skin. Luckily it could be corrected, he had soothed, by a touch of judicious surgery. Imagine! He'd mentioned plastic surgery just like that, casually, as if she were Elizabeth Taylor or somebody. Indeed, now that she had her figure back and could pass for thirty, or thirtyish – well, after the judicious snipping she could – there was no reason why she shouldn't try out for films. *Mon Dieu*, Shepperton Studios was just around the corner! Her American accent in the Wyebridge Players' *You Can't Take It With You* had been praised to the skies by the *Surrey Advertiser*, no less. She could write a script herself, based on one of her short stories – and star in it! She'd write it now, just as soon as she'd had a coffee and a fag. First thing to-morrow, she'd telephone the Studios about a screen test. Maman did her brittle, New England, Katharine Hepburn laugh into the mirror. It frightened her. Her jowls, under-lit by stabs of lightning, trembled. She quickly averted her gaze towards her delicious, dehydrated ankles.

The Tennis Club bar was empty, as it often was around lunchtime, except for Roger who was watching the way Lorraine's sweater stretched over her really very, well, loveable bosom; and Lorraine, who was stretching upwards to place clean glasses on the shelf above the counter.

'Pint, Mr Cholmondeley?'

'Please, Lorraine. And it's Roger. Please.' She nodded. 'You're looking lovely today, Lorraine.' He realised as he said it, on automatic pilot, that it was in fact true: she looked lovely. Slightly less… *obvious* than usual, perhaps. Blonde hair less bouffante; lipstick less pink; skirt still short, but less so. Unfortunately.

'As is my wont, Roger.'

'Indeed, Lorraine. Ha-ha. I say, you haven't got any of your sandwiches, have you? I'm ravishing, ha-ha.'

'No, Roger. But I have baps.'

'And what have you put in your baps, Lorraine?'

'Corned beef or egg and salad cream, Roger. Suit?'

'Rather. One of each, please.' Her high heels clicked as far as the cubby hole at the end of the counter. She returned with a brace of well-stuffed baps. 'Thanks, Lorraine.'

'*De nada*, Roger.'

'Blimey, Lorraine. You speak Italian as well as… as everything else.'

'Spanish, Roger. Six months in a bar in Sitges. Not working today?'

'No point, Lorraine. Nobody wants what I make any more. I've lost my old orders. No new ones coming in.'

'The silicon chip, I suppose.'

'Did *everyone* know about those bleeding things apart from me?' It was a *cri de coeur*.

'No, Roger. It's just that, working in a bar, you hear things.'

'I wish you'd of told me, Lorraine.'

'You would not have listened, Roger.'

'Too true.' He sighed. 'Another pint, please, Lorraine. And one for yourself.'

'Not for me, Roger. Not on duty.'

'Sorry. I forgot.'

'You're feeling sorry for yourself, Roger.'

'Too right, Lorraine.'

'It's your workers I feel sorry for. All laid off, I suppose?'

'Down to a skeleton staff,' admitted Roger. 'Whole bang-shoot'll be shut down in three weeks. Should do it now, really, but I can't face it.'

'I don't as a rule feel much sympathy for the filthy capitalist running dog, Roger; but I make an exception in your case.'

'Do you, Lorraine? Well, thanks.'

'You'll be all right, Roger.'

'I suppose so. It's just difficult to see how.'

'What does your wife say?'

'Nothing. She doesn't know. Or doesn't want to know.'

'Yes. She knows and she doesn't know. Like the whole of Europe during the Holocaust. It's the human way.'

'I say, Lorraine. Steady.'

'I apologise, Roger.'

'No. You're right. Anyway, she knows. The disappearance of my car was a big clue.'

'The red Italian job? That must've been a blow.'

'Do you know, Lorraine? I thought it would be. But, in a way, it wasn't. I mean, it wasn't even mine really. It was the firm's. And besides I'm just as happy bumbling about in an old banger. It was more Cheryl's idea, the Italian job. I could never help thinking: "What would Dad say?" He hated anything flash, Lorraine. He was a clever man, my Dad. He could've been anything. But he was happy as a skylark flogging meat out the back of a van at the end of the promenade in Southend-on-Sea. I used to help him in the holidays. We'd load up at Smithfields and drive out at four in the morning. You could taste the salty air in the dark. I'll tell you another thing, Lorraine. I haven't told a soul this. My name isn't Cholmondeley – it's Chumley, C-H-U-M-L-E-Y. Chas Chumley was my Dad's name, and it was good enough for him. It was my Mum who changed it.

She had aspirations, Lorraine. She reckoned she was a cut above the working classes. She was respectable, spoke posh, pushed me into Grammar School, hated the smell of meat and never forgave my Dad for not bettering himself. But he was happy. She was the one who was never happy, Lorraine. Cheryl's Mum was the same. She married an Irish farmer, Brendan, from Mayo, who was broke and came over to build the Seven Sisters Line – you know, the Tube. Cheryl and I have the same dark secret, you see: we're both, wossname, parboiled.'

'*Parvenus*, Roger.'

'That's it. Johnny-come-latelys anyway. Now I'm Johnny-up-the-creek. It must be a punishment for getting above my station.'

'And for wearing yellow cravats, Roger. Are your parents still alive?'

'Nah. Poor old Mum copped cancer of the colon from clenching her buttocks all her life, pardon my French. Dad was washed out to sea by a rip tide while he was angling off the Isle of Dogs.'

'Strewth, Roger.'

'Not a bad way to go, though. Dad's, I mean. Wouldn't mind it myself. I leaned out over the lake here the other day, half hoping that bloody crocodile of a pike, if it exists, would leap up and drag me under. No such luck.'

'You're a twit, Roger.'

'You can say that again, Lorraine. What's your surname?'

'Baskerville.'

'What? Like *The Hound of the*? All this crying for the workers – and you're an aristocrat! No wonder your nose is so... so *Baskervillian*.'

'Thank you, Roger. Yes, I suppose we were once aristocrats. Probably Norman since it was actually *de* Baskerville. But we plummeted down the social scale and into the working class generations ago, I'm happy to say. The Ruling Class, like every dog, has had its day. However, we're not here to talk about my ancestry. We're here to sort you out. You must talk to your wife today, Roger, and form a plan of action together.'

'I can't, Lorraine. I'm too ashamed. When I hinted to Cheryl that things were not going as planned – that a certain tightening of Italian leather belts might be in order – she only said: "Roger," she said, "I am never going to be poor again." So that was telling me.'

'Well, you won't be poor, Roger. A man like you, with your experience and talent, can always get a good job. And if I were your wife I'd muck in and get a job, too.'

'Ah but, Lorraine,' said Roger sadly, 'you are not my wife.'

9

IT was Saturday morning, the time when, traditionally, ritual battle took place. The apples were rotted to perfection. George was up early, transporting his pungent arsenal by wheelbarrow out along the cliff path to the clearing deep within the Tennis Club wilderness. It was hard going on the slippery path, especially where it had partially subsided into a dip beside the wonky fence. The lean-to camps were conveniently built within taunting distance of each other. Sometimes open warfare broke out in duels with bamboo swords and dustbin lids. There had been a Thirty Years' War of water pistols until mothers, sick of drying clothes, had put a stop to it. Similarly, flour bombs. The Great Mud Pie debacle had escalated the conflict to a new level. 'Little do you suspect, you puny Englander,' thought George, the linguistic influence of both Nazi storm-trooper and the Mekon mingling happily in his internal monologue of destruction, 'that VENGEANCE WILL BE MINE!'

His dispositions made, his plans laid, George beat off through the undergrowth to commune with the tigers. Pressing himself to the wire, he called softly to them. Only one of them, lying quite near and licking its chops, showed any interest, grunting a little but disdaining to do more than flick its tail. 'May the spirit of the tiger enter me,' George intoned mentally, 'for the coming fight.' The tiger looked at him. Its smouldering unblinking stare bored into him, filling him with power. He was ready.

'Oi, fish face. Come over here.'
'Whaddya want, mush?' replied the Enemy suspiciously, advancing a few paces from the safety of his camp.
'Look what I've got in this crate.'

'Balls' ache, Blyte.'

'No. Honestly.'

'What?' The Enemy's curiosity was his weakness. Already he was edging farther into the open, and closer to George's lean-to.

'You'll see,' said George pleasantly. 'Come on. It's dead snazzy is this.' Hands in pockets, the Enemy strolled as if unworried towards him.

There is an etiquette of war. When you are about to pelt the Enemy with squashy rotten apples, you have to lure him within range. If possible, *well* within range. But you can't fire at point blank range. There has to be a sporting chance, a possibility of missing.

George opened up when the Enemy was twelve feet away, scooping the apples out of the crate and hurling them in rapid-fire at his head. In his excitement, he threw too wildly and hard – and missed. He had better luck as the Enemy, yelping, scampered back to the shelter of his camp – one apple glanced off his shoulder, leaving an ugly stain on his jersey; another splattered satisfactorily on the back of his left thigh.

George dashed to a bush at the back of the Enemy's camp where he had stashed a fresh supply of apples. His best chance to splat Bradley full in the face had gone. If he was to achieve his goal, he must keep calm and aim carefully. Sure enough, the Enemy, believing George to be at his front entrance, was trying to break out of the less well-constructed rear of his camp. George greeted the emergence of his head and limbs with a deadly salvo. That there were some palpable hits was evident from the Enemy's retreat; but the ultimate strike remained elusive.

'You bloody liar, Blyte! Treacherous, pie-faced moron! You'll pay for this!'

As the Enemy cowered in his lair, George took a jumping jack out of his pocket, lit it, and ran full tilt at the Enemy's camp. He tossed the firework inside, *en passant*, and continued his run around to the other side where Hugh's duffel-bag, filled with the last of his ammo, hung concealed behind a tree. He scooped it up and donned it in a single movement as he hurtled full circle back to the front entrance of the Enemy's camp. The multiple explosions of the jumping jack alternated with the yells of the Enemy who, panicking, bolted out like a rabbit. The first apple hit him square in the chest and stopped him in his tracks. The second smashed him full in the face, knocking his glasses to the ground. He let out a cry of pain and, half blinded, fell to his knees, groping for his specs. Victory, absolute and crushing, was George's.

Blood rushed to his head. Power crazed him. The Enemy on his knees, grubbing about in the dirt, was a worm – less than a worm, a red ant. George moved coldly forward and, from a diabolically close range, flung a last apple hard at the Enemy's unprotected head. It exploded in his hair. Bradley screamed. He leapt to his feet and came howling towards George, fists clenched, arms windmilling, eyes screwed up, face streaming with tears and apple juice. George backed away in alarm, and then broke and ran for safety. Bradley did not follow him but made for George's camp. He began to pull it down in a frenzy, screaming:

'I'll get you, I'll get you! My dad'll get you! My dad'll get your spastic dad!'

'Bradley. Don't,' called out George. 'Leave it alone. Look, I'm sorry. Okay? I'm sorry.'

Bradley paused to yank his shirt out of his trousers and wipe his face with the front tails. 'Your dad's a… a pile of donkey poo. A big smelly pile of poo.'

Now, while George had more than once thought the same thing about his father, he was not about to let anyone outside the family think it, let alone voice it.

'Take that back, Cholmondeley, or I really will finish you off,' he threatened, advancing menacingly on the Enemy. Bradley held his ground, fists clenched and eyes narrowed, no longer crying.

'I won't take it back because, actually, it's true. Your dad stinks like a pile of poo. He fucks other people's mothers.'

George stopped dead. He had never knowingly heard this word before, but it had a strange snazziness. It winded him.

'Whaddya talking about? What's it mean, *fu*…?' He couldn't say the word. It lay like a sword on his tongue. It foreshadowed a knowledge he knew he had to possess, yet dreaded to possess.

'Doesn't know what it means,' taunted the Enemy. 'What a baby. What an ignoramus. Doesn't know the facts of life.'

'*You* don't know what it means. You're the pea-brain.'

''Course I know what it means. It means, for your information, smelly-nappy babykins, it means when a man takes ladies' pants off and pokes about. It's what your precious Dada does.'

George wanted very badly to smash the Enemy's mouth in. But he found that he couldn't move his legs. His head was boiling with shame at the extremity of the slur. He'd never forgive it. He turned away lest he burst into tears, and walked very deliberately towards home.

'What's the matter, nappy boy?' jeered the Enemy. 'Can't take it, eh, mush?' Then, when George did not look back, 'What's the matter, Blyte? You don't have to go off in a baby sulk. Look, you *got* me, okay? I admit it. I *admit* it. It was pretty snazzy. I didn't mean it about your dad, okay? Look, I'm putting your camp back...' But George couldn't hear for the blood throbbing in his ears.

Now that the nights were drawing in, the palaver of the Moo's bedtime was, if anything, worse – the long patches of shadow which the hall light could not penetrate were even longer and darker and potentially more crowded with the malevolent spirits that could only be dispelled by switching on the upstairs landing light. It was one of Bernie's duties to escort the Moo through the gauntlet of horror; but unluckily she was as prey to dark fancies as he was. Thus neither would precede the other up the stairs, fearing that the other was no longer behind them or, worse, was – but had been snatched by a bogey. So they edged up the stairs next to each other with cries and reproaches: 'Don't go so fast!' 'I'm not – you are!' 'Don't push, you little divil.' 'I'm not pushing – it's Something Else pushing!' 'Holy Mother of God!' and so on. Once, in a not-to-be-repeated experiment, George had crept up behind them with a damp cloth on a stick, and pressed it against Bernie's cheek. She had screamed and clutched the Moo, who screamed even more loudly and flailed about, fortuitously knocking George over and sending him, bellowing with laughter, bumping all the way down to the bottom of the stairs.

Tonight, however – it was Saturday night – the Moo did not go to bed because it was Bernie's night off and he had been given special dispensation in order to help her prepare for the Young Catholics' Hop. By the time she was ready, lit from above this time as she made her descent, the rest of the family (bar Dada, who was working late in Town) was summoned to the hall by the Moo's warnings and

120

exhortations as he shepherded Bernie's astounding costume down the staircase.

Either Bernie's style was the fashion in Ireland or else it was that of England some years ago – most likely it was her own. Certainly, the dress she had acquired with advance wages begged from Maman, with money sent by the faithful Pat Tim, and by never buying ordinary clothes, had never been seen anywhere by the amazed Blytes. It was an extraordinary confection of tight low-cut bodice in maroon satin, and a great circle of pink skirt fluffed up by layer upon layer of buoyant petticoats. On the arms, long white gloves; on the legs, sheer 15 denier nylons; on the feet maroon satiny pumps. The raven hair was piled up and pinned; the swan-like neck and shell-like ears flamed and sparkled with cheap but effective jewels. As this apparition floated sedately towards them, a flushed Moo fussed around behind the skirt, attempting to manoeuvre it without mishap down the stairs. Bernie was both Cinderella and her own fairy godmother.

'*Elle est formidable, quoi!*' gasped Maman.

'Away with you!' laughed Bernie, 'I know I look like a big fluffed-up chicken, but, sure, I can't help meself.'

'You look stunning, Bernie,' said Janey.

'Ah God, no. I'd say I'd never get a man in a get-up like this. But who cares? I couldn't resist the petticoats!'

'There's a lot of them,' remarked Hugh lamely. He was still glowing from his afternoon shopping trip to Kingston with the au pair; still dreamy from his audacious purchase in the matter of footwear; still dazed by the cigarettes he had smoked in the back stalls of the James Bond film, *Dr No*.

'Well now, I can hear my ride. I'll be off so. Come here to me now, the Moo, till I give you a kiss. Why the worried face, mein Fuehrer? This kit is no serious matter. Ah well, have a kiss anyway. C'mon now, Janey. Mwah, mwah. And Hugh. Wasn't it great gas we had today? You'll be too old for a kiss, but where's the harm?' Hugh was partially paralysed by the waft of Bernie's perfume, and finished off by the press of her soft warm lips to his cheek. His ears popped as if he'd jetted up to a thousand feet.

Unnoticed by the Blytes, Bernie's ride was indeed throbbing in the drive. It seemed only natural when it turned out to be, of all things, a Bentley. The au pair climbed in and the car, quiet as a magic carpet, bore her away to the wonders of the Young Catholics' Hop.

George was lying awake. He was in a state of emotion. It had been a day of, well, surprises was not quite the word. After lunch, Dada had happened upon him, moping in the garden.

'What's this?' he had asked rhetorically. 'What is the best little brain in the family up to?'

'Nothing, Dada.'

'Well, mein Fuehrer, I have to go to the office later on; but meanwhile, like you, I have nothing on. I suggest we take ourselves off to a matinée at the Wyebridge Odeon.'

George had been so amazed and delighted at this impulsive suggestion – he never had Dada to himself, nor was he allowed to see films except for his birthday treat – that he almost forgot the horrible confusing encounter with the Enemy. Indeed, it was totally wiped from his mind when the film turned out to be that snazziest of war films, *The Longest Day*.

The Allied forces were trapped on the Normandy beach now, their backs to the sea, facing heavy fire. Beside him in the dark, George felt a tremor. He turned to Dada. His father was shaking. Not just his head or hands, but his whole body was racked by spasms of trembling, making his seat rattle. Luckily there were only a few people in the cinema.

'Are you ill, Dada?' whispered George.

'No, no.' But sweat was pouring down Dada's pasty face.

'Let's *go*, Dada.'

'I'm all right. I'm all right.' But when George made a beeline for the exit, Dada followed him.

Outside in the street, Dada breathed deeply until the colour returned to his face.

'Ha-ha,' he laughed apologetically. 'Got the shakes, mein Fuehrer! Best not to mention it, old chap. It upsets Maman.'

'But what… what *was* it, Dada?' George was still pale from the shock.

'It's the sound of the shells. Brings it all back, you see. Ha-ha. The mortars and so on. Shells whizzing over. It doesn't bother me at all, but it makes my body behave in that odd way, you see. Can't seem

to control it, ha-ha.' To George's horror, Dada's lip was trembling. 'Sorry to spoil the film, old chap. We'll go for a Wimpy to make up –'
'I'll wait in the car,' he said quickly, nipping off.

Strange to discover that Maman was not the only one with nerves. He hadn't been able to believe that Dada could ever do what the Enemy had said he'd done; but now, lying awake, he began to wonder.

Maman opened her little pill box and looked uncertainly at the purple hearts. In fact, the slimming pills were less purple than a sort of electric blue. There'd been a bit of a furore in the papers about them, but only as regarded unruly youngsters taking too many without a prescription. She herself wasn't supposed to take more than two a day; but how could a thing that made her feel so *well* be harmful?

The younger children were in bed; the older ones were in their rooms. Bernie would not be back till late. It would have been an ideal time for a quiet evening in with her husband. Why he had to work late on a Saturday was beyond her. It was, frankly, an awful bore. But, then, it was, she supposed, the price of his promotion to senior management, with its pay rise, health plan and Zodiac.

She switched on the television set in the corner of the breakfast room. Eamonn Andrews was perspiring on one channel, while, on the other, Hughie Green was mugging like a demented man at the camera. She switched it off. Poor Dermot, working so hard. She'd have a lovely hot dinner waiting for him no matter what time he got home. It would be a surprise. But first she would take another pill. The more she took, the quicker she'd be slim. And, besides, she *ought* to take an extra one because, without it, her nerves were liable to get the better of her. As it was, she was troubled by the impression that a huge creature, at once as heavy as lead and as insubstantial as a shadow, was rearing up behind her. If she wasn't quick, it would come down on her and crush her. She had to speed up. The colour of the pills was almost ultraviolet, like the haze above bluebells. She swallowed one with a sip of water. And then another, in case.

That lamb mince in the meat safe needed eating. She would make an English shepherd's pie! Imagining Dermot's look of delight, she set to with a will. It was a labour-intensive dish, but it

123

could be compiled in a jiffy if the separate ingredients were cooked simultaneously and thrown together at the end. It was a bonus side-effect of the pills that they endowed her with a surplus of energy and confidence, ideal for throwing together pies.

Enthusiastically she began to peel potatoes. But perhaps it would be better if the mince was simmering meanwhile. Firstly it had to be seared. She put on a frying pan with a dollop of dripping and returned to the potatoes, only to remember – *zut alors* – the onions. They should simmer with the meat. She began to peel them, but the skins didn't come away cleanly and had to be picked at endlessly with her nails. It went on forever. Tears blinded her. No wonder – the kitchen was full of smoke. The dripping was burning. She whipped the pan off the gas ring and threw in the mince which spat ungratefully into her face. The eyes of the potatoes regarded her malevolently. She stabbed and twisted to remove them. Then she threw them, half-peeled, into a saucepan, added cold water and put them on the stove's back ring. As she searched for an Oxo cube, she smelt burning. The meat was, to put it mildly, over-seared. She threw it in another saucepan. Now, where were the onions? She couldn't believe that they weren't ready. Hadn't she spent hours on them? They were barely peeled, let alone chopped. She began to chop with a vengeance. The onions skidded under her fingers. The knife bit deep into her thumb. She looked at the blood in surprise. It was dripping on to the floor. She held her thumb over the pan of mince – *en français, le mince? Le mincé?* – while she thought what to do. She wrapped a tea-towel around the wound, and that reminded her of a crucial ingredient: bay leaves. She was out of the back door in a trice, and groping her way through the darkness to the bay tree, or shrub. Or bush. She stubbed her slippered toe painfully on something hard. She felt at her feet and encountered the steel contours of the Fuehrer's German helmet. *Merde.* Pardon her French, ha-ha. She picked it up and flung it away from her in the direction of the hedge.

It was cold outside. The sky was lightly frosted with early stars. Maman stood beside the bay thingy and looked up at them. There was the Plough. You could find the Pole Star if you traced a straight line from the handle. Or was it a line from the other end? She tried both, but the stars were fidgeting about and difficult to focus on.

If she could only find her Pole Star, the sky's constant, she could get herself oriented and everything would fall into place. Was *that* it, there? Or there? She couldn't be sure. She felt a bit panicky and began to scan the whole sky wildly as if the Pole Star would suddenly announce itself.

More time than she thought must have passed because, when she opened the back door, she was almost knocked flat by the fog billowing from the kitchen. She crawled to the stove with the gory tea towel pressed to her mouth and nose, and managed to switch off the gas rings – one lit, which had boiled away the water and burnt through the smoking potato pan; and one unlit, which had filled the room with gas. Surprising really that it had not ignited and blown the house up. Maman threw the potatoes and their pan into the garden, burning her good hand in the process. Then, as an afterthought, she threw after them the raw blackened *mincé*. The bloody onions she put in a newspaper and dropped into the waste bucket under the sink. She put another damp tea towel around her burnt hand. She felt better.

She looked in the cupboard for another pan and there, now that they were no longer needed, were the Oxo cubes, the letters forming the face of a village idiot. Next to them was a tin of 'Old Oak' ham. She smiled. Prince Flasheen Eyes had a weakness for 'Old Oak' ham. Unfortunately the key that rolled back the lid was missing. Maman attacked the tin with an ordinary tin opener, with no success apart from a small explosion of ham jelly at one end. Her muffled hands were less of a help than a hindrance. The thing to do, she decided, was to go and smoke a Strand or two in the drawing room, and to re-think her whole strategy. Perhaps she wouldn't make Dermot dinner after all. She didn't know what time he'd be in and, God knew, she had a million other things to do.

When Dada returned home, he found his wife in the drawing room. Sheets of paper were strewn about the floor, all of them written on, but many with only one or two sentences. The one nearest to his foot was inscribed: 'Murray Mints, Murray Mints, the Too-Good-to-Hurry Mints.' There were also the pieces of two jigsaws on the Turkish rug, with some bits fitted together, other bits forced. Maman was pacing about, smoking and talking rapidly under her breath.

125

She registered his presence but did not at first take in what he was saying to her. He spoke earnestly, even affectionately, for some time. 'Ça ne fait rien,' she heard herself saying. 'It doesn't matter.' And, 'I see.' Dermot had seemed relieved. He had even kissed her on the forehead before going up to bed.

Maman did not go to bed. She sat up in the drawing room, smoking and listening to her internal engines running down. At dawn, they stopped. The huge and heavy beast that shadowed her, silently reared up. Instinctively she reached for her pills. But then she thought: 'What is the point of being slim now?' She carried the pills to the lavatory and looked into the depths. By rights she should be down there. For she had always suspected that she might be little better than *merde*; and now that had proved to be the case. There was no point in keeping up this farce of slimming. She was, by nature, a tub of *merde* and she might as well resign herself to it. One by one she flicked the pills, like pieces of herself, into the pan. In the Hereafter, she thought, we will all be slim. For the flesh will melt; and, lo, we shall all be weightless and I, the skinniest of spirits. The black beast's claws sank into the back of her head. She could do nothing but bow before it. She pulled the lavatory chain and, pressed down by an intolerable weight, dragged herself towards her bedroom.

10

IT was Sunday morning. The children were up early, sitting around the breakfast room table in their pyjamas, to hear about Bernie's evening as they munched toast and drank tea. For George, Bernie's tales of her nights off were better than *Bunty*. The Moo was less certain. He preferred the stories about Ireland best: about Pat Tim and his tractor; about Declan, the IRA man – a Sloppy Club candidate if he was any judge; about the drinking and the lock-ins and the crack; even about the Good People, who were not always Swinging, far from it, but Dodgy; who sometimes came between the Moo and his sleep. But the way she told the stories was always good. Even Luh'le Shuggy got up for them.

'I won't do the Twist,' Bernie was saying. "Tis an ugly dance. I'll only jitterbug and jive – that class of dance – so me petticoats can swish about and knock the eyes out of the heads of the lads. And I'm after dancing with several of the lads now, but there's one I have me eye on, Kevin Brady, the one with the power of eyelashes and the lovely smile, showing a head full of his own teeth, Pat Tim take note, only he's with that Janine Freeman of the long white arms and the flashy jewellery, I can talk, mind. But she has a face like a hatchet that frightens Kevin, I can tell. Anyway, I'm dancing with Liam Flynn, who has me brought to the dance in his Bentley, that you saw, I hope, and didn't your jaws hit the floor? But, sure, I have to come clean, the car is not his own but his boss's and he does be chauffeuring it. And Liam is trying to kiss me, while Father Mulligan himself is sharpening his eyes on us. But I don't mind because where's the harm in a kiss? And I'm feeling great because of the whiskey Liam's lashing around from a flask when Father's not looking, although he's not above a drop himself, and that before Mass – can't you see his eyes sloshing about during the elevation? – when Kevin comes over to Liam and says will we all go over to a place called Tolworth Towers in the Bentley when the dance is finished? And I can see that Liam likes Kevin, and he says yes, no bother, if we have a whip round for a bit o' petrol. But Janine is baring her teeth at Kevin and saying isn't it a bit late for Tolworth Towers and wouldn't it be lovely to go home, Kevvy darling, just the two of us, snuggled up on your Lambretta? But Kevvy darling says: 'Leave i' ou', wollya? When joo las' 'ave a go in a ruddy Bentley?' – he talks in that funny way, attractive though, like French, but niver a haitch nor a 't', cocky I suppose you'd call it – what, the Moo? Cockney? Ah God, yes, that's it, cockney – anyway we have Janine out-voted and we're off so, in the Bentley, Janine clinging to Kevin for dear life and nibbling at him whenever she gets the chance, to show he's hers, the poor craytur. And when we get to Tolworth Towers, it's not a big house or anything I was expecting. 'Tis a ten-pin bowling alley. Did you ever try the ten-pin bowling, Shugs? You should. It's great gas. You put on these smelly slidey slippers and you fling this great ball, with holes in for your fingers, down an alley all smooth like a parky floor. The idea is to knock all the pins over. If you knock all ten, it's a strike; but if you leave two, one on each side, the divil himself couldn't get them both. Anyway, Janine's hopeless at it and I'm not much better for all that Kevin is guiding my hand and breathing on me cheek and smelling of nice soap instead of Old Spice – Pat Tim, you should take note o' the soap – while Janine's gnashing her teeth and swinging her white arms about to draw Kevin back, but it's hopeless, the man is lost, and who can blame him, for amn't I the girl? But, sure, I don't forget Liam, and I make him show me how to bowl a bit and I give him plenty to smile about, because he's a good lad and, you never know, things may not work out with Kevin, who has no Bentley when all the story's told. Still, I sit up front with Liam on the way home like a Christian, with Kevin and Janine in the back seat, but Janine not clinging any more but in the corner, grinding her teeth and her shoulders all hunched, God love her. And Liam drops her off at her house and takes Kevin back to his Lambretta and brings me back here, where – block your ears now the Moo – I let him kiss me because he's a nice lad. But I'm no sooner waving him off when I hear the Lambretta. Ah, Pat Tim, you should trade in your tractor for a Lambretta that'll whisk you through the cold air of the night, in full view of the moon, while you hang on to the boy in front – God, it has a Bentley beat any day – and carries you up on the Golf Course with the bright stars pouring over you and the soft sand beneath you… Ah, the Lambretta is a heavenly thing. If Jesus had a Lambretta, he'd be after having no trouble at all attracting Apostles among the girls of Nazareth. Now, who's going to take the tea up to your Ma and Da? Okay so, Janey. Yes, that's it, the Moo, you help your sister…'

Dada sat up in bed, yawning, as the clink of teacups woke him. Janey drew the curtains. The Moo prodded the humped form beside Dada.

'Are you asleep, Maman? I'll get in, shall I? We'll have a story, like Bernie's.' He began to climb over his mother, heading for the comfortable slot between his parents.

'Go away,' came Maman's weary muffled voice.

'Well,' said the Moo, withdrawing. 'That is not very sloppy.' He began to sing *Does your chewing gum lose its flavour on the bedpost overnight?*

'Be quiet,' said the remote voice.

'Why?'

'Leave your mother alone, the Moo,' said Dada, coming to. 'She has a bad head this morning.'

'Poor Little Lorna,' crooned the Moo, stroking the few inches of visible hair.

'Leave me alone.'

'Don't be a bore, Maman,' he scolded.

'Maman am a maniac.'

'She *is* a maniac, Dabs.'

'She takes pills to make her fat.'

'*No*, you flabby fool, Dabs – to make her *thin*.'

'Dabs am going to eat pills. Dabs am going to eat all the pills in the medicining cabinet. The clever pills am making Dabs's brains go up.'

'*No*, Dabs,' said the Moo, genuinely shocked. 'You must never touch anything in the medicine cabinet. You might take poison by mistake and die.'

'Dabs wants to die. Dabs am a tragic figure. She am going to die and everyone am going to be sorry. But Dabs am forgiving everyone because she am being an angel,' said Dabs dreamily, settling herself under the eiderdown facing her parents. The Moo didn't dignify her speech with a response. He merely contented himself with detaching Spiv from his harness and lunging across the bed at Dabs. 'Ow! Ow! Spiv am murdering Dabs. Dabs am coming back from the dead to haunt Spiv.'

'Don't be a flabby eejit, Dabs. You'd make a spastic ghost. You couldn't frighten the skin off a rice pudding.'

'Dabs could. Dabs can be werry frightening. She am making a werry good ghost,' said Dabs huffily.

'Wrong again.' Spiv struck.

'Ow! Ow!' There was a pause.

'Dabs won't die, will she, Janey?'

'No, of course not, the Moo. Dabs is just being silly.'

'Yes, she is, isn't she? She is silly beyond belief, and a nit.'

Hugh wandered in, reading *An Introduction to Zen Buddhism*. He slumped down on the yellow sofa. George followed, yawning, and inserted himself head first under the eiderdown next to Janey and Dabs who were facing their father. The Moo, determined not to be thwarted, clambered over Dada's legs in order to loll with professional sloppiness between Dada and the mound that was Maman.

'Well, well,' said Dada, 'now that we are all gathered as usual on this fine Sunday morning, I have something to say to you.' It was not so much his words as his smile that alerted the children to something untoward. Called by the Moo the Horrid Smile, it was a rictus of false sincerity which Dada applied to his face when committing public outrages, such as the time when – despite the direst of warnings – he performed a U-turn in the Mersey Tunnel on the way to the Holyhead ferry for Ireland. At once, George emerged from under the eiderdown; Hugh looked up from his book; and the Moo instinctively attempted a diversionary tactic:

'Dada, can I have a raise in pocket money? Please?' he begged, cunningly adding a favourite expression of Dada's: 'A shilling doesn't go far these days.'

'That's not fair,' said George. 'If he has a raise, I ought to have one too, Dada. Two shillings is, you've got to admit, a spastic amount.

The Enemy gets seven and six. It's not fair. How am I s'posed to conduct a decent war on two bob?'

'If it comes to that,' added Janey, 'how am I to become a famous artist on five bob a week? It doesn't even pay for charcoal and sketch pads.'

'Shut up, the lot of you!' There was real bateyness in Dada's voice. And batey was a short hop to loss of temper. With Maman apparently *hors de combat*, no one felt up to defusing Dada's anger. An obedient silence fell, broken only by the faltering, melancholy notes from the flat above as Sabrina tortured the Moonlight Sonata. 'Well, well, that's better. Now. There is good news. Your Dada is going to move out of this house and live somewhere else where he will no longer be an irritant to your mother's nerves and an embarrassment to you all.'

'That is not good news,' said Janey. 'That is very bad news.'

'Never fear, my beloved daughter. You will all see me often – perhaps more often then you would prefer, ha-ha. And you will all receive your pocket money as usual.'

'Zer Fuehrer hass not given any personnel permission to leave zis house. You vill remain here, Herr Dada, until furzer orders,' commanded George, springing from the bed and marching up and down the bedroom while returning the Nazi salute of an imaginary Nuremberg rally.

'I don't like this,' said Janey. Tears came to her eyes.

'Don't worry, Janey,' consoled the Moo. 'Dada's only having a joke with us. Tell 'er, Maman. Everything's Swinging really, isn't it, Maman?'

Maman heaved herself at last into a sitting position.

'No,' she said. 'It's Dodgy.'

'Dada doesn't love us any more,' said Janey.

''E *does*,' reproved the Moo. 'He does. He *does*.' Spiv struck her for emphasis but, each time, more feebly until the hitherto vicious creature seemed to be stroking her and the Moo, to be weeping.

'Now come on, kids,' said Dada heartily. 'Don't make such a fuss. We must all be grown-up about this. Your Dada loves you all very much and will always look after you.'

'But if you love us,' hiccuped the Moo, 'why are you going away?'

'I have said, the Moo. I have become redundant as anything

other than a dispenser of money. It has been painful for me to confront this fact, but I have never been one to shirk truth in any of its forms. I have been forced reluctantly to conclude that you will all be better off without me. It will be sad, of course, to leave; but I do so in the knowledge that it is for the greater good of all.'

'Why is it that no one seems to agree with you?' asked Janey.

'I don't deny that I am touched by your apparent grief, my darling daughter – although I notice that the Young Master has yet to show his hand – but it is only the shock of my announcement. These tears are but a *seeming* grief, and will not last beyond lunch, I warrant, when you will all doubtless begin to rejoice in your liberation from a tedious fond old Dada.'

'You are saying, are you, Dada,' asked Hugh, 'that your decision to leave is entirely selfless?'

'Well, well, Luh'le Shuggy. You speak at last. But only to ask a trick question. As you know, no truly selfless person can, by definition, claim to be thus. But I forgive your duplicity. This is a momentous turning-point in our family history and it behoves us all to speak the truth without flinching. So I answer you with a frankness and candour you could do worse than to emulate: I freely admit that an iota of selfishness may have entered into my decision. For, as I grow old, I have begun to yearn for a little time and space for myself. Like the ageing Hindu who leaves behind his profession, his family, his possessions, everything, and takes to the road with nothing but a loin cloth and begging bowl, I long to put worldly concerns behind me and to ravel up the threads of my soul in preparation for death.' Dada's eyes were misty as they contemplated the Infinite.

'Dass iss gutt,' said George, as if in agreement. 'Herr Dada vill fuck mitt Frau Cholmondeley.' He added for good measure: 'Fuckenzi schnell, schnell.'

There was an appalled silence in which Hugh, staring at his book, distinctly heard the sound of one hand clapping. Dada turned a funny colour. The Fuehrer's pronouncement seemed to wake Maman from her trance. Out of long habit, she quickly addressed her husband:

'Be calm, Dermot. He doesn't know what he is saying. Mein Fuehrer, you have used an abominable word. Never repeat it. Even in German. And that goes for all of you.'

'Yet it's a word that seems to go to the heart of the matter,' mused Hugh.

'That is a typical utterance, Luh'le Shuggy,' said Dada bitterly. 'Typical. Oh yes, you are all very intellectual, I'm sure. Very superior. And whose hard-earned money has made you so, hmm? I have never made any secret of my own lack of education. And I did not begrudge you the finest education money can buy. First you fritter it away and now you repay me with insults and injustice. No, no, let me speak for once. Not one of you ungrateful brats has ever given a single thought to my comfort or happiness. I am nothing to you but a *milch* cow, as the Fuehrer has it – an endless stream of pocket money, and, after that, nothing, less than nothing, save an object of mockery and a figure of fun. Has any one of you ever done a single thing I asked? Have you, Luh'le Shuggy, mended the cliff fence? Hm? I see by your insolent expression that you have not. It was too much to ask. No wonder I look elsewhere for a crumb of consideration. And you Janey, have you ever made me so much as a cup of tea, without my begging and bribing you?'

'I've made tea for you,' said Janey hotly.

'A miniature cup of tepid water in company with five dolls when you were aged three does not qualify under any rules whatsoever, including those of the Geneva Convention, as making your poor old thirsty Dada a cup of tea. No, no, I haven't finished. And you, mein Fuehrer, the best little brain in the family, of whom I had such hopes, for whom I nurtured such dreams – you do not pass the simplest examination at school, you are idle, you waste my money, you may as well leave school now and… and join the army. Join the German army. Why not? You account as nothing your Dada's suffering during the War, suffering and fighting so that you may be free to live a life of idle Fascism. No doubt during the next war you will be happy to kill me, your loving and indulgent Dada, and to dance in jackboots on his grave. Is that what you wish?'

'No, no, Dada,' cried George, distraught. 'I'll try harder at school, I promise, I won't be a German any more – '

'Well, it is a little late for that, my son. You will not change now –'

'I will, I will !'

'You don't hate me too, do you Dada?' enquired the Moo with big round tear-filled eyes.

'I do not hate any of you, the Moo. On the contrary, I love you. I am just saying. That's all. I hold nothing against any of you, and least of all you, the Moo. You are too young to have shown the vicious nature of your siblings, though I dare say I've been treated pretty shabbily in the matter of the Sloppy Club. But let that pass. I will say nothing on that score. It remains a matter for your own conscience, the Moo. I only hope that you will not live to regret the cavalier nature of your blackballing policy.'

'Please join the Sloppy Club, Dada.'

'Well, well, we will discuss it. Meanwhile, I shall be leaving this house within the week. That is all. There is nothing more to be said on the subject. It is for the best. We must all strive to be rational and adult. It is not the end of the world. I am not going far. You will see me and, God willing, come to appreciate when he is absent the father you held in contempt while he was present.'

'But Prince Flasheen Eyes loves Little Lorna forever,' said the Moo stubbornly.

'Prince Flasheen Eyes will certainly stay married to Little Lorna,' said Maman in a monotone. 'She is a Roman Catholic.'

'Hardly, mavourneen,' said Dada. 'Little Lorna is well and truly lapsed, ha-ha.'

'A Catholic is never *that* lapsed. We will not be divorcing.'

'Is that a threat, ha-ha?'

'It is a fact.'

'I can't get through to Maman,' said Hugh, lighting a stub of cigarette. 'She just lies there like a lump. Dada's gone off. To the Tennis Club, he *said*.' They exchanged looks. 'Who's that you're drawing?'

'Nobody,' said Janey. She was sitting on her bed, working on a charcoal portrait. Hugh craned his neck round for a better look.

'It's George Harrison.'

'It might be,' said Janey, whose feeling for the Beatle grew more tender every day. Sketches of him had begun to supplant those of Theo littering the bedroom floor.

'Well, it looks like him.' He strolled over to the mirror above the mantelpiece and combed his hair forward. There was still a lot of growth needed for his Beatle style. 'I don't look like John Lennon,' he said in a burst of bitter honesty. 'Who was I kidding? Also, Dada's right – my hair's too thin and weedy. Bum boy hair.' He snatched up the fox's brush which was nestling in a pair of plimsolls under the bed. The Fuehrer had severed it from the dead fox he'd found in the rhododendrons, and presented it to his sister for outstanding bravery, hypothetically speaking, on the hunting field. 'Pooh! It's a bit whiffy!' he said, draping the brush across his forehead.

'Thick red hair at last,' said Janey. 'Dada will be proud.'

'I ought to start a group. It'd be fab to make enough dough so that Maman wouldn't have to depend on Dada. I could think of a better name than "Beatles".'

'The Bumboys.'

'*Enfin*, Janey, *c'est malheureux*,' quoted Hugh.

'Dabs am going to be a backward vocalist.'

'You said it.' He stuffed the fox's brush into his shirt so that it stuck out like heavy chest hair, and moved restlessly over to the window to dispose of his cigarette butt. Down below, on the lawn, Theo was crouching between the two silver birches as the Moo placed his football on an imaginary penalty spot and withdrew. He tilted his chin up in a way that made Hugh smile because he had so clearly copied the tic from Theo. The Moo trundled in and, despite his size and weight, struck the ball with surprising grace. It whistled past Theo's outstretched fingers. The Moo did a little dance of triumph.

But where were the red toadstools that he had been keeping an eye on? The fly agaric? They were no longer there. Nor, by the look of it, had they been smashed by the football. They had been removed. Eaten, perhaps, by an animal. Hugh was regretful. Not that he'd been going to *do* anything with them exactly. It was just that, well, it would have been incredible to have written to Bloggs: 'Oh, by the way, I've cleansed the Doors of Perception, like A. Huxley, by eating toadstools. Wm. Blake was right – things really are infinite...' If only he weren't such a coward.

'Anyway,' he said, 'Dada's not going anywhere. He's all talk, isn't he? And he's scared stiff of Mrs Cholmondeley. He'd hardly fuckenzi mitt her.'

'Yes, he would. You saw the look on his face. And he didn't deny it.'

'Well, okay. He might have done. She's quite sexy, after all.'

'No, she's not.'

135

'Well of course you wouldn't think so. You're a girl.'

'All the same, she's not sexy. She's men's idea of what sexy is, but she isn't really.'

'You seem to know a lot about it, Janey.'

'I don't. Not really. It's just that you can't imagine Mrs Cholmondeley… *snuggling*. Like Maman does. Her hair's too brittle. She's not cosy. And Dada likes cosiness.'

'D'you think Dada'll twiggez-vous? He will, won't he? He's not a complete clot. He won't really leave. He's just feeling a bit neglected.'

'I'm afraid she'll make him,' said Janey gloomily. 'He has a slavish streak – what's he always saying about the Nazis?'

'"Either at your throat or at your feet."'

'Exactly.'

'But what about Dodgy Roger the Loggia Bodger? He's not going to like any hanky-panky between his missis and Dada. He'll clock Dada one. Then Dada will lose his temper and kill him.'

'Dodgy Roger the Stodgy Lodger will not be doing any clocking. He's too busy getting drunk and ogling Lorraine at the Club. He's unhappy. Oglers generally are,' she added world-wearily.

'Theo never ogles,' mused Hugh, examining a spot on his forehead in the mirror. 'But why not? I mean, has he ever had a girlfriend?' He pulled out his tube of Clearasil and dabbed a bit on the spot. He stepped back to survey the effect. 'It's supposed to blend in with your skin, but it makes you look like you've got beige leprosy.'

'I think Theo's saving himself.'

'For you, you mean.'

Janey tilted her head forward so that her hair swung over her face, hiding her cheeks.

'Of course,' she said defiantly. Then: 'I see Theo going out with an elegant woman dressed in a little black number, with a cigarette holder. Audrey Hepburn-ish. She'd know a lot about music and art and things. Not like me.'

'You know he likes you, Janey. You're the only one he treats as a grown-up. Including the Aged P.s.'

'No, he thinks I'm a child. I *am* a child. Look at me. Look at *this* –' she fingered a strand of lank hair – 'and *that* –' she bared her teeth to reveal the steely grin of Foody Fenella.

'Theo doesn't judge by appearances.'

'Everybody does.'

They fell silent, Janey re-charcoalling and Hugh re-Clearasilling. Then he tapped the glass case on the mantelpiece.

'Speedy! Speedy Gonzalez! Where are you? Come on, shake a leg. God, slow worms are the most boring pets ever.'

'They're not. Speedy may not be vivacious, but he has depth of character.'

'What if Theo were to marry Bernie,' said Hugh, 'and then they adopted us? That would be Coolville.'

'We'd have to kill the Aged P.s.'

'Natch.'

'Actually, we won't have to kill them. Dada's off with La Chummy and Maman's nerves will finally be shredded, and the men in white coats will take her away.'

'That's not funny.'

'What's the matter, Shugs? God, you're not blubbing, are you?'

'No.' He turned his back on his sister for a bit, and then said: 'It's just that… that she'll never survive without Dada. Her inferiority complex means she's got no confidence. She'd be helpless.' In his heart, Hugh was as frightened for himself as for Maman. If Dada went he'd be responsible for her, for everything, and he wasn't up to it.

'She'll be all right,' reassured Janey. 'She's tougher than she seems. And she's getting thin.'

'Thin – and mad. Those pills are a bloody liability.'

'Well, she's dumped them now. They were sitting in the bog this morning. It took three flushes and some fancy brush work to get rid of them.'

'No wonder she's just lying there. Like a lump.'

'She's sleeping them off.'

'No, she isn't. I think her nerves are stretched to the limit. She's on the edge. Someone should call a doctor.'

'He'd only give her more pills. It's best if she just sleeps.' They thought about Maman for a while. '*I* know what!'

'What?'

'We'll consult Nana. She'll know what to do. Go and round up the boys.'

'Better leave them out of it. You know what happened last time.'

'We need them. We can't get hold of Nana with only the two of us. Why don't we get Bernie along? She'll keep them calm.'

'That might work,' admitted Hugh.

Although the pain in his innards was bad, Charles was determined to walk it off. It would take more than a bit of discomfort to make a chap break his routines. He liked his routines. He stuck to them. When a chap had spent three years in the whimsical hands of murderers, a chap might be forgiven for wanting a smidgen of predictability in his life – wanting to know, for example, whether he had a better than even chance of surviving the day.

It might be argued (as, indeed, the trick cyclist he'd seen once after the war had argued) that it was this very lack of predictability, namely the daily fear of death, which had driven the iron spike into Charles's heart, and made it go numb. At any rate, he had henceforth not really liked other humans, apart from Theo, who was the apple of his eye; and he certainly didn't trust them. What he liked were animals in general and, in particular, dogs. If he had not kept a dog before it was because they tended to up and die too soon, and to break what was left of a chap's heart. The Colonel, however, had been thrust upon him – had even adopted him – and he was not a man to turn his back on such a thing no matter how, well, challenging it seemed.

However, he dimly recognised that the qualities he respected in Colonel Bogey were also those that sorely tried him. The fellow was unpredictable, dammit, but this was also evidence of his independence – his free spirit, eh? – which helped to prevent Charles's routines from becoming too rigid and life-stifling. He admired the way the Colonel asked for nothing – patting, stroking, feeding, walkies – but accepted these things as his right, at most acknowledging them with a cursory salute of the tail. Yet Charles was dismayed by the fellow's refusal to recognise that rights entailed obligations: there was something chilling about the fellow's disinclination to reciprocate. In short, while he found the Colonel's companionship restful, he could wish at times that it wasn't so… *impersonal.* God knew, he didn't resent the Colonel's secretive excursions to Wyebridge – a fellow didn't have to go shouting his business from the rooftops – but he couldn't help feeling that they

138

represented on Bogey's part a want of confidence in him, amounting almost to disdain. He made it clear that Charles was not wanted on his trips and would be, in any encounter with his associates or acquaintance, *de trop*. Thus their walks, as if together, to the Tennis Club took on – in spite of all the attendant anxiety – increased significance. Today had been unusually satisfactory; for, despite the usual jockeying for position, the Colonel had consented to take the same route as himself, around the lake, instead of beetling off to Bugger Lamb and the drinkers on the terrace.

In her bedroom, Janey had drawn the curtains and lit the candles. The three boys and Bernie trooped in. The house was silent. The five of them sat around the space Janey had cleared on the floor. She opened the box and took out the ouija board and its planchette. Shaped like a tiny grand piano, it was worn from much use by Maman's mother, who had been a noted medium in the Thirties.

'I don't like the look o' this,' said Bernie. ''Tis Dodgy surely.'

'They're only spirits, Bernie,' said George. 'They can't hurt you.'

'Frankly, they can even be a bore,' added the Moo.

'We could eat a chocolate against the weakness,' said Bernie, taking one out of the large box she was holding to her, and offering it around. Whenever she could afford to, Bernie brought a box of chocolates back from shopping trips, such as the one she'd taken yesterday with Luh'le Shuggy. If Maman knew about the chocolates, she would ban them or else insist that the children choose one per day as a treat. Thus they had to gather in secret and to gorge, drawing lots for the Savoy Truffle and giving the one with the vile orange centre to Colonel Bogey. Such orgies were followed by days of dearth when Bernie was broke. But as soon as wages were advanced, or Pat Tim sent cash, or a boy at the Church Social could be persuaded to part with five bob, the good times rolled again.

'We'd better fast before we talk to the spirits, I think,' said Janey. 'We can have a choc afterwards.' Obediently, Bernie replaced her chocolate in the box and put it aside.

The smooth polished board shone in the candlelight. All the letters of the alphabet were painted in a slight arc along one edge. At either end, contained in neat boxes, were the words 'YES' and 'NO'. Janey placed the planchette in the centre.

139

'You put your finger on, Bernie, like this,' instructed the Moo, placing the tip of his finger lightly on the planchette. The others followed suit. 'But you mustn't push it,' he added sternly.

'Holy Mary and all the Saints…'

'In the name of Jesus,' intoned Janey, adding for Bernie's benefit, 'and of the Virgin Mary, and of all the Saints, we ask to speak to the spirit of our grandmother.'

'Nana,' clarified George.

They waited in silence, apart from the sound of the Moo breathing heavily through a slightly blocked nose. Suddenly, the planchette jerked. Bernie let out a small scream.

'Holy Jesus, Mary and Joseph!' she said, crossing herself with her free hand. 'My skin has come up in bumps!'

'It means a goose has walked over your grave,' said the Moo scientifically.

'It's all right,' said Hugh. 'The Fuehrer pushed it. He always does to start with.'

'I do sometimes,' admitted George, 'just to gee them up. But I didn't that time.'

'Shut up,' said Janey. They waited a bit longer. 'Nana? Are you there? Talk to us please.'

The planchette began to move slowly until it touched 'NO'.
'Who are you then?' asked Janey. The planchette began to whiz round in circles so that their fingers could hardly stay on it. Then it pointed to a string of letters in quick succession.

'B-U-R-S-T-C-L-' spelt out Hugh. 'I know where this is going.'

'Yes, it's Burst Cloud,' said George.

'That's the name of Nana's spirit guide,' Janey explained to Bernie. 'He was an Apache when he was alive.' Bernie nodded speechlessly, torn between fear and fascination. 'Hello, Burst Cloud. Can we speak to Nana, please?'

'NO'

'Why not?'

'B-R-A-V-E-S-A-Y-I-B-O-R-E.'

'Now look what you've done, the Moo,' hissed Hugh.

'Sorry,' called out the Moo. 'This is the Brave speaking. The Moo-Brave. You're not a bore, Burst Cloud. It was a mistake. Can we please speak to Nana? Oh go on, please?'

140

'NO'.

'Oh God,' breathed Bernie. 'It's a divil, isn't it? Oh God forgive me, I'm talking to a divil.'

'Sssh,' whispered the Moo. 'He's not a devil. 'E's good. Though actually he *is* a bit of a bore.'

'M-U-S--G-O,' spelt out George. '*Must go.* Must you? Oh, wait...'

'S-H-E-C-O-M-E-S.'

'Who comes? Nana?'

'NO – T-H-E-O-L-D-O-N-E.'

'*Theo L. Done?*'

'No, you clot. The Old One.'

'Oh.'

'Is it me or is it getting cold in here?'

'Ah God.'

'That candle has gone out.'

'Oh dear, perhaps we should...'

'Who is the Old One?' asked Janey. No reply. 'What's your name?'

'D-E-A-T-' Bernie screamed and, snatching her finger away, made for the door. The planchette swivelled, as if accusingly, and shot off the edge of the board.

'Dod-*gy*,' breathed George.

'What's DEAT?' asked the Moo.

'God knows,' said Hugh hastily. 'We'd better pack it in now, I think. The spirits obviously aren't in the mood.'

'I expect Nana is busy today,' agreed Janey.

Only George remembered Bernie's box of chocolates as the party, shaken, dispersed.

Charles stopped as usual at the spot where the lake shelved unfathomably away into darkness. Seized by that dread which powerfully attracts even as it repels, he craned over the water's surface and peered down into the black depths. Vertigo overtook him and, dizzy, he slipped towards the water. For a heart-stopping second he thought he was going to overbalance, and fall in. He saw himself clearly, thrashing about in the lake, unable to claw his way up the muddy bank, sliding under, inhaling water, his limbs quickly numbed, the waters closing over his head.

He closed his eyes. It was horrible. But it was also curiously liberating. Even comforting. It would be over so quickly. There'd be no feeling in his body. And after a few short moments of panic as water instead of air filled his lungs, he would become acclimatised, euphoric, drifting down like leaf mould to be embraced by the warm darkness below. Even the pike would be his friend, helping him to settle in the soft comfortable mud, initiating that quiet natural breaking-down of the body to which all are subject, its gentle lips dispersing his flesh until, delicately absolved by millions of micro-organisms, his bones alone shone like pearls.

As he gazed into the water, the image of his adorable wife, dead these twenty years, rose up to greet him, the untameable wisp of black hair falling over her left eye, just as it always had. He smiled. Death was not oblivion, but reunion. He felt it in his pearly bones. When he turned back on to the path to resume his circumambulation, his heart lifted to see that, of all things, Colonel Bogey was waiting for him. Not appearing to, of course – he was sniffing in a shrub absent-mindedly – but he was there, close by, like a confirmation.

11

In honour of his new boots, Hugh put on a tie, constructing a Windsor knot under the smart button-down collar of his blue shirt. Then he looked at his feet again, as he did every couple of minutes, in order to savour the sight of them encased in the utterly fab, elastic-sided Chelsea boots. He'd thought that Maman would go mad when she saw them yesterday. They were hardly the sensible shoes he'd been ordered to buy. But she merely gazed at them for a few seconds, and then kissed Hugh. You just couldn't tell with Maman these days. Dada, however, would definitely go mad – if he noticed them. Hugh was counting on the tie to distract him. Dada noticed ties, not footwear. He went downstairs and joined the others in the hall for Lunch Inspection.

'You have made no attempt, the Moo,' Dada was saying, 'to tidy yourself. Here, take my own brush and stand in front of the mirror in the cloakroom, and give your hair a good brush. You are old enough now, the Moo, to perform such simple tasks for yourself.'

The Moo ignored the proffered brush and crossed the hall to the stretch of wall next to the playroom door, where he stood, the tip of his nose just touching the wall. Dada sighed.

'Well, perhaps we will make do with a cursory inspection today. You all look reasonably presentable. If only Janey would move her hair from her face. Well, that is better, Janey. But there is no need to look at me in that fashion. If you cannot keep a civil expression in your eyes, then perhaps you had better cover your face again. I see that you take my ironical suggestion literally. Very well. You may, if you please, go through life entirely screened by hair like some sort of Abominable Snowman. Really, I do not care any more. It is a matter for yourself. I have tried to help you, but you block your ears and

143

cover your face against me. Well, on your own head be it. Where the hell is the roast? Really, Bernie is no better than your mother. Now, mein Fuehrer. You have muck on your face I cannot overlook. I don't have to taste it to know that it is chocolate, something you have been expressly forbidden to eat between meals.'

'But, Dada, we never have chocolate *at* meals so what am I to do?'

'Well, your logic does you credit, mein Fuehrer. However, you must learn to subordinate it to obedience. I know who is responsible in this house for dispensing chocolate at all times of day and night, and I shall be speaking harsh words to Miss O'Flaherty. Meanwhile, your punishment will be to forgo your snippet. Stand still and do not pull faces. Are you going to remove that mess from your face, or am I going to spit on my handkerchief and remove if for you? I thought as much.' He turned to Hugh. 'Now. The Young Master. You are looking, I dare say it, very neat, Luh'le Shuggy. I am surprised and pleased. It may be that your smart attire bespeaks a guilty conscience, but I will give you the benefit of the doubt because I am a fond, foolish old man who indulges his children perhaps to a disastrous extent.'

At that moment, Bernie swept through the hall, bearing a steaming joint of roast beef that, unlike Maman, held no terrors for her, cooking as she had from an early age for up to four brothers and three sisters.

'Not before time, Bernadette,' admonished Dada, tapping his watch. 'And we will have to have word about chocolate and its distribution.'

'Okay so, Mr Blyte. But I don't advise you to eat any just now – it'll spoil your appetite. Hello Handsome,' she said to Hugh, flashing a meaning look at his boots and waggling her eyebrows.

Hugh smiled wanly at her. Yesterday's happiness already belonged to another remote time, almost another world. Part of his compulsive glancing at the beauty of his boots was a ritual for recapturing the orderly cosmos that prevailed before Dada's world-shattering announcement. In that other happy world, he had gone shopping with Bernie in Kingston. Maman had given them money on top of Bernie's advance wages for Hugh to buy sensible shoes, and Bernie, pillow cases – of which there was a mysterious shortage.

They had laughed on the bus all the way to Bentall's where, instead of pillow cases, Bernie bought, in full view of him, a class of black underwear whose existence Hugh had not suspected. She also bought presents for the children, of course. She favoured bright and shiny things; and the recipient duly felt illuminated by something of Bernie's innate glamour and luminosity. She bought the Moo a tiny exquisite silver sword (in reality a paper knife) and George, a chrome expanding watch strap which he now wore snazzily on his upper arm in the manner, he claimed, of a Celtic warlord. For Janey, dangly clip-on earrings with sparkly jewels she could hide under her hair. In a surprise lapse of her decided tastes, Bernie also bought a Jaeger silk scarf, which she later presented instead of pillow cases to a wild-eyed Maman – who laughed hysterically and, almost tearfully, embraced her. Bernie took advantage of this momentary weakening to openly hand out Mars Bars, Bounties, Kit-Kats and Crunchies to the children, while leaving undeclared, of course, the large box of chocs she had brought to the séance.

Together they had looked at sensible shoes. But Hugh had been unable to take his eyes off the dazzling pair of Chelsea boots, absolutely the latest thing, their restrained chisel-toes superseding the dated spivvy winkle-picker. Bernie had egged him on. He lost his head. He bought them. He walked on air, swanking down the street with Bernie laughing beside him, and, twice, leaning against him.

Then, at a matinée of *Dr No* – Ursula Andress in white Bikiniville, *hell's teeth* – their hands had simply clasped one another under the shared bag of popcorn, as if it were the most natural thing in the world.

'Come a*long*, Luh'le Shuggy,' ordered Dada. 'The joint is cooling. Bring your youngest brother with you.' The Moo remained facing the wall.

'I'm afraid I can't, Dada. The Moo holds no brief for me. I'm powerless to influence him.'

'That's enough, the Moo,' Dada called out from the dining room doorway. 'You have made your point, whatever that may be. Now come along. Lunch is on the table.' But the Moo did not stir. Eerily, he did not even blink. His extreme immobility unnerved Dada. 'What do you suggest, Janey? Might Dabs have some influence?'

145

'Dabs brains am down. She am asleep.'

'Apparently not,' said Janey. 'But the Fuehrer will quite easily chivvy the Moo out of this mood, won't you, mein Fuehrer? Make the Moo laugh.'

'I vill not make ziss feeble and pathetic Moo-*schwein* laugh,' said George, advancing on the Moo in an exaggeratedly evil manner. 'I vill tweak him till he squeaks like ein stuck pig, und zen I vill take ein big pair of badger-tongs for ze baiting of ze badgers, und I vill – *mitt great delicacy* – remove ze offensive leetle unterpants of zis Moo-beast, and I vill… *stimulate his follicles.*' George feinted at his brother, trusting that he would flinch and squeal, for follicles could not be stimulated, as it were, in cold blood. But the Moo remained catatonic. And although George went very close to him and whispered in his ear sentences which would cause the unshockable hair of Dada himself to start from his head, the Moo stayed as unmoved as if he could neither see nor hear.

'Well, well, we shall leave him,' said Dada. 'He will soon tire of this game.' More loudly he said: 'Come away, mein Fuehrer. Let your brother sulk.' And, forgetting his previous threat, 'You shall have his snippet.'

'Is your good lady not joining us today, Blyte?' enquired Charles Hamilton, ostentatiously folding up Colonel Bogey's lead and cramming it into the pocket of his tweed jacket.

'She is indisposed,' said Dada.

'She is not Swinging,' said George.

'She has the googie withers,' said the Moo.

'No, she has *not*, the Moo,' said Hugh.

'She am acquainted with grief,' said Dabs.

'Oh, so Dabs has woken up now, has she?' said Dada sharply, blowing out his cheeks in preparation for the Knife-Sharpening Face.

'The Colonel will be here any minute. He was right behind me a moment ago,' said Charles, his words drowned by the clash of carving-knife against steel.

Theo leant towards Janey. 'The Moo… ahem… not, um, lunching?'

'He's in a state. Probably because Dada has said he is leaving us.'

'Good, er… Lord…'

'What's that you say, Theo?' grated Dada from between clenched teeth, being in the middle of changing from the Sharpening to the Carving Face.

'Ah… um… one gathers… er, pastures new.'

'I see that my children are eager to tell the world of their father's imminent departure. They do not mention, I suppose, how they have conspired to drive him to this decision. No, that would require a respect for truth. But let it pass. I say nothing.'

'There's no point in leaving, Dada,' said Janey. 'Maman will not give you a divorce.'

'It really is quite nippy out,' said Charles. 'I remarked on it to the Colonel…'

'Perhaps… your permission… respects to good, um, lady?' requested Theo, rising from his chair.

'She sleeps at present,' snapped Dada. 'Nor do I imagine that French conversation is what she requires at this moment. Still, while you are up, Theo, perhaps you would do me the kindness of finding out if the wretched Moo is ready to grace us with his presence?'

Theo slipped out into the hall. Presently, he could be heard softly singing in a fetching falsetto:

'We are the Sloppy Boys
We like to make a Sloppy noise
Plerff burp plop fart
A Sloppy noise is quite an art
Burp plop fart plerff
Us chaps is made of Sloppy sterff
Fart burp plerff plop
Even the cops can't make us stop
For we are the Sloppy boys
We like to make…'

After another verse, the Moo's wheeze of reluctant laughter could be heard.

'Theo has a hit record there, if I'm any judge,' said Hugh.

'I can only apologise for Theo,' said Charles.

'Very… *cliquey*, these Sloppy Club members,' sniffed Dada.

Theo reappeared, holding the Moo's hand. They took their places at table.

'The Moo will have 'is snippet now,' said the Moo airily.

147

'The Moo certainly will not,' contradicted Dada. 'You have some neck, the Moo – demanding snippets after making such a spectacle of yourself. In fact, there are to be no snippets for anyone today. I am heartily sick of the lot of you, ungrateful weedy-haired brats. I shall be glad to be rid of you.'

'I've changed my mind,' said the Moo, with an aplomb that drew admiring glances. 'I don't want a snippet after all.'

'Well, that is good, the Moo. That is just as well when you consider that the snippet which will not now be forthcoming, would have been your last snippet on this Earth.'

'I don't care,' said the Moo, his eyes moistening and mucus appearing at his nostrils.

'Leave the Moo alone, Dada,' said Hugh. 'He is upset, as you very well know.'

'That is precisely what I do not know, Luh'le Shuggy. The Moo has displayed an aloofness, a lack of feeling, which has dismayed his poor old Dada.'

'Quite the reverse, Dada, as you see.'

'I see nothing of the kind. I merely see a child snivelling for a snippet. I see no depth of emotion. Not one of you can express the simplest feeling in a plain and sincere fashion.'

'I think the Moo is doing so now,' said Janey.

'Well, well, perhaps he is learning something after all. Perhaps he is learning, as the rest of you will do well to learn, what it is to put oneself in the place of another, to suffer what another suffers, instead of forever looking after Number One. Oh, it is my fault, I know – I have provided for you a life of ease and luxury. I have spoilt you, and so you lead selfish lives. It is little wonder that you cannot begin to imagine what it is like for me, your devoted father, to be wrenched from the bosom of his family and from the home he has built up over many years with sweat and tears and hard-earned cash.'

'But we aren't asking you to go,' reasoned George.

'We shall be though, at this rate,' murmured Hugh.

'If you go,' hiccuped the Moo, 'who'll do the carving?'

'I will,' said Hugh.

'You can't do the Face,' said George anxiously. 'We'll starve.'

'So that is what I am to you, the Moo? Simply the man who puts meat on your plate. Well, well. Now we see the true colours of a Moo who –'

'Dabs am werry sad that Dada am leaving,' interrupted Dabs.

'Well, well, that is something I suppose. Although it is a sorry comment on you all that it takes an imbecile to show a little maturity and compassion.'

'Yes, Dabs am sad, but she am happy that Dada am whisking the bootiful Mrs Chummalummy off to the Bogs to live happily ever after. Aaaah,' sighed Dabs sentimentally, 'call Dabs a Romantic fool but –'

'Is this a cretinous attempt at some sort of sarcasm?' said Dada suspiciously. 'Well, even supposing I recognised the existence of these so-called Bogs, I am not, for your information, returning to them, let alone with Mrs Cholmondeley, whom you will leave out of this altogether or – I give you fair warning – I will *lose my temper*.'

'Ah, here's the Colonel!' exclaimed Charles with relief.

Colonel Bogey paused in the doorway to regard Charles dourly and, without a reply, padded over to Dada.

'This dog will be the only one I shall miss,' he said, ostentatiously carving a hefty slice of beef and delivering it into the Colonel's mouth. 'He at least knows the meaning of gratitude.' As if in contradiction, the Colonel waited for a moment to see if more meat was forthcoming; and, when it was not, he smacked his lips noisily and strolled out of the door, nearly tripping Bernie as she bustled in with the brick of Wall's vanilla ice-cream.

'Holy Mother of God!' She crossed herself involuntarily as she put the ice-cream on the sideboard. 'Isn't he a quare one, the Colonel?' She glanced nervously behind her. 'He's no *right* dog, I'd say. You wouldn't want to be meeting him on a lonely road on a dark night.'

'The Colonel's all right,' the Moo assured her. 'He's a member of the Sloppy Club.'

'And that wouldn't be the only Club he'd be a member of.'

'What's this?' cried Charles. 'What are you implying, Bernie?'

'Wasn't I up at the Tennis Club, taking the air with the Moo, and didn't we see that ould fella, the Secretary, drinking at a table on the terrace?'

'We did,' confirmed the Moo.

149

'And wasn't Colonel Bogey next to him, and he up on a chair like a Christian?'

'He was, and Colonel Lamb poured beer into an ashtray. And Colonel Bogey drank it.'

'They have a lot in common,' surmised George. 'Colonels and that.'

'Well, they were certainly colloguing away like army buddies,' said Bernie on her way out. 'Though we were too far away to hear what was said.'

'Good grief,' said Charles. All his early optimism collapsed. That the Colonel should choose to socialise with Bugger Lamb already beggared belief. That he should do so behind Charles's back was unforgivable. He had reckoned the Colonel capable of many things, but this two-faced behaviour was something new. It was nothing short of a betrayal. He felt again the sharp stab of pain in his stomach, or thereabouts, and nearly cried out. He had not succeeded, it seemed, in walking it off. The doctor had referred him to some sort of innards specialist at the hospital. He had gone, under duress. There had been 'tests'. X-rays, blood samples – those sort of shenanigans. He had an appointment next week to hear the results, but he wondered if he'd bloody bother to go. They'd probably only want to open him up and poke about; and Charles had seen enough of innards and such in the War.

'I shall not be staying for dessert,' said Dada, rising from his chair and looking at the company in a challenging way.

'What are you going to do about Maman?' asked Janey.

'I? I am not going to do anything about Maman. She sleeps peacefully.'

'I doubt that,' said Hugh.

'You needn't worry, children. Your mother and I had a long adult discussion last night and we agreed that my leaving was for the best.'

'Maman seemed less certain this morning,' said Hugh. 'I'm afraid her frayed nerves won't withstand your departure. I'm afraid they'll snap.'

'I think I may be supposed to know your mother rather better than you, Luh'le Shuggy, and she is a good deal more robust than you give her credit for. You forget that she survived a World War.'

'I wasn't aware that the German army marched on Surrey.'

'I'm sick and tired of your impertinence, Luh'le Shuggy, and I will not stand here while you exercise it.' He turned on his heel and stalked out of the room, only to return a minute later. 'Who has taken the keys to the Zodiac?' No one spoke. 'Mein Fuehrer, you have taken the car keys and poked them through the crack in your bedroom floorboards. Admit it and I shall not beat you.'

'That was years and *years* ago, Dada. And it was combs, not keys,' protested George. 'Keys I buried.'

'Well I remember it, mein Fuehrer. Anyone else and I might have thrashed them within an inch of their lives. As it was, your mother had physically to restrain me. So. You have buried my keys?'

'*No*, Dada. I'm telling you. I learnt my lesson. But I'll help you find them. I'm coming with you.'

'You are not, mein Fuehrer. You are to stay here and finish every last scrap of your meal. Is that understood?'

'Yes, Dada.'

'I must have left them in the car,' said Dada to himself as he turned to go.

George began to wolf down his Wall's, wincing at the pain of the ice-cream on his ill-brushed teeth. 'Dada won't leave without me,' he reasoned. 'I'm the best little brain in the family.'

'He's not leaving forever this minute,' said Janey. 'He's not going for a week or so, he said.'

'I expect we'll see a film,' pursued George, his mouth working.

'Um… your, er, Maman,' murmured Theo to Janey. 'Might one perhaps… tempt… *soupçon* ice, er, cream?'

'A good idea, Theo. But I'll take it to her. She may not want you to see her not, well, looking her best.'

'Ah… quite… absolutely… message, er, understood.'

'Spiv'll probably manage it if she doesn't want it,' said the Moo.

Janey took a bowl of ice-cream upstairs and tapped on the door of her parents' bedroom. There was no reply. She went in. The bed was empty. She looked for Maman in the bathroom and lavatory and then, at a loss, she wandered along the landing and gazed moonily out of the window. She could see Dada walking purposefully down the drive towards the garage. He stopped and cocked his head, as if listening. He seemed about to walk on to the garage when he was distracted by the ominous yet exciting sound of a powerful car, raising the pitch of its engine as it swerved into the quiet of Chestnut Avenue. Janey trained her eyes eagerly on the garden hedge and, sure enough, a glint of chrome, a flash of glossy paintwork, a blind blacked-out window – all proclaimed the swift apocalyptic passing of her jet-black Mini. Dada also stared at the hedge. Then he stared at the garage doors. At last, executing a precise late cut to an invisible outswinger with an imaginary cricket bat, he walked quickly down the remainder of the drive, out into Chestnut Avenue and turned right, towards 'Ponderosa.'

As soon as he had finished his ice-cream, George got down from the table – there was no one left whose permission he had to ask – and ran off in pursuit of his father. He was just in time. He could hear the Zodiac's engine – although, strangely, the garage doors were closed. He heaved them open, noticing that, inside, a roll of old carpet had been wedged along the bottom. The garage ponged to high heaven, like a gas leak. He paused to admire the mechanical ingenuity with which the garden hose had been strapped with masking tape into the exhaust pipe, and then inserted through the side window of the car. He began to feel distinctly sick. Through the miasma inside the car he saw that Maman was sitting, if that was the word, in the front passenger seat.

In the drawing room, the depleted party was drinking coffee.

'I'm rather worried about the Colonel's health, Hugh,' Charles was saying. 'He has looked distinctly peaky these last few days. I can't help wondering if there is something amiss that an early diagnosis might prevent from turning into something nasty.'

'If you think so, Mr H.,' replied Hugh uncertainly. 'I s'pose we could take him to the vet –'

'Now, er, now... Papa,' soothed Theo, watching the Moo who was on the floor at his feet with Dinky toys, retreating into Jack Pluff's realm, which, for all its extreme violence, was safer than the world. 'Nothing wrong... Bogey... in the pink...'

'Perhaps,' conceded Charles. 'But he's not himself. All this boozing with Bugger Lamb, pardon my French. Not a sign of health, I suggest.'

'I wouldn't take that too seriously, Mr H.,' Hugh assured him. 'The Colonel has always been a social animal. His diary always seems to be full. But he likes it best to be quiet at home, especially with you, I'd say.'

'Would you, Hugh? Well, you might be right at that,' said Charles, looking heartened. 'But, between you and me, I've never gained the fellow's confidence, you know. And, frankly, it's a sore point.'

'If anyone... you...,' Theo contradicted. 'Just that... Bogey... secretive, er, nature...'

'Well, that's certainly true,' sighed Charles, staring mournfully out of the long bay window. There was a silence, broken only by the Moo aaarghing under his breath.

'Couldn't help, er, old chap... noticing...' said Theo to Hugh, pointing at his eyes and then at Hugh's feet. 'As Fuehrer... um... "snazzy"...'

'Oh, they're only Chelsea boots,' said Hugh dismissively while colouring with pleasure. He added: 'I bought them with Bernie. She's good-looking, isn't she, Theo?'

'Er... rather...'

'I think she goes out with quite a lot of blokes. Not all of them, well, *that* suitable, I think. I worry a bit. I don't s'pose *you'd* take her out, Theo? I mean, you're not *too* old for her or anything. You'd steady her a bit...'

'More, er, you than me... I'd say...um Hugh old chap – hep cat... so forth.'

Hugh laughed. 'I wish I were, Theo. But I'm too young for her. I mean, I know she likes me. But not, well, in *that* way. It's not surprising. I mean, look at her. She's, well... But you could... you know. I mean, it's none of my business, Theo, but you ought to have a girlfriend. I mean, you could easily get one.'

'Ah... um... alas, one's heart... spoken for... old chap...' Theo lowered his eyes, his left hand absently stroking the Moo's preoccupied head.

'I guessed as much,' said Hugh. 'Would it be too nosy to ask –'

But at that moment, George burst into the room, wearing his army surplus gas mask. His frantic gesticulations did not immediately make themselves intelligible. Theo was the first to react. He ran like the wind, with George puffing in his wake. At the garage, George found that the gas mask not only failed to work, it also filtered out what little oxygen remained. Luckily, as a veteran of the lead smelter's craft, a period of unconsciousness was a mere bagatelle to George. He came round after a minute or so, just in time to see Theo laying Maman out on the gravel drive, clasping her green face and apparently kissing her blue lips.

12

IT was Saturday. The children had somehow gone to school, and Dada to the office, for the past two weeks. Hugh had mostly stayed in bed, and the more so because Mrs Cholmondeley had been in and out of the house at intervals, and he had been loath to run into her. This morning, roused by the sound of the Zodiac setting off – Dada was working all weekend to prepare for an important board meeting on Monday – he got up early and began to dress himself in front of the window which overlooked the drive.

Colonel Bogey appeared from around the side of the house. He liked to take the air first thing, and to prepare himself for the rigours of the day. However, he seemed unsteady on his pins, looking about with a vagueness very different from his usual brio. Perhaps Mr Hamilton was right, and the Colonel was sickening for something. Just then, George appeared from the same direction. He was carrying one of his lead-smelting saucepans and, to judge by his stealthy movements, he seemed to be stalking the Colonel. Every time the Colonel lifted his leg, the Fuehrer darted forward with the pan. After several false starts, during which on one occasion he actually overbalanced, the Colonel managed to urinate copiously. At once the Fuehrer was on hand to niftily catch the wee-wee in his pan. Hugh wrinkled his nose. What fresh squalor was this?

He went down to the breakfast room. Janey was already sitting at the table, her head in her hands. Bernie could be heard next door in the kitchen compiling her trademark mountain of toast and pot of hot red tea. She was singing:

Rattling roaring Willie, oh he's off to the fair
Rattling roaring Willie, to buy some other ware...

'Why's 'e rattling and roaring, Bernie?' asked the Moo's voice.

'Because he's a big eejit, the Moo.'

'Like Dabs?'

'Like Dabs but noisier and with more spit and slobber around the mouth, I'd say.

If I were to sell me fiddle the world'd think I was mad

Oh many's the ranting day this fiddle and I have had – Now!' she broke off, coming into the breakfast room with the Moo in her wake and plonking the platter of toast on the table. 'And good morning to the pair of yez.' The grubby slip she usually wore had been supplemented in the crisper weather by an old sloppy joe of Janey's which, being a little small for her perfect figure, made Hugh's eyes water.

'Good morning, Bernie,' intoned Janey and Hugh.

George appeared, looking innocent.

'What were you doing, molesting Colonel Bogey?' demanded Hugh.

'Nothing.'

'Is it nothing, squalid child, to be snatching his wee-wee from under his very nose?'

'Jaysus, Luh'le Shuggy!' exclaimed Bernie. 'How's a person to eat with that class of dirty talk going on?'

'Sorry.'

'It's just an experiment,' explained George. Hugh shrugged.

'I miss Maman,' announced the Moo.

'I know, darling,' said Bernie. 'We all do. I miss my own Ma.'

'Is she dead?'

'Both my parents are dead, God be good to them – ah, don't be filling your little eyes with tears, the Moo. Come here to me now till I kiss them off you – mwah, mwah – there! Isn't that better? And aren't me poor ould Ma and Pa lepping about like lambs in the lush green meadows of heaven? So there's no cause for tears or alarm.'

'But *how* did they die, Bernie?' asked the Moo, rallying.

'About my Ma's death, the Moo, I'll say nothing. 'Twas too horrible, and your ears would fall from your head to hear about it. But my Da, now, he died of fatness. He was the fattest man in Ireland, I'd say. Probably America as well. It took a pair of JCBs to dig his grave and lower him in.'

'How'd 'e get so fat?' The Moo's eyes were as big as his mind's eyes, trying to encompass the scene.

''Twas on account of the Hungry Grass.'

'What's *that*?'

'Well now. You remember I was telling you about the Good People?'

'The *Sidhe*,' said George with a technical air.

'*Ssssh*. It's they who are putting the glamour on a bit of sod to lead you astray – you've only to tread on it, and you've no idea where you are. You might be wandering for days. Annyway, the Hungry Grass is a similar case. If your foot touches a patcheen of grass the Good People are after putting the glamour on, straight away you're slaughtered by a terrible hunger. This happened to my Da. One moment he's walking across a field at the back of Pat Tim's, the next he's raging into the house, careening around the kitchen, stuffing his face with whatever he can lay his hands on. And Pat Tim's people know at once that the Hungry Grass is over him, and they send out Pat Tim for as much food as he can gather, for won't my Da die if he's not fed? The desire itself is so desperate that it'll kill a man. But my sweetheart returns in no time at all with all the food in the townland, and my Da is saved. For the Hungry Grass passes off as quickly as it comes. But it left my ould Da in a sad state. He was niver the same, like he had a fear on him that he'd not get enough to eat; and so he ate all the time – every day a power of bacon and spuds, bread and brack going into him until he was hefty as a herd of Mullingar heifers. We'd a massive chair built especially for him. Ah God, the man was fat. There was one time, I remember, when –'

A knock at the back door interrupted her. 'Who could that be?' George scampered next door to find out. He came back wide-eyed.

'Dada has gone mad.'

'We know that,' said Janey and Hugh in unison.

'No, I mean really mad. Come and look.'

They all gathered in the cramped kitchen to watch the two cheerful workmen removing the meat safe and its table from the capacious larder. In their place they installed a tall white machine which, as soon as it was plugged in, began to breathe stertorously.

'Bonkersville,' murmured Hugh. 'Dada would never normally lash out on such a luxury item as a refrigerator.'

'Fridge,' said George. 'You say "fridge", if you're modern.'

'So this is modernity,' mused Hugh, watching the Moo opening

157

and closing the fridge door ever more minutely in an effort to catch out the light that went on when the door was opened. 'I don't think I like it.'

'That thing has sent a chill running through the house,' said Bernie. She shivered.

'It's not chilly,' said George. 'It's just that you're all afraid of change.'

'I'm not,' said Hugh. 'I'm just slow to adjust. I haven't got over the Zodiac yet.'

'Well, you'd better speed up, Luh'le Shuggy,' advised George. 'When things change they change faster and faster. They snowball.'

'If things have got to change,' said Janey, 'I'd rather have a pony than a... fridge.'

'I'd rather have a fridge,' said the Moo. 'It'll make ice lollies.'

'Also,' added George, 'you can store chopped-up bodies without any tell-tale pong.'

'Squalid child.'

'Bluebottles can still get in a fridge,' said the Moo.

'But would they survive in the cold?' wondered Janey.

''Course they would,' asserted George. 'The bluebottle is tough as old boots. When they drop the Bomb and kill us all, there'll be nothing left except bluebottles. And dry rot, of course.'

'And Dabs,' said Dabs smugly.

'You're so feeble you'll be the first to die,' said the Moo witheringly.

'Dabs am a born survivor, like dry rot.'

'But with less brain,' insulted George.

'The dinosaurs didn't have much brain,' said Janey in support of Dabs, 'but they survived for millions of years.'

'Well, that's true. The brontosaurus had a brain the size of a mouse,' conceded George, recalling the wisdom of Arthur Mee. 'The impulses it sent out were too weak to reach as far as its back legs, so the brontosaurus had a second brain in its bum.'

'That is something you have in common with the brontosaurus, mein Fuehrer,' said Hugh. 'It accounts for your brain damage – every time you sit down –'

'Best little bum in the family,' squeaked Dabs.

'*Actually*, Luh'le Shuggy,' said George, 'we all know that it is you who has his brains in his bum because, as you have just proved, that is the place all your words come from.'

A nasty scene might have developed, had not the fridge proved to be simply the cold and formal envoy of an even more stately personage: Mrs Cholmondeley.

'Hello, children. Here I am, just as your father promised.' She was wearing a pearl-coloured silky dress, cut low and arguably too short in the skirt for a mother, unless she were going to a cocktail party; an impression enhanced by the impeccable make-up and strong perfume. There was quite a long silence. At last Hugh said:

'Dada... father didn't mention your coming to me. Did he to you, Janey? Or you, Bernie?' There was a shaking of heads.

'He may have mentioned it to me,' said George, 'but I wouldn't remember because I don't pay attention.'

'Never mind,' said Mrs Cholmondeley, 'I am here now. To look after you.'

'It's all right,' said Janey quickly. 'I mean, thank you – but we can look after ourselves. Plus, there's Bernie.'

'There is,' confirmed the au pair.

'Bernie looks after the Moo,' said the Moo complacently, 'with toast and stories.'

'I'm well able to mind them,' added Bernie, placing a protective hand on the Moo's large head.

'No seriously, Bernadette,' laughed Mrs Cholmondeley, 'I do not doubt that you do your best. But you are not their mother.'

'Are you going to be our mother?' asked George curiously.

'I hope that you will think of me as such.'

'We already have a mother,' said Hugh.

'Of course. I meant temporarily. It is unfeasible for your father to leave home under the circumstances, so he and I have decided that I will look after you while your mother's nerves are mending.'

'In the loony bin,' supplied George.

'What a thing to say, George. She is in a very nice and very expensive nursing home in Bournemouth, as I think you very well know.'

'Poor Maman. The Sea Hare will make her better,' quoted the Moo, picturing it easily.

'We wouldn't dream of depriving Sabrina and Bradley of you,' said Janey in a grown-up way.

'Of course not, dear. Children!' She called through the door. Her offspring came in, carrying a camp bed between them.

Sabrina looked about her confidently, gratified but unsurprised by the attention. Bradley stared defiantly at George whose mouth began to fall open: the Enemy's National Health specs, with the blanked-out lens, were gone. Instead of them he was wearing huge glasses with thick square black frames, just like Hank Marvin of The Shadows.

'Bradley will be occupying Hugh's old bed in the boys' room. And George, you must learn to be better behaved. Now, Bradley – give George your gift.' Bradley stood in front of George and handed him a sheaf of comics. Both boys were breathing audibly. George glanced at them. They were American, which was good; and they were called *Creepy Tales,* which was better.

'They're reasonably snazzy, actually,' offered the Enemy. George nodded.

'Good,' said Mrs Cholmondeley. 'Now you two will get on with each other. And that goes for Moe as well.'

'Who's Moe?' wondered the Moo.

'Are you not Moe?' replied Mrs Cholmondeley crisply.

'No. I am… THE MOO.'

'There is no need for that sort of emphasis, dear. And the name is absurd. I cannot possibly call you that. What is your real name?'

'My real name,' said the Moo with pride, 'is… is…' His lip trembled. 'I've forgotten! I don't know who I am any more,' he wailed. Hugh crouched beside him:

'Your name, the Moo, is Montgomery. *You* remember.'

'Oh yes.' The Moo brightened at once. 'Mo… Mom… Moogomry.'

'Near enough. And remember: you are named after the greatest field marshal since the Duke of Wellington. So you need not be afraid of anything.'

'I cannot call the child "Montgomery",' said Mrs Cholmondeley, irritation getting the better of her. 'It is ridiculous. I will call him "Moo" for now.'

'*The* Moo,' corrected the Moo.

'Very well. *The* Moo. Now, Jane. Sabrina will be in your room. As you see, we have brought a sturdy camp bed. I do think it would be a nice gesture on your part, dear, if you were to give up your bed to Sabrina, and to take the camp bed yourself. You do not dance, do you, Jane, and so you do not have to be so careful about your spine. Also, I might just mention that your room is, not to put too fine a point upon it, a sty. I cannot believe your mother would approve. You will tidy it this afternoon, please. Hugh, I confess that I was surprised to find your room next to Bernadette's. But we will leave things as they are for now.' Hugh hung his head with a shame whose origins he couldn't put his finger on.

'I like sleeping next to Luh'le Shuggy,' said Bernie.

'That is my point, Bernadette. And that is what you call him? It is a quaint pet name, I suppose. Do you think it appropriate to address your employer's eldest son in such a familiar fashion?' She looked Bernie up and down in silence, all the children seeing Bernie's eccentric and scanty attire through Mrs Cholmondeley's eyes. Hugh's obscure shame deepened. 'We will have to find some decent clothes for you, Bernadette. Incidentally, do you change the pillow cases?'

'I do,' replied Bernie in a voice made small by Mrs Cholmondeley's bare-faced scrutiny. 'Fresh ones whenever they're needed.'

'But you do not, I notice, remove the old ones. I counted seven on Mr Blyte's pillow.'

'Ah God. Are they to come off?'

'Mrs Chummy will sleep in the spare room,' assumed the Moo.

'It is "Mrs Cholmondeley", dear. Can you say that for me?' The Moo considered.

'No.'

'I think you can, dear. With a little bit of effort. We will try again later. And stand up straight, please. I detest sloppiness.'

There were sharp intakes of breath. The Moo drew himself up slowly.

'Sloppiness is next to godliness,' he quoted from the new Sloppy Club manifesto he was working on.

'No, dear. Cleanliness.' The Moo began to laugh. Janey intervened quickly:

'I'll make up the bed in the spare room for you, Mrs Cholmondeley.'

'Thank you, Jane. But not just for the present, I think. And under the circumstances you may all call me "Cheryl".'

'That's your bed,' said George. 'This is mine. That's the Moo's.' Bradley put down his suitcase and bounced experimentally on his bed. 'You can have the bottom drawer here for your smelly clothes.'

'The other drawers are full of your *spare school clothes*, I suppose, Blyte. That you wear during the holidays because you love school so much, and long to meet a teacher in the street, and say "Ooh, sir, sir, can I have some extra homework to do in the holidays, please, sir, please."'

Sensing that Bradley was venting feelings that were not to do with him, George was unable to take the taunt personally and so did not retaliate. 'I'm not going to bother to unpack,' Bradley went on, kicking his suitcase under the bed. 'I won't be here long. I'm going to live with my Dad – hey, what's in this box?' He pulled out a cardboard box his suitcase had struck. George had forgotten that he kept the box under Hugh's unused old bed.

'Leave it alone,' he said. 'It's private.'

'It's got comics inside.'

'*Don't you dare touch them, Cholmondeley or else I'll –*'

'*Bunty,*' said Bradley.

'They're my sister's.'

'Oh, Blyte. Oh dearie me, Blyte. We both know that you are lying...'

It was humiliating beyond any possible riposte. George could think of nothing to do but turn tail and run away – run to the refuge of Janey's room.

But next door, in Janey's room, the situation was hardly any better.

'I've cleared your desk for you, Jane,' said Sabrina brightly. 'It was *covered* in dirty stones and messy birds' nests. Pooh! I think my gonks look nice on it, don't you, arranged in a row like that? Oh *do* look, Jane!' Janey stopped making up her camp bed and turned her face heavily in the direction of the hideous stuffed troll-like creatures that had replaced her Nature Collection. She wanted to protest. More, she wanted to cry out to the heavens. But in the face of Sabrina, it seemed pointless. You didn't know where to begin to explain how precious the stones and nests, the shells and feathers had been. All her anger glanced off the shiny uncomprehending surface of Sabrina and was reflected back on herself in the form of a dull painful lethargy. 'This one's Marigold Gonk, and this one's Big Daddy Gonk, and this little one is Tommy Gonk because it was given to me by Tommy Price who's got the most terrible crush on me!' To Janey's surprise, Sabrina giggled – 'girlishly', thought Janey, by which she meant 'almost humanly'. 'I can see why you leave your drawings on the floor for people to walk on. They're not really proper drawings at all, are they? Men with onions, men with guitars and so on. I think you must be Man Mad, Janey! One or two are quite good. I'll keep the ones I like, shall I? I won't throw away the rest, they'll make useful scrap paper. For lists and so on.' The sound of tearing paper was too much for Janey in her depleted state. She rounded on the younger girl.

'My nem eez FOODY FENELLA and I jerst lerv to smuzzer leetle girls wiz beeg slobbery keesses…!'

'I know you Blytes have a rather unique sense of humour,' said Sabrina, unflinching before the advance of Miss Fenella. 'But actually, Jane, that is rather disgusting. You should always rinse your plate after every meal.' The sanctimonious dimple in her chin expressed both her disappointment with Janey and her goodness in correcting the older girl's aberrant behaviour. 'I'm lucky enough to have perfect teeth. Only three fillings, believe it or not. Do you want to see them?' She opened her mouth confidently.

Foody Fenella uttered a strangled snarl as she was stuffed back into the mouth of Janey, who promptly fled the room to take refuge with Hugh. However, she was stopped at the door by the sound of familiar vowels within. She tip-toed away and then ran to the playroom.

Hugh was in the middle of going back to bed in order to recover from the Cholmondeley invasion. He had been side-tracked by the decision to smoke the banana skins he had carefully dried and shredded in accordance with instructions laid out in the *Head Transplant* that Bloggs had sent him. They were supposed to stone you – no, make you stoned. Anyway, he was sitting cross-legged on his bed, wearing only a shirt and underpants, and rolling the finely chopped skins in a sheath made of five Rizlas when there was a tap on the door.

'May I come in?' called out Cheryl.

'Jesus wept.'

'Was that a "yes"?'

'*No.* Just a minute.' He guiltily scrabbled up the makings of his reefer and was in the midst of stowing them under the bed, his bottom in the air, when Cheryl walked in. 'I – I – I'm… I'm just…'

'So I see,' said Cheryl. She dropped an eyelid in one of her dummy's winks. A shock of embarrassment passed through the length of Hugh's body.

'I – I mean, I was just… I wasn't doing, you know… If you'll just give me a sec…' He was acutely aware of his vulnerable white legs and his none-too-pristine Y-fronts.

'Don't be silly! Nothink I haven't seen before!' She winked again. She was in a skittish mood. 'I thought we might have a little chat, Hugh. There is a sense of my having got off on the wrong foot, and I would like to make amends.' She threw herself across the end of the bed and, with her head resting on one hand, smiled up at him like a tigress through long false eyelashes. The scent of menthol cigarettes and of one or two gins mingled headily with her penetrating perfume.

'Erm. Yeah. I'll just put some trousers on.'

'You have better legs than your father!' She laughed, and patted the surface of the bed near to her. Nevertheless, Hugh struggled into his trousers and perched at the pillow end. He wondered if he could make a dash for it. He could bolt for the bog, claiming a sudden bout of googie withers; which, if things went on as they had begun, might turn out to be no less than the truth. 'Do not look so frightened, Hughie. I am not going to seduce you!' She smiled more widely. Her teeth were white and sharp, and there were, surely, too many of them. 'Unless you would like me to! Would you, Hughie? Oh, you are blushing. That is so sweet. But of course you do not want to be seduced by an old hag like me, who must seem a hundred years old to you. Do I seem a hundred to you, Hughie? I suppose I must do, compared to your dolly birds…' She gave a mock-rueful *moue* and ran a finger down her neck as far as the cleavage of her clingy silky dress. Hugh also noticed that the too-short dress had ridden up rather in the course of her flinging herself down, and that she had not redressed it. Against all reason and nature, his treacherous amoral renegade loins suddenly pulsed like a bilge pump and began to swell. 'No, seriously, a handsome young man like you must have a flock of dolly birds after him.'

'Erm...'

'No, no, you do not have to tell me. I am not one to pry. Only, if by any chance, Hughie, you are a little shy about girls or perhaps find them a little intimidating – no, do not blush, it is only natural, today's girls can be, I will not say promiscuous, but quite shockingly forward compared to my day – always feel free to come to me. For advice or a frank talk. Will you do that for me, Hughie? You can say anything to me, you know. I am quite unshockable! For example, when it comes to, well, "that side of things", I can –'

'I think I can hear Dada's car in the drive,' interrupted Hugh with a preposterous lie born of despair. His loins, as if realising the enormity of their venal lapse, had penitently retreated like whipped curs to the farthermost reaches of the Y-fronts.

'No, dear. Your father is at his office until late. The poor lamb works so hard. I gather you are not always patient with him, Hugh. You must try. He has had a hard life. I know how difficult it can be for an immigrant. My own father came to this country from Ireland. And, like yours, he worked like a coolie to give me a good standard of living. Unlike yours, however, he was not encumbered by a demanding wife. You do not mind if I am candid with you, Hughie? You are old enough now to face certain truths, I am sure. In fact, it may be a good thing that your mother's nerves are now out in the open. No one in your family realises, I believe, what a tremendous strain they have been on my Dermot. I say nothing against your mother, but a fool can see that Dermot has been tried beyond endurance. He has not been properly fed for years. Of course, we would all love to lie in bed all morning and day-dream about writing little stories – I can only hope that you do not take after your mother in that respect, Hugh, although I have to say the signs are ominous – yes, we would all like to fritter away the days in fantasy, but some of us prefer to face reality. Some of us put our families first. Do not get me wrong, Hughie – I am no saint. But I sincerely believe I can put my hand on my heart and say that I value the happiness of others, and especially your dear father, above my own. And I intend to look after you and your brothers and sister just as lovingly as if you were my own children, no matter how much resistance I am met with. All I ask in return, Hugh, is a little help with this heavy responsibility. I do not think that any of you will ever be truly happy without some discipline in your lives. Jane, I hate to say it, is a surly girl, while George is hopelessly unruly and Moe –'

'The Moo.'

'Yes, yes. Well, he is almost out of control. We cannot have that, can we, Hughie? The children look up to you and so I count on your support. After all, you are no longer a child. No, seriously, Hughie, you are a fine good-looking young man, and if I were a few years younger…!' Hugh's cowering loins shrank and tightened into a granny knot. 'Well. I have said sufficient. I am old enough to be your mother. All the same, I hope you will not look upon me as a mother, but as someone you can talk to, without awkwardness, as we are talking now. I will say no more. I think we have an understanding, do we not, Hughie? The kind of understanding which does not need words. Come over here, you silly boy. No? Must I come to you? Very well. I understand. I notice that you are perspiring a little, Hughie, and this tells me that you are a teensy bit over-awed by our new relationship. You must not be. You must feel that you can come to me at any time and simply put your arms around me like this. I will not misunderstand. I will not read into it more than is there. Perhaps you will have a teensy wash before lunch? And if you wish to give me a little kiss – there! – just so, on the lips, that is nothing to be ashamed of, nor any cause of the slightest embarrassment for we are perfectly comfortable with each other now, Hughie, are we not, like old friends? I am so glad we had this little talk. And now I must love you and leave you – no, don't ask me to stay – I cannot for I cannot trust Bernadette to plan and execute a proper meal for the children. I might just add, Hughie, that you would do well to show Bernadette a *leetle* less attention. She does not always, to put it mildly, quite understand her place. I do not blame her. She is Irish, and not as we are. But it would be as well not to encourage her. Besides, I am sure I can find a nice girl for you, Hughie! One who does not push herself at, frankly, rather rough Catholic boys. Yes, I am determined to take you up, Hugh, and –'

'Erm, excuse me – sorry, I must dash…' Hugh and his loins, now shrivelled beyond reclaim to the constitution of a walnut, lunged towards the door, snatched it open and thundered downstairs.

'Do you like having me as a sister, George?' asked Sabrina. George gaped. He had run into his sister's room but, as in some nightmare, she had been replaced by Sabrina.

'You aren't my sister.'

Sabrina laughed dismissively. 'Do you think I'm pretty?'

George stiffened. 'I don't know.'

'Well, George, look at me.' Reluctantly he did so. Sabrina looked like Stella the ice-skater in *Bunty*. Sort of glistening and pink, both succulent and repellent, like glazed ham. 'Well?'

'Up to a point,' he said carefully.

'Wouldn't you like me for a sister?' she wheedled.

'I already have a sister.'

'Not a dolly bird, though. Not a *pretty* sister.'

'Janey's pretty.'

'Jane's nice, but she's not *really* pretty, is she? You and I look a lot alike, don't we?'

'No.'

'We do. You look more like me than Jane. You're quite nice-looking, George. We could be brother and sister.'

'No, we couldn't.'

'If you won't have me as a sister, I'll tell Bradley about how you're always kissing me.'

'I'm not.'

'Ooh, fibber. You kissed me when we played Nurses that time.'

'I didn't. You did it to me.' He could not even say the word. Fear made his heart thud.

'Well, you *liked* it. You wanted more.'

'No,' said George, breaking out in a muck sweat.

'Yes, you did.' She changed to a huskier tone. 'I could kiss you again now, if you wanted. If you'll just let me be your sister.'

'No. *No.*'

'Ooh, I wonder what Bradley will say when I tell him you've been kissing me.'

'I did not.'

'I wonder what *Cheryl* will say.'

'Well, go and tell them, Sabrina. I don't care.' He looked defiantly into her too-blue eyes; but in the face of their painted stare, his gaze faltered. Bitterly he looked away. Sabrina had won. She wouldn't tell immediately – she might never tell – but the possibility would hang over him like a sword from now on so that sleep would be a stranger to him, and dread his constant companion.

'Would you like to play with my gonks, George?' He shook his head and, turning on his heel, relinquished the field.

In the playroom, the Moo was busy crayonning on the wall. He was adding an exciting episode to the Bayeux-like frieze of Jack Pluff's adventures. In concert with the Sea Hare, who was firing a bazooka, Pluff was attacking a Mini Minor. In the next frame, a woman with pink trousers and red lips was flying out of the exploded car and about to plummet into the smiling jaws of an expectant Fray Bentos. The Moo barely looked up when Janey arrived out of breath to fling herself down on a mattress; then Hugh, to fling himself flat on his back on the sofa; and, lastly, George, white and strained-looking, to lament:

'The Chummy Bums have taken over the world! We'll just have to live here. Let's barricade the door.' The others looked at him sympathetically but, as if exhausted, did not move. George spread-eagled himself on a bean bag and lay still, apart from the occasional involuntary thrashing of his legs as memories assailed him.

'I am going to kill Cheryl Chummy Bum,' remarked Hugh at last. George sat up with a look of interest.

'It would be better to hire an assassin.'

'I've only got about ten bob. What sort of an assassin could I get for that?'

'A sloppy one,' said the Moo, thinking that Jack Pluff would do the job for less than ten bob. Fray Bentos would do it – indeed, *had* done it – for a couple of pork chops.

'Foody Fenella threatened Sabrina,' said Janey. 'She didn't even flinch.'

'*Himmel,*' said George, impressed.

'She has nerves of steel,' said Hugh.

'While my nerves are in shreds!' Janey's imitation of Maman, being in poor taste, drew a stern look from the Moo.

'I s'pose that now you are sharing a room with your Enemy, mein Fuehrer,' said Hugh, 'you have kissed and made up. Two squalid little boys in love. It is the pits.'

'At least I'm not soppily and weedily in love with a wet Mexican girl,' retaliated George, but without conviction.

'I've given up the Mexican girl,' yawned Hugh. 'I'm going to form a group and make a hit record.'

'Like Freddie and the Dreamers,' sneered George, knowing his brother's contempt for the comical Liverpudlian combo.

'No, *actually*, you gormless blob of squalor – like The Kinks.'

'*Na-nana-na-na. Na-nana-na-na,*' growled George in a fair rendering of the opening chords of *You Really Got Me*, to which they had all thrilled when The Kinks, dressed in their red hunting coats, had rocked the *Ready, Steady, Go* studio to the rafters.

They all sang *You Really Got Me* for a while, with varying degrees of accuracy, until the Moo said:

'Luh'le Shuggy, read Maman's letter again.'

'All right.' He fished a folded sheet of paper out of the back pocket of his trousers, and cleared his throat:

'"Darlings!

What a 'Dodgy' business, quoi? I'm so sorry my nerves let me down, but you must *not* worry in the slightest because I am already on the mend and will be home before you know it, Gareth says. Gareth is my doctor, Dr Rhys, who has made many things clear to me. It turns out that Dada was mistaken because, according to the latest science, there's no such thing as 'nerves'. Fancy that! All the same, I've given up the ciggies and the slimming pills which, it turns out, were not *at all* good for me, so I shall be fat again, boo-hoo, but never mind. I've even stopped taking Dada's miracle Valium which Gareth, who is very strict (!) also disapproves of. And, do you know, I feel as if a mist in front of my eyes has lifted, and I can see more clearly – when I'm not asleep, that is, because I sleep a lot. But I am sloppier every day, the Moo, and walking by the sea, reading, and even writing bits and bobs which Gareth says is good for me rather than a waste of time. He likes what I write – at least, he says he does! – and pooh-poohs my inferiority complex, which is bracing. I have a room with a sea view that I share with a

Miss Bickerstaff from Bolton, who is most amusing" –'

'She means Barking,' interrupted George gloomily.

'It is *not* a loony bin, mein Fuehrer,' said Janey.

'"She keeps me cheerful with some very clever music hall 'turns' from her professional days. Her Gracie Fields is as tuneful as her Great Bombasto is surprising. I am so sorry, darlings, about my behaviour in the Zodiac. It was all a stupid mistake. I was so nervy and run down I scarcely knew what I was doing. You were so clever and brave, mein Fuehrer, to save me."'

'It was Theo's artificial respiration that saved her,' commented George.

'"I'll have lots of stories to tell you and Spiv, the Moo darling, when I get back, and I miss you very much. I miss you all. Luh'le Shuggy and Janey, you will look after the boys, I know, and be sensible. Do not bait Dada, Luh'le Shuggy, but be patient with him; for he means no harm really. He's just confused. It is only a Seven Year Itch sort of thing, I think – though Twenty-One Year Itch is more like it!"'

'Wait till she hears about the Chummy Bum invasion,' said George darkly. 'That'll push her over the edge.'

'We won't be telling her about that, mein Fuehrer,' warned Hugh. '"Tell Bernie," he went on reading, "that she is to cook green vegetables three times a week or at least twice. Brussels sprouts are cheap and plentiful at this time of year. I have been reading that they contain vitamins and iron which growing children require. Give my love to the Boys upstairs. I have written to Theo whom, as you know, you can rely on.

My love to you all, darlings.

A bientôt, Your Maman xxxx"'

Hugh replaced the letter in his back pocket. There was a general silence. He rose from the sofa and went over to the Moo who was standing very cast down, with his nose touching the wall.

'Who's that fellow taking out the Mini with his bazooka?' he asked the Moo, whose eyes had now filled with tears. 'He's got very long floppy ears.'

'Nobody,' said the Moo in a trembly voice.

'I like the dog with the savage smile. He's going to eat that woman falling out of the sky!'

'He's not a dog. 'E's a wolf. He's called –' He stopped himself in time from uttering the sacred name.

'Let's play a record,' said George. 'You choose, the Moo.'

'I don't want a record.'

'Dabs wants a record!' cried Dabs. 'Dabs will have her *favourite* record, which am the Choo-Choo Song and it am being sung by Dabs's *best* person, Big Eva!' The Moo could not let this imbecility pass.

'It's *Little* Eva, Dabs, you big flabby fool. And it's not a spastic Choo-Choo Song – it's called *The Locomotion*. Don't you know *anything*? And you only want it because it's my favourite record. Why do you have to copy everything I do?'

'Dabs doesn't,' squeaked Dabs. 'The Moo am copying Dabs.'

'That is… that is … *such* a lie, Dabs.'

The opening saxophones of *The Locomotion* blared out of the Dansette as George placed the needle on the record.

'Dabs am doing the Choo-Choo dance,' claimed Dabs, waving her arms in the air.

'That's not how you do it, Dabs, you steaming great nit,' shouted the Moo. 'It's like *this*.' He began to work his arms like a steam engine's pistons and to chuff forward.

'*Everybody's doing a brand new dance, nah-ah-ah*,' sang Little Eva.

'*C'mon baby, do The Locomotion*,' chorused the children, joining the Moo and chuffing along in a line facing the bay window. '*A dada-dada-dada, if you'll just take a chance, nah-ah-ah (c'mon baby, do The Locomotion)…*' Soon, even Dabs was making, under Spiv's violent tuition, the proper moves (*You gotta swing your hips, nah-ah… c'mon baby – jump up… jump back! Woe I think you got the kna-ack…*).

But Little Eva was barely two-thirds of the way through her instructions, superfluous in the Moo's case but very much to the purpose in Dabs's, when there was an abrupt ripping sound, like a violent burp, and then silence. The four children, arrested in mid-chuff, turned as one. Sabrina was bending over the Dansette.

'You've scratched the record,' said George. 'That's a… a…' He groped for the words to express the enormity of the crime, and fell back on the language of Bernie: 'a mortal sin.'

'Well, what do you expect with such a funny little record-player?'

replied Sabrina unrepentantly. She straightened up and regarded them all with her head slightly on one side and with a smile slightly tinged with sadness. 'Never mind. I expect Cheryl will bring our radiogram over – that's a radio and gramophone combined,' she added kindly. 'But I can make do with this meanwhile, I suppose.' With a coy sideways look she held up the LP she was carrying and waggled it alluringly. 'I've brought you some real music as a treat.' The children watched in silence, as if helpless, as she fitted the record on to the turntable, switched the dial from 45rpm to 33 rpm, and lifted the stylus half-way across the spinning disc:

Doe, a deer, a female deer,
Ray, a drop of golden sun…

With a fixed smile, Sabrina began to prance, flicking her pony tail and, at key moments, moving forward to mouth the lyrics exaggeratedly at Janey and George whom she had identified as the weak links in the Blyte chain, with an even lower embarrassment threshold than Hugh and the Moo. But even the latter did not know what to do with themselves or where to look – if any of them had been able to look at each other, they might have been able to break the circuit of embarrassment. As it was, they were paralysed, trapped, forced either to stare dumbly at the walls or to watch Sabrina dancing with expression – until they were unexpectedly delivered by Cheryl.

'Come along now, all of you.' She clapped her hands. Janey turned off the music with relief. 'Come along and wash your hands before your meal. It is a pity none of you dances, like Sabrina. Perhaps she will show you some steps.'

'The Moo dances,' said the Moo. 'At least, he used to,' he added darkly.

'Have you been drawing on the walls, dear?' said Cheryl in a clipped voice. 'What *would* your mother say?'

'She would say: "Aren't you clever, the Moo darling?"'

'It is *not* clever, Moo dear, to draw on walls. And you shall not have any pudding because I will not be spoken to in that fashion. In addition, it will do you no harm to lose a little weight.'

'You need weight to be sloppy. And I don't like pudding,' said the Moo untruthfully.

'Well, that is good because cheeky little boys do not get pudding.

Does anyone else not care for any pudding?'

'I don't,' said George.

'Good. Then there will be all the more for the rest of us.'

'I rather think I'll forgo the pleasure of your pudding myself on this occasion,' drawled Hugh in a tone of voice opposite to what he felt.

'Me too,' muttered Janey from behind her hair.

'I expect Janey is watching her figure,' said Sabrina. 'Like me.'

'I am surprised that Janey *has* a figure,' said Cheryl. 'It certainly cannot be deduced from the clothes she wears. And please remove your hair from your face when you are speaking to me, Jane.'

There was a muttered sound from Janey which may have been 'I'm not.'

'And I am disappointed in you, Hugh. I thought we had an understanding. Obviously you are too young after all to be treated in an adult way. Perhaps you avoid pudding in the belief that it will rid you of spots. I am afraid it will not. Spots are simply inevitable for the adolescent with greasy skin...'

'You mustn't mention Luh'le Shuggy's spots,' reproved the Moo. 'It upsets him.'

'He's sensitive,' added Janey. 'He's a writer, you know.'

'So I gather,' said Cheryl. 'But for how long, we wonder, when he is thrown into the real world and has to put food on his own table?'

'I don't expect I'll be eating until I'm an old man of at least thirty,' said Hugh modestly.

13

IT was bedtime at the end of what had seemed to the Blytes a very long day.

The Moo and Bernie had goaded each other up the dark stairs, and Bernie had stayed with him while he put himself to bed. She had told him a story about Pat Tim and his bellicose billy-goat until the Moo's eyes had closed.

Now it was the turn of George and Bradley, who met at the bathroom basin under strict orders from Cheryl to brush their teeth and wash their faces – in other words, a challenge to their powers of duplicity.

'Don't tell me, Blyte,' Bradley was saying scornfully, 'that you *actually* brush your teeth, you baby.'

''Course not,' said George. He deftly squeezed a small blob of toothpaste into his mouth, briefly swilled it round with water, and spat. 'There.' He breathed into the Enemy's face. 'Foolproof.'

'Minty breath might fool your Mum, mush, but it won't fool mine. You're heading for a clip round the ear.'

'I think not, Four Eyes – I can lie with a straight face. I don't go all shifty like you, pushing my specs about.' The Enemy sighed with long-suffering tolerance.

'Look and learn, Blyte.' He picked up George's toothbrush. 'Feel the bristles.'

'Yeah. So what?'

'Wakey, wakey, Blyte – they're *dry*, see? She feels your bristles and if they're dry, she knows you haven't brushed.'

'*Donner und Blitzen,*' said George. He had to hand it Mrs Chummy Bum. 'Okay. So you wet the brushes and *I'll…*' He smeared a dab of toothpaste in the basin to suggest recent and copious usage.

'That is actually quite good thinking,' approved Bradley.

'It'd be easier to brush our spastic teeth,' grumbled George.

There was a light tap on Hugh's door. Slumped on his bed, writing his novel on his knee, Hugh stiffened with horror. Hell's teeth, was there no escape? He decided to remain very still and silent in the hope that whoever it was would go away. He reviewed his evening's work:

Rex Darkling was tired. Mortally tired. He had tired of Lady Isabella and her incessant amorous demands. He was tired of the money and lionising his best-selling existential novel had won him. It may well have been the most profound and searing indictment of modern society since the suicide of Socrates, but to Rex, it was simply a bore. Wearily he took up his pen. "Chers Monsieurs," he wrote, "I thank the French Academy for offering me the highest honour at its disposal, but I fear I cannot accept. Please give the large cash prize to the Poor of Paris..." In the street far below the Notting Hill penthouse, children were playing hopscotch and cricket. The sound of their innocent laughter floated up through Rex's superbly-restored Baroque windows, and mingled with J.S. Bach's eighth symphony which was playing quietly on the walnut-veneered radiogram. All the children would be dead soon. When they dropped the Bomb. Not today, perhaps; or even to-morrow. But inevitably. And soon. There'd be no more laughter in the streets after that. The world would be one big mushroom cloud. And good riddance.

He turned to look with distaste at the leggy blonde girl on the king-size water-bed, wearing only a slip and a velvet choker. If only he could be innocent again like the children! The girl returned his look with dumb admiration. She was as magnificent and sensual as a jaguar in the way she totally inhabited her astounding body. How he envied the simple peace of such a blank unreflecting mind! The telephone rang. Wearily he picked up the receiver. "No, I don't care what Colour Supplement you represent. I don't give interviews any more." He replaced the receiver. The blonde moved with feline grace from the bed and began to caress his neck and shoulders. "Leave me," said Rex wearily. "I cannot," she murmured huskily, moistening her index finger in her full mouth and drawing it slowly down the length of –

There was another tap at the door. Hugh tried to ignore it. He was not happy with what he had written. He was mortally tired of Rex Darkling, who was taking an age to reach the point of suicide. Perhaps the bird on the bed could kill him now, and embark on a crime spree. Plus, a sex spree. That would cheer the bleeding book up a bit. Perhaps she had a twin sister. That would cheer Rex up, to have an affair with twins. Siamese twins. Joined at their curvaceous hips. *They'd* show bloody D.H. Lawrence a thing or two.

There was a third tap on the door, which opened. Sabrina came in. She was wearing a pink, flimsy, gauzy garment which only reached to a point just below a pair of brief panty-type things, leaving her smooth golden legs bare. She was like something out of *Tit-Bits*, the only place where Hugh had previously glimpsed the fabled Shortie Nightie. And here it was, so to speak, in the flesh. Sabrina was smiling at him prettily. Her hair was tied up with ribbons into two cute bunches, and she was wearing – hell's teeth – red lipstick.

'I've brought you an ickle present, Hugh,' she simpered, bringing out from behind her back an indescribable creature from hell, sort of like a werewolf Humpty Dumpty. 'Say "Hello" to Matt Monro Gonk, Hugh,' she said, settling herself Cheryl-like across the end of his bed. 'He sings beautifully! Don't you, little Gonk? Yes you do!'

'Have you brushed your teeth, George?'
'Yes, Mrs Cholmondeley. I mean, Cheryl.'
'Bradley?'
'Yes, Mum.'
'Well, lights out then.'
'I usually read for a bit,' said George, reaching for his *Creepy Tales.*
'Not tonight, George. It is late.'
'It's not my bedtime yet, actually.'
'Do not make me repeat myself, George. You will go to sleep. Now, get into bed.'
'But I'm too hot.'
'Do not be tiresome. It is a chilly night. Now, get in.'
'But I'm *boiling*.'
'Very well. If you wish to freeze, you may. Now, lights out.'
The boys both had bedside lamps which they switched off

simultaneously, leaving only a wedge of light shining from the landing through the half-open door. Then, as Cheryl reached the far end of the landing, that light too was switched off.

George lay awake in the dark on top of his bed, freezing, missing Maman, wishing that he could animate Goose to clear the recesses of his bed of the snakes which he was certain had sneakily returned. He must have dozed because he was jerked into full consciousness by a ghostly figure, like a white sheet, flitting past his bed and out of the room. George shivered. He was even colder than before. He decided to investigate.

The passage was very dark, but he was reassured by the distant expostulation of Dada's voice downstairs. He groped his way forward. The bathroom light was on. He peered around the door and was greeted by an untoward spectacle.

Janey lay on her back, on her unforgiving camp bed, in the corner of her own room, in the dark, staring at the ceiling, while rivulets of tears flowed down the watershed of her face, soaking the pillow on either side. It was too early for her to go to bed, but then again there was not much to do after Mrs Chummy Bum's 'hay tea'. Television was not allowed because it was bad for your eyes or for some other part of you. Record-playing was out because it was too loud, and would wake the Moo who slept above the Dansette and could in fact sleep through a World War; or else, later, it would keep the Enemies awake; or else because it would be a pleasure and consolation to her. And besides, all the children had to be out of the way by the time Dada came home so that he and Mrs Chummy could dine alone and in splendour, if Mrs C.'s perfume and black evening dress were anything to go by. 'Dear Jesus,' she prayed. 'Please bring Maman back soon. And let the Chummy Bums go away and leave us all, and especially Dada, alone, and never be heard of again. Thanking you in advance, love Janey.'

She had wanted as a last resort to read in bed with some Horlicks. But Horlicks was too heavy last thing, apparently. Plus, it was ruinous to the teeth. So no joy there. And then Sabrina was in the room, prancing and primping and, oh, chattering on and on, until Janey had been forced to feign sleep. Sabrina had promptly slipped out in her Shortie Nightie, doubtless to torture some other unsuspecting soul, and would inevitably come clumping back just as Janey really was dropping off. It was *murder*. If only, if only Theo could receive the desperate telepathic messages she was beaming through the ceiling. If only he would swoop down and swaddle her in a thick blanket and carry her off to his big, warm, comfy double bed. If only the black Mini would come screeching up the drive and bear her away to a bright future. If only Jesus would put forth his hand and restore order and sanity to this hell-hole of muddle and madness. If only... The two saddest words in the language of Shakespeare.

'I 'ave failed you, my leetle friend,' said Foody Fenella sadly out of the dark.

'Yes, you have rather.'

'I am *désolée... désolée...*'

'Matt Monro Gonk is absolutely my favourite gonk, Hugh, and I've brought him for you. Are you going to sing a song for Hugh, little gonk? What? You're too shy? Aaaah.'

'Go away, please, Sabrina.'

'Don't you want a gonk of your own?'

'No.'

'But he's a WUVVERLY gonk! Aren't you, Matt Monro Gonk? Yes, you are! No, seriously, Hugh, I want you to have him. He'll bring you luck with your writings.'

'I don't need luck. Take the thing away and go. I'm busy.' He pretended to resume working. There was a sniffle. Sabrina had thrown an arm across her eyes. Hugh did not like this one little bit.

'*Now* what's the matter?' he asked irritably.

'Please don't hate me, Hugh.'

'Why should I hate you, Sabrina?'

'Because I'm not clever or interesting like you, Hugh.' There was no easy reply to this, so Hugh said lamely:

'I don't hate you. Now, if you don't mind –'

'So you like me? Just a little bit?'

'Yes. Now, will you please –'

'I was hoping you'd like me a little more. Once you got to know me.' She leaned towards him, wiping away her tears with the backs of her hands. For a second, just before he quickly averted his eyes, Hugh fancied that he saw down the front of her nightie – saw a perky little bosom which, hell's teeth, was still visible in outline through the gauzy material. A klaxon went off in his underpants. His appalled loins, suddenly torn between instinctive tumescence and rational shame, briefly reared up – and then shrank down again, crawling away to lie even more doggo than they had that morning. 'We could spend more time together, Hugh. I'd like that. Wouldn't you? I wouldn't annoy you, Hughie. I'd just want to be with you. I could watch you writing. I'd be as quiet as a little mouse. Can I, Hughie? Can I watch you?' She brought to bear upon him the twin beams of her astonishing, freshly-washed cobalt-blue eyes. Then she shifted her position, putting a supporting hand, as if unawares, on his leg. Hell's *teeth*, thought Hugh. And: *Hughie.*

'Well, Sabrina, it's a nice thought but, you know, writers like to be alone when they're at it. Besides, it would be very boring to watch!'

'I wouldn't be in the least bored,' said Sabrina, making her eyes big and uncrossing her long golden legs. *What if I put my hand on them?* Then, *what are you THINKING of, Hugh? Are you MAD?*

His genitals contracted beyond all recovery. What Black Art did the female line of the Cholmondeleys possess that they routinely shrivelled loins for a year and a day?

'Come along, Sabrina. You're a child.'

'No. I'm not.'

'Just go away. You're too young for… for…' He didn't know how this sentence ended. He could feel his testicles blackening already. How long before they dropped off?

'I'm very grown up for my age. Everyone says so. My friend Melinda, she's only a month older than me and she has a boyfriend who's eighteen. Older than you.' She patted his leg pointedly. 'Don't you find me the teensiest bit attractive, Hughie?' There was an affecting little break in her voice.

I admit that there is something perversely attractive about your spooky doll-like appearance; but the idea of ME and a child of THIRTEEN… well, it's at best squalid and at worst obscene, thought Hugh.

'No,' he said.

'I'm so sad,' said Sabrina, leaning towards him, offering herself for comfort. Hugh closed his eyes. 'You'd find me attractive if I were Bernie. You wouldn't turn her down for being only thirteen.'

'That's enough, Sabrina. Go. And my name is not "Hughie".'

'All right. *Hugh*. But you're wasting your time, you know, making doggy eyes at Bernie. She has lots of boyfriends. Men with motorbikes. And cars. I hear them. They park outside 'Ponderosa'. Bernie doesn't get out –'

'Bugger off, Sabrina.'

'Yes. I will. *Hugh*. But I don't think your father is going to be pleased to hear that you use such bad language.'

Sabrina flounced from the room. Hugh put his face in a pillow. His heart, which he usually managed to keep cloaked from the image of Bernie with other men – his heart was bleeding. He banged his face into the pillow. A spotty youth with greasy skin could not hope to compete. Bernie held his hand as she would a little brother's. Of *course* she did. What had he been *thinking*?

He sighed and, always the true artist, turned wearily to amend his manuscript:

… the blonde girl on the king-size water-bed, wearing only a pink flimsy Shortie Nightie *and a velvet choker…*

Looking oddly mole-like without his commanding specs, Bradley was standing at the bathroom basin, his pyjama trousers around his ankles, scrubbing with a nail brush at his sheet. He turned convulsively and peered myopically at George with red-rimmed eyes.

'You can leave that, Cholmondeley,' said George casually. 'I'll get you another. Pyjamas too.'

'Mum'll kill me when she finds out.'

'She won't. We'll stash the evidence under my bed and tell Bernie. She'll sort it out. She won't snitch.'

Bradley looked so helpless without his specs, and so grateful, that George couldn't help adding: 'Don't worry, mush. Our whole family gets googie withers on a regular basis.'

'What's that?'

'What it sounds like. Dada's always wee-weeing in his bed.' Bradley sniggered.

George restored him to his bed with a clean dry sheet and a pair of his own pyjamas. He lay on his back in the dark. He felt a tremendous sense of victory. Not in the old sense when, to have discovered the Enemy in the aftermath of a bed-wetting would have been to humiliate and vanquish him forever. No, he sensed a victory over their differences, and a recognition of a common humanity. For who is not liable under pressure to wet their bed out of the blue? The Enemy was but a man, a vulnerable human, as he himself was. He felt much as he imagined Attila had felt when, in AD 452, according to Arthur Mee, the great Hun, backed by his slant-eyed horde, had Rome at his mercy; but, after a private word with the helpless Pope Leo, had inexplicably wheeled his troops away and spared the Holy City.

'Blyte. I haven't done that for years.' Bradley's voice came with difficulty out of the darkness.

''Course not.'

'I 'spect it's the sudden change and that. Also...' He hesitated.

'What?'

'Nothing.'

'What?'

'Well, I usually have this thing I sleep with. You know. I'm used to it.'

'What thing?'

'You know. A sort of stuffed thing.'

'What? Like a teddy bear, you mean, Cholmondeley?'

'A frog, actually, Blyte.'

'A frog.'

'Yes.'

'Well, where is this *frog*, Cholmondeley?'

'In my suit case. I had to smuggle it in.'

'Well, why didn't you unpack it?' asked George, knowing very well why. 'You'd better get it now.' He heard Bradley get out of bed, unclip his case and settle back into bed with a sigh. 'Has the frog got a name?' He couldn't resist a touch of sarcasm.

'Yes.'

'What?' There was a pause, as of someone struggling with themselves. Then there was a suppressed laugh.

'Froggy.'

'Froggy?' George also started to laugh but didn't quite know why.

'Froggy,' confirmed Bradley, failing now to suppress his laughter.

'That's nothing,' said George. 'Mine's called... *Goose.*'

'Goose?' Bradley nearly choked. 'You've got a *goose?*'

'No-o. No-o,' hiccuped George. 'That's not the funny bit. The funny bit is he's not … a goose –' here he roared into his pillow while Bradley giggled excitedly, saying: 'What is he? What is he?'

'He's a…' spluttered George. 'He's a… a *sock.*'

It was too much for both of them.

'Wha'? Grrr,' complained the Moo, before sliding back down the helter-skelter of sleep to the sound of stifled guffaws.

'I'm going to read my comics,' said George when at last the hysteria had subsided.

'So am I,' said Bradley. 'Here. Put my dressing gown on.' He flung it over. George wrapped himself up gratefully, and shone his torch eagerly on to *The Terror That Comes In The Night*. Bradley's torch shone redly under his blankets.

Suddenly the room was bathed in light. Cheryl was standing in the doorway with her finger on the light switch.

'Did you think that I would not hear the commotion you are causing?' she asked. The boys did not reply. 'Did I not expressly forbid you to read, George?' She snatched up his comic and torch. 'I cannot abide disobedience. Your father shall hear of this. Now get into bed properly.'

'But –'

'*Get into bed.* No, properly. Put your knees down. That's better. And what are you hiding, Bradley?'

'Nothing, Mummy.'

'That is not true. I can see by your face.' She yanked the covers back. Bradley was holding a copy of *Bunty* in one hand, and his torch in the other. Nestling against his neck was Froggy. Cheryl smacked him across the face. 'That is not for reading after lights out. It is for lying to me.' She held up the *Bunty* and shook her head in a puzzled way. Then she held up Froggy. 'I thought we had agreed that you were too old for this,' she said. 'George does not have a stuffed toy. You do not want him to think you are a sissy, do you?'

'No, Mummy.' Bradley's voice was wayward with the effort of holding back tears. He was rubbing his cheek.

'Well then. Not a peep out of either of you. Goodnight.' There was a silence. 'I said "Goodnight".'

'Goodnight, Mummy.'

'Goodnight, Mrs Cholmondeley.'

'It is "Cheryl", George.'

'Yes, Cheryl.'

For a few minutes after she had left, George and Bradley lay in a darkness and silence broken only by the Moo's incoherent sleep-talking: 'No...Mam... no... aaargh... Pluff!...' Then soft footfalls were heard. A voice whispered:

'O'Bond here. Bernie O'Bond. Oh-oh-seven. Licensed to Thrill! Does this belong to anybody?' A beam of torchlight lit up Froggy, and he dancing.

'Me,' said Bradley.

'He was on the landing windowsill. He looked awful lonely. Here!' Bernie fired Froggy into Bradley's bed. The torch beam played over George's clenched face. 'You don't look too comfy, mein Fuehrer. Will Goose do a sweep?' Her soft hand pressed briefly against his cheek, then burrowed under the pillow where the dormant Goose lay. In a flash he was all savage activity, flipping up the blankets and laying waste with snarls to whatever lurked beneath, even nipping George's toes in his enthusiasm for snake-killing, which made George giggle nervously. 'Okay so. All clear. Mission completed. Bernie O'Bond signing off. Oh-oh-seven. Licensed to kiss boys.' She kissed George and then, whisking over to Bradley's bed, ordered: 'C'mon now. Face the music.' Bradley presented his smarting cheek, which was kissed with a loud smack. Then she was gone.

George breathed out contentedly. Bradley did the same.

'Bradley,' said George.

'Yeah, George?'

'You know that time in the camps when Sabrina was there, playing nurses and that...?'

'You mean that time she kissed you? Errrggh, eh?'

'Yeah. Errrgh.'

'To be honest, George, there are times Sabrina scares the pants off me.'

'I know what you mean. 'Night.'

''Night.'

'It's a filthy world,' said Roger, pushing his empty pint glass towards Lorraine with whom he was alone in the Tennis Club bar. She was still dressed in white; but this time it was a piquant little lacy mini-dress. Large pink plastic earrings dangled from her exquisite ears.

'Is it, Roger? You are referring, I suppose, to the social and economic injustice which infects the world, and which only the death of capitalism can cure?'

'By God, Lorraine, that's bloody marvellous. Where'd you learn to talk like that?'

'At Kingston Tech., Roger, where I took a degree in Sociology.'

'Bloody marvellous.' He watched her easing beer out of the tap. 'I didn't understand a word of it, but it sounded bloody marvellous. Why are you a barmaid? Why aren't you the chairman of bloody Shell or something? I'd love to put a tiger in your tank, Lorraine,' he added, quoting the popular advertisement for Shell petrol.

'Because Shell is a Dutch company, Roger; and, besides, I like being a barmaid. You meet all sorts and conditions of men –'

'I bet. Men in all sorts of conditions,' agreed Roger.

'And you contribute only marginally, if at all, to the exploitation of the masses by a corrupt capitalistic system.' She smiled prettily at Roger and, flipping open her compact, adjusted some strands of the back-combed yellow hair, and then refreshed her glossy white lipstick. Roger watched her, mute with admiration. That was the thing about Lorraine: she was a marvel, bloody well-assembled, a... *whole* woman, with a wholeness that amounted to more than the sum of her parts, bloody marvellous though those parts were.

'I'd love to be a bloody pinko, Lorraine. Do you think you could teach me?'

'Just because I am conscious of social ills, Roger, and do not wish to compound them, it doesn't mean I'm a Communist. As a matter of fact, I'm politically unaffiliated.'

'Are you, Lorraine? By God, I'd love to 'filiate you, Lorraine. You're a bloody marvel.' Lorraine laughed kindly.

'Am I, Roger? That's very perceptive of you.' She smoothed her dress over her hips. Bloody Swinging hips, if it came to that. 'This is your last pint, Roger,' she said, handing him the drink.

'Don't say that, Lorraine. It casts a pall. As long as I can believe that this is the penultimate pint and not the ultimate, I can cling to sanity.'

'It's after hours, Roger, and Colonel Lamb would have my guts for garters if he knew I was serving you.'

184

'Bugger the old bigot, Lorraine. The question is: are you *ever* going to have a drink with me?'

'Yes, Roger. I am.'

'That is *bloody* marvellous, Lorraine. I'd better start planning the whole thing. Now let me guess what you'd like... Double Babycham? No. Cherry Brandy? No. Something sophisticated, I expect, like a White Lady or a vodka and orange – wossname – a spanner.'

'A screwdriver, Roger. And what I am partial to is a pint of Newcastle Brown.' Roger groaned with pleasure.

'I wish we could swap places, Lorraine. I would love to serve you a pint of Newcastle Brown.'

'The Tennis Club doesn't stock Newcastle Brown, Roger. However, I have a supply in the flat, and you can come up there now and serve me a pint.'

'*Can* I, Lorraine? That would be... that would be...'

'Yes, Roger – bloody marvellous. However, I'm well aware that you are a bit drunk and that you will make a pass at me. Now, I may let you kiss me once or, if it goes well, twice. But that will be all. I will then walk you home.'

'That would be heaven, Lorraine. But I don't only want to kiss you, you know. I want to go out with you. I promise to get a job. I'd love a job in a bar.'

'Well, that's very nice, Roger. But it's not your lack of a job which causes me to hesitate. You will understand that it is less than alluring to be asked out by a man who has taken to drink because his business has failed and his wife has left him.'

'Call this "taken to drink", Lorraine? I'll show you "taken to drink"!'

'Exactly, Roger. You make my point for me.'

'Do I? God, you're bloody marvellous. I'd stop drinking in a second for you, Lorraine. Do you know what I like about you, Lorraine?'

'You like everything about me, Roger.'

'D'you know, Lorraine,' said Roger, amazed. 'You're right. I *do*. But most of all, Lorraine, I like your nose. That is one bloody marvellous hooter, Lorraine.'

'Thank you, Roger. I find it useful for looking down at people with.'

'You are a witty woman, Lorraine. I like talking to you. You're much cleverer than me, but you don't squash me. I've never talked to my wife like I talk to you. I always seem to be minding my Ps and Qs when I talk to her.'

'Will she come back to you, Roger?'

'No. She won't come back. Because I'm broke. I thought for one horrible moment that, when the business went belly up, she'd offer to stick by me. I should have known her deepest nature would prevail. I feel sorry for her, to tell the truth, because I'm not sure that Blyte bloke has enough dosh. Actually I feel sorry for *him*. He's got no idea what he's in for. I'm not drinking because I'm sad, Lorraine – I'm drinking because I feel guilty at being so relieved that she's gone.'

'What about your children?'

'That is a tricky one, Lorraine. I love my kids. I really do. But, you see, they're born, sight for sore eyes, you're over the blessed moon, more love than you can shake a stick at, so on, you work for them every hour God sends, time flies, you look up from your desk and they're grown up, Sabrina looking at you funny as if you were a bloody stuffed dodo or something. It unnerves me, Lorraine. I lose confidence. I should've been at home more when they were little. They don't tell you that, though – they tell you to go out and work and bring home the bloody bacon to wifey and the babies. Now, I wish I'd been a barmaid. And it's no better with Bradley, my boy, he's always off on his own, or with the Blyte boy, and if I speak to him he looks bored or embarrassed or both. And I want to give him a big kiss, Lorraine. But he'd only be even more embarrassed – and I can't give him a big kiss anyway because I'm too embarrassed. Wouldn't it be bloody marvellous, Lorraine, if there was no embarrassment? If we didn't have to waddle about with our bloody buttocks clenched?'

'One's buttocks are not clenched, Roger.'

'I can see that, Lorraine. Bloody marvellous buttocks, Lorraine.'

'This is a moment when a little more embarrassment on your part, Roger, would become you. Now, Newcastle Brown for me and strong coffee for you, I think.'

In the small hours of the morning, Hugh lay awake in the dark. The muddle of the day – the menacing Cheryl, the macabre Sabrina – was taking sleep away. He felt... besmirched. He wanted to pray –

to pray that everything might be restored to the time before Dada and Maman had fallen – but words wouldn't flow. They were as desiccated as his shrivelled loins.

Suddenly Hugh became alert to a sound like a whimper. It gradually increased in volume to a low moan. It was either quite loud and distant or, worse, near and quite soft. 'It's the wind,' he told himself, although he knew it was not. The sound grew louder, and rose in pitch to a strangulated wail. His scalp crawled. The wail broke up into a kind of prolonged sobbing. 'Bloody vixen,' hoped Hugh. But while a vixen could sound like a woman being murdered, this cry seemed neither animal nor human, but beyond the human, contaminating the sleep of everyone in the house.

The Moo dreamt that Fray Bentos was trapped in a burning building. Janey dreamt of the little mermaid who, for love of a mortal man, shed her skin and walked screaming on to the strand, where every step was like treading on knives. George dreamt that he had caught the big pike; but, as the fish turned its head on a long skinny neck to look at him, George knew that to look on its face would be to go mad. Only Cheryl woke; and, momentarily desolated by the mournful sound, shivered. For the first time in years she thought of her father and his stories of the old country.

The dire, long-drawn-out sobs were intolerable. Hugh wanted to leap out of bed – but didn't. A strange lethargy overshadowed him as if he were paralysed within a waking dream. Just as he was on the point of forcing himself up, the horror of not knowing the source of the sound more terrible than knowing, the sound ceased.

There was a tap on the door. His trance of fear was broken.

'Come in.'

A figure in white darted to the side of his bed.

'I woke frightened,' said Bernie. 'There was something not right. It put the heart across me.'

'There was a sound,' said Hugh. 'The wind, I think.'

'There's no wind.'

'Well, it's okay now.'

'I'm still scared. Will I hop into your bed for a minute?'

'You can't do that, Bernie.'

'Ah, sure, don't be squalid, Luh'le Shuggy. Where's the harm? Shift over.' She gave him a push and, climbing in, arranged his left arm around her neck and snuggled her head against his shoulder. 'Now!' she said with finality. Hugh could feel her body all the way down his left side.

'Jesus,' he said.

'Sorry. Did I pinch you? Isn't this grand? I feel safe now.'

'Yes.'

'Ah, Shugs. Aren't you the lad?'

'I suppose I am.'

Bernie fell asleep almost at once. Hugh lay awake, listening to her breathing, keeping watch, holding his painfully numb arm immobile, like a trophy. She smelt like Eden before the Fall. His sensation of taint was washed from him like oil from feathers; and slowly, sweetly, life spread its wings again within his withered loins and carried him upward on a slope of calm air into the blue. Desire, thought Hugh, is by its nature limitless. And while we may be tempted to imagine that something or someone – Bernie, for instance – might consummate it, in truth we have all trodden on the Hungry Grass, which no earthly food can ever finally assuage.

14

I T was Sunday morning. Bugger Lamb had slept badly and woken early, disturbed by bad dreams he could not shake off. No matter how hard he tried to grasp and unmask them, they always flitted away just beyond his reach. He drank a cup of tea and decided to go into the Club. He'd catch up with some paperwork. There were plenty of membership applications to be vetoed, and he ought not to get behind with them.

The first bloody streaks of dawn were appearing in the eastern sky as he stood on the terrace. A light went on behind the drawn curtains of the bedroom in Miss Baskerville's flat above the bar. He decided that a brisk constitutional might be just the ticket – a fast circuit of the lake would soon bugger the unpleasant residue of those dreams. On the point of striding out, something caught his eye on the far side of the lake. Was there someone on the bank, where the path gave on to the water's edge, at the lake's deepest point? He strained his eyes in the grey light. Yes, someone seemed to be hunkered down at the pike-haunted spot, like an embodiment of his elusive dreams. Who could it be, so early? Not a member. Someone up to no good, he'd be bound. Some bugger.

As the light imperceptibly intensified, it seemed to the Secretary of the Tennis Club that the motionless person, if it were a person, was female. Was it a trick of the light, or did she have the most extraordinary long grey hair? If it was one of those gyppos who'd had the nerve to camp in the grounds last spring, he'd give them what for. Yet Bugger Lamb did not move, but continued to watch the figure, still as a tree-stump, crouching beside the water. A sudden breath of wind rippled the surface of the lake and made him shiver. He was just beginning to think that he was mistaken – that the figure was indeed a stump or bush – when it made a sudden jerky movement of its skinny limbs, like a spider, and began to bat the water with its bony hands.

'No, no, no,' said Bugger Lamb to himself, turning away. He thought that, on the whole, his morning walk could wait and that a strong cup of tea was in order, perhaps with a little something in it.

'Children!' bellowed Dada. 'Report to me at once.'

Obediently, his offspring began to arrive one by one in their parents' bedroom, where Dada was sitting up in bed, drinking tea. Beside him, looking like a Fifties' film star in a powder-blue satin night gown and matching bed-jacket, sat Cheryl Cholmondeley, wearing a mask of full make-up and a slightly fixed smile.

The Moo came in first and, out of habit, climbed under the eiderdown at the end of the bed, facing Dada and Cheryl. Janey arrived next. She walked towards the bed, checked herself, turned and sat down on the yellow sofa, swinging her hair across her face to hide it. George was the third to arrive, absorbed in an armful of transistor radio parts which he spread on the carpet and sprawled beside. Sabrina and Bradley were absent. Roger had called for them early, and had taken them off for the better part of the day.

'Well, well. That's more like it. I am happy to see you, my children. It's not too much to ask, I hope, that you show your faces here for a moment on a Sunday morning to please your poor old Dada who works so hard and late all week to put food in your mouths? He won't keep you long because of course he understands that you lead busy lives of your own and cannot be expected to spare more than a passing thought for the one who enables those lives – no, no, that is as it should be: I wish my children to indulge selfishly in their own childhood for they will soon enough have to face the harsh cares of the adult. So let them be carefree while they may! Where is Luh'le Shuggy?'

'He is dressing himself,' said the Moo. 'He's coming.'

'Well, we cannot always be waiting on the convenience of the Young Master. I have something to say and I will say it now. While other men enjoy the Sabbath's respite, your father has to go to the office again. Naturally, I leave Mrs Cholmondeley in charge. I understand that she has kindly said that you may call her "Cheryl".

That is friendly, is it not? I do not have to tell you that you will do as she says without argument or fuss. You will pay her the same respect that you pay your mother. Is that clear?'

'I should think that we'll pay her more respect than Maman,' said George, 'since we pay Maman hardly any respect at all.'

'The Moo respects Maman. She is a member of the Sloppy Club.'

'Oh really?' said Dada. 'I understood that she had been disbarred for unsloppy behaviour.'

'She's back in.'

'I see. So, to sum up, it does not matter how flagrantly irresponsible a person's behaviour is, the said behaviour is deemed sloppy merely at the whim of its president? Isn't this despotism of the worse kind?' There was a pause while the Moo considered the question.

'She's back in.'

'Well, well, in that case, the Moo, if membership depends merely on the caprice of a president –'

'The Sultan of Sloppy,' the Moo reminded him.

'A sultan whose fitness for the post I beg leave to call into question – but let that pass – then I think it would be a nice gesture, the Moo, if Cheryl were to be inducted without delay into the marble halls of the Sloppy Club.' The Moo looked at Janey.

'What's 'e say?'

'Dada wants you to make Mrs Cholmondeley a member,' she interpreted.

'She's not sloppy,' said the Moo.

'Indeed I am *not* sloppy,' confirmed Cheryl.

'Of course you aren't, ha-ha-ha,' laughed Dada. 'But in this instance, you see, the term "sloppy" is not to be taken literally. It has other levels of meaning, all of which finally exist in the mind of the Moo alone. But, generally speaking, it is a term of approbation, describing some desirable, um, state of being...' Dada's voice tailed off rather, as he ran up against the puzzling ontology of sloppiness.

'And you, Dermot,' said Cheryl with tightening lips, 'are you... "sloppy"?'

'Oh yes. Very. The question remains: why does the Moo not recognise this? I do not say that he does recognise my sloppiness but wilfully refuses me admittance to the Club. That would be sinister in the extreme – although I have to say that I am sometimes at a loss for an alternative explanation. There really ought to be clearer directives in the matter of sloppiness so that a candidate might have some idea as to what constitutes it and how to achieve it. In fact...' Dada was beginning to ramble when, fortunately, Hugh appeared in the doorway and said at once:

'So that is where my precious transistor radio has got to.'

'I'm mending it,' said George. 'It was going to be a surprise for you. That is the sort of person I am: kindly.'

'It was not broken,' said Hugh evenly.

'Well, being dropped in the bath hardly did it any good,' replied George accusingly.

'I did not drop it in the bath.'

'Well, *someone* did.'

Hugh clenched his fists and then opened them again, dropping his hands hopelessly to his sides. Then, his lips turning rather pale, he addressed the parental bed:

'You called, Dada? Well, here I am. Good morning, Maman. Oh, I see that it is not my mother in bed with my father. It is Mrs Cholmondeley, our neighbour, who has taken Maman's place. And very nice she looks, too.'

'She *does* look nice,' confirmed the Moo. 'All shiny like a robot. We must call her "Cheryl", Luh'le Shuggy. Dada says so.'

'Well, that is a bonus,' said Hugh.

'And what exactly is all... *this*, Luh'le Shuggy?' asked Dada with studied pleasantness.

'All what, Dada?'

'Your apparel. The jacket. Not to mention the shirt. To say nothing of the trousers.'

'What's troubling you, Dada? Don't be afraid to say.'

'Well, Luh'le Shuggy. Let us begin with the jacket. I can forgive it, for all that it has coloured stripes. It might at a pinch be construed as quite doggy. The shirt, however, is – there's no other word for it – *pink*. And the trousers are low-slung to the point of obscenity.'

'They're called hipsters, Dada. They are something you may already have heard of, namely *fashionable*.'

'I see. And whence, pray, did this... *ensemble* emanate?'

'It's not an ensemble, Dada. It's fab gear. And it comes from Kingston where I shopped this week with Bernie at a...' Hugh braced himself. 'At a… boutique.'

'At a *what*? A *boutique*? No son of mine will shop at a boutique, whatever that may be.'

'I fear a son of yours already has, Dada.'

'And the results are deplorable, Luh'le Shuggy. You are clearly unaware of how ridiculously effeminate you appear, like some nancy boy.'

'Isn't that what you sent me to Public School to train as?'

'Ha-ha-ha,' laughed Dada, falsely.

'Actually,' continued Hugh, 'what you see before you is a Mod.'

'If Luh'le Shuggy's going to be a Mod,' said George, 'then I'm going to be a Rocker.'

'Well, you have the squalid greasy hair for it,' admitted Hugh. 'But you're rather short in the 1000cc motorbike department.'

'I may not have a motorbike, but you don't even have a spastic little Mod scooter with all those silly mirrors for back-combing your hair in.' Hugh tried to look too dignified to reply.

'Did Bernie put you up to this, Luh'le Shuggy?' asked Dada suspiciously.

'No, Dada. I'm afraid it was all my own idea. I'm tired of living in the olden days. I don't want to live in the nineteen fifties any more. I want to live in technicolour. Bernie only lent me some money.'

'I see,' said Dada, at a loss as to what to say next. Mods, boutiques, hipsters – it was a foreign language. He felt that he was being drawn out of his depth. 'Well, you will not parade yourself around my house while there is breath left in my body, looking like – I do not wish to say it but you have forced my hand, Luh'le Shuggy – looking like a species of bum boy.'

'Really, Dermot.' Cheryl spoke up for the first time. 'You do not understand teenagers. You are not With It.'

'I'm perfectly With It,' protested Dada. There were hoots of laughter.

'The way in which you phrase your claim, Dada, proves the reverse,' said Hugh.

'Oh, very clever, Luh'le Shuggy. But, you know, this sneery way of talking does you no credit.' Dada began to heat up alarmingly. 'You march in here, bold as you please, dressed up to the nines like some Christmas fairy and you expect me –'

'Dabs am werry With It!' squeaked Dabs, stalling Dada's momentum. 'Dabs am a Mod.' The Moo gave a snort of boundless contempt.

'You, Dabs,' he said, 'are a flabby fool. With brain damage.'

'Dabs am singing all the Mod songs.'

'You can't sing a *single* song, Dabs, you imbecile.'

'Dabs can when her brains am up.'

'Go on then.' Dabs's shifty eyes swivelled about. Then:

'*There Dabs goes, just a-walking down the street, singing DOO-WAH-DOGGY-DOGGY-DINS-DOGGY-DOOS.*' She beamed with self-congratulation.

'*No, Dabs.*' Spiv was apoplectic with frustration at being too far away to strike. 'It's *doo-wah-diddy-diddy-dum-diddy-doo*, you steaming great nit.'

'What is it you are saying, Jane?' asked Cheryl in puzzlement.

'Me? Nothing.'

'It is Dabs who speaks,' said Dada, as if that were sufficient explanation.

'Dabs...?'

'A clot,' said George.

'The village idiot,' amplified the Moo.

'But a cult figure,' suggested Hugh.

'I see,' said Cheryl, far from doing so. 'It is a game. With silly voices.' There were muffled squeaks of protest from behind Janey's hair, followed by merriment from the other children. 'Did you say somethink, Jane? Perhaps you would care to share the joke?' The general laughter increased. 'I think that is enough, children. I do not want to have to ask your father to take steps.'

'Take no notice, my dear.' Dada's tone was conciliatory. 'Dabs is a law unto herself. Or itself. Pay it no mind.'

'Well,' said Cheryl, put out, but determined to haul matters back on to home ground. 'I think Hugh looks quite the ladies' man in his new get-up. I am not surprised that he rather lost his head while shopping with Bernadette. I think he carries a bit of a torch for her, Dermot. I am really quite jealous at the sight of his modish – perhaps I should say Mod-ish – attire. Dressed to kill, eh, Hughie?' She winked wickedly at Hugh.

'I wish I were,' muttered Hugh, hanging his burning head.

'I am only sorry,' Cheryl continued brightly, 'that Bernadette has not seen fit to do something about Jane. Since it is time – you will agree, Dermot – that she dressed less like a tomboy and more like a young lady. Never mind. I will take her in hand myself.'

'Please...' Janey mumbled miserably. 'Please don't.'

'It would honestly be no trouble. I can just see you in a nice tight little skirt – your legs are not all that bad – and you will soon catch the eye of young gentlemen.'

'Oh, oh,' despaired Janey, under her breath.

'And it really is time you had a proper bra. I expect you would prefer Sabrina to help you in that department, and not some old woman such as myself! I will have a word with her. No doubt she will advise you on other items of underwear.' Her tone grew kittenish. 'You will feel quite different in your first suspender belt – but I expect you two girls will discuss that between you. I am not one to interfere. I expect you have longed for a sister to share girls' secrets with. And now you have Sabrina, who will soon have you looking like a fashion plate! The boys will be buzzing around you, Janey, like –'

'Ow! Ow!' Dabs's outburst was so anguished that even Spiv was alarmed. Her cries could be heard receding down the passage as Janey dashed to her bedroom, and then approaching again like a police siren as she ran past her parents' room, down the stairs and out of the house.

'A good example of the Doppler effect,' said George appreciatively.

'She has gone to throw herself off the cliff,' surmised Hugh grimly. Then, seeing the Moo's stricken face: 'Not really, the Moo. I'm joking.'

'You wretched children always *take on* so,' complained Dada. 'You all have your mother's nerves. Here is Cheryl, like a breath of fresh air, willing to help Janey make the most of herself – willing to help us all – and the ungrateful brat behaves as crazily as Grace Poole.'

'I think you mean the first Mrs Rochester, Dada.'

'Do I, Luh'le Shuggy? Do I? I think I know very well whom I mean, do I not? I mean Grace Poole, the mad woman who cackles all night in *Jane Eyre*!'

'The point is, Dada, that she does not. Jane Eyre only thinks she does.'

'Well, Jane Eyre and I are of one mind. And why you, Luh'le Shuggy, always presume to know better is itself something of a conundrum. I rather think, in this instance, that, while you may well know better than your poor old uneducated father, you do not know better than Jane Eyre herself who, after all, tells the story and therefore should know very well who is, and who is not, cackling all night. Really, Luh'le Shuggy, your superior air is most unbecoming and, as now, not always well founded. You will do well to take stock of yourself and amend your attitude.'

'No, seriously, listen to your father, Hugh,' chimed in Cheryl. 'Frankly, I am surprised at how lenient with you he is. If I were your parent I would not tolerate your back-chat, however smart you imagine it to be.'

Hugh sank to his knees, pitched forward on to all fours, and began to crawl out of the room.

'What are you playing at, Luh'le Shuggy?' demanded Dada.

'You have successfully reduced me to the rank of a lowly cur and I am going to live with Colonel Bogey, if he will take me in.'

'This is not comical, Luh'le Shuggy. You are only making a fool of yourself,' said Dada.

'You let yourself, and your father, down,' sorrowed Cheryl.

'The Colonel won't have you,' said George.

'He will,' said the Moo. 'And I'll bring you dog biscuits and sloppy orange juice, Luh'le Shuggy.'

'Thank you, the Moo. That and the occasional worming is all I ask,' said Hugh lugubriously, crawling through the bedroom door and mournfully wagging in lieu of a tail his hipster-clad behind.

'It's more difficult than it looks, mending a radio,' said George, sifting the pieces through his fingers.

The Moo was in the larder. He was intermittently aware of Mrs Cholmondeley and Bernie talking in the kitchen, but he was not paying attention to them, so intent was he on trying to coax a sleepy bluebottle into the fridge.

'Quite apart from your sloppiness,' Cheryl was saying – the Moo was gratified at her appreciation of Bernie – 'you are impertinent…' He frowned. A dim sense of foreboding made him concentrate more deeply on the task in hand. Bernie was speaking now, but inaudibly, as if something were pressed over her mouth. 'No... no need to work out your notice,' Mrs Chummy was droning on, 'well, unfortunately... Mrs Blyte is not here, so it is left to me... quite capable, thank you, of minding a few children... that sort of remark, Bernadette, is exactly... your services are no longer...' Sounds of distress suddenly alarmed the Moo who poked his head around the door. Bernie was wiping her eyes with a tea towel. She caught sight of him and, flashing him a smile of reassurance, fled from the kitchen.

'Why are you making Bernie cry?'

'I am not. She is simply over-wrought. Now, off you go.'

'What's "over-rort"?'

'Bernadette seems to suffer from nerves, that is all.'

'Like Maman.'

'I imagine so, yes.'

'Is Bernie going away?' The Moo's lip was trembling.

'She is only an au pair girl. She has to go at some point.'

'Yes. To marry Pat Tim. I'm going to visit them, and Pat Tim will let me drive his tractor.'

'Well, that is something to look forward to. Now, off you go and play.'

'But she's not going yet.'

'I am trying to make you a nice lunch, Moe... Moo.'

'The Moo.'

'Yes, yes. Now, I am extremely busy, so go outside and play while I cook. But do not go far. Stay where I can keep an eye on you from the window.' Cheryl was, she had to admit, a trifle nervous. She wished to show Dermot that she was well able to cope with his unruly family. This would have been daunting even with the help of the wretched Bernadette who would now, no doubt, stay sobbing in her room throughout the preparations for a large lunch and be no help at all. Still, it was perhaps, in the end, a small price to pay for control over a household which, she could see, was simply *impossible* as things stood. Additional help would, of course, be required; but she would hire a proper housekeeper, one who knew her place, when the dust of Bernadette's departure had settled. Also, an entirely new kitchen to replace this dark hell-hole would have to be installed without delay.

197

'Can I have a dog?' asked the Moo, who had not meanwhile gone out to play.

'You already have a dog, Moo – *the* Moo.'

'Colonel Bogey isn't exactly a dog. I mean a proper dog like Lassie who'll save your life. Or a sort of wolf-type dog like Fray Be –'

'Like who?'

'Nothing. No one.'

'Well, we'll see.'

'That means "no".'

'Out you go now, dear.'

'The Fuehrer says that Dodgy Roger is going to come round and stimulate Dada's follicles.'

'I do not know what you are talking about, dear. Now off you go before I become annoyed.'

'You sound annoyed already.'

'Do you wish me to smack you? Is that what you wish?'

'If you smack me, Spiv will smack you. *Ouch.*'

Since Spiv seemed unwilling to live up to the Moo's threat, they both trailed miserably off, wishing that they could put Mrs Chummy Bum in the fridge with bluebottles; wishing Maman were home.

'Mark my words, Moo,' Cheryl called after him, 'and don't wander too far from the house.'

The lunch was on and under control. Cheryl suddenly remembered the unhappy Moo, who was not visible from the kitchen window. She hurried out to look for him. The day was as grey and still as the endless Sundays of her childhood. She felt rather oppressed, as if the anxiety which formed the backdrop to her life were about to advance on her, like the girls camouflaged as great Birnam Wood in her school's production of *Macbeth*. 'Come on, girl,' she said to herself. 'Brace up.' She saw, with relief, that the Moo was kicking a football about on the lawn. As she turned back towards the house, she noticed an unsightly tin bath full of water lodged in the flower bed against the wall. She bent over and looked into it. The neatness of her reflection was cheering. As she straightened up, a hot silver curtain fell hissing like a steam train past her face and exploded in the water. She leapt back, almost falling over in her high heels.

'Watch out,' said George's voice mildly and belatedly. She looked up at the second floor window from which the boy had just tipped a large saucepan full of molten lead. She had been inches away from an abrupt and painful death. She found it hard to catch her breath. The lead in the water was beautiful. Cooling in the air on the way down, it had already half congealed into a bizarre elongated shape when it hit the water and was fixed. 'It's Action Sculpture,' explained George, hanging out of the window. 'I'm going to sell it to the Tate Gallery.' Cheryl nodded. She was too shocked to remonstrate with him. She remembered the god-awful noise she had heard in the night, and wondered vaguely if her father was all right. She hadn't even spoken to him for – what? – two years or so. Perhaps she would give him a call that afternoon. The lead in the tin bath, shining like the drowned corpse of a twisted angel, was discomfiting. It reminded her of something, but she didn't know what. She only knew that she did not want to look farther into it.

Hunched in her duffel coat, Janey sat on the damp verge outside the house and garden, furiously sculpting the lump of wax. She kept her ears peeled for the revving of the Black Mini, hoping it would zoom past, like a talisman, to reinforce the spell she was pressing into the wax along with three of Cheryl's blonde hairs.

She was interrupted by Colonel Bogey who, pausing only to raise his eyebrows at her, padded off in the direction of the Tennis Club. He was followed by Mr Hamilton:

'That's right, sir – we'll head for the Club,' he called out for Janey's benefit, raising the Colonel's lead to show that he was taking the dog for a walk.

'Are you leaving us, Mr Hamilton,' asked Janey, pointing to the hold-all he was carrying.

'How did you know? Oh, I see – this. Ha-ha. No, just my, er, squash kit and so on.'

'You've forgotten your racket.'

'Eh? What on earth do you mean?' He seemed irked by her helpful remark. 'Oh, I see. No, no, I'm not actually playing, just… stashing my gear at the, er… so on.'

He had no sooner walked briskly away up Chestnut Avenue in the wake of Colonel Bogey, than Theo's feline footsteps crunched lightly on the gravelled drive.

'May one… not disturbing…?'

'Oh no, Theo. You never disturb me. Do sit down.' Janey slipped the effigy of Cheryl into her pocket and curled her fingers around it.

'Everything, um… tickety, er, boo?'

'Not really. Mrs Chummy Bum has been tormenting me, Theo. She has threatened to buy me underwear.'

'Lingerie… always, um… horrific.'

'It's no joke, Theo. Well, I can see that it *is* funny. But the worst thing is, there's a part of me that *would* like to dress a bit more, well, you know, sort of…'

'Er, fabbily…?'

'Yes, because, you won't have noticed, but I *am* growing up, you know.'

'Werry much so… er, attractive young… um, so forth.'

'I know you're only saying that, Theo. But thank you. I mean, I don't want to dress *up* to attract beastly men or anything, which is all that she and her squalid daughter ever think about. I'm just sick of wearing the same old stuff every day, and looking a fright. But now I *can't* change or else they'll think they've won.' She turned to him with urgency and looked into his eyes – a thing, she realised, she hadn't done for ages, what with shyness and him being a teacher at school, and her thinking about him and drawing him more than was strictly necessary. '*Do* you think I'll ever be attractive, Theo?' She regretted the outburst immediately and turned away, wanting to die.

Theo's hand, light as an owl's wing-beat – so light she might have imagined it – brushed for the briefest moment against her hair.

'Already… the most…' he murmured. And she knew with great certainty that he meant it.

'Well, that's enough of my inferiority complex,' she said in a pulling-herself-together way. 'I'm just emotionally scarred, Theo, by that woman. I wish she hadn't moved here. I can't help wishing she were – well, it's no use wishing, I s'pose. I *s'pose* you find *her* attractive, Theo? Men seem to.'

'*Au contraire*… absolutely… Dodgy… Word "hideous"… not too strong…'

'Steady on, Theo. Don't go mad. She *does* have a hypnotic effect on men. You should see Dada's face when he looks at her. It goes all soppy. It's beyond embarrassing. He's not a bad man – he's just so… suggestible. And he wants to feel young and… *doggy* again. Poor Dada. But the worst thing is –' she took a deep breath – 'on the day when Maman, well, you know… I saw Dada walking down the drive, and then he stopped and listened. Then the Black Mini came roaring by, and he was distracted, and he walked away from the garage. But what if he'd heard the Zodiac's engine running?'

'Surely, um, not. Your Dada… not, er –'

'But, but what if he *did* hear?' she repeated. 'He would have, I *know*, rushed into the garage, but the thought of *her* came into his mind and…' She could not, after all, bring herself to fully admit what she had suspected that day. 'That's what she'll do in the end, you see, Theo,' she tailed off. 'She'll make murderers of us all.' She wanted to put her head on Theo's shoulder and close her eyes and stay like that until… well, until. Instead she held the tears back behind her eyes by pinching Cheryl's head between her thumb and forefinger. 'If only Maman were here…'

'Not to, um, worry… one has… er, modest plan… dark secret, so forth…'

'Your secret's safe with me, Theo,' said Janey, not believing for a moment that he had any sort of plan, but grateful for the effort to console her. She put her arms across her raised knees and buried her face in her duffel coat sleeves. When she looked up, she found that Theo had ghosted away.

Janey finished her little wax model of Mrs Cholmondeley, the strands of hair running through it like arteries. Quite a decent likeness. Especially the shapely legs and slender ankles. She thought of Maman's poor swollen ankles, the grief of her life, and, seized by hatred and pity, picked up a sharp stone and scored two deep gashes across those of Mrs Cholmondeley.

Charles Hamilton stepped into the gap in the undergrowth at the edge of the lake and peered into the black water. It was less uninviting than he had anticipated. He knelt down and examined the bank. It was, he guessed, just steep enough, and slimy, for him to be unable to claw his way out if he should happen to lose his nerve; but, in any case, he was taking no chances. He unpacked the chain and padlock from the hold-all. He had practised with it. He had learnt to bind it tightly around his legs so that he would not be able to thrash them about; and to tie one arm to his body, leaving the other free to loop the chain around his neck and padlock it so that any change of mind would be of no avail. The chain not only bound him – it was heavy enough to carry him down to the bottom.

Charles was at a low ebb. The pain in his innards had got worse. Yesterday, blood had come out of his rear end. He did not need to hear the results of the hospital tests to know what that meant. At best he could expect to be subjected to butchery. He had sworn a long time ago in the jungle that, if God spared him, he would never again allow his life to be put at the mercy of anyone other than himself. He had only meant to make a recce this morning, but he was tempted to do it now. Get it over with. Colonel Bogey had, agreeably, accompanied him on the first part of the lake's circuit; but then they had run into Bugger Lamb who had all but ignored Charles while greeting Bogey with great bonhomie. The bloody fellow had actually wagged his tail and, worse, abandoned Charles in order to escort Lamb back to the Club house. Well, Bogey had made his choice. So be it. Perhaps it was better this way. For two pins Charles would have wrapped himself in the chain right away and, with one easy topple, plunged headfirst into blissful oblivion. It was only the thought of Theo which prevented him. He had made several attempts to write a letter. So difficult to strike the right note. But he'd finish it this afternoon, and then return to the lake. Better in any case to do it in the twilight when there was sure to be no one about. Carefully, he stashed the chain under a bush and covered it with leaves. Then he picked up his empty hold-all and set off for his Sunday lunch.

Dermot had gone into the Tennis Club for a sandwich and a stiffener before the drive up to Town. Dan Rose and Eugene McCarthy were sitting at the bar, dressed in immaculate whites and laughing in a manly way with what looked like a new barman. Dermot felt irrationally intimidated. He broadened his shoulders and stepped forward with a confident air.

'What's your poison, old man?' enquired the new barman. It was Roger.

'Be da Holy Floy!' exclaimed Dermot. 'You've gone up in the world, old man.'

'Just standing in for Lorraine. She's entertaining my kids in her flat.' He indicated the floor above with a tilt of his head.

'Well, half of Red Barrel for me. And I was, er, sorry to hear about your factory, old man. You'll miss it.'

'No, I won't.'

'What? A high-flier like you, Cholmondeley...?'

'Too high a flier, Blyte. Too near the sun, see? Wings melted. Like that bloke. Wossname? Biggles – that's the Johnny.'

'Listen, Cholmondeley...' Dermot glanced at Dan and Eugene, who were regarding him with unnerving interest. 'No hard feelings, eh?'

'I don't know, Blyte. I'm having a bit of a look at my feelings. The best I can say is, they're mixed.'

'Did Lorraine leave anything to eat?'

'Oh yes, a nice knuckle sandwich, I shouldn't wonder. The odd slice of fist pie, as warmed up by me.'

'Ha-ha-ha. No, seriously...'

'Who says I'm not being serious?'

'I wouldn't try any funny stuff if I were you, old man. I've got witnesses...' But the two witnesses were now gazing non-committally into their drinks. 'I was in the War, remember.'

'Ah yes. Get you. Bap be okay?'

'Yes. Yes, bap.'

'Coming up, old son.'

'We've got to be adult about this,' appeased Dermot.

'Have we, old son? Well, I dare say you're right. But it's not going to be easy for us, is it – being adult. Because, you see, we've had no training in it. I'm making a start now. But *you*, old son – let's be honest, your kids are more adult than you. And, by the way, you're not getting my kids. Let's be quite clear on that one. As for my missis, she spending your dosh yet?' Dermot thought uneasily of the expensive unnecessary refrigerator.

'Not yet, ha-ha-ha. Your trouble is, Cholmondeley – was, I should say – you don't know how to handle a woman like Cheryl. No offence, old man. You did your best. But things change. *C'est la vie*. We'll laugh about this one day. How much do I owe you?'

'Nothing, old son. Have this one on me. You'll be digging deep into your pockets soon enough.'

'Sour grapes, old man. Half a crown cover it?'

'Keep it, old son. And keep my wife. I mean it. But take a tip from me: don't ever let your income drop.'

'Yippee!' cried the Moo. 'Chicken! Spiv loves chicken, don't you, Spiv? Look at him. 'E's crafty. 'E's going for the parson's nose.' Spiv was indeed slinking on his belly over the edge of the table and towards the steaming carcass. 'Go on, Spiv. Get 'im. Get that chicken by the nose. Aaaargh!' The strangled cry was caused by Cheryl's smart backhander which swept Spiv, together with the Moo's arm, off the table. She picked up the carving knife and fork.

'I'd better carve,' said George. 'It's not a woman's job.'

'Thank you, George, but this knife is too sharp for a small boy to use.'

'I may be small but I am the best little brain in the family. Ask anyone, except Luh'le Shuggy. Ask Theo.'

'Where *are* the Hamiltons?' asked Cheryl in a vexed tone. She wasn't sure why she was required to feed the lodgers; but Dermot seemed to expect it.

'Plus,' pursued George less than truthfully, 'Dada said I could carve whenever he was away. I'm the only one who can do the Carving Face, you see.'

'Be quiet, George.'

'You'll just have to teach Mrs Cholmondeley the Carving Face, mein Fuehrer,' said Hugh.

'I do not think that will be necessary, thank you, Hugh.'

'But it's *crucial*,' protested George. 'It wards off evil spirits. If you don't do the Face, the chicken will be possessed. It will rise mysteriously into the air and then, suddenly, it'll fly at the Moo's throat, sicking up its stuffing all over –'

'That's *enough*, George. Sit up properly and put your serviette on your lap like a grown-up.'

'What's my... serviette?'

'She means your napkin,' said Hugh.

'Ah, here you are. At last,' said Cheryl with tightish lips as Charles, Theo and Janey came into the dining room. 'Will you sit here, Mr Hamilton? And you, Theo, next to him and Moo. And you, Jane, next to Mr Hamilton.'

'I always sit next to Theo.'

'What is that you say, dear? I cannot hear you when you do not articulate your words and hide your face behind your hair. Perhaps you would be civil enough to brush it aside and to look at me when you are speaking? Ah, I see you have decided to sit where I originally placed you. You were simply amusing yourself by being contrary for the sake of it. Well, with your permission, dear, we will all get on with our meal.'

'Spiv hasn't eaten for days,' the Moo confided to Theo. 'He's ravishing. 'E's ready to tear the parson's nose off the nearest human being. Look out, Theo – here 'e comes!'

'Oh, oh… similarity Dabs… werry frighty… Spiv… cruel jaws, so forth…'

'It's all right, Theo. I won't let Spiv get you,' reassured the Moo, clawing Spiv back and muzzling him with a podgy hand. 'Spiv and me will take some chicken to Bernie.'

'That is a kind thought,' said Cheryl, 'but I think not. She is not hungry.'

'She is. Crying always makes you hungry.'

'Bernie crying?' exclaimed Hugh.

'"Her services are no longer…"' quoted the Moo.

'Where is Bernie? Didn't she cook the lunch?'

'I'm afraid she did not,' replied Cheryl. 'Which, I am afraid, is rather typical.'

'I'd say the obverse was the case,' said Hugh, his bombast betraying his distress.

'I do not follow you, Hugh, dear. Nobody does. I am simply saying that however jolly you children find Miss O'Flaherty, from the responsible, adult point of view she leaves much to be desired.'

'She leaves nothing to be desired.'

'I understand why you say that, Hugh dear, and I overlook your discourteous tone because of your infatuation with the girl.' Cheryl winked. 'However, puppyish feelings unfortunately do not affect the reality of the matter, namely Miss O'Flaherty's poor work record. I do not mention her, let us say, outside activities – which set a very bad example to impressionable children.'

'What "activities", Mrs Cholmondeley?'

'The Roman Catholic Church Social. Do I need to say any more?'

'Bernie is entitled to a day off and some social life.'

'I think you are being deliberately obtuse, Hugh. But we will not discuss the au pair's promiscuity in front of the children.'

'What's promise cutey?' asked the Moo.

'It's enjoying yourself,' said George. 'I think.'

'Mrs Chummy am having a mind like the bluebottle's legs,' opined Dabs suddenly.

'*No*, Dabs, you big eejit. The bluebottle's legs are dirty,' the Moo reminded her.

'Normally I would ask you to leave the table, Jane; but since I have taken a lot of trouble to prepare this meal, you will do me the courtesy of sitting here and eating it. I will have a word with your father when he returns.'

'Dada likes Bernie,' mentioned George.

'Well, *I* like Bernie,' said Cheryl, pulling her lips back in a smile. 'We all do. It is a sadness to us that she has chosen to return to her native land.'

'Bernie going?' The Moo allowed himself to take in this intelligence at last.

'No, the Moo,' said Hugh. 'She is not. Dada would not deprive us of Bernie.'

'First Maman, now Bernie. It is a bloodbath,' murmured George.

'Well, Hugh, you are right to try and soften the blow. If I have a fault, it is a fondness for plain speaking. We will say no more of Bernie's departure until your father has time to break the news gently.'

'Bernie's going and Maman's never coming back,' said George forlornly.

'Shut up, mein Fuehrer,' said Janey.

'Maman's coming back, isn't she, Theo?' asked the Moo, his lip trembling.

'Of *course*, the Moo... Back very soon... all well... Sea Hare, so forth.'

'Theo is right, the Moo,' said Cheryl. 'Your mother is certainly returning. Although how soon exactly... Well, let's not spoil our lunch with gloomy thoughts –' She was interrupted by the clatter of a knife and fork on a plate. Charles Hamilton had dropped his cutlery and was doubled over, a lick of hair falling over one eye.

'Papa!' Theo half-rose, while Janey shot out a protective hand. At once, Charles righted himself.

'Good Lord! Sorry everyone. Sudden stab of... indigestion. Won't put me off my chicken, Mrs Cholmondeley, what? Certainly not. In fact, tremendously good of you to stand in for Mrs B. while she's, er... We're lucky dogs, eh, Theo? It's a treat to have chicken, isn't it, children?'

Only Theo, gazing with concern at his father, noticed the greyness of his face and its film of perspiration.

'I do not think that Mrs Blyte quite realised how inexpensive chicken has become,' Cheryl was saying, beginning at last to cut into the plump bird with unwomanly expertise, 'now that they are bred by the thousand in convenient batteries. She imagined that they still cost what they did in the bad old days when poultry was allowed to peck around in unhygienic farmyards, growing stringier by the day. Anyone would think it was still the nineteen fifties!'

'Colonel Bogey!' cried the Moo. Glad to be distracted from a frightening confusion over Maman and Bernie, he slid off his chair and put his arms around the new arrival's neck. 'Colonel, you're not sloppy enough. That's better. Ooh, did you see that? He nipped Spiv. Watch it, Colonel, or I'll chuck you out of the Club for bad attitude. That's it – kiss Spiv. You love Spiv really. Eeergh, you're slobbering, Colonel. Mrs Chummy, Colonel Bogey wants 'is snippet.'

'*Not* Chummy, dear. Return to the table, please. Pick up your napkin. And do not encourage the dog.'

'*I* wouldn't mind a snippet neither,' added the Moo. Cheryl looked blank.

'A snippet, Cheryl,' explained Hugh, 'is as it were a *bonne bouche*, which Dada customarily dispenses as an appetiser. We older children, Cheryl, are of course willing to forgo it in the light of new circumstances; but it would be Draconian, I think you'd agree, Cheryl, to deprive Colonel Bogey and the Moo – to say nothing of Spiv – of the *amuse-gueles* on which so much anticipatory slavering has been lavished.'

'One day you will cut yourself on that tongue of yours,' warned Cheryl.

'And if there *were*, Cheryl, the teensiest shred of chicken skin left over for a snippet all of my own, I would be undyingly grateful.'

'Act your age, please, Hugh. There will be no more of this snippet nonsense. You children will eat your meal like civilised people.' She rapped on the table for emphasis, like a schoolmistress who senses that a class is getting away from her.

'All right... Papa?' enquired Theo anxiously.

'Eh? Fine, fine. Everything ship-shape. Miles away, that's all. But thanks for asking, my boy. Thank you.'

'This chicken is a bit of a disappointment,' mused George.

'Is it possessed?' asked the Moo, failing to mask genuine alarm.

'No. But it is... something.'

'It is not something,' said Cheryl sharply. 'It is good wholesome food. Eat it up, George, and if you cannot say anything sensible, say nothink.'

Everyone ate in silence for a while.

'It is,' pursued George, chewing meditatively, 'sort of... flabby.'

'Dabs-like,' proposed the Moo. There were some minuscule squeaks of indignation from Janey's direction, but nothink Cheryl could pin on her.

'It *is* a bit Dabs-like,' agreed Hugh. 'It is certainly not chicken as I remember it from the old days.'

'What does the Dabs-chicken say, Dabs?' the Moo enquired eagerly. Dabs appeared slyly, with narrowed eyes and loose mouth, on Janey's partially hidden face.

'It am saying: "HELP! HELP! I'VE LORST ME GIBBERLETS! WHERE AM ME GIBBERLETS?"'

The Moo went sloppy with laughter. 'It's *giblets*, Dabs, you nit,' he corrected weakly, barely able to lift Spiv, let alone strike.

'Be *quiet*. All of you,' snapped Cheryl. 'You make me quite sick. I am quite sure that Mr Hamilton and Theo do not want to hear this painfully childish rubbish.'

'Eh?' said Charles, starting. 'Oh, I don't mind, to be honest. But I *am* rather out of my depth among young people. Bogey is more my level. Although, I don't think I'll be taking him for walks any more.'

'Don't say that, Mr H.,' said Hugh, noticing Charles's sadness. 'If you don't walk him, no one will – no one else *can*. I mean, you're the only one apart from the Moo who the Colonel even gives the time of day to.'

'It's good of you to say so, Hugh. But it's no longer strictly true. Colonel Bogey has transferred his allegiance to someone new. The Secretary of the Tennis Club, to be exact. Privately, I suspect foul play – cajolery and possibly bribery – but as a gentleman I'm bound to say nothing. Twenty-five years ago, before the War, I'd have given Lamb a good pummelling, I can tell you. But now, well, I haven't the heart and, worse still, I haven't the guts.'

'Papa… case of… er, mislaid… gibberlets,' commented Theo. Several of Janey's peas went down the wrong way.

'If you cannot control these fits, Janey,' said Cheryl, 'then you must leave the table until you can.'

Theo was all concern, craning across his father to assist her.

'Here, Janey… water… and here… one's serviette…' Strangely, this only seemed to make her choking worse. Cheryl addressed him:

'Sabrina will miss your piano lessons, Theo.'

'Discontinuing…? Not, um, happy…?' He was surprised.

'Perhaps I have spoken out of turn. I assumed Mr Blyte had informed you and your father.'

'What? What's this?' said Charles.

'It is not for me to say. Any decision about your leaving the flat must be Mr Blyte's alone.'

'No, no. Some misunderstanding. Theo is – we are not leaving the flat.'

'I fear that you will have to,' said Cheryl gently. She smiled with infinite sadness, like the Virgin Mary.

'Question of, er, rent…? Gladly increase…'

'No, Theo. It is not a question of money. But I have said too much. It is better if Dermot explains.'

'He has said nothing to me,' said Charles. 'Are you sure of your facts, Mrs Cholmondeley?'

'Alas, yes. I ought not to say another word, but if it will help to cushion the blow, I might mention that Mr Blyte has it in mind to accommodate a certain person in the flat.'

'Good God! *You*. He's going to give the flat to you.'

'Not I, Mr Hamilton.'

'Then who?'

'Why, to dear Mrs Blyte, of course. She will need somewhere to convalesce. Clearly, she cannot be left alone in such a delicate state, and so we need a suitable place where I can keep an eye on her.'

'Like Grace Poole,' said Hugh.

'I suppose you think that I cannot understand your literary reference, Hugh? Well, I am going to surprise you. Grace Poole is the mad woman in *Jane Eyre*, and I take exception to this slur on my sanity.'

'No, you're thinking of – oh, it doesn't matter.'

'I think you will find that real life is very different to your little world of books, Hugh.'

'Not always,' said George, thinking of Arthur Mee and his wide grasp of real life.

'I shall shortly be taking coffee in the lounge,' said Cheryl brightly. 'Who is going to join me?'

But, mysteriously, no one did join Cheryl in the drawing room except George, who appeared with a mug of steaming fluid.

'Don't drink that coffee, Cheryl,' he said anxiously. 'It's Nescafé. I've made you some real coffee.'

'I do not think I want an enormous mug-ful, George.'

'I made it specially,' said George, crestfallen.

'Well, I will do my best in that case,' said Cheryl. The Blyte children could be so charming when they wanted. What a pity they did not want to more often. However, they would not be too difficult to master. And, if some part of her wished for something more – to win them over, perhaps – then this gesture of George's was a place to start. She supposed that the coffee was his way of saying sorry for the near-lethal lead incident earlier, and she took a large swallow to show that there were no hard feelings.

'Is it all right?' asked George eagerly.

'Yes, dear. Very nice.' In fact, it was a little bitter. But not undrinkably bad. As George continued to gaze at her expectantly, with an unnerving fixed and sickly smile, she sipped away with a will.

15

As he signed the letter, he sensed a shift in the order of things, as if the idling machinery of death had been put into gear. He had been out walking, turning his decision over in his mind, just to be sure. Now he was sure. He'd probably be dead in any case within a few months – weeks, even – from whatever canker was gnawing his vitals. Better by far to spare Theo his lingering demise. Besides, Theo had to find somewhere else to live, and he'd manage better without the dead weight of his father holding him back. Best not to delay, then. Best to seize death by the scruff of the neck.

Charles read his letter through. He was in no danger of being disturbed – Theo had gone off on some mysterious errand after lunch, indicating that he would be back late. Colonel Bogey was similarly engaged on one of his secretive missions to Wyebridge; but the less said about him the better. The trouble was, the note sounded like a business letter. He had even signed it: 'Best wishes for the future, Charles Hamilton.' It was absurd. The trouble was, he had been away so much when Theo was a boy. Then there'd been the War, imprisonment, etcetera. So, by the time he had got back to England, Theo was practically an adult, off to Paris for his music, having buried his mother alone.

Charles had never said how proud he was of his son; how much he loved him. He had wanted to, but a fellow didn't, well, go on about such things. Sincerity always seemed to strike the wrong note, like a modern vicar. He *would* say the words, he had told himself, when the time came; but now that the time *had* come, the words wouldn't. What had started as a shyness he assumed he could always overcome, had become the very fabric of their relationship. It now seemed false to start gushing at the eleventh hour, even in a letter.

'Be assured, Theo, that I have always…' He crossed the sentence out. 'Be assured, my dear son, that you have always been to me…' It sounded stilted and pompous. But so would anything intimate. He and Theo were bound by reticence. The farthest he would, or could, go was to sign the letter: 'Your loving Papa.'

He made a fair copy and propped the letter on the piano's music stand. Then he stroked the keys. Oddly, two or three notes down on the left hand were silent. How could Theo not have noticed? Charles lifted the lid of the baby grand and peered inside. Sure enough, some of the longest wires appeared to be missing.

'Whacha doing?' said Bradley, mooching over with his hands in his pockets.

'You're back then,' stated George, not looking up from his excavation of the sand pit. He'd got tired of Cheryl, who just sat there, staring at her hands. This new scientific project was much more interesting.

'Yeah. I wangled a bag of crisps off Lorraine for you. Whacha doing?'

'Fab. I'm filing my teeth into points.'

'No, really.'

'What's it look like, bird-brain? I'm shovelling all the sand out. Why're you back early?'

'Sabrina wanted to. 'Sides, Dad wanted to be alone with Lorraine.'

'She's a bit of all right,' commented George, uncertain of the meaning of his words.

'Yeah, she's all right. We played Cluedo. Quite snazzy actually.'

'I expect they wanted to… snog and that.'

''Spect so. I'll help, shall I?'

'Start the other side. Use the trowel. Your Dad's not as bad as mine, though. When it comes to birds,' reflected George.

'She's not a bird. She's my Mum.'

'Okay, okay – keep your Y-fronts on. I meant, she's not his wife.'

'No, but she's only gone two secs and my Dad's getting off with Lorraine.'

'Yeah, but it's not as if she's someone else's *wife*. And she *is* Lorraine. Who's all right.'

'Look. My Dad's a lot worse than yours, mush,' decided Bradley.

'No, he isn't. My Dad gets off with someone else's wife and then bangs *his* wife up in a loony bin.'

'Strewth. Is it a loony bin?'

'They *say* it isn't.'

'All right. You win. Your Dad's worse than mine. What are we building?'

'A marine research laboratory.'

'You what?'

'We take out all the sand. There's nice concrete underneath. See? We fill the empty pit with water and stick stuff in. Frog spawn, plants, animals and that – newts, snails, sponges, probably.'

'Sea horses!'

'Ye-ah. Probably.'

'Fab.'

'Too right it's fab. We can charge people for entry. We'll clean up.'

Mounted on his powerful palomino, the Moo was a Pony Express rider, galloping hard through a narrow gorge in Arizona, while Apaches fired arrows at him from the cliffs above.

'C'mon, boy,' panted the Moo, digging his heels into the back of the battered old sofa in the playroom. He drew his six-gun and shot up at the Indians, three of whom fell to a gruesome death. Their blood-curdling cries were echoed by the Moo himself. Alongside his horse, bearing a remarkable resemblance to Spiv, ran the gallant Fray Bentos, lent to him for his dangerous journey by Jack Pluff himself. Just as well for, rounding a bend, a war party of six Red Indians barred the way; and the Moo's gun was empty. As he reloaded, holding the reins in his teeth, Fray Bentos leapt at the leading brave, who was about to shoot the Moo in the heart, and savaged him. He had ripped the throat out of a second and was starting on a third, when the Moo coolly saved him the trouble by dispatching four Indians with four extraordinarily accurate shots. They were out and away, free as air! Breathing hard, the Moo slid off the sofa's back and lay down for a well-deserved rest.

'You sure are an ornery critter,' he said, patting the smiling Fray Bentos. Then he closed his eyes and, exhausted, fell fast asleep.

≈

Cheryl was feeling, well, a little queer. She had not moved from the settee, nor did she have a clue as to what time it was. To judge by the already failing light, it was much later than she would have credited. There was something about her hands she could not take her eyes off. They seemed luminous, the red nails praeternaturally vibrant and sharp, like bloody talons. She curved the fingers and the result was almost frightening. As if her eyes had acquired X-ray properties, she fancied she could see the blood flowing through the beautiful pale blue veins just beneath the surface of her skin. She was so absorbed that she did not even look up when someone came into the room.

It took her a while to register what the person was saying to her because the words seemed, oddly, to bypass her ears altogether and to imprint themselves directly on to her brain, where they manifested as a series of images. What she saw there, played out as if in 3-D technicolour Cinerama – more real than real life – was horrifying: it was the Moo, trundling with a determined expression on his face, towards the end of the garden and, more significantly, the cliff path. Cheryl realised that this was a picture painted by the messenger, who had now gone. But the scenario went on spooling through her mind with a life of its own. She saw the Moo emerge on to the path, begin to run along it, stop, peer at a gap in the fence, force himself through it, misjudge the nearness of the crumbling cliff-edge, tip forward – *oh God!* She let out a scream and sprang up. Dermot had entrusted her with his precious children. She could not even look after them for a single day without one of them dying.

From his vantage point, perched on Janey's windowsill, with the window ajar to let out his cigarette smoke, Hugh watched Cheryl teeter as fast as her high heels would allow, across the lawn towards the rhododendron bushes at the end of the garden. He saw her turn and gesticulate at the house, possibly towards the very window he was sitting in. She was shouting something.

'Mrs Chummy Bum's in a state,' he remarked to his sister, who was lying on her – on Sabrina's – bed, chewing the ends of her hair. 'She's belting across the lawn and shouting.'

'I can hear. Just about. What's she saying?'

'It sounds like "Ooo" or "Mooo." Silly cow.'

214

'Maybe she's lost the Moo.'

'I hope she's not going on to the cliff path in those shoes. You never did make that danger notice, did you? You're as bad as me.' He looked at his cigarette with distaste. 'I don't really like these menthol jobs.'

'Serve you right for nicking them.'

'I didn't nick them. They're Cheryl's butts. She only smokes half a fag at a time. Very extravagant.'

'Do you think the Moo's out there?' wondered Janey.

'No. He knows he's not allowed.'

'Then why is she all in a kerfuffle?'

'Hell's teeth, I'd better go.' But as he sprang to the floor, the subject in question appeared at the door, rubbing his eyes.

'Have you seen Spiv?' asked the Moo. 'I was asleep and when I woke up Spiv had escaped.' He indicated the ribbon across his body and the lack of Spiv on the end of it. 'Or been stolen,' he added darkly. 'Dada'll kill you if he sees you smoking.'

'If Mrs Chummy goes on to the cliff path and turns an ankle...' worried Janey.

'She's got good ankles. Besides, I doubt if I could catch her now.'

'You could if you ran.'

'Hell's teeth.'

'You'd better.'

'Yes.' And Hugh set off in pursuit of Cheryl.

Charles felt a bit foolish, standing there trussed up in a chain. He had managed, though, to loop the chain around his free arm and then, by grasping the last links in the fingertips of his already tied arm, to bind the free arm as well. It remained only to snap the padlock shut, to shuffle forward half a pace on his bottom – he was in a sitting position – and to slip silently into the watery gorge. If he hesitated, it was only because he had momentarily envisaged the great pike, tearing at his face. But that was absurd. He didn't even believe in the existence of the fish.

He strained his eyes to see across the lake, through the twilight, to the terrace. He didn't want to risk being seen or heard – he'd already made a complete recce of the lakeside. There was no one about. His index finger crooked itself over the padlock: one little

215

press and he'd be as helpless as a swaddled baby. He closed his eyes. But just as he was about to seal his fate, he heard a disturbance back along the path. In a flash, cursing under his breath, he flipped the loose end of the chain off his arm and unwound it from his body. The loosened chain dropped at his feet. He kicked it into the bushes before strolling back along the path with as nonchalant an air as he could muster. The sound came closer. A largish creature – about the size of a wild pig, estimated Charles – was crashing towards him on a collision course through the undergrowth. He stopped at a point where he judged the creature would emerge. The path widened out here, almost into a clearing. He waited with, he had to admit, some trepidation. Wheezing breaths could now be heard, and painful grunts that sounded not unlike human speech – that sounded, in fact, not unlike "bugger".

And so it was: Bugger Lamb burst into the clearing. He was very out of breath and his colour was alarmingly high. At his side, equally out of breath, was Colonel Bogey.

'Evening, Lamb,' said Charles with a civility he did not feel. 'What goes on?'

Bugger Lamb clasped Charles by the lapels, unable to punctuate his wheezing with any words. His mouth worked soundlessly, his eyes bulged, his breath smelt of sour meat. He jabbed a finger in the direction he'd come from. Right on cue, with a lazy rolling gait, there blazed out of the bushes a fully-grown Siberian tiger. Not the most sizeable, perhaps. But big enough.

'Nobody move,' said Charles carefully. The tiger approached in a leisurely way, as if he were out for a Sunday constitutional. His burning eyes appraised the little group with scientific detachment.

'Bugger that,' panted Bugger Lamb. He began to back away from Charles. Colonel Bogey watched him, tongue hanging out, and then looked up at Charles with a questioning expression.

'Stay,' said Charles. The Colonel looked doubtful. He moved a foot towards Bugger Lamb. 'No,' said Charles. 'Heel.' Suddenly, and for the first time in his life, Colonel Bogey came smartly to Charles's heel.

The tiger advanced to within four paces, continuing to regard them with professional interest. Its spicy smell caused a whimper to escape the Colonel. At the same moment Bugger Lamb broke.

He made a dash for the water's edge, doubtless, thought Charles – who seemed to have plenty of time for thought since everything was occurring in slow motion – doubtless because he believed, quite erroneously as it happened, that tigers were unable or, at least, unwilling to swim.

The tiger accelerated like a Ferrari. Its stripes bunched briefly like a concertina and then it was a fire-bomb, sailing through the twilight. It landed soundlessly and with great precision on the Lamb shoulders. The Secretary of the Tennis Club pitched forward.

'Oh bugg –' he began. But his last words, as predictable in death as they had been in life, were never completed, his neck having been snapped by teeth even before he had hit the ground. The tiger did not, as Charles hoped, begin to feed. It was obviously not hungry but only playing. It seemed fascinated by the twitching of the Secretary's legs; and, while it batted at them experimentally, Charles took the opportunity to retreat a couple of steps, pushing back the Colonel who was pressed, trembling, against the backs of his legs. Immediately the tiger turned its attention on them. A rumble, as of distant thunder, infinitely menacing, sounded in its throat. Charles and the Colonel were rooted to the spot. The hair on their bodies rose in unison. The tiger lowered its body and began to slink towards them, its shoulders working up and down like a catwalk model.

Cheryl followed the path into the giant rhododendrons. It was like a cave inside. Out of breath, she wove and ducked between the knotty stems. They seemed to move and convulse like a speeded-up film of plants growing, yet they never changed. What was *happening* to her? Was she going mad? Worst of all, she kept seeing things, unpleasant things, in the corner of her eye; but when she swung around to pin them down, there was nothing but seething foliage. There! Now! Her heart gave a jolt as she glimpsed a skinny figure with long grey hair. But when she looked again it was nothing but a rhododendron trunk and its shadow, a trick of the light.

Out on the path she glanced to left and right. Which way? Recent drizzle had left the path wet. It shone oddly, like quicksilver. She could see something lying on the path to her left, and headed towards it. Her eyes seemed to home in on the object, like binoculars. It was the wretched Moo's stuffed toy. Her heart renewed its pounding.

Her flesh turned spongy on her bones. If Spiv was there, the Moo was nearby. But where? He would never be separated from his pet unless – was that a gap in the fence? A gap big enough for a small boy to…?

She began to run towards the small stuffed toy, its arms raised in gay abandon or, as it now seemed, in horror. She felt a sharp pain across her ankles, staggered, lost her balance on a dip in the path, and tumbled forward. To break her fall she twisted sideways as she crashed into the fence and felt it give under her. She closed her eyes.

When she opened them again she was lying on her back, staring at the leaden sky. She moved slightly, and the fence beneath her gave a little more. It was bent outwards, almost at right angles to the cliff, with her spread-eagled on top of it. There was nothing underneath her except the ground, nearly two hundred feet below. She could see it clearly, as if she had eyes in the back of her head. Pebbles could be heard trickling down the cliff-face. She dug her fingers into the fence and tried to edge forward, feet first, back on to the path. The simple bracing of her body caused a further avalanche, and the almost horizontal fence jolted sickeningly downward another degree. She could not move an inch.

A breeze riffled over her. Moreover, it seemed to pass easily through her body. It occurred to her that she had nothing to fear, for the simple reason that she was light enough, like thistledown, to fly. In the distance, she could hear Hugh's voice calling like a wood pigeon. The grey sky began to glow, grow golden – and she realised that she was looking at a vast steppe covered in golden moss; and across that endless plain, to a muffled drumming of hoof-beats, surged herds upon herds of beautiful reindeer. In spite of herself, she smiled. The fence collapsed.

The tiger stopped in front of him. Charles Hamilton gazed deeply into the eyes of the tiger, who returned his gaze with the sublime indifference of a god. Charles was mortally afraid. Yet, as the silent communion went on, his fear gave way to exultation. He was about to be initiated into the great secret of death. He had seen the way the tiger had killed the Secretary: so efficient, so elegant – so much more dramatic and swift than the death he had planned for himself. He felt a kind of kinship with the animal, who was, after all, only the agent of Providence. Looking into its divine eyes, he was suffused with, well, a sort of peace.

'Come on then, sir,' he said. The tiger ran its huge rough tongue around the outside of its jaw, but made no move. 'Come *on*, man.' Charles opened his arms to emphasise both his helplessness and willingness. The tiger concertinaed promisingly, and snarled. Charles's heart was beating fit to burst with a kind of wild joy. His only thought was to wonder whether the Colonel would have the good sense to leg it as soon as the tiger sprang.

But Colonel Bogey had other ideas. He suddenly barrelled out from behind Charles's legs with a series of deep, impressive, well-controlled barks. The big cat started, as if in mock fear, and broke the mesmeric stare it was directing at Charles. For a second it seemed at a loss in the face of this odd noisy pudding of a creature with his raised hackles and floppy ears. Then it lifted a great paw that quivered as claws came out of it. Charles saw at once that the Colonel would be eviscerated by its merest swipe. He did something queer.

While the tiger was looking at Colonel Bogey, Charles marched smartly forward and punched it on the nose. The tiger blinked and licked its lips. Charles punched it again. It jumped back five feet, all four paws in the air. Charles began to shout even more loudly than the Colonel was barking. In tandem they advanced on the beast. It seemed to smile. Then it turned on its heel and sloped off.

Charles and the Colonel looked at each other. Then, as one, they began to run in the opposite direction. They ran and ran. They did not stop for bush or briar but ran straight through. They didn't stop for the keepers from next door who were combing the grounds in pursuit of the escaped cat. They merely shouted and barked, pointing the way, and kept on running. They ran around the lake, across the drive of the Tennis Club and into the first grass court, slamming the wire door behind them. Safe in the cage of the court, they fell panting and laughing into each other's arms, rolling around and around in ecstasy on the manicured grass.

16

'I killed her,' said Hugh.
It was the following morning. Everyone had been questioned
last night, their stories recorded, their whereabouts ascertained.
Now Hugh was in the drawing room with Detective Chief Inspector
Derek Crail. He was a heavy man with jowls and a thick moustache.
Like a detective in a black-and-white B-film, he wore a three-piece
suit and carried a hat and mackintosh which he now laid carefully
down on an armchair and patted. 'At least, it was my fault. I should
have mended the fence. Dada told me to. But I didn't.' Hugh was
rather red in the face, possibly close to tears.

'And 'ow… how is your dad this morning?' asked the policeman
who liked, when possible, to pronounce his aitches.

'Still sedated.'

'I'm not surprised. He knows how to kick up, doesn't 'e? What a
carry-on. Very highly-strung gentleman.'

'Well, his… his… girlfriend had just died.'

'True. But as a matter of fact, son, neither you nor your father are
responsible for maintaining the fence. It's a public footpath.' Crail
groomed his heavy moustaches with slow, symmetrical movements
of the middle fingers of each hand.

'Still,' said Hugh. He had told his meagre story last night: how he
had pursued Cheryl; how he had emerged on to the path; how there
was an empty space where a section of fence should have been; how he
hadn't dared to look over the cliff but, guessing what had happened,
had sprinted back to the house to look for Theo; how he had been
unable to find him but had found Charles Hamilton instead, looking
as if he had escaped from Bedlam; how the emergency services had
been called. He had not mentioned, however, what he had seen

whilst tip-toeing towards the gap. As if reading his thoughts, the Chief Inspector said:

'And you didn't notice anything unusual on the path?' Hugh almost panicked. Did he *know*? He couldn't, could he?

'Yes. Come to think of it, I did notice something: Spiv.'

'A spiv, eh?'

'No. Spiv is my brother's stuffed toy. A sort of fox.'

'And where is this Spiv now?'

'Well, I gave it back to the Moo.'

'You picked up a piece of evidence from the path and you didn't mention it yesterday.'

'Sorry. I forgot. I was a bit, you know...'

'And how did this Spiv character get on to the path?'

'I don't know. Perhaps the Moo dropped him there. I mean, he's forbidden to go on the path, but kids don't always do as they're told.'

'Except that I'm pretty certain that young Montgomery did not in fact go out on to the cliff yesterday.'

'Well, in that case...'

'So you've no idea 'ow... how the toy got there?'

'Well *I* didn't put it there if that's what you're getting at.'

'Now, now, son. No need to take on. I wasn't getting at anything. It's just that...' The policeman hesitated. 'I 'aven't mentioned this to anyone else, but there was, so to speak, an hanomaly on Mrs Thingy's body.'

'Mrs Cholmondeley.'

'Exactly.'

'What sort of anomaly?'

'Cuts. Quite nasty. On the ankles.'

Hugh summoned up all the informal training he had acquired at Public School in order to keep his face blank. At the same time, the piano wires he had found tied almost invisibly across the cliff path, just before the treacherous dip – these same wires were burning a hole in his jacket pocket.

'Maybe you should ask Mr Hamilton about them.'

'Oh I 'ave, son. I have.'

'And what did he say?'

'He said he'd made the cuts himself with a machete prior to throwing the lady off the cliff. Then he'd thrown the machete into

221

the lake at your Tennis Club. Which is where 'e fell in with the tiger as ate that Colonel Lamb.'

'Well then,' said Hugh.

'Two deaths more or less at the same time. Extremely untidy,' commented Crail, himself a tidy man.

'A strange coincidence.'

'Only thing is, son – I don't believe a word of Mr Hamilton's story. As stories go, it's not a good one. He made it up as 'e went along. I mean, he turns up at the scene of the accident, he looks as if 'e's been dragged through a hedge backwards, covered in scratches and grass stains. He's laughing and babbling about a tiger; and, in the same breath, swears blind 'e's topped Mrs Doofah… Cholmondeley. Turns out he doesn't know the first thing about it. Well, of course, I'm obliged to take him down the station and bang 'im up for the night, but the fact is, son, it's two other blokes I'm interested in…' In fact, the Chief Inspector had been all for writing off the death as an accident, had Charles not rolled up, confessing to the murder and thus putting homicide on the agenda. However, the obvious culprit – the cuckolded Roger Thingy Doofah – had a cast-iron alibi: a bar full of Tennis Club members. '…namely, the two as lives upstairs in the flat. I'm especially interested in this bloke young Montgomery was telling me about, geezer as calls hisself' – he referred to his notebook – '"Colonel Bogey". Don't summing strike you as odd about that name?'

'Yes, but –'

'He doesn't quite fit the picture. Would 'e 'ave… have any reason to hold a grudge against Mrs Cholmondeley?'

'Well, he might have, but, you see –'

'What *sort* of a grudge?'

'Well, she called him smelly. And disgusting. And he *is* rather smelly. But –'

'What? Sort of tramp, is 'e? Gyppo?' Crail was all suspicion.

'No, no. He's a dog.'

'What? An *actual* dog?'

'Yes.'

The Chief Inspector crossed out several items in his notebook.

'And now, what about this Theodore Hamilton – "Theo"- is he a dog? Or a cat?'

222

'No. He's a man.'

'And are you still saying you don't know where 'e... he is?'

'Yes. I mean, he went off yesterday afternoon and he never came back. No one knows where he is.'

'Often do that, does he?'

'No, never. I mean, he might do. He probably does. I... We don't keep an eye on his movements, you know. He can go where he likes.'

'What exactly is 'is relationship with your family?'

'None. I mean, he's a friend.'

'A friend of your father's?'

'Not so much father's. More mother.'

'I understand your mum's under the doctor.'

'She's in a... nursing-home in Bournemouth. For her nerves.'

'And does she see a lot of Mr Theo?'

'Yes. Well, we all do. He lives upstairs, after all. She has French conversation with him. Used to have.'

'"French conversation". I see. So Mr Theo wouldn't take too kindly to your father, ahem, playing away from home?'

'?'

'Your father 'aving a bit of 'anky... hanky-panky, so to speak, with Mrs Wossname... Cholmondeley?'

'He wouldn't like it, no. None of us like it... liked it.'

'A lot of people had it in for Mrs... Cholmondeley.'

'They wouldn't kill her.'

'Maybe not, son. Maybe not. Only, your sister mentioned that Mrs C. told both the 'Amiltons to 'op it. To leave their habode.'

'There was nothing definite. We only 'ad 'er... had her word for it. I'm certain Dada wouldn't have kicked them out.'

'Although Mrs C. seemed certain he would.'

'Yes.'

'So our... Hamiltons'd 'ave... have a good reason to want Mrs C. off out of it. Especially our Mr Theo.'

'Honestly, sir. Theo wouldn't harm a flea.'

'His father thinks he committed murder.'

'*Surely* not...'

'Why else would Mr *Hamilton* Senior confess to an act of 'omicide he obviously didn't do, except to protect someone 'e thought 'ad... had done it, someone close to him – someone who's now mysteriously done a runner?'

'If he had done it, I'd have seen him at the cliff. Probably. I was hard on Mrs Cholmondeley's heels.'

'It says 'ere in my notebook that you was at least four minutes behind Mrs C. –'

'Look. She just *tripped*. The path's Dodgy there. It dips. It was wet and slippery. She was wearing high heels. The fence was wonky – as I should know,' added Hugh bitterly.

'All right, son. Don't work yourself up. You may be right at that. Only, you understand, I 'ave to pursue every line of enquiry. There was the fox, remember. And the cuts to the ankles.'

'Anything could have made them. The fence, nails, stones...'

'I dare say you're right, son. The thing is, what if something were tied across the path? A bit of wire, say? There *was* a sort of a mark, like, on a broken post.'

'*Jesus.*'

'Sorry, son?'

'I mean, Jesus, you're a good detective.'

'We try, son. We try. And if you wouldn't mind not blaspheming? It goes against the grain with me, you see.'

'Sorry. It's just that, if there *had* been anything tied across the path, I'd have run into it myself. I'd have seen it.'

'Unless someone had removed it.'

'They wouldn't have had time.'

'Oh I'd say there was time enough, son.'

'They'd have left footprints. Did you check for footprints?'

'We're policemen, son. Footprints is our bread and butter.'

'I expect there were a lot.'

'Surprisingly few. Some kids –'

'George and Bradley are up and down there all the time.'

'So I gather. Then there were hers, o' course. And yours.' There was a pregnant pause. 'So if I was to ask you again if you saw anything tied across the path, your answer would be...?'

'No.'

'And if I was to ask you if you removed anything...?'

'No. No, of course I didn't.' In fact, the two wires had been quite tricky to remove. Hugh had nearly cut his fingers getting them off the rhododendron trunk.

'So, to summarise: if I was to look in your pockets now, I wouldn't find anything resembling wire?' Hugh's casual laugh sounded much too loud to him. The sweat trickled down his sides.

'You can look if you like.'

'That won't be necessary, son. I'm only saying. If there was wire involved, the miscreant would have fixed it up from the bushes and covered 'is tracks. He wouldn't have left big prints like your number sevens! No, it's Mr Theo Hamilton as needs to answer some questions.'

'Did you find his footprints?'

'Not yet, son.' The Inspector pictured Theo, musician and French speaker, a louche geezer in a slouch hat, catching the boat-train to Paris where he could use the 'language of love' he had honed on Mrs Blyte. 'And you 'ave no idea where he is?'

'No. But there's bound to be a simple explanation.'

'I 'ope so for 'is… his sake. Well, son, that about wraps it up for now. There's just one more thing – Miss O'Flaherty hasn't got an alibi. Says she was in her room all afternoon, writing a letter to some foreign bloke –' he looked at his notebook – 'Pattim. Says she was sacked by Mrs C. that morning.'

'So you're saying she had the opportunity and the motive.'

'Well, that's as may be. What do *you* say?'

'I say that it must have been obvious even to you that she is as innocent as the day is long.'

'No need to take that tone, son. I'm only doing my job.'

'Yes. Sorry. But Bernie – you can't really think…'

'Between you and me, son, I don't. Well, I'll be off back to the station. See if Mr Hamilton is in the mood to tell us where 'is son is. It doesn't much matter. We'll find 'im… him.'

While Hugh was being interviewed by the policeman, the remaining children, including Sabrina and Bradley, were seated at the breakfast room table with Bernie. They were all pale, with dark rings under red eyes. Time had slowed almost to a standstill. It seemed an age since Cheryl had died; and yet, according to the clock, only about seventeen hours had elapsed. There had been no question of any of them going to school – just as Dada had, of course, missed his important board meeting – and so they did not know what to do except stay instinctively in the vicinity of Bernie. But she was herself in shock and, not knowing what to do, made them sip hot sweet tea and in the Moo's case sloppy orange juice. Little by little the situation was beginning to sink in. Sabrina broke the silence:

'I expect Bradley and I will live here now,' she sighed.

'Well,' said Janey, picturing a life sentence of sleeping on the narrow camp bed while Sabrina imparted make-up tips, 'I expect you can stay for a while, but your Dad will be missing you.'

'No, he won't.'

At that moment the Moo began to sob. He could no longer suppress the awful fear that had been gnawing at him. Deep down he suspected that it was impossible, but a part of him believed there was an obvious cause of Cheryl's death. Oh yes, they could talk about a tragic accident ect. but who was the only witness to the event? Who was loitering on the cliff path, his arms lifted in joy, a long smile on his face? Who had uniquely left the Moo's side for the brief interval during which Death had struck? It all added up. Weakly the Moo held up his inseparable companion.

'It was Spiv! Spiv did it!' He buried his face in the murderer's body and wept.

'Ah no, the Moo,' said Bernie, stroking his head. 'Spiv did nothing. Lookit, he's not big enough nor strong enough – and he's never spiteful.'

'He can be vicious,' said George thoughtfully.

'The point is,' said Janey in a clipped voice, 'Spiv is a stuffed toy. For God's sake, the Moo – you *know* he's only a toy. Has no one in this house got the smallest grasp of reality?'

The Moo stared at Spiv. Conflicting emotions passed across his big sad face.

'You're only a toy,' he said wonderingly.

'C'mon, Brad,' said George. 'Let's go and work on the Marine Laboratory.'

But when the two boys arrived at the sandpit which, the day before, they had filled with beautiful translucent water, the sand artfully sculpted around it to simulate dunes, they found that it was empty.

'It's gone,' said Bradley. 'It's gone!' He sounded as though he couldn't get over it.

'*Donner und Blitzen,*' said George. 'It's all drained away. Through those cracks. See? Bloody old sandpit. We'll have to think of a way to plug 'em up.' But Bradley wasn't listening. He walked unsteadily into the damp pit, staggered, and fell to his knees.

'It's gone. It's gone. What am I going to do now? Oh –' and he began to cry uncontrollably.

'I killed her,' said Janey in a low voice.

She had intercepted Hugh after he had shown Chief Inspector Crail out of the front door, and led him into the playroom.

'Yes, of course you did,' replied Hugh tetchily. He was still shaken by his interview. 'You killed her with mind-rays from a distance of three hundred yards. Don't be a clot, Janey.'

Mutely, and with a tragic expression, Janey held up the wax effigy of Cheryl.

'No.' Hugh shook his head. 'Don't start. There's no witchcraft about this. Cheryl just fell. If anything, it's my fault for not mending the fence.'

'But... but *why* did she fall?'

'People trip up. That's all. She had heels on. The path was slippery. Something *may* have got tangled in her ankles – she had cuts, apparently – but we don't have to put sinister interpretations on –' He was stopped by Janey's stifled shriek. She held out the effigy, pointing to its ankles. They had been sliced across. It was unnerving, to be sure. 'Hmm. Well. I have to admit that these... marks are, hmm, suggestive.'

For a second, Hugh had a sort of vision, as if from on high, of a world in which there is no cause and effect but only interconnecting images, such as a wonky fence, some piano wires, a wax effigy, a wet path, Spiv, a pair of high heels – all of which, by a kind of cosmic sympathy, a web of destiny, made up the total meaning of Cheryl's demise.

'I killed her,' repeated Janey, the words muffled by the wodge of wet hair she had in her mouth. She covered her face with trembling hands. In the face of her despair, Hugh returned to the realm of causality. He had vowed to tell no one of his discovery on the path, but now he had no choice.

'Listen, Janey,' he whispered urgently. 'It wasn't you. It wasn't

227

even me. Look. I found these.' He took the wires out of his pocket and held them up. 'They were tied across the path. They were meant for Cheryl. She must have gashed her ankles on them and... and, well, gone over the edge.'

They looked at each other. Neither had to say it – the trap had the Fuehrer written all over it.

'*No*,' said Janey. 'He would never do such a thing. I mean, never deliberately. The Fuehrer's not a...' Hugh shrugged.

'You remember the guitar strings he nicked off me? The Fuehrer's always had a soft spot for garrotting.'

'How did he know that *she*...? And not someone else?'

'Well, someone told Cheryl that the Moo was on the cliff path. Someone put Spiv there to cause panic. It was diabolically clever.'

'The Fuehrer *is* clever.'

'Best little psychopath in the family.'

'We should tell someone.'

'Yes, we should.' They both thought.

'Are we going to?' asked Janey.

'No. I've already lied about the wires to the Chief Inspector. The thing is, the Fuehrer would never *mean* to kill anyone.'

'Of course not. He was just experimenting, as usual. A bit like me with the effigy.'

''Course he was.'

'You know what he's like.'

'Yes. And it would still have been okay if I'd fixed the bloody fence. Besides, everyone wanted her gone. None of us is exactly innocent, least of all Dada who visited this whole pestilence on us in the first place. The trouble is, they're after Theo. How're we going to save him without shopping the Fuehrer to the cops?'

'Oh God, Luh'le Shuggy. *Theo*. It could have been him, you know.'

'How can you say that, Janey? You of all people.'

'It's just that... he told me... he had a...*plan*.'

'What plan?'

'He didn't say. Only that I wasn't to worry about Mrs Chummy.'

'He didn't do it, Janey.'

'Oh, I hope he didn't. He couldn't. But then why has he run away?'

~

But, it turned out, Theo had not run away, far from it, for he turned up in the kitchen, where the children were eating lunch, with a woman they did not at first recognise, wearing as she was an unfamiliar hat, and looking fit and trim. The Moo, who had been carving Fray Bentos-shapes out of his luncheon meat slices, looked up at her and then looked away, continuing his handiwork with heavy breathing. It was George who shouted 'Maman!' and leapt to his feet to embrace her.

'Maman!' echoed Sabrina, doing likewise. Maman hugged both children with appropriate degrees of warmth.

'Darlings! I'm home!'

'God love you, Mrs Blyte! You look *grand*.'

'Thank you, Bernie. I feel grand. And how is my the Moo? Did you miss me, darling?'

'No,' said the Moo, not looking up. Hugh and Janey arrived, drawn by the commotion. Wordlessly they embraced their mother who was beginning now to shed tears.

'I mustn't be silly,' she laughed, wiping her eyes. 'But it is too, *too* divine to see you all. I do believe you've all grown! I've missed you *so* much.'

'But *how* did you get here?' asked Janey.

'Theo, of course. He came down to Bournemouth yesterday on the train. And I talked to him, and to Gareth, my doctor; and, this morning, I discharged myself – and here I am!' She reached behind her and grasped Theo's hand where he stood in the doorway.

'Oh Theo!,' exclaimed Janey. 'So *this* was your plan.' She burst into tears.

'Yes. Well done, Theo,' said Hugh in a manly way. 'But, God, of course – you've no *idea* what's happened.' At once he drew Theo aside and began to speak urgently to him.

'Mrs Cholmondeley fell off the cliff, Maman,' explained George.

'What are you saying, mein darling little Fuehrer? Of course she did not.'

'She did,' said Janey, recovering herself.

'Ah, she did,' said Bernie.

'*Mon Dieu!* Is she hurt?'

'Yes,' said Janey.

'Dead,' said Bernie, adding, 'God be good to her.'

229

'*No. Enfin, c'est incroyable.*'

'Spiv missed you,' announced the Moo.

'Did he, darling? Well, I must kiss him at once!' She scooped up Spiv and the Moo with him, and kissed them both with passion, making the Moo laugh reluctantly. Then she edged around the table to where Bradley was sitting, blank and silent, and cupped his face in her hands before kissing him violently as well, causing his glasses to skew.

'You mustn't worry about anything, Bradley,' she said, hugging him.

'No,' added Sabrina primly. 'Maman will look after us now.'

'Of course I will.'

'Forever and ever,' said Sabrina serenely.

'Well, for the time being. Where is your father, Sabrina?'

'The poor man,' said Bernie. 'He's had the police after him. And now he's recovering.'

'With Lorraine,' said Sabrina.

'Lorraine's nice,' expanded Bradley.

'I see. Theo – where's Theo?'

'He's gone to the police station, Maman,' said Hugh. 'Mr Hamilton confessed to murdering Cheryl. But he didn't of course,' he added quickly, seeing the faces of the young ones, who knew nothing of Charles's confession. 'He just went a bit mad for a minute on account of nearly being killed by the tiger as ate Colonel Lamb.'

'I see that I have some catching up to do,' said Maman, plumping herself down on a chair as if her legs had given. Bernie put tea in front of her. She drank deeply, while everyone watched her, beginning to recall nervously how and why Maman had been taken away.

'You're looking slim, Maman,' said Hugh. His mother smiled gratefully but sceptically at him.

'So, no school today?'

'Under the circumstances, Mrs Blyte, I thought – we all thought…'

'Of course. Where's Dermot?'

'He's asleep.'

'At this hour?' No one answered. Then Janey said:

'He was in a bit of a state yesterday.'

'I can imagine,' said Maman.

'So the doctor gave him some pills to quieten him.'

'He did wake this morning,' admitted Bernie, 'but then there was a class of groan coming out of him I didn't want the children to hear, so I gave him a cup of tea and another couple o' pills and there hasn't been a peep out of him since.'

17

'I killed her,' said Dada.

The Blyte family was assembled in the drawing room where – Roger having waived all rights – the funeral gathering had taken place after the body of Cheryl Cholmondeley had been burnt at Kingston crematorium. Once Theo's absence had been explained, a verdict of accidental death had, after all, been pronounced, just as Chief Inspector Crail had suspected all along. The few mourners (if such they could be called) had dispersed, except for a funny little Irish man who preferred to sit in the breakfast room with Bernie, drinking whiskey, and striving to establish, as the Irish always do, the labyrinthine way in which they were connected, as they always are. Sure enough, the man, Brendan O'Kelly, who turned out to be Cheryl's father, had a second cousin who was related by marriage to Bernie's mother's sister-in-law. As Hugh went into the breakfast room on his way to re-filling the tea-pot, he caught the tail-end of their conversation. In an extraordinary accent of pure blackthorn Irish overlaid with a forty-year patina of Hounslow, Mr O'Kelly was saying:

'... and whin I 'eard it keenin' oi t'ought me toime 'ad come. I t'ought Mister Debt 'ad caught op to me. Bot. Oi wuz wrong. He took me only dorther – 'erself an 'ard woman – inshtead.'

'I heard it too,' said Hugh. Bernie and Mr O'Kelly turned to look at him; but there was no curiosity in their faces. He became conscious of how jarring his voice was to their murmured conference. 'Sorry,' he said.

'Ah well,' said Mr O'Kelly.

Hugh went back to the drawing-room just as Dada was claiming to have killed Cheryl, and Maman was exclaiming '*Pas vrai!*'

'Not *literally*,' said Dada, his irritation suggesting a return to himself from the man who had kept to his bed all week. 'I mean, I blame myself. I know I should not, but I find I do. I cannot help it. Oh, God help me.' He buried his face in his hands.

'Don't torture yourself, Dermot,' soothed Maman. 'It serves no purpose.'

'No, no, I and only I am to blame. It doesn't matter that Luh'le Shuggy so calamitously failed to mend that fence – and after I had asked him to, *begged* him to, all to no avail – nor that Janey failed to assist Cheryl in the care of the young ones – no, I blame myself. I should never have left her to cope alone. If only you had been here, Little Lorna, none of this would have happened. Oh why did you leave your Prince Flasheen Eyes? Why did you leave all of us, macushla? How *could* you abandon poor Cheryl to a pack of murderous brats?'

'How could I indeed? What *was* I thinking of? How could I have been so negligent?'

'Well, well, I dare say we are all sorry. Sorry beyond words. But what was she *doing* on the cliff path, in the wet, wearing high heels? It was madness. What devilry, what witchcraft possessed her to try and run in those conditions? Madness, madness. A lovely woman, in her prime, untimely ripped from me, ripped from us all.'

'Not, on the whole, ripped from Maman, I suggest,' murmured Hugh.

'What's that you say, Luh'le Shuggy? Are you accusing your mother of a deficiency of feeling? That is not something that has ever before been levelled at her. If anything she has always had an excess of feeling. She suffers whatever her loved ones suffer. She suffers acutely for her Prince Flasheen Eyes now. Ah, mavourneen, do not, do not – I am determined to suffer this tragic loss alone. And when, perhaps, after many months, I feel able to raise my heavy head and to hear once more the sweet birds sing and to smell the good air –'

'Bernie has made up a bed in the spare room for you, Dermot. It sounds as if you are ready to take to it.'

'I thank her. I thank you, my dear wife, for being so understanding. What a blessing it is to have you back. Of course, you are not cured of your nerves – how could you be after so short a period of time? – but you are at the very least alive, as others

233

are not. Alive and, as always, sensitive to the needs of your Prince Flasheen Eyes. For, yes, he must needs be alone in the spare room; but it will not be for always. Time brings balm for bleeding wounds. Bruised hearts heal faster than we think.'

'They seem to be pretty much healed already,' said Janey.

'Well, well, my beloved daughter. That is good. I do not say you are unfeeling. You are merely young. Green leaves quickly cover over the cut limb. But you will pardon your poor old Dada if his sad dismembered trunk takes a little longer to put out new shoots and to wave them in the sunlight.'

'Is Dada using metaphor or hyperbole?' asked George, who was being encouraged to name these things at school.

'Pathetic fallacy,' suggested Hugh. 'In every sense.'

'Come here to me, mein dear little Fuehrer, with your mind that is always enquiring,' urged Dada, holding out limbs attached to his trunk. 'Best little brain in the family. Here's a kiss from your fond Dada. We look to you, mein Fuehrer, to cheer the grim hours and to lighten our mental darkness with your bright, honest and forthright countenance. You have never been a murmurer nor a sneerer, have you, my son? It's not your way. You are incapable of a devious thought or an underhand deed.'

'Except,' intervened Hugh. 'Except when it comes to stealing my possessions.'

'Possessions!' cried Dada. 'You talk of possessions at a time like this, Luh'le Shuggy? Your gross materialism does you no credit. Sometimes I wonder if you are in fact the fruit of my loins.'

'Is Luh'le Shuggy a fruit?' the Moo also wondered, looking up from his crayonning.

'Of course he is,' said Maman.

'Of course he is *not*,' said Hugh.

'Metaphorically you are, I think,' considered George. Hugh would normally have taken up the gauntlet of such a squalid remark, but nowadays he couldn't look the Fuehrer in the eye. He still couldn't decide what to do with the venomous piano wire he carried around with him. He had several times meant to confront his brother, but his nerve had failed. It was a can of worms he quailed at opening. What on Earth could George possibly say? The boy had the grace, it was true, to look troubled and subdued; but then so he should.

'Ah, how glad I am that calm now reigns after the storm,' sighed Dada moistly. 'How glad that we can all be exactly as we were before. You need have no fears about the refrigerator, Little Lorna. Your Prince Flasheen Eyes has not yet paid for it, and so it can be rapidly sent back, restoring the blessed status quo.'

'Oh no,' lamented George. 'That means I'll have to give up the meat safe. What'll I cram the Moo into now, when we play Jap prisoners-of-war?'

'The Moo suffers horribly,' added the Moo proudly.

'Don't worry, darlings,' Maman reassured them. 'The refrigerator will be remaining. It represents at least one instance where we will not be returning to the blessed old days, *n'est-ce pas*, Dermot?'

'As you wish, macushla. Personally I doubt that it will protect us as surely from rot and the bluebottle as is generally advertised; but let that pass. If you believe that it will lighten your burden even a fraction, then the expense is well worth it... And now, tell me, the Moo, what it is that you are drawing for your Dada? Bring your picture here to me so that we can enjoy it together. It is first class, the Moo. Although, it is on the violent side of things. This tall heroic With-It fellow, bristling with weaponry, is a clear, if fanciful, representation of your father, is it not? Fetch me your red crayon, the Moo. You have omitted to supply me with the proper mass of red hair, and have applied it instead to this measly ill-groomed fellow lying on the ground. What is he saying? "Yaroo. Gurgle." As well he might, being savaged as he is by a fierce dog. Which of us would be more articulate under the circumstances?'

'It's not a *dog*, Dada. It's a wolf. *Obviously*.'

'Your crayonning paper has typescript on the reverse side,' noticed Hugh. 'Where did you get it, the Moo? Hell's teeth, it's not *my novel*, is it, you horrible little John Thomas?'

'*Enfin*, Luh'le Shuggy!' exclaimed Maman. '*C'est malheureux.* What do you *mean* by using such language? *Vraiment*, I should smack you.'

'But Maman, what would you say if someone crayonned all over your novel?'

'It's not your weedy novel,' said the Moo. 'It's paper I found at the back of the summerhouse. In a trunk.'

'Then what's that writing on it?' Hugh snatched the Moo's art work and began to read aloud:

'*As they danced, pressed together like a single person, they felt the spotlight dancing with them so that, when the Master of Ceremonies suddenly announced in a blaze of light that they were the winners of the Spot Dance, Alice was scarcely surprised, as if the moment, the prize – and, yes, the man – had been forever destined to be hers.* Well, this is not my story.'

'No,' said Maman. 'It is mine.'

'There are more,' said Hugh, leafing through the Moo's pile of paper.

'Mavourneen,' said Dada. 'I can explain.'

'These are the stories, children,' continued Maman, 'which I wrote years ago and entrusted to your father. Who promised to show them to his friends and contacts in the publishing world, with a view to their publication. Alas, they were all rejected. More than once, it seemed. It was something of a blow to my hopes and to my belief in myself as a writer – indeed, in myself as a person.'

'And so you put them away in a trunk in the summerhouse,' said Janey, 'to be rediscovered by future generations.'

'No,' said Maman. 'I never saw them again after my own Prince Flasheen Eyes had taken them away.'

'Little Lorna,' said Dada gently. 'I did not want you to see them. They would only have been a reminder of failure. You were not strong. Your nerves would not have stood it. See how affected you are even now? Your loving Prince Flasheen Eyes put your stories away to spare you.'

'Yes, I see. But you put them away before you showed them to any publishers.'

'Mavourneen! How can you say such a thing?'

'Because it is true.'

'How can you possibly say that?'

'Because I know both myself and you a good deal better since my stay in the loony bin.'

'Told you so,' said George.

'I assure you, macushla, that a so-called loony bin does not cost the sort of money that the Pine Winds Rest Home cost me.'

'Very well. A posh loony bin. For which – do not misunderstand me – I am in retrospect truly grateful. Through my conversations with Gareth, my doctor, I came to realise much about my life of which I was unaware, including the fact that you, Dermot, are capable of hiding my stories away.'

'Why on Earth would I do such a thing?'

'Probably out of fear that I would be successful and become the centre of attention.'

'But I dreamt of, longed for your success.'

'That's what you tell yourself, but it's not true. Any success of mine would have averted attention from yourself and reduced my dependence on you. You would have found this difficult to bear.'

'Now you are simply being hysterical, my dear. You have discharged yourself prematurely from Pine Winds and this is the result. Perhaps I should summon the doctor. Perhaps it would be for the best if you were taken back to the Rest Home, for all that it may break the bank. But money is not a consideration here. The cure of your nerves, together with the feverish fancies they breed, is paramount.'

'It's odd,' said Janey, 'but I'm beginning to believe less and less in Maman's nerves.'

'She is not displaying them now,' added Hugh, 'when perhaps she has most reason to do so, in the light of Dada's deception.'

'How dare you accuse me of deception when, from first to last, I had only your mother's welfare in mind. If I had submitted her sad little stories to publishers, they would have been dismissed out of hand with monstrously cruel remarks. Your mother would have been utterly crushed. At least I was able to break the news of their rejection tenderly, so that she suffered as little damage to her nerves as possible.'

'But the stories were not in fact rejected,' Janey pointed out.

'That is neither here nor there,' retorted Dada. 'With respect, Janey, you have never been a mistress of logic. The facts are these: (a) of course her little stories would *certainly* have been savagely rejected, *ergo* (b) she would have been driven to suicide, if (3) I had not taken considerable pains to spare her that ignominy and humiliation.'

'Glancing at the stories now,' said Hugh, doing so, 'they seem rather intriguing. I wish *I* possessed the power of delineating character in such few apt words...'

237

'Yes, yes. They were not bad in their way, I recall,' said Dada, 'but to one who, I dare say, has some real command over the language of Shakespeare, they are, really – though I don't like to say it – you have forced it out of me – they are almost pitiably slight, the plots naïve, the characterisation thin.'

'They may be as you say,' said Maman. 'I would have liked a second, more professional opinion.'

'Well, well, perhaps I *was* a little hasty. Perhaps I am one who loves not wisely but too well. You must forgive a poor husband who tries only to act in your best interests. You will forgive him, who always puts you and your feelings first; who, appalled at the very thought of your dear, dear little face falling as you read another and another bestial rejection from heartless publishers, tried to soften the blow.'

'Knowing myself, I probably will forgive you, Dermot. But not for the reasons you suggest.'

'Well, well, let's call it water under the bridge in that case. Besides, the stories would have earned next to nothing. And we don't need the money, thanks to my successful career. Writing is no way to make a living – take note, Luh'le Shuggy.'

'All the same...' said Maman thoughtfully.

'Dada is not altogether wrong, Maman,' said Janey. 'The memory of your episode in the Zodiac is fresh in our minds. Who knows if such an episode wouldn't have occurred much sooner if you had suffered literary disappointment?'

'It would not,' said Maman shortly. 'You forget that I was deranged by sleeplessness and starvation brought on by the criminally irresponsible dispensation of drugs by a Harley Street quack with fewer morals than a peddler of snake-oil. A friend, incidentally, of Prince Flasheen Eyes.'

'Hardly a *friend*, macushla,' demurred Dada.

'Nevertheless, Maman,' continued Janey, 'which of us is not scarred by the image of you, suffocating within the closed garage? I see it as clearly as if I were standing at the landing window, looking down on the drive, looking down at the garage doors –'

'Behind which the Zodiac of Death was throbbing,' added George helpfully –

'And I often find myself wondering how far away exactly can the car's engine be heard when the garage doors are closed...'

'I heard it some way off,' said George.

'Mein Fuehrer has acute hearing,' said Dada. 'Best little ears in the family. His Dada's poor old ears, so badly shell-shocked in the War, could never detect the faint hum of a luxury saloon behind fastened doors. You mustn't be morbid, Janey. It does no good to entertain these horrid fantasies. Your mother is safe and well. That is the main thing. I understand that you have all suffered a shock, a series of shocks, and none has coped better or been a greater support than you, my beloved daughter. And I'm delighted to say that, as a reward, your mother and I have decided to buy you the pony you have so often pestered us for.'

'We have decided no such thing.'

'Indeed we have, mavourneen. We discussed it at length. Do you not remember? Ah, perhaps you do not – that dark period of drug-dependency we must draw a veil over...'

'We did not discuss it – I suggested it and was overruled by you on the grounds of expense.'

'Ha-ha-ha. Not at all, Little Lorna, not at all. But even if I had, cannot a fond father change his mind, and bestow gifts on a thoroughly deserving daughter, especially if it helps her to lay to rest disturbing images and neurasthenic fantasies concerning the past?'

'A pony might help, I suppose, Dada. But there can be no guarantee. Certain memories are hard to erase.'

'And yet memories are so often unreliable and hard to distinguish from imaginings, the two becoming mixed in a farrago of fairy tales.'

'I find that, on the contrary, Dada, my memory is accurate. And long.'

'Well, well, that is good. Long may you remember how generous your hard-working old Dada has been to you. How hard he has laboured to keep this family together in the face of dire events and hostile fate. How fervently he intends – if he is spared – to care for his children and his wife, who is miraculously returned to him. You may say that he does not deserve such a blessing. But, on the other hand, you may agree that perhaps his error was not, after all, so great. He was led astray, to be sure, by a beautiful temptress, and suffered a moment of madness, nothing more. It is, of course, unthinkable that he could ever have wished her dead – we all feel the loss of her – yet he cannot help but discern a kind of holy Providence at work, whereby the deceiving angel has, like Lucifer, been expelled and my own dearest wife by the grace of God brought back to me, as it were resurrected. We have all been purified by the ordeal; all utterly, utterly changed.'

'With one notable exception,' remarked Hugh. 'As your speech so amply demonstrates.'

'I understand why you say that, my son and heir,' replied Dada, regarding Hugh with the sad, kind eyes of a St Francis of Assisi. 'You are of a younger generation who eagerly manifests every little change of mood. Oh yes, it is charming in the young to wear their hearts on their sleeves and to show every emotion on their unformed faces. But your father is of an older, sterner generation, whose watchwords are strength and reticence. He shuns outward show. He holds himself in. No matter how violent his inner transformations, he gives – as now – no vent to them. Whereof we cannot speak, sayeth the sainted, er, Einstein, thereof we must remain silent. You are looking at a man for whom, as for the noble King Lear, "The Rest is Silence."'

'I wonder why I feel so doubtful that that is what I am looking at,' mused Janey.

It was Sunday. As was the custom, the children began to filter into their parents' bedroom. The Moo was already in the double bed, cosily ensconced between the two adults, when George arrived. He was carrying Hugh's striped Mod jacket, severely maimed and modified. The seam at the back was torn, the buttons had been removed and holes crudely pierced where they had once been. Leather shoelaces, tied together, had been interwoven between these holes and the true buttonholes. Further laces had been bound tightly around the cuffs, effectively sealing the holes where the hands appear. He brandished the garment in triumph.

'I made this for you, Maman. Nifty, *nein?* Will you get up and try it on?'

'In a minute, mein Fuehrer. I'm just enjoying a quiet cup of tea.'

'Oh, *please*, Maman. It won't take a sec. Make her get up, Dada – oh, 'morning, Theo.'

'Good, er... mein Fuehrer... trust... slept well...?'

'Yes, thanks. Can you make Maman get up, Theo?'

'Perhaps... Lorna... Fuehrer... take trouble...?'

'Oh, very well. Now what is this, mein Fuehrer?'

'No, no, Maman. You put it on back to front – that's it – and it laces up at the back. It's a straitjacket, you see. In case you go barking mad again, Maman. I'll be able to restrain you.'

'Well, that's thoughtful of you, mein Fuehrer. Thank you. I suppose my arms cross over like this, and are tied behind me with those clever thongs attached to the sleeves?'

'Exactly. There! Trussed up like a Christmas turkey. Try and thrash about. Go on. See? You're helpless.'

'I can kick, though.'

'Ouch! Hmm. I must think up some leg restraints. Maybe a *bolas* type of thing to bring you down in full gallop like an Argentine horse...' He removed the straitjacket from his mother and sat down on the floor to fine tune the lacing.

Janey appeared, yawning, in the doorway. She stopped, gaped, stifled a scream and went out again. When she re-appeared she was very composed.

'Good morning, Maman. Good morning, Theo,' she said carefully, throwing herself lengthwise along the foot of the bed, compelling Theo hurriedly to retract his feet.

'Good, er...'

'And how are you this morning, Janey darling?' Maman enquired rather formally.

'A little taken aback,' said Janey, 'but otherwise quite well, thank you. Very well, in fact. I cannot help noticing that Theo wears silk pyjamas.'

'Not, um, meet... your approval...?'

'No, no. They're very nice. Swinging. Fab. I might almost say snazzy.'

'Sloppy,' said the Moo. He added comfortably: 'Theo is our Dada now.'

'Is he, Maman?'

'No, of course not, Janey. Dada will always be Dada. It is just his position as my husband which is under review.'

'You said you could never divorce Dada. Being a lapsed Catholic and that.'

241

'I have not said that I'm going to divorce anyone. Don't put words in my mouth, Janey dear. I merely thought that I would try a different arrangement of the men in this house, in view of circumstances which have come to light. It may turn out that the religion I've neglected may turn out to be less binding than I formerly thought. It may not.' She added irrelevantly: 'I always wanted to speak French in bed.'

'*Ah chérie... comme tu es... belle, hein?... si merveilleuse...*' murmured Theo, taking Maman's hand and raising it tenderly to his lips.

'What's this?' asked Hugh, arriving at that moment in his short paisley-patterned dressing gown. 'Theo in Dada's place? Hand kissing? French? Have I wandered into some squalid Maurice Chevalier porn film?'

'You sound affronted, Luh'le Shuggy,' commented Maman.

'Do I? Do I? Well, well, perhaps I am affronted. I don't know.'

'He sounds like Dada,' said the Moo.

'*Sank 'eaven for leetle girls*,' sang George, not looking up from his handiwork.

'I do not sound like Dada,' retorted Hugh.

'You do a little, dear,' said Maman.

'I'm just trying to adjust to a new and challenging situation. You gave me no warning of this, Maman.'

'I'm sorry, Luh'le Shuggy. It was a spur of the moment thing.'

'And you didn't think it appropriate to conceal your new, ahem, sleeping arrangements from the children?'

'I thought that there had been enough concealment on the whole,' said Maman. 'And the children seem to have adjusted rather more quickly than you.'

'What does Dada say?'

'Dada doesn't know.'

'Hell's teeth. Well, I find that I've adjusted now. 'Morning, Theo – *Jesus wept*, is that my favourite jacket you're shredding, mein bloody little Fuehrer? I can't *believe* it.'

'Shush, shush, Luh'le Shuggy,' reproved Maman.

'You threw it out, Luh'le Shuggy,' protested George. 'It seemed a pity to waste it.'

'*Threw it out?* I did *no such thing*. It was hanging up on the back of my bedroom door.'

'It was on the floor. Thrown out,' said George.

'It was *not*. All right – it may, *may* have fallen off its hanger, but it was not thrown out. *Obviously*. And what were you doing poking about in my room? I ought to bash your head in. Maman, can't something be done about the Fuehrer? Why is he allowed to ruin my life? Can't you control him? Hell's teeth, stop me someone because, so help me, I'm going to bash his head in –'

'Quick, Luh'le Shuggy – put the straitjacket on,' said George, holding out the article, 'before you do something you regret!'

'No one seems to realise,' said Hugh furiously, advancing on George, 'that the Fuehrer is a beastly little psychopath, capable of any crime. If you only *knew* what he –'

'O-oh,' said George in a subdued and urgent voice. 'Here comes Prince Flasheen Eyes.'

'Did no one think to bring me my tea?' complained Dada, rubbing the distinctly unflasheen articles as he entered the room. 'I suppose it is too much to ask that one of my children should –' There was a long silence, on the pregnant side.

'It's a meeting of the Sloppy Club,' said the Moo inventively but apprehensively. 'Go away, Dada. You're not invited.'

'My eyes indeed tell me that I am not, but can I believe them? Am I dreaming, macushla, or is that, of all people... *Theo* in my bed?'

'Our bed, dear. And you can see very well who it is.'

'It is Theo, Dada,' confirmed the Moo, rubbing his plump cheek on Theo's upper arm.

'Good, er... morning, Mr... um...' assayed Theo, politely raising his tea cup.

'Well, well. This is all most amusing, I'm sure. But I should not have thought that this was quite the moment for practical jokes and such. I understand that you, mavourneen, are still perhaps a little hazy about reality, a little highly-strung in the aftermath of your recent luxury rest-cure, and thus having difficulties in judging what is and what is not in the best of taste. But I should have thought that you, Theo, would have known better. Cut along back to your flat, there's a good chap, and we'll say no more about it.'

'He's all right where he is for the moment,' said Maman.

'What are you saying? This is grotesque. I am speechless. Come out of there, the Moo. I will not have a son of mine snuggling up to a silk-clad species of sissy.'

'Hush, dear,' said Maman. 'And, incidentally, that is another thing – the Moo is not strictly speaking your son.'

'Oh very good. Very good indeed. And whose son does your feverish imagination suppose he is, pray? The bum boy's, I suppose.'

'If you mean Theo, then yes.'

Everyone was silent while their separate minds worked. The Moo was first to grasp the essence of the thing:

'So, Theo is my Dada?'

'Yes.'

'Yippee!' The Moo scrambled to his feet and began to bounce up and down on the bed, pointing his finger at each of his siblings in turn. '*You*, Luh'le Shuggy, are from the Bogs! *You*, mein Fuehrer, are from the Bogs! *You*, Janey –'

'They are *not* from the Bogs,' cried Dada; but the Moo was unstoppable.

'You're all from the Bogs except me. *I'm* from... Where am I from, Theo?'

'Um... mother's side... ultimately... Holy Land... via, er, Germany.'

'The Holy Land! Germany! I'm probably related to Baby Jesus! And Hitler! No wonder I'm the Sultan of Sloppy!'

Dada's face was the colour of raw liver. He advanced to the bed, breathing loudly through his nose. He put his face near to Theo's.

'You... you...,' he hissed between clenched teeth. But for once, words failed. He held up a fist and drew his arm back to strike. With a quick short jab, Theo hit Dermot on the nose.

'Your hands, Theo!' shrieked Maman.

Caught off balance and by surprise, Dada rocked on his heels and teetered five steps backwards. His arms windmilled briefly. Then he sat down with a bump on the floor, his legs stretched straight out in front of him. He licked the blood which trickled from his nose and over his top lip.

'I'm fairly certain,' he said, 'that I'm going to lose my temper.'

A *frisson* passed like electricity through the assembled company. The Moo slipped under the bedclothes and moved closer to Theo; Janey rolled on to the floor, and sat with her back braced against the foot of the bed; Hugh retreated to the yellow sofa; George held his straitjacket nervously in front of him; Maman sipped her tea.

'Um… sorry.'

'Well, you should have thought of that, Theo. Now it is too late. You have torn it. I am losing my temper.'

Dada began slowly to rise like a piston-driven engine working up a head of steam.

'You're going to stop him, Maman,' hoped George.

'Yes, stop him, Maman,' echoed the Moo, his words muffled by blankets.

'I think it might be best,' said Hugh, trying to sound calm.

'Do you know, children,' replied Maman, 'I've had twenty years of stopping the temper. I don't know that I can be bothered any more.'

'If people still said "Dodgy",' said George, 'I'd say "Dodgy".'

Strange noises began to be heard within the depths of Dada. Violent belly noises which rumbled up towards his head.

'This is frightening,' said Hugh.

'Yes,' said George. 'But it *is* interesting.'

Dada's shoulders were lifting up to his ears, which changed colour from vermilion to a livid white.

'It's strange,' said Janey, 'but I'm not feeling at all as I imagined I'd feel.'

'Hadn't we better take the children out?' wondered Hugh.

'Let them stay, I think,' said Janey. 'They may as well know the worst.'

'He might kill someone.'

'I'm beginning to doubt it.'

''E looks like Tom,' said the Moo, peering over the bedclothes. 'In Tom and Jerry. When smoke comes out of 'is ears.'

And indeed, smoke was, metaphorically at least – or perhaps pathetically fallaciously – beginning to hiss from Dada's pale ears. His contorted face was horribly mottled with red and white blotches. Purple veins stood out to a dangerous degree.

'Theo,' said the Moo apprehensively. 'Is his head going to explode?'

'One hopes… the Moo… not. Touch and, um… go.'

For a long moment Dada was as still as a gargoyle, frozen in his rage, sparks flying from his mane of hair, the upward rumbling growing in volume like a huge breaker approaching the shore. His mouth opened. Everyone's mouths opened in sympathy, their bodies instinctively flinching back and bracing themselves against the imminent world-annihilating roar.

But Dada's mouth simply opened wider and wider, the expression in his blood-bolted eyes turning to surprise and then panic. From out of his throat came a little squeak.

'Dabs am werry frighty,' mentioned Dabs kindly, but unconvincingly.

'Is that *it*?' asked Hugh, as Dada sank to the floor again.

There was a knock on the door, and Bernie's head appeared around it.

'Hello. Is this a bad time, Mrs Blyte? Only I wanted a word.'

'What is it, Bernie?'

'Ah God, Mrs Blyte. I'm only pregnant.' Hugh let out a strangled cry.

'Well,' said Janey, 'Bernie has provided us with the drama we were counting on Dada for.'

'It's not funny,' said Bernie, her eyes filling with tears.

'What's the matter with Bernie?' asked the Moo, upset.

'She's going to have a baby,' said Maman.

'Oh that's very sloppy of you, Bernie,' approved the Moo.

'You mustn't worry, dear. It's not the end of the world. Mr Blyte will telephone your people and discuss what is to be done.'

'Bernie's parents are dead,' the Moo reminded her in a worried voice.

'This is no time for your nonsense, the Moo, dear. Now, help your poor father to his room, Luh'le Shuggy and Janey. Lunch will be at two o'clock sharp.'

18

DADA was not up to making any 'phone calls, so Hugh did it. The ringing tone sounded a continent away. There was a click.

'Hello. This is Coolmore 9. The Post Office. Mrs Quealy speaking.'

'Hallo. This is Hugh Blyte. I was hoping to speak to Mr or Mrs O'Flaherty. But I seem to have the wrong number.'

'Is that Bernie's employer? It's a pleasure to speak to you, sir. And how is Bernie now?'

'She's fine, thank you. And, actually, I'm not her employer – I'm the son of the employer.'

'Little Shoggy, is it? Well, how're you? I was devastated to hear about your poor mother's death, God be good to her. Bernie wrote us all about it. And the poor baby Moo left motherless –'

'It wasn't my mother who died, actually.'

'Was it not? Who died then?'

'It's a long story.'

'Sure, I've plenty of time.'

'The thing is, Mrs Quealy, I'm 'phoning from England, and time presses at this end. So perhaps you could give me the O'Flaherty's 'phone number.'

'This is the number for the O'Flahertys.'

'Didn't you say it was the Post Office?'

'That's right. They've no 'phone. No one has a 'phone, except meself and Doctor Prendergast – and he never answers the thing in any case, so –'

'How can I speak to the O'Flahertys?'

'I'll run over and fetch them.'

'Won't that take rather a long time?'

'Ah God, it's no trouble. Hold the line, please.'

Hugh was left holding a receiver filled with a sound like the sea. Bernie stood next to him, waiting.

'Mrs Quealy,' he said, 'is fetching your parents.' She nodded. 'How far away do they live?'

'Not far.'

'Dada's going to go mad when he sees the 'phone bill. Why did you say your parents were dead?' Bernie looked puzzled. 'You know, why did you lie?' he asked. Bernie thought for a moment but nothing came to her. She shrugged. Hugh realised that he was looking at someone more mysterious than he had thought. The language they held in common fostered the illusion that they shared a common culture. 'Your Dad's not even fat, is he?'

'Well, he's not a thin man.' Hugh shook his head. Truth for Bernie was a moveable feast, only adhered to when it was more colourful than her version of the world, or as a last resort. What a wonderful girl she was. His anger evaporated on the instant. You could no more be angry with Bernie than with the strange, ambiguous *Sidhe*.

'May I ask who's baby it is?'

'Ah God, Luh'le Shuggy, I'm not sure. One o' them eejits at the Socials. I wish I'd been harder on them now. 'Twas only a bit o' fun. I wasn't bothered half the time, but they were all so desperate for it, God love them.'

'I wish it was mine.'

'Oh, Luh'le Shuggy, so do I.' She put her arms around his neck and laid her head on his shoulder and cried for a little while until Mrs O'Flaherty's voice was heard. Hugh handed the receiver to her and tip-toed away.

'I'm pregnant, Ma,' he could hear her saying. 'Ah God, don't take on… No, Ma… yes, I'm sure it's mine… No, I'll tell Pat Tim myself… Mrs Blyte says it's not the end of the world… and how's Da? Did he? Well, isn't that like him, the big eejit. Had he drink taken? Well, that'd explain a lot…'

'…and Lorna opened the front door. There, stood a young dark-eyed stranger…'

'Theo,' said the Moo dreamily, drawing the sheet higher over their heads and gazing through the window patch that seemed to frame the diffident features of his biological father as a younger man.

'Yes. Theo. Who blushed and mumbled: "Advertisement… flat to rent… self and, er… father…?" And at once, without even knowing that he was musical and spoke French, Lorna said: "Do come in. The flat is yours if you'd like it." For she knew, even as she did not know, that destiny was showing its hand to her that day, and that something momentous would be the result.'

'The Moo,' said the Moo confidently.

'Well, yes. The Moo, certainly. But not immediately. Not at that moment. At *that* moment Lorna knew only that this strange dark-eyed young man…' The Moo closed his eyes and let his mind go blissfully blank, a canvas on which Maman's lively voice painted bright pictures that grew animated as they merged with his dreams. The Moo was asleep.

When Hugh and Janey went into the playroom for a record session to help them absorb the morning's surprises, they were immediately assaulted by the sound of Sabrina's show tunes and by the stench of burning plastic. Sabrina was miming to her music; Bradley and the Fuehrer were melting 45s with a Zippo lighter and sculpting them into wavy-edged bowls. Hugh leapt across the room, snatched a soft disc from his brother's hands and peered at the centre label. He let out a howl of anguish:

'My records! The Everly Brothers! How *could* you?' Sabrina was sufficiently impressed by his bellow to turn the record player off; and, in the ensuing silence, George spoke:

'I'm putting them to good use,' he claimed defiantly. 'You never play them so we're making them into Art.'

'Of course I play them. But that's not the point – they're my old records, *my* records, my childhood. They're… precious.' Hugh was clearly too upset even to bash George's head in. He just stood there, turning the ruined record round and round in his hands as if he might mould it back into flatness. 'I can't understand you, George' – there was a break in his voice – 'I honestly think you're deranged. You don't care what you destroy. I'm beginning to be sorry that I protected you from the police.'

'What did he do?' asked Bradley, pushing his black spectacles up on to the bridge of his nose.

'He… He knows what he did.'

To everyone's surprise, George burst into tears. It was so rare a sight that, in spite of himself, Hugh's fury abated. Through his sobs, George blurted out:

'I killed her… I d-didn't mean to… I killed your Mum, Brad… I… I'm so sorry… so sorry.'

Just then, Dada appeared.

'Where is the hosepipe, mein Fuehrer?'

'In the garage, I expect, Dada,' replied George, hastily concealing his tears. 'Maman had it last.'

'When will she learn to put things back in their proper place?' asked Dada rhetorically.

'She was a little indisposed at the time, Dada,' said Janey. 'If you recall.'

'Everyone in this family is always ready with some feeble excuse. And where are the car keys?'

'In your pocket as usual, I expect, Dada,' said George.

'Yes, well, it is lucky for you that here they are,' said Dada, fishing them out.

'Are you going somewhere, Dada? With the hosepipe?' asked Hugh.

'The journey I embark on, Luh'le Shuggy, is a long one. Yet it will take but a moment.'

'Well, lunch is at two o'clock,' Janey reminded him as he went out again. The children looked at each other.

'The Fuehrer didn't kill your Mum, Bradley,' said Hugh. 'He just feels guilty. We all do.' He bent down and whispered in George's ear. 'Don't say another word. I've got the piano wire. No one can prove a thing.'

But George only began to weep again. Once the dyke of guilt had been breached, the waters of confession could not be stemmed:

'It was an experiment. That's all. I did it just like I was supposed to. Only, I hadn't got a reindeer, of course. So I used Colonel Bogey instead.'

'What are you blathering about, you squalid child?'

'The toadstool. The fly agaric. You have to feed it to reindeer and then drink their wee-wee. I fed it to Colonel Bogey and collected his wee-wee in a pan. But I thought it might be too strong for a boy, so I gave it to a grown-up. I gave it to Cheryl, in her coffee, to see what would happen. And she must have jumped off the cliff, thinking she could fly, like that girl in California on the news. Oh, oh, oh.'

'But that's not all, is it, George?' said Janey gently, but sternly.

'What? Yes, it is. I promise. I don't know anything about what Luh'le Shuggy said. About piano wire.'

'What piano wire?' said Bradley, alarmed and bewildered.

'Do not be too hard on my Fuehrer,' interrupted Sabrina, sounding uncannily like her mother. 'I am sure it was only a prank. The main thing is, to get rid of the piano wire, if you have it, Hugh.'

'Why should I get rid of it?'

'Fingerprints,' said Sabrina. 'The Fuehrer's fingerprints will be all over them.'

'You said "them", Sabrina. How do you know there's more than one piano wire?'

'You said there was,' smiled Sabrina.

'No, he didn't,' said Janey.

'Well, I assumed.' Sabrina put her head on one side and looked at them sweetly and even slightly pityingly. 'Obviously I am wrong.'

'No. You are not wrong.'

The truth was dawning, with great clarity, simultaneously in the minds of Hugh and Janey.

'Perhaps you're worried,' said Janey, 'about your own fingerprints.'

'Me worried? What would I have to worry about?'

'You had a piano lesson on the Saturday,' said Janey.

'No, I didn't. Theo changed it from the morning to the afternoon, but when I went...'

'Exactly. When you went,' said Hugh, 'you found that he wasn't there because he'd run away. Or, rather, hadn't run away, but had gone to Bournemouth. And Mr Hamilton was out. The flat was empty.'

'It's no good trying to pin the blame on me,' said Sabrina, 'so as to save your precious brother.'

'I don't know anything about piano wire,' protested George, wiping away his tears at this interesting development.

'We are beginning to believe you,' said Janey. 'It is Sabrina who knows all about piano wire.'

'You can't prove that.'

'No, but I expect the fingerprints experts can.'

'There won't be any prints. The wire's too thin.'

'Well, we'll see,' said Hugh, pulling the wires out of his pocket. 'I'll take them to the police now.'

'Is that a good idea, Hugh?' wondered Sabrina. 'After all, *your* fingerprints are all over them now. Everyone will think you did it, not a little girl like me. I'll tell them you did it. I'll tell them I saw you on the cliff path. I *did* see you, tying the piano wires across. I'll tell them –' But she was stopped in full flow by Bradley, who let out a yell and then ran at her with flailing fists.

'*You* did it, Sabrina! You killed Mum. You killed Mum.' Sabrina was knocked backwards by the velocity of his attack, which stopped as abruptly as it had begun. Bradley sank down on to a mattress and, pulling up his knees, hid his face in them.

The rest of the children looked at Sabrina, who was rubbing the side of her face.

'So you stole Spiv off the Moo while he was asleep and put him on the path. And then you told your mother that the Moo was up there,' said Hugh, thinking aloud. Sabrina shrugged.

'I'd never have thought of it if Bradley wasn't always going on about garrotting George with piano wire. It's his fault as well. You can't just untie them, you know. I had to cut them with special pliers Mr Hamilton has. The first one nearly took my eye out,' she complained. 'I didn't think it would work,' she added in a small voice. 'I just wanted to be in your family. Where it's cosy and… and funny. I just wanted a kitchen not all metal and clean but warm and cobwebby.'

After some time, George said:

'Should we save Dada?'

'I suppose so,' replied Hugh absently. He was sitting next to Bradley on the mattress, holding one of his wrecked Everly Brothers' records. He looked around him. Eighty per cent of the people in the room were murderers. If not in fact, like Sabrina, then as good as. His negligence, Janey's spells, the Fuehrer's hallucinogenic experiments – who could say what the decisive factor had been?

'It'll take him quite a long time to rig up the apparatus,' said Janey. 'He's not as handy as Maman.'

'I wouldn't be surprised if he botches the whole thing,' agreed George. 'Still…'

'Still,' said Hugh. 'We'd better stop him before he gets brain damage.'

'Although,' said Janey, 'Dada as a vegetable might be rather sweet.'

'I don't understand any of you,' said Bradley.

'Dada's gone off to commit suicide,' explained George.

'Why aren't you stopping him?'

'I don't know. I expect we will.'

'We're having trouble really believing in it,' said Janey. 'But don't worry, Bradley. I'm sure one of us will do something any minute now.'

'I'll go,' volunteered Sabrina.

'No, you won't,' said George. 'You might help him. You're good at rigging things up.'

'I won't. I wouldn't. I love your Dada.'

'Well, we all love him,' said Hugh irritably. 'In a way. Don't we?'

'Yes,' said George.

'In a way,' said Janey. They all thought about him.

'It's not all his fault he's like he is,' said Janey. 'He's got an inferiority complex, coming from the Bogs.'

'And he was shaken up in the War,' added George. Then: 'I'll go. I'm the best little brain in the family. Plus, I have the experience.'

'No,' said Janey decisively. 'I'll go.'

As she approached the garage, Janey stopped at the spot on the drive where, from the landing window, she had once seen Dada stop and execute the cricket stroke. She cocked her head and listened, just as Dada had cocked his head before the Black Mini had roared past, distracting him. But today there was no Black Mini; there was only silence. Perhaps Dada had changed his mind. Janey found herself wondering whether, if he had not – if she could hear the Zodiac, as he must have heard it – she would proceed.

She went towards the closed doors of the garage, and still she heard nothing until she was only a few feet away. Only then did the hum of the Zodiac's engine reach her ears. She suffered a rush of remorse that she could ever have suspected her father of... well, of hearing the car's engine when Maman had been... Remorse and gratitude.

Hurriedly she pulled the doors open and yanked the hosepipe

out of the side window. Dada was looking distinctly green. He began to cough.

'What took you so long?' he spluttered, with real annoyance.

The spare room was darkened. The Moo poked his head around the door, and addressed the humped form in the bed.

'Are you dead, Dada?'

'Perhaps you wish that I were, the Moo,' came the muffled reply.

'No, Dada,' said the Moo, negotiaing the bowl on the floor beside the bed for Dada to be sick in. 'I want you to be well. Here. Drink this.'

'What is it?'

'Sloppy orange juice.'

'That is only available to Sloppy Club members.'

'The Sultan of Sloppy invites you to be a member, Dada.'

'Never. Never as long as that… that *person* is a member.'

'Do you mean Theo, Dada? He's a sort of Dada too.'

'I cannot bear to hear you calling another "Dada".'

'He hasn't been my Dada for ages and ages, ever since I was little, like you, Dada. Theo is only my sloppy Dada.'

'Are you saying that I'm your *real* Dada, the Moo?'

The Moo considered. 'You're the Dada I'm used to. If you died, Spiv would cry.'

'Would he? Well, well, I will consider your offer of Sloppy Club membership. It is long overdue, I might add, but I say nothing on that score. Now is not the time for raking over the past. I have walked through the Valley of the Shadow of Death, and I have emerged into the sunlight, purged, purified, reborn and ready to –'

'Here is your Sloppy Club badge, Dada.'

'Well, thank you, the Moo. I accept it in the spirit of reconciliation in which it has been tendered. I dare say I am man enough to live with the other members, providing we are not cheek by jowl – Colonel Bogey in particular is no nosegay – yes, I think I have acquired through my long dark night of the soul sufficient wisdom to rise above the petty cares of this world and to grow, and move forward, and –'

'That'll be two shillings, please,' said the Moo.

'That… that bestial nancy boy only paid sixpence!'

'The cost of sloppiness has gone up, Dada.'

'You will be a financier, the Moo,' said Dada, not without admiration.

But if Dada was indeed subject to inner transmogrification, as he claimed, it was the outer change that was the more striking. When he woke the next morning, feeling restored, he was startled by the sight of a brown squirrel nestling on the pillow beside him, not three inches from his face. He jerked away with a shout of fear. But it was not a squirrel, nor any sort of animal.

By the time that Maman, alerted by his wild cry, arrived in the spare room, her husband was silent, sitting up in bed, and turning over in his hands a mass of hair, of a colour which he had traditionally insisted was red; but which, as perhaps he was clearly seeing for the first time, was in fact brown with the odd auburn strand that caught the light. In short, whether from recent shocks or through the insidious action of unmanifested temper, Dada's hair had fallen out; and, apart from a residual band of hair around the perimeter, his head was bald.

part Three

19

IT was, inevitably, Sunday. Janey, the Moo and George were already disposed here and there about the parental bed when Hugh strolled in, smoking a Player's No. 6.

'Ah-ha,' said Dada. 'Here is the Young Master, cutting quite a dash as usual. No doubt he has returned briefly from our capital city to the bosom of his family in order to avail himself of a square meal. Well, well, he is welcome, no matter how eccentric his appearance – you wear a species of necklace, I observe, Luh'le Shuggy, and your hair sweeps over your collar. If this is a forlorn attempt to emulate your father, it will not serve – hair must be thick, lustrous and upwardly amassed as mine is, and not hanging lankly over the ears like some degenerate oik of a pop singer.'

'Your hair certainly cannot be said to be lank, Dada,' replied Hugh, regarding the stiff candy-floss-like confection that covered his father's pate. 'It is a triumph of art over nature. To say nothing of the victory of vanity over common sense.'

'Say, rather, Luh'le Shuggy, that it is merely a re-creation of my natural condition. Is it vanity to supply for myself what nature originally bestowed upon me?'

'Nature's gift has been somewhat enhanced, if memory serves,' demurred Hugh, gazing in wonder at the violent redness of the hairpiece. 'I marvel that Maman's nerves can stand sleeping beside such a folly.'

'It has been testing,' admitted Maman. 'But I've been won over by your father's reckless bravery in wearing it. And if you must smoke those vile little ciggies, Luh'le Shuggy, open the window a crack and sit by it.'

'And how are Mr Davis, Mr Lang and Mr Dick, the recipients of frequent cheques drawn on my bank?' asked Dada. Davis, Lang and Dick was the name of Hugh's tutorial college in London.

'No one has ever seen them, Dada. But my tutors are satisfied with my progress, I think. I got another alpha this week. For my essay on *King Lear.*'

'At last! Luh'le Shuggy is acquainting himself with the language of Shakespeare! Soon we shall be conversing on equal terms, my son. How eagerly I look forward to that day. I will consider the monies lavished on a London crammer well spent.'

'Also, I have heard the result of my interview at Balliol. They will give me a place if I get two "A"s and one "B" at "A" level.'

'Is that good, darling?' asked Maman.

'It's fine, Maman.' They exchanged a smile.

'Does that mean that you will get these As and Bs, Luh'le Shuggy?' asked Dada.

'Yes.'

'Well. To think that a son of mine will be going to the world-famous Oxford University. The son of a humble, but hard-working immigrant who has, I dare say, succeeded beyond all expectation despite his comparatively lowly origins –'

'In the Bogs,' expanded the Moo.

'*Not* in the Bogs, whatever they are,' said Dada tersely, 'but... elsewhere. Ah yes, to think that Luh'le Shuggy's begowned figure will be strolling indolently through the picturesque quads of Oxford colleges, where Kit Marlowe and Jack Milton and Ludo Wittgenstein have strolled!'

'All Cambridge men, Dada, but never mind,' murmured Hugh, flicking the ash from his No. 6 out of the window.

'One supposes that you will be running up bills at the College bar and at your tailor's for port wine, tail coats, etcetera. Well, well, I dare say funds can be made available. I won't have it said that a son of mine was looked down upon by Lord Snooties from Eton and Harrow.'

'They are more likely to be whiz-kids from Manchester Grammar, living off the fat of maximum grants,' said Hugh.

'Well, you must choose your own friends and associates, Luh'le Shuggy. But do not shun the scions of noble houses with their spats and amusing teddy bears through some misguided labour-party belief in the intrinsic value of working-class boys.'

'No, Dada. I promise not to entertain in my rooms any undergraduate of a rank lower than belted earl.'

'You may mock at me now, Luh'le Shuggy, but you will see the value of my advice in later life.'

'How's the novel going?' asked Janey shyly. She was a little awkward with her brother now that he had started a new life in an exotic location.

'It isn't. I have abandoned Art in favour of Life for the time being.'

'And this... Life, Luh'le Shuggy,' said Dada. 'It is to be found in Notting Hill?'

'Very much so, Dada.'

'Why do I dread to think what that means?'

'I hope you are eating properly, Luh'le Shuggy?' said Maman. 'Do you cook? Or does Bloggs cook?' Hugh rolled his eyes. 'Well?' insisted Maman.

'We both cook,' groaned Hugh. 'But mostly the birds do.'

'The "birds"? The "*birds*"? What are these birds?' exclaimed Dada.

'Have you got a bird, Luh'le Shuggy?' asked George wonderingly.

'As a matter of fact, yup.'

'He means, I suppose, that he is stepping out with a young lady,' surmised Dada. 'Do *not* tell me, my son, that you are sharing premises with one.'

'No, Dada. I'm sharing a room with one.'

'Be da Holy Floy!'

'I hope you know what you're doing, Luh'le Shuggy,' said Maman.

'Yes, Maman.'

'You are being... careful?' she said meaningly.

'One word, Maman – the Pill.'

'*Pas devant les enfants*, Luh'le Shuggy.'

'That's two words,' observed the Moo.

'Had we better not forbid this behaviour, mavourneen? Is it not rather too – well, Bohemian is the polite word – for a boy of Luh'le Shuggy's age?'

'It seems a bit late for that, Dermot.'

'Luh'le Shuggy's living with a bird!' George couldn't get over it. 'No wonder his spots have gone.'

'Is she a dolly bird, Luh'le Shuggy?' asked the Moo, unclear as to the exact nature of the distinction.

'She is a part-time model.'

'A "model"!' cried Dada. 'You mean, I suppose, that she is no better than she should be. Good grief, Luh'le Shuggy. I suppose I ought to be grateful that you are not a bum boy' – '*Enfin*, Dermot!' – 'but I have to say that taking up with "models" is scarcely any better. You found her in a Soho gutter, I dare say, and immediately began to lavish my hard-earned money on her, wasting it on wines and baubles.'

'Actually, I met her in the Victoria and Albert Museum. I have a picture of her here, if anyone is interested.'

'I am,' said Janey. Hugh drew some pages from a clothing catalogue out of his pocket and handed them round, saying:

'Don't show them to Dada, who has impugned the character of the girl I love because he has a mind like a Cairo sewer.'

'She is most attractive, darling,' said Maman. 'Her little crocheted outfit is very daring, though.'

'Those are not her normal clothes, Maman. She's modelling them.'

'She *is* a dolly bird,' confirmed George. 'You can nearly see through her dress and she's wearing kinky boots.'

'She has a lovely smile,' said Janey.

'She has a lot of sloppiness,' approved the Moo with a professional air.

'She is swarthy,' said Dada, craning his neck to look at the picture Maman was studying.

'She is dark, Dermot, not swarthy.'

'She is a negress,' decided Dada, throwing up his hands.

'Don't be ridiculous, Dermot.'

'She's actually half-Mexican, Dada.'

George and the Moo burst out sniggering in unison:

'Luh'le Shuggy's in love with a Mexican girl!' they chorused.

'Yes,' said Hugh, with dignity.

'So, to sum up,' said Dada, with an expression of despair, 'my son and heir is living in the most disreputable part of London, with a reprobate male called Bloggs, who can be nothing but the most bestial influence, and with a so-called model, who is at best a dusky foreigner and at worst a swarthy – I mean, these skimpy tight little garments with indiscreet holes in them are all very well, but what one may ask is she wearing underneath? I *mean...*'

'Don't be filthy, Dermot.'

'Well, I mean – is this how you live, Luh'le Shuggy? In physical and moral squalor?'

'Yes, Dada – although in Notting Hill we tend to call it Blissville.'

Charles Hamilton and Colonel Bogey arrived simultaneously at the fork in the path on the perimeter of the Tennis Club lake. They looked at each other and grinned. No longer was there a jockeying for position, an unseemly power struggle. The Colonel was content to go whichever way Charles suggested. It seemed to be his pleasure nowadays simply to accompany Charles on walks, either at his side or, occasionally, a little behind. Charles had only to murmur 'Heel' for the Colonel to adopt the heel position. Never obsequiously nor, it had to be said, promptly; but he came to heel. However, it was a command but rarely issued: Charles would not, after all, have the Colonel be anything other than his own man. It was simply a case of playing master and dog when social convention – as now, approaching the Club house – demanded.

'Would you mind, old chap, if I put the old lead on you for a minute or two? Just as we go into the bar, you know, for form's sake?' The Colonel obligingly stopped and proffered his head. Then he led Charles into the bar where, to Charles's surprise, the Committee was gathered to inaugurate Bugger Lamb's replacement.

'Hi, Charles. Hi, Colonel,' Dan Rose greeted them. 'Have a glass of bubbly. I was just about to propose a toast.' He raised his voice. 'Ladies and Gentleman! As Chairman of the Committee, it is my pleasant duty to ask you to raise your glasses to our new Secretary, Roger Cholmondeley, and to his lovely bar staff and fiancée, Lorraine.'

'To Roger and Lorraine,' cried Charles, taking a swallow of champagne and patting the Colonel.

'Rough,' commented Colonel Bogey.

The acidic drink caused Charles to wince with pain. His stomach, according to the test results, was in a bad way – although it was something called Inflamed Bowel which was causing the acute pain and the bleeding. Far from being life-threatening, however, it was a minor condition that could be cured by milk puddings and, above all, by a cessation of anxiety. Not something you could just switch off after thirty years; but, fortunately, something that was already diminishing after his momentous survival of death by tiger; by the knowledge that Theo was innocent of murder; by his discovery that his son loved him as he loved his son; and by his new relationship with the Colonel – who had at last initiated him, even made him a partner, in the secret business he conducted throughout the byways of Wyebridge. On the whole, Charles Hamilton was – he hesitated to use the unfamiliar word – happy.

'Well, gosh. Thanks, Dan,' Roger was saying. 'I'm going to do my best to give this place a bit of life. We need new members, and I'm not going to be as, ahem, exclusive in vetting applicants as my predecessor. Every race, creed and colour of person will be able to slaughter each other at mixed doubles, or my name's not Roger Cholmondeley. Which, by the way, it isn't. From now on, it's C-H-U-M-L-E-Y.' While the Committee applauded, Roger whispered to Lorraine:

'This job should be yours, my darling. You're the boss really.'

'Of course, Roger. Unluckily, that has been the way of things all down the centuries. While Secretaries of Tennis Clubs commit themselves to a policy of equality for all races, creeds, etcetera, they do not extend this courtesy to women. Luckily I do not give a fig because I would rather shave my head and poke my eyes out than be the Secretary of a Tennis Club.'

'My God, Lorraine. You're bloody marvellous. Let's sneak up to the flat and discuss dialectical materialism with hardly any clothes on.'

'Your duty lies here, Roger.'

'I'd never have got this job, Lorraine – and I couldn't do it – without you. You're the Jeeves to my Wooster.'

'Thank you, Roger. I endeavour to give satisfaction. Now, I'm going up to the flat. And when you have closed the bar at two o'clock, you will find me waiting for you with a hot cup of tea and wearing only a smidgen of black lace.'

'Oh Lorraine, Lorraine…'

~

'Well, well. And how is my beloved family going to spend this fine sunny morning while Prince Flasheen Eyes cooks a sumptuous luncheon? Your beautiful mother is, as usual, taking herself off upstairs for some educational French conversation with my fellow Sloppy Club member, but what about you, mein Fuehrer? How is the best little brain in the family going to occupy himself?'

'I'm going to muck about with Brad at the Club. We've got a plan to land the Big Pike. The trick's in the bait: corned beef. Can Brad stay the night again, Maman?'

'If Roger and Lorraine don't mind. And don't come back from the Club with fingers missing. That would be the last straw.'

'And what has happened to the little girl who used to torment us by banging on Theo's piano? Will she require board and lodging also?' asked Dada.

'Sabrina hardly ever comes back,' replied George. 'Her boarding school is very strict.'

'I'm going for a ride on Crackerjack,' said Janey, referring to her pony.

'The Moo is collecting Sloppy Club fees from all members,' said the Moo, looking around at his family with a meaning expression. 'And then 'e's going to give the money to Bernie for her baby. Also, for buying crisps on the ferry crossing.' Bernie was returning to Ireland the next day.

'Well, that is … admirable, the Moo,' said Dada, taken aback. 'We will all, I'm sure, contribute handsomely to the baby-and-crisp fund.'

'And this afternoon,' continued the Moo, 'Theo is taking me to the football. I'm leaving Spiv behind. He's a hooligan.'

'And I'm taking Janey shopping this afternoon,' said Maman. 'So I'll be taking the Mini, Dermot.'

'Of course, macushla. Perhaps you would like me to chauffeur you?'

'No, thank you. Janey and I have girls' things to buy and you would be bored.'

'Dabs am going too, and buying snazzy Mod clothes. Dabs am looking like the Shrimp,' averred Dabs optimistically.

'You are too flabby and too thick,' the Moo corrected her.

'And Dabs am buying a little tam o' shanter,' she went on undeterred, 'to put on Dada's lovely new hair.'

265

'Well, that is thoughtful of her,' said Dada. 'And how does our Oxford man intend to fill his day?'

'I'm going to finish my essay on T.S. Eliot. "Humankind cannot bear very much reality." Discuss.'

'Well, in the first instance, you must say that his statement is true, Luh'le Shuggy. It would be unethical of me to help you with your homework, but I think I may say that humankind cannot, as a rule, face unpalatable facts. You may hold in your mind's eye, like a beacon, as you write, the image of your father who, God knows, has never flinched from unwelcome truths.'

'As your magnificent head of hair so stridently attests.'

'You are not to be disrespectful to your father, Luh'le Shuggy,' reproved Maman. 'Not as long as he is paying for your education, at least.'

'Sorry, Maman. It's just that I have emotions left over from recent events which, if they can't find expression, may fester and cause me to become embittered in later life, and perhaps to lose my hair with horrid suddenness.'

'Nevertheless, you will repress your emotions.'

'Does it strike no one as strange that the son, who has led a life of consummate ease, feels entitled to be bitter when it is the father who has felt the poisonous sting of betrayal by a wife whose fair seeming masked a perfidious heart?'

'I don't think you are well advised to take that tack, Dermot,' said Maman with a look.

'Of course. You are, as so often, right, mavourneen. You are not to be blamed. We all have our little moments of madness, without knowing why. A twisted nerve, as the Bard says, O, a ganglion gone astray. Thus in the great scheme of things, our momentary lapses are perhaps not so wicked. Let me be the first to sound the trump of forgiveness. Let us draw a veil over past misunderstandings. Above all, let love henceforth be our watchword.'

'I may need a little more time,' said Janey.

'Ah Janey, my beloved daughter. Don't harbour unkind thoughts to wrinkle your pretty face. Let us, you and I, bury the hatchet.'

'Well, all right, Dada. But I cannot guarantee to forget where it is buried.'

'Well, that is a beginning. You have lifted your hair from your face, I notice, in earnest perhaps of a new openness. May I hope that, once again, we will be opening our hearts to one another?'

'No, Dada, because we never did.'

'That's scarcely a kind thing to say to your poor old Dada. I sometimes feel that Dabs has more of the milk of human kindness in her veins, for all that she is an imbecile, than you have in your clever but cold heart.'

'That may be true, Dada. Dabs takes after you in the area of sentimentality.'

'I don't think Dabs takes after me in any particular. But I will let it pass for the sake of our new spirit of concord.'

'Dabs wanted to kill you,' said the Moo simply. 'But Spiv stopped her.' He patted his companion proudly.

'It would have been interesting to see what means a creature of Dabs's limited capacity would have employed to kill Dada,' said Hugh.

'In all fairness,' said George, 'she can be cunning when her brains are up.'

'Indeed she can, mein Fuehrer,' said Dada. 'And it is characteristic of you, the best little brain in the family, to steer us all on the fair course. Do I take it that Dabs has overcome her homicidal urges? Ah, I see – she is silent now, leaving me to speculate on her current position.'

'She is silent, I expect,' speculated Hugh, 'because her brains am currently down and thus unable to sift complex thoughts and feelings. Meanwhile, Dada, it wouldn't do to put her dander up.'

'Dabs can be werry dangerous when her dander am up,' quoted the Moo.

Janey had enjoyed her ride, cantering across the heathland to the west of St Michael's Hill. She had groomed Crackerjack, tied on his blanket and left him in the paddock, formerly the orchard of 'Ponderosa', which Roger had lent her whilst letting the house and garden to a rich building contractor. It was not quite lunch time and, besides, Dada would shout when the meal was ready, so she put her duffel coat on over her riding kit – it was sunny, but chilly – and went out to sit on the verge of Chestnut Avenue and to moon for a while.

She was a bit sad that Hugh had left home. Things would never be the same. But he was keen for her to come up to Notting Hill for a Madman's Ball, thrown by the staff of *Head Transplant*. She couldn't possibly, of course, what with dolly birds on the Pill, men smoking hashish, intellectuals and so on – it was too nerve-wracking. Maman *was* buying her a fab trouser suit, which would be just the job; but still.

'Mind… join…?'

'Oh hello, Theo. No, do sit down.'

'Glad… chance to talk… your Maman and I… so sorry…'

'It *was* a bit of a shock, Theo.'

'Your Maman… me… long time… love… so forth.'

'Yes, I understand. The trouble is, schoolgirls can have the most awful crushes. They're silly, I know, but they feel real to us. So I was a bit hurt.'

'You and I… always had… certain, um… Definitely real…'

'Well, I'm glad, Theo. Glad you felt something, too. But don't worry, I'm already getting over it.' She smiled up at him. He cupped her face impulsively in his warm piano player's hands and looked into her eyes. He seemed about to speak; but, then, as if having second thoughts, he bent his head and kissed her, Foody Fenella and all, on the mouth until she saw stars.

When she opened her eyes, he had gone and Bernie was sitting beside her.

'Sure, you look like you need a bit of a chocolate,' said Bernie, offering the box she was holding.

'Yup. Thanks.' They sucked in companionable silence for a bit, enjoying the feel of the low wintry sun on their faces. Chestnut Avenue was very quiet.

'I hope you don't mind me asking, Bernie, but, you know, I need to understand these things – did you use, er, contraception?'

'What? That Protestant divilry? Don't be filthy, Janey! I used the ould rhythm method, o' course.'

'What *is* that, exactly?'

'Well, sure, you get on top, I think. Then it doesn't count.'

'Are you sure, Bernie? It doesn't sound very scientific.'

'Ah well, it didn't work annyway.'

'Have you confessed to the priest?'

'Are you mental?'

'Aren't you supposed to confess your sins?'

'Ah God, no one tells the priest what they're up to.'

'What do you tell him then?'

'You just make up a few little sins, like everybody else. Eating a Wimpy on a Friday, that class of thing. "Impure thoughts" is as far as anyone'll go. If you go any farther with Father Spillane at home, he starts fiddling with himself in the confessional, the poor ould gobshite.'

'What are you going to call the baby?'

'Well now. If it's a boy, I'll call him the Fuehrer. And if it's a girl, definitely Dabs.'

'You don't want to *Blyte* the poor child!'

'You're right there. I'll let Pat Tim decide.'

'Will he still marry you?'

'O' course he will, the soft eejit. Have another choc.' Janey took the box and studied the drawing of the chocolates, and their names, on the lid. Cream Tangerine, Montelimar, Ginger Sling, Coffee Dessert…

The deep roar of a powerful engine sounded. A car pulled sharply around the corner and stopped in front of them. It was the Black Mini. Janey's heart skipped several beats. As if in a dream, she stood up and, in three steps, found herself beside the driver's window. She tapped on the opaque, blacked-out glass. The window opened. The man inside looked at her quizzically, and then smiled a crooked sort of a smile.

'Do you live here?' he asked.

'Yes.'

'I've moved in up the road.'

'I know. I've seen your car before.'

'And I've seen you before. Out here. Making daisy chains.' The man had an accent, strange, flat, but also very, very familiar.

'Have a chocolate.'

'Ta very much. Which is the best?'

'They're all nice. But nothing compares to the Savoy Truffle.' She picked it out and passed it through the window.

'Fab,' said the man. Then, 'would you have any use for this?' He produced an LP from the passenger seat. 'It's new,' he added. 'Not out yet.'

'Will you write on it?' She pulled a coloured pencil out of her pocket and passed it in. The man scribbled. 'Thanks.'

'See yer,' he said cheerily.

'See you.'

The car took off.

'What in God's name was that about?' asked Bernie. Janey passed her the LP. 'Holy Mary, Joseph, Jaysus and all the saints! It says "Love from"!'

'Men,' said Janey. 'They can't resist me.'

It came to her that she would, after all, go and stay with Luh'le Shuggy in exotic Notting Hill. She would go to the Ball.

'It says "*Love from*",' repeated Bernie, incredulously.

'Yes,' said Janey. '"Love from George".'

She opened her duffel coat and slipped the shiny, new, not-out-yet Beatles' album inside and held it over her heart.

Other books by Patrick Harpur:
A Complete Guide to the Soul
The Philosophers' Secret Fire: A History of the Imagination
Daimonic Reality: A Field Guide to the Otherworld
Mercurius; or, the Marriage of Heaven and Earth
The Rapture
The Serpent's Circle

Lightning Source UK Ltd.
Milton Keynes UK
UKOW051522260613

212835UK00001B/32/P